# THE CROSSING POINT

*Also by Gerda Charles*

THE TRUE VOICE

# The Crossing Point

GERDA CHARLES

CONTEMPORARY FICTION
EYRE & SPOTTISWOODE
LONDON 1961

FOR MY MOTHER

*Dearest and best of parents with*

*love and blessings*

*This Contemporary Fiction edition was produced in
1961 for sale to its members only by the proprietors,
Readers Union Ltd, at Aldine House, 10–13 Bedford
Street, London W.C.2 and at Letchworth Garden City,
Herts. Full details of membership may be obtained from
our London address. The book is set in 11 point Bembo
type leaded and has been reprinted by The Shenval
Press Ltd, London, Hertford and Harlow. It was first
published by Eyre & Spottiswoode Ltd.*

# Author's Note

Every novelist has problems over and above the actual labour of creation. One of them is the perpetual worry as to whether, in creating his fictional world, he may not inadvertently have hit upon some combination of facts such as actually exist in real life. For any writer who is venturesome enough to embark on a novel with a specifically Jewish theme and an urban setting this hazard is immensely increased. The Anglo-Jewish community is a comparatively small, enclosed society. Though in the creation of characters, names, backgrounds, situations or even geographical locations I have taken every possible precaution to avoid the duplication of anything in real life, there is still the possibility, within such a restricted range, of invention coinciding with fact. One cannot check every name, every circumstance. . . .

Let me say, therefore, most emphatically, that every character, every incident and every institution in this book is a pure creation of the imagination. Apart from references to such bodies as the Beth Din (which in this context are about as personal as would be a passing reference to the London County Council) the people, the establishments and the organizations together with the events which happen or are referred to within these pages, are absolute fiction. Whether they carry conviction on their own level—that of imaginative truth—is quite another matter. I can only say that I hope they do.

GERDA CHARLES

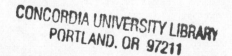

# Chapter One

## I

FROM THE MOST CENTRAL POINT OF LONDON TO THE
suburb of Manor Green is a distance of about six miles. The
district holds within its boundaries Manor Green West, a
neighbourhood of fine, impressive houses and leafy roads; Manor
Green East which is today, if not exactly slum, certainly dreary with
its monotony of small, drab, late-Victorian streets; and, somewhere
between the two, Manor Green Garden Suburb, a large area entirely
built over with uniform, somewhat flimsy, but not entirely dis-
pleasing modern villas.

The inhabitants on the whole match the particular section in
which they live, though with some overlapping round the edges.
The lower middle class, the artisans and small tradesmen, live in the
East; the middle middle in the Garden Suburb; and the upper middle
(though now much infiltrated by classless, and very often stateless,
one-roomers) in the West. Sprinkled thickly across the whole
borough, but with a double concentration in the Garden Suburb,
are the Jews.

There have been Jews residing in Manor Green for over a hundred
years during which time, in order to cater for their spiritual needs,
three synagogues have been erected. The suburb as a whole is shaped
like a partly opened fan with the hub at its northernmost point and it
is at this point, within a street or two of being outside Manor Green
altogether, that the Ferne Road Synagogue stands. It is a large and
imposing building of pale-cream stone with something of the
Orient in its style. Cupolas and a certain oriental floridity of decora-
tive stone carving had been fashionable perhaps for a year or two
towards the end of the last century when this synagogue was being
built. Or possibly the wealthy merchants whose money had built it
had had what was to prove a last, expiring flicker of grandiosity
before their descendants succumbed docilely enough to Western
conceptions of "taste". Certainly its nearest rival at Pelham Close,

9

built fifteen years later, exhibits none of this fleshy exuberance: indeed, in its sombre magnificence and general air of shadowy, dimlit decorum, it would not disgrace a cathedral town in the staidest of English shires.

Ferne Road Synagogue, standing where it does at the junction where the three fairly sharply divided areas of Manor Green converge, draws its congregation freely from all of them, though a third competitor for souls, the synagogue at Dorchester Terrace, which was erected only two years ago in the middle of the Garden Suburb, has drawn off many of the members of both the older congregations. This has not so far caused any real resentment in either Ferne Road or Pelham Close, partly because each house of worship still has a long list of would-be seat holders and partly because both the older synagogues, though often divided by immense feuds in the past, were able to come together in a united, mild contempt for Dorchester Terrace which—apart from belonging to a different circuit of synagogues and so incurring much the same reaction as two Odeons might feel for a Gaumont—served also to arouse such feelings of benevolent disdain as any bumptious redbrick university might in Oxford or Cambridge.

The only congregants either synagogue regretted losing to the glaringly new (literally red-bricked) edifice in Dorchester Terrace were not the youngish married couples from the brightly painted, pebble-dashed, little houses in the Garden Suburb, but the sprinkling of older and more orthodox members who found the long walk to and from the older foundations on Saturday mornings, an increasing strain. The less orthodox members not caring greatly—and with each year caring less—that it is forbidden the Jew to ride or drive in any form of transport on the Sabbath, were in the habit of driving blithely up to Ferne Road in their, for the most part, extremely handsome cars, taking part with enthusiasm in all the more vociferous parts of the service and driving equally blithely home again to eat their Sabbath chicken with the cheerful consciousness of pious duty well done. Each Saturday the rich members of the Ferne Road congregation, as they drove home, reflected with pleased self-righteousness on their own tactful consideration towards their Rabbi. For had they not (even when it was raining) parked their cars, not outside the synagogue where his eye might fall on them and be offended, but round the corner, decently concealed amongst the trees of Veryan Square; which rather resembled on Saturday mornings the show rooms of some highly superior automobile company.

The Reverend Leo Norberg, the Rabbi whose feelings the congregation were (in this instance) so tender about, was quite aware of Veryan Square and in fact made a point of preaching at least twice a year—there were a number of appropriate texts—on the use or rather abuse of the motor-car on the Sabbath and what kind of example was this to the children?

A large proportion of the congregation usually occupied the time he took over this sermon (as they did over most of his sermons) with a mental review of the week's trade and resolves to get hold of Silverman after the service and find out if those premises were suitable for heavy machinery.

The women, segregated, after the Jewish fashion, upstairs in the Ladies' Gallery, counted the number of mink capes or looked suspiciously at each other's pretty daughters, and the daughters, both pretty and plain, looked at the young men downstairs.

One Saturday morning in January, as Rabbi Norberg came out on to the porch of his synagogue after the service, a heavily-built woman encased in a largely-flowered dress and a three-quarter length ranch mink coat came up to him. Behind her the Rabbi, even as he responded to her somewhat effusive greeting, noticed that the president of his congregation, an imposing and large-stomached man and one of the few who still wore a silk hat to the Sabbath, had stopped to speak to the honorary treasurer; another silk hat.

Sir Robert Bart-Grune looked benign; the honorary treasurer, plain Mr Bertrand Schelling but an almost famous barrister, was smiling. So, the Building Fund dispute had, if not disappeared (which was really too much to hope for), at least subsided. The Rabbi, relieved, bent his attention to Mrs Goldenbird.

"That was a terrific point you made in your sermon, Dr Norberg," she was saying in the voice peculiar to many Jewish, middle-class women, a voice in which resonance, vulgarity and attempted refinement all fought a strangling battle with each other. "I couldn't agree more. Our young people. . . . It's so necessary to give them more

Judaism to think about than . . . I mean, Jewish culture . . . after all, I'm always telling my daughter . . . it's not just a religion, it's a way of life, isn't it? You haven't met Doris, of course. But my poor husband, God rest his soul, used to say exactly the same. I don't mind telling you, Dr Norberg, that that's one of the reasons I sold my house and believe me what a beautiful house, my drawing room alone was thirty-two feet, and pears *that* size in the garden, over forty fruit trees, and took a flat here in Manor Green. That was my main reason. It's no good if you've got growing up children to live away from your own people, is it? You really must meet my daughter. She's a sweet girl. I'm not saying it because she's my own. It's the truth. Whoever meets her . . . she's friendly to everyone. Just chats to anyone. So about this Guild of yours. If you'd just introduce her round a bit. You know. Such nice young people everyone tells me. Cream of young Jewry. I almost wish I could join myself!" And she gave him a coy, self-conscious glance which sat oddly on her heavy features and put up a hand to her hair which, brightened to a brazen copper-brown, supported a twelve guinea pea-green hat. She was about forty-seven.

She paused and Leo, his brain from long practice catching up on what his ears had heard some moments before, said, "Certainly," while his eyes still watched the animated talk between Bart-Grune, Schelling, and young Victor Bart-Grune who had joined his father on the synagogue steps. "But of course, Mrs Goldenbird. I should be delighted to see your daughter at the Guild."

"You'll introduce her?" she said quickly and then, archly: "Not just to the *Guild*. It's a nice young man or two I'd like her to meet! *You* know," and she lowered her voice to a throttled whisper. "A nice young professional man. Or not so young. It doesn't matter." Catching the direction of the Rabbi's gaze she stared with a look of calculating longing at young Bart-Grune then, with a slight shrug as if to say: "Not that. That's too much to expect," she went on: "After all, a girl has to meet a few men. You will look after her, won't you?"

"But of course——"

"Such a handy girl," she said, her big, fleshy mouth smiling back from her formidable teeth. "There's not a thing in the house I swear to you she can't do as well as I can. A young girl like her!

12

And I don't mind telling you, Dr Norberg . . . she won't be short. I'm not one to hold back over a few pounds. *Everything* she can do; cooking, baking, well educated . . . believe me, she deserves a good husband."

Mrs Goldenbird stopped speaking rather abruptly and gave Leo a meaning look, then tried to extract the meaning by gazing rapidly into the distance over his left shoulder.

Suddenly grasping what she was about—if he hadn't been only half listening, with his other ear cocked to the Bart-Grune-Schelling conversation (could the Building Fund dispute really have died at last?), he would have recognized her gambit earlier—he felt himself becoming more alert while simultaneously taking a step back.

Doris was being offered, cooking, baking, money, lovely girl and all . . . to *him!*

"I'm sure she does," he said hastily. "Of course she must meet some nice young men. I'll do what I can, Mrs Goldenbird. I'll see . . ." he broke off to greet some of his congregants.

"You've only to have a talk with her and you'll see for yourself. Now why not come and have tea with us one day? What am I saying? Why 'one day'? Why not this afternoon? Come for tea this afternoon."

"Oh, I . . . " he said trying to think of a quick, good excuse.

"Come on! Come on!" she said with massive archness. "Don't say no. I know what you do on Saturday afternoons. You do like everybody else! You have a good sleep. Well! come for tea after your sleep!"

Just for a moment the Rabbi hesitated. For a moment an old voice whispered in his mind, "Perhaps. Perhaps. Perhaps." Perhaps out of all the Mrs Goldenbirds of the last thirty years, *this* Mrs G. is going to hit the target. Perhaps Miss Doris Goldenbird (and his thought lingered on the syllables which suddenly became momentous to him . . . Doris; Doris Goldenbird; my wife, she used to be Doris Goldenbird . . .) such a good cook, was to be his fate? Then he remembered with an almost regretful relief that he did indeed have another engagement for tea that day. "But do tell your daughter to come along a week tomorrow evening. The Guild meets every other Sunday, you know. I'm giving the lecture myself that evening but I'll look out for her. Not at all. Not at all," as she thanked him and, getting away with some difficulty—she had laid a possessive, diamonded hand on his arm and was looking up at him with bold, persuasive eyes so masterfully that an even more horrifying suspicion flashed across his mind that she was doing a bit of angling on her own behalf and wouldn't mind presenting Doris with a stepfather instead of a husband—he ran down the steps and walked nearly all the way home with his own beadle before he could be sure he had shaken her off.

## 2

It was with some pleasure that, a couple of evenings later, Leo heard his housekeeper's voice in the hall talking to Joel Fredlander as she admitted him. He came into Leo's study a moment later, a very short, very fat man carrying with him despite his size a slightly woe-begone, vulnerable air. His face was both fat and lined, his tiny nose, curved like a comma, latched to the middle of it, his small, blue eyes blank, sardonic, sad.

"How a—a—are you, Joel?" said the Rabbi expansively, getting up and shaking hands. "I thought Wednesday was your day in town?"

"So it is but I had to come up and see Tarsch off."

"Again?"

"This time His Excellency has received a call to South America. Apparently they can't raise funds without him. Not during the English winter they can't. What d'you bet when atomic warfare breaks out on earth the President of the Congregation on the moon will suddenly discover he needs Tarsch to conduct a Zionist campaign!"

Joel settled himself with a thump into his armchair.

"How does he do it in Heaven's name?"

"Nerve. Good looks. Gift of the gab. Or what have you?" Joel said with a shrug. "Looks mainly, I think. I understand they have special Red Cross attendants on duty every Saturday morning outside the *shool* when he's preaching to deal with all the fainting women."

"What about Mrs T.? Doesn't she object?"

"Mrs T.—our dear Evelyn (did you know her real name was

14

Annic, by the way?), though by no means a fool I might tell you, finds life as Mrs Solomon Tarsch pretty good. She knows bloody well that Sol can't wander even if he wanted to. Our revered Rabbi . . . head of the Hebrew Academic Institute, figure of international Jewry . . . besides, she's got the dough!"

"You mean to say he did actually marry for money?" said Leo, always interested in motives for marriage.

"Sure. You're not going to tell me he took that frozen lettuce leaf for any other reason!"

"I suppose it's just conceivable——"

"Listen," broke in Joel. "Let me tell you something about our Sol. I've known him for years and I've been living under the same roof with him for some time now. He's tough. Pretty tough. Like the rest of his family. Good-looking, shrewd, capable. . . . I could tell you a thing or two about his old man, old Moses Tarsch. When that family were kids they were routed out of bed at six in the morning, summer and winter, and set to study *Chumash* for two hours before breakfast. No fire. No mercy. When Moses said 'breathe' they breathed, and when he said 'stop' they stopped. He never earned more than three pounds a week in his life and he went through three wives and had fourteen children. Two wives and eight children he abandoned somewhere. Nobody knows what became of them. But before he died he saw four sons at the top of their professions and his daughters married to two of the richest Jews in Britain. Not bad going for an obscure, bearded Jew from a dirty little slum in Glasgow. How did he do it? How do the Jews do anything? But that's the push Sol and the rest of them inherited. Not that there weren't murders when any of them came up against the father. Look at Zella. Broke her heart crying on her wedding day. She didn't want Haslom with all his money; who would? Moses forced her to marry him. As soon as he died—but not before, mark you!—she divorced him. *What* a beautiful girl she was. I knew her well at one time. Friend of Irene's." His voice sank on the last words, his eyes became smaller, glazed and distracted at once.

There was a silence.

"Heard from Irene—or of her?" said Leo at last in a casual tone.

"Had a letter from Janette," he said lumbering his round form over to get at his other pocket. "She wants to take a holiday, she and Irene. In Switzerland. Thinks her daddy might like to know."

"And is daddy going to cough up?"

"If it were Irene alone I'd see her in hell. But I can't let the kid. . . . Look," he said producing a crumpled envelope and taking a snapshot out of it. "Doesn't she look a picture? Look at that figure for only fourteen. Slim as a reed. And look how tall she——"

"Now then," said Leo impatiently, "Don't start that old-fashioned Jewish thing, making a fetish out of height. Jews like us are always eighty years behind the times. In Victoria's day" (Leo's accent, normally an excellent English one, just occasionally betrayed him as now: "Victor—r—rehria" he said, thickening and swallowing the 'r') "the ideal woman was always tall, had a bust like a shelf, abundant hair and twelve children."

"My daughter, Janette, nor, come to that, my ex-wife, Irene, neither of them have busts like shelves," said Joel but without much spirit. "And as for twelve children, she hated me enough to get a divorce after five years. What is strange, when you come to think of it is that she waited that long."

"I've told you before. You should have got back at her. Sued her for restitution of conjugal rights or whatever they call it."

"And made public still more hate; more shame; more disgust?" he said heavily. "What's it matter anyway? I'm done for, Leo. Done for. What am I? What's left? Teaching to a lot of students who want degrees, not knowledge. Philosophy! Ha! who wants philosophy, words in a book? Not me. Not me. I want my life back again. A home of my own, not a room in an institution. I want to be a Headmaster again and sit at the head of my own table again. Friday night, Saturday, Sunday . . . never less than twenty, thirty people to lunch, to dinner. Remember, Leo?"

"I remember very well," said Leo, shrugging. There was a faint lack of sympathy in his manner. "I remember even better how I envied you sitting there with your pretty wife—such a good hostess, Irene, you can't take that away from her—and looking so . . . established." He nodded his head slowly. "I envied you. Ah, I envied you! I still do."

Joel gave a soundless, scathing laugh. "Still!"

"Oh you can laugh," said Leo, holding out his hand vertically, the fingers spread out, "but you've *had* it. No one can take that away. You've *had* something; experience; pleasure; marriage; a child." He turned his hand till it was palm upwards, horizontal and questioning between them. "What have I had? Tell me that?"

"You haven't done so badly. Prestige, good salary, perks. Fine house. You don't starve!" he said with a quizzical look at Leo's portly figure which in some way contrived to look prosperous and authoritative where his own excess flesh looked puffy and degenerate. The two faces were equally unlike, Joel resembling nothing so much as a weary, sagging owl, where Leo's bold, massive, Semitic features looked bull-like and swarthy despite his greying hair.

"Well—— why didn't you marry?" said Joel. "What's stopped you all these years? Plenty of girls. Nice girls."

"*Nice* girls!" said Leo in sudden fury. "You too! I'm sick to death of nice Jewish girls. I'm sick of the girls, I'm sick of their mothers. I'm suffocated with their chicken dinners, I'm drowned in their chicken soups. I *don't want*," he said shouting "nice girls and chopped liver. I want lobster and champagne and pale skins and thin cheeks and flat chests!" He stopped and burst out laughing and after a moment Joel also began to laugh and the two fat men in their two fat, leather armchairs, facing each other across the blazing fire, shouted cheerfully at each other.

"Ah! a *feinë gelechtë*," said Leo sobering. "You can laugh . . . but it's bitter . . ."

"I know what you really want," said Joel. "What you need is a nice, little widow, good housekeeper, not too young, say about thirty-five . . ."

"No I don't," said Leo loudly. Then he added a shade awkwardly: "Funny thing, Joel, I couldn't fancy a widow. More than once I . . . this peculiar Jewish dislike I have of anything not the best. Somehow, a widow . . . the idea smells of second-hand. No. I've waited so long. I'll wait a bit longer."

"What for?"

Leo shrugged. "God knows. Someone, something . . . something that isn't Manor Green. You think a Rabbi hasn't any right to such sentiments. Well—— I'm a man aren't I? I've a right to my own tastes. And the Manor Green girl isn't one of them. 'A ni—i—ze gairl from Manor Grin'," he said parodying the Yiddish accent.

"*Nicht zo* a beauty," he went on still in burlesque, "*ober mit chein*. The minute they trot out that word '*chein*' (it might have meant charm originally but now it means anything including a light hand with sponge cake) I know the girl's got a face like the back of a cab. No thank you; I've had enough. If you knew how sick I am of 'smart' girls, of 'nice' girls, of 'well-dressed' girls, of 'good-at-business' girls, of 'lively' girls, 'sweet' girls, 'wonderful-worker' girls . . ."

"In fact, girls!"

"Yes! It's girls I'm sick of. Give me anything but girls; a moon maiden, a goddess, a nymph, a witch even! But no girls. And no widows! By the way, talking of widows . . ." and he went on to tell Joel of his encounter with Mrs Goldenbird. "Maybe I'll introduce *you* to Doris," he ended up.

"Toss you for her. Loser to take Ma!"

"All jokes aside," said Leo. "Are you going to spend the rest of your life knocking about from job to job, eating your heart out for that bitch? Take your own advice. Marry again. Live a decent, settled life once more. You could get a fellowship any time you liked."

Joel shook his head. "Thanks," he said. "You're right of course. Thanks. But no. I can't marry. I'm a failure in marriage. Besides . . . I repel women. No woman could bear me near her."

"I've never heard such blithering rubbish in my——"

"No. No," said Joel in a high, wandering voice. "It's true."

Leo looked at his pale, defeated eye and changed the subject. "Have you heard the latest about Ringler?"

"Your *chazan*? That brilliant intellect! What now?"

"My 'cantor' as my president, Sir Robert, insists on calling him —Englischë snob!—decided to take it into his head (where there's certainly plenty of room for a new idea) to sing *Uv'nucho Yomar* and a lot more not to the usual," Leo hummed a few bars of the traditional, liturgical tune, "if you please, but to bits of Puccini, Verdi, and so on. An old game of course but he's taken it beyond all limits. Fancies himself, Ringler. Thinks he ought to be in Grand Opera at Covent Garden instead of wasting his talents in Ferne Road. Anyway, it's been going on for weeks and at the last board meeting the whole thing boiled up into a first class row."

"Who's objecting?"

"Sir Robert . . . because the Bart-Grunes are 'musical' and they can't bear Bizet massacred; Schelling . . . because 'our traditional tunes, our old Hebrew melodies should be retained'," Leo mimicked Schelling's precise, rather pompous enunciation, "and all the more English element from sheer, crusted Toryism."

"What! You surprise me! What about the *frumë*?"

"I was surprised myself! It turns out the more strictly orthodox members of my congregation, bless them, *like* a bit of Puccini mixed in with the *Kedusha*. The simpler, sentimental Jewish soul *likes* to have its religion as it might be an opera. Dramatic, highly-coloured, tuneful . . . you know. They have an idea that's how life really is; all this twentieth-century greyness they're living in is a sort of temporary mistake. They're all for arias. Schelling and Mandelbaum nearly came to blows over it—at least Mandelbaum did."

"I always did see Schelling as a Morris dancer somehow," said Joel.

"More English than the English! I know! Anyway, there we are. No sooner out of the Building Fund fire than we're into the *Chazanishë* frying pan!"

"I must come up for the week-end," said Joel. "I'd give a lot to hear Ringler singing *Ain Comocho* to 'Your tiny hand is frozen'."

"And giving his *Tallith* that important twitch just before his top note! Seriously, the congregation's split clean in two over the business. Impassioned letters . . . passionate counter-attacks . . . it's taking me all my time to keep one impartial foot in each camp. But about the week-end . . . you'll come and stay with me? Come next week. I can promise you a good *Shabbos*— or *Shabbat* as Sir Robert would say!" the Rabbi concluded in a sarcastic voice.

"Or 'the Sabbath' à la Schelling!" said Joel.

"When talking to a 'co-religionist' as they would both no doubt put it. To anyone else I'm pretty sure it's 'the Day of Rest'!"

"If an *Israeli* says *Shabbat*——" began Joel in the peculiar, sing-song intonation the Jew adopts at the beginning of a discussion, "that's all *right*." He dropped his voice sharply on the last syllable.

"But for *me* . . ." answered Leo in the same tonal idiom, and giving a little thrusting away movement with his hands, "I stick to

*Shabbos.* So I'll expect you for *Shabbos* then," he said briskly in his normal voice.

Joel stood up to go. "If I can get away," he said, "I will. Good night. Better hurry or I'll miss my train. Why they have to stick a Hebrew Academic Institute in the middle of a Kentish marsh I don't know."

"To remind you that the Jews were chosen—to suffer!" said Leo.

## 3

Though of British nationality for over forty years, Rabbi Norberg had not been born in England but in Lithuania, the small principality at one time half under German and half under Russian influence but now completely swallowed up by the Soviet Union. His birthplace, a small country town, was always a source of great pride to him. The little town, as indeed the whole of that small country, was for most of the nineteenth century the centre (for Jews) of a cultured, comfortably-off middle class, on a level, *vis-à-vis* international Jewry, with say Cambridge or St Andrew's. It is not known precisely why Lithuanian Jews should have developed this instinct and talent for both learning (*Hebrew* learning as distinct from the more secular culture found amongst the German or Spanish Jews) and pleasant living, but so it had come about. It was from Lithuania that there came the long procession of distinguished Rabbis noted—and this is what still gives the Lithuanian Jew a particular power in the modern world—not only for their piety and culture but also for a certain kind of liberalism, a humane flexibility which, allied to their impressive academic power, gave a particular and happy ease to the transition many of them were called upon to make between eastern and western Europe.

Not dissimilar from the Chinese in some ways, the Jews have their share of ancestor-worship which in turn gives rise to its own peculiar snobbery. In Europe it is the Jew of Spanish or Portuguese extraction, considered, not only by themselves, as the most aristocratic of all, who rather condescends to the German Jew who in general holds himself as belonging to the Junker class and in his turn looks down upon the Lithuanians who occupy a social strata corresponding roughly to the professional upper middle class—

professors to the German generals and Spanish dukes. Below them come the Russians, the Austrians, the Czecho-Slovaks, and the Hungarians, all more or less equal; a rung below stand the Rumanians, often disliked and distrusted by the others and, at the very bottom, the Poles, despised by everyone.

This rough and ready grading with, of course, huge qualifications, cross-fertilizations and innumerable exceptions to prove the rule (from the Poles, for instance, have come some of the greatest figures in world Jewry) still holds with surprising tenacity amongst those descendants who have long ago become part of the fabric of what is known as Western civilization.

Although brought over to England at a very early age, Leo, true to his Lithuanian ancestry, had never thought of becoming anything else but a Rabbi. His father had been one; so had his grandfather; and his great-grandfather had been a highly distinguished and famous Rabbi, a renowned teacher in the great Jewish seminary which had been a centre of learning for the whole of the Semitic Europe of his day.

Brought up in the unusual position—for a Rabbi's son—of only child, Leo had gone through school, university, Hebrew training for his rabbinical degree and subsequent posts in suburban or provincial synagogues with equanimity. At the age of thirty-four he had been "called" to Ferne Road and there, both his parents dying soon afterwards, he had stayed.

Within his heavy frame he was a man of some vitality and it was this rather than the perhaps more useful quality of committee-man's patience which had enabled him to ride the periodic storms (with their own over-excitable Jewish quality) which are apt to sweep any ecclesiastical organization. But, added to this was his genuine love for what might be termed "intellectual Judaism". If his sermons were not always listened to throughout, they were held in respect. What he said in the pulpit was not, as with many of his co-ministers, geared to the lowest intellectual capacity of his listeners. Neither was it heavy with innumerable dead-weight, moral observations. And, as Schelling, the almost-famous barrister, had been heard to observe: "At least his grammar and syntax are impeccable. Not like Bolman at Dorchester Terrace." Which was hard on Reverend

Bolman who was dutiful and indefatigable but whose sermons were apt to contain passages like this: "Therefore we must take care not only that every Jew can be encouraged about this great task but that every child is instilled in the earliest example as soon as he is observational as this is the vital beginning through which the key to the foundation is laid."

Of the strength and validity of his faith Leo was absolutely convinced. No part of it irked him though, born a generation earlier, it might have done. He was fond, for instance, of dancing and liked the company of women and nothing in the modern code of rabbinical behaviour barred him from either. Sixty or seventy years ago an orthodox Rabbi might well have been frowned upon for so much as shaking hands with a woman. Now, his fondness for dancing occasioned only the most infrequent lift of an eyebrow and had given rise only to one consequence; the nickname, not used so much of late, of "the waltzing Rabbi". He was the more surprised therefore, on reviewing his conversation with Joel Fredlander, at his own outburst over "lobsters" (which, like all shellfish, are forbidden food to the Jews) "and champagne".

"What on earth," he asked himself that night after Joel had gone, "made me talk such nonsense?" And he lay awake with the question nagging him for some time. When he stopped thinking about lobsters it was to reflect upon the half-lie he had told Joel. No, it was not exactly a half-lie. It was . . . he did not know quite how to define this many-faceted attitude of his towards "girls".

It was not true for instance that he collectively despised them. He had proposed to more than one in his time. He did not despise marriage but on the contrary longed for it. He had even allowed himself—at the expense of some mockery from his own sardonic element—to be persuaded by the professional matchmakers (still a perfectly legitimate business activity conducted on all levels of Jewish life) to meet a likely girl or two, though without result. Only a few months before, such an encounter had taken place. Leo smiled, but half bitterly, to himself at the recollection. . . .

4

Old Sir Oswald Gould was fed up. He stumped about his flat

with its beautiful view on the Bayswater side of the park, shouting at his wife.

"Is it *my* fault?" he cried. "What more do you want me to do? Twenty thousand pounds and a directorship in the business isn't enough? What do want from me——? that I should go down on my knees to some young *tanzer* and say 'Do me a favour. Marry my daughter'?" He held out his hands in a vicious, mock-pleading gesture then lifted them, clenched, to his temples. "*Och und vay*" (Sir Oswald only dropped into Yiddish when he was feeling either indignant or democratic) "that I should have to beg——"

"Who said anything about begging? You can't do things in a nice way?" said Lady Gould, getting up and going over to the window. She was a tall, big-boned woman half a head taller than her stocky, little husband.

"We've done 'in a nice way'," he retorted, "and where are we? How old is Muriel? Thirty-two. How much longer before she gets a husband?"

"Well that's exactly what I'm saying, isn't it?" she said exasperated. "That's exactly why I want to call in Levinson."

Sir Oswald shrugged his thick shoulders. "I should have to call in a professional *shadchan* for my daughter!"

"Plenty do it," she said, drawing the rich, stiff, green brocade hangings across the window. "I tell you I'm ashamed to go anywhere these days. Always the same question: 'What's doing with Muriel?' I can't stand any more of it I can tell you. I'm so ashamed I could die every time. You think I want to go to Levinson? But what else can we do?'

He raised his eyebrows consideringly. "How much does he want?" he said after a pause.

"Five per cent."

He gave a scandalized hiss. There was another pause. Then he shrugged again as if to say: Well, if that's what you want then do it.

"I'll ask Levinson to call," she said.

There were probably "agents" in the Stone Age who, in return for the promise of a particular marrow bone, were ready to give information on the whereabouts of a herd of bison. The human race in fact cannot get on without the entrepreneur. He is as much a part

23

of the body of mankind as the nervous system is of the human physique. And in one sense, in one of his many Protean guises, the Jew is man's nerve, extending and touching everywhere, the message carrier between disparate parts, the connecter without whom the whole flies apart. He is the "agent" incarnate, the supreme middle man without whom, despite all the theories of high-minded economists, all the blastings of honest idealists, we cannot exist.

Mr Levinson, agent for matrimonial joy (a very good selling line on occasion), like many another of his kind did not rely solely on one kind of goods. Matrimony was good and the commission, when it arrived, handsome: but there was in this commodity always the risky human element of personality to be reckoned with. Mr Levinson therefore carried on at the same time his bread and butter trades: in this case, watch repairing with side lines in chromium re-plating, an occasional re-silvering job and, most paying of all in certain London suburbs where the fashion remained for some years, manufacturers' agent for peach coloured mirror glass. This line was especially useful to Mr Levinson as providing a great number of contracts for matrimonial joy. Many a five per cent came his way via the mirror in the lounge, the table in the hall, even, in one case, the four bathroom walls a client with two daughters and a lawyer son wanted completely covered with the flattering glow.

A few evenings after the previous discussion he came sidling into Sir Oswald's drawing room, a thin, small man with sharp, regular features and very brown skin. At first sight he looked healthy, twinkling, alert. At second sight one noticed the humped, meagre back, the small, brown, ingratiating fingers, the vulpine mouth with its broken teeth.

"Good evening, good evening, good evening," he said, still standing sideways as if afraid to confront the stiff, handsome room full face. He had taken off his hat but now, seeing that Sir Oswald (who prided himself on his orthodoxy) was wearing a skull cap, he put it on again quickly. Lady Gould entered and, uncertain whether to take it off again in English-style good manners or keep it on in deference to Sir Ralph, he hastily tipped it backwards then forwards again.

"Sit down, sit down," said Sir Oswald, and turning his back he busied himself at the sideboard with a bottle and glasses.

Mr Levinson sat down.

"A kümmel?" said Sir Oswald approaching with a glass.

"I won't say no," said Mr Levinson. Then, his natural perkiness asserting itself: "*Nu!*" he said holding up his glass as the others sat down with theirs, "*A guten! To a mazeltov in the near future!*"

"Let's hope so, Mr Levinson," said Lady Gould with a hasty glance at her husband. They all three drank.

There was a long pause during which Sir Oswald, his head sunk between his shoulders, stared at his knees and twisted the cut crystal wine glass in his fingers. Lady Gould alternately sipped and fidgeted and Mr Levinson tried to assess the value of a cabinet of very ugly wedding-present silver facing him.

"Yes. Yes," said Sir Oswald suddenly looking up. "Not far off from *Yomtov*. Which *shool* do you go?"

"Northern District. A beautiful *shool* a minute from my house. You've never been? Ach, you must come. Everything we have, a Ladies' Guild, a school for the children, a Synagogue Hall like you couldn't see another in the country like it.'

Sir Oswald gave a short nod and relapsed into silence again.

Lady Gould, with a look of baleful impatience at her husband, took the bull by the horns.

"Mr Levinson," she said in her restricted, nasal voice, with its coarse yet strangely self-conscious undertone. "I'm sorry my daughter isn't in to meet you but she had to go out this evening. Young girls . . . you know how it is. Always running about here, there and everywhere. So many friends . . ."

"Of course, of course," he said. "*Jungë leit*, I know how it is. My own daughter, bless her, fourteen years of age, she's already running all over the place. Please God," he said, "eighteen and I marry her off. A girl should get married. For boys . . . we—ell," he spread his hands, "not so important. A boy has his career to think of, his position. But a girl! A girl must be married."

"That's what I keep telling Muriel. But you know what it is . . ." she sighed, "young girls think oh, there's plenty of time . . . I want to enjoy myself . . . *you* know."

Mr Levinson looked grave and respectful.

"Of course," he said, "it's not always so easy. A girl like your daughter . . . I haven't seen her . . . I'm sure a fine girl, good family

25

. . . it's not always so easy for such a girl to find the right one. Mind you, she *can*," he added hastily, "for everyone there's always someone. Isn't that so? Sometimes it takes a little longer finding, sometimes a little shorter time; it depends. But there's always a right one. And with a little help——" he made an encouraging gesture.

"That's exactly what I *always*," she said leaning forward, "always say. A little push in the right direction. . . . My daughter's not the kind to push herself, Mr Levinson."

"The reserved type," he said.

"Exactly! You've hit on exactly the right word. Muriel's very reserved. And you know what men are. Unless you push something right under their noses they just don't see it."

"I know just what you mean. Men in solid, good positions, not so young any more maybe, tired of running about . . . and yet they don't settle down."

"All they need is a good push," she said again.

There was a momentary silence.

"If only you knew of someone like that for my daughter, Mr Levinson. Maybe we could give him a push together," she said laughing.

Mr Levinson looked at his hat which he had absent-mindedly taken off after all and placed on his lap.

"Who knows?" he said, "I might meet exactly the right one tomorrow, next week . . ."

"If you did . . ." she said quickly, "if you *did*, I needn't tell you how grateful we'd be . . ."

"A pleasure! A pleasure! If I can make two people happy. . . . Why not?"

"To do such a *mitzvah*, such a good turn . . ."

"It is the Almighty's will that we must help each other . . ."

"I wouldn't want you to do it for nothing, Mr Levinson," she cried.

"Lady Gould. I'll tell you the truth. For my part I want nothing. To bring happiness to you, your husband, your daughter . . . do I want money? But I'll tell you . . . for me, as I'm saying I want nothing. But for my family, *meinë kindë*, four bless them and the boy thirteen next year—for them I need. For them I take from

26

you—but, *but* only the cost of expenses. For now. You know how it is, not everything falls to you in a minute. You have to look around, go to a few places, inquiries . . ."

"How much?" said Sir Oswald suddenly roused by the commercial note from where he had been sitting silently and forgotten.

Mr Levinson looked deprecating, smiled with all his broken teeth and said: "Fifty pounds."

"Fifty pounds!" said Sir Oswald sitting bolt upright. "For expenses," he cried, outraged.

Mr Levinson spread his hands, shrugged his shoulders, smiled modestly . . . and said nothing.

Lady Gould, herself shaken, rallied. "Of course," she said, "in a delicate matter like this we wouldn't bargain. But Mr Levinson . . . fifty pounds!"

"Fifty pounds down *now*. But it comes off the five per cent. Only five per cent altogether, Lady Gould. Is that such a lot for a child's happiness? I understand from my good friend who recommended me that your daughter's dowry is twenty thousand? Yes? So, for a fifty pounds you would sacrifice a daughter's happiness? Besides . . . I give a guarantee."

"Guarantee?" said Sir Oswald who, as a successful business man, was strongly suspicious of guarantees.

"But of course! A guarantee absolutely that I find your daughter a bridegroom."

A confusion of ideas, a vague sense that guarantees, always suspect, were doubly so in such a matter, mingled with a peculiar feeling, engendered by Mr Levinson's firm confidence of manner, that he could leave the matter, with all its attendant worries and wife-nagging, safely in the marriage-broker's hands and give himself a bit of peace, all warred inside Sir Oswald's mind.

He caught his wife's eye which was trying to convey to him desperate assent while simultaneously appearing non-committal to Mr Levinson, and saw he would have to give in. And yet . . . the idea stung and violenced all his business instincts. Not in this way did a tobacco baron who had fought his way up from a Northern slum do a deal.

"I'll give you twenty-five," he said at last.

"God forbid," said Mr Levinson throwing up his hands, "God

forbid that I should bargain over a young girl's happiness. For me
..." his voice took on a tearful note, "for me—I ask nothing. But
for my children ... my wife ... as I wish you joy from your grandchildren, Sir Oswald, if I say forty it is for them. But below forty
—no!"

Lady Gould tightened her lips and flashed a sideways menace at
her husband who, helplessly weakening, closed at thirty-five.

"*Nu!* With *mazel!*" said Mr Levinson, shaking hands with great
rapidity as soon as he had pocketed the cheque. "I let you know.
In a few days I let you know." And he departed with another quick
look at the silver cabinet and an offer to do a bit of re-plating if ever
they should need it.


By what—had he known it—was a temporary stroke of luck for
Mr Levinson, his persuasive overtures to Leo to let himself be introduced to Muriel Gould happened to coincide with one of Leo's
periods of depression which within the last year or two had been
occurring more and more frequently. More alarmed than he allowed
himself to notice by this gradual change in his normally sanguine
temperament, he had found himself listening to Mr Levinson and
finally agreeing to meet the girl. He was the more amenable because
he knew well enough the obvious fact that sex and emotional
loneliness both were at the bottom of his increasing low-spirited-
ness. In other words, it was high time he was married; a conclusion
he had reached long ago but which was now, with every day that
passed, beating with ever-heavier blows upon his consciousness.

And yet—even while he was nodding his head and agreeing with
the marriage-broker's arguments and arrangements—a wry, painful
pang seemed to slice his heart in two. "Not this way," his romantic
self whispered. "Not like this!" echoed the mid-twentieth century
sophisticate with a self-conscious, horrified laugh. And then——
"Why not?" from the practical forebears of his blood. "Why not?
Do not the French ... and Royalty ...?"

"And if it has to be," he said to himself, "why not the money
too?" And he repeated to himself several times the words "twenty
thousand pounds, twenty thousand pounds"; although, when he
tried to think what he would do with such an amount, he could
think of nothing he did not have or could not do within reason

already. Yet the very ring of the words held a kind of golden pleas-
ingness.

No amount of gold plating unfortunately could englamour
Muriel Gould. Nor could the excellent dinner to which he was invited, ostensibly to discuss some charitable foundation in which Sir
Oswald had entangled himself as patron, smooth over the girl's
painful, gauche attempts to interest him. He was not without heart.
He saw and suffered, but could not, under the heavy yoke of his own
pained embarrassment, help with the girl's agonized attempts to
appear attractive in a situation which, however often she was
obliged to endure, she would never take in her stride. The plain
heavy-figured girl with thin legs and thick waist, chattered and
chattered in her high, flat voice, trying desperately to conceal her
constant, tepid, vacant unhappiness with a babble of meaningless
words, mostly about her "interests", a word which all three of the
Goulds repeated often. "Interests in common," said Lady Gould
frequently at inapropos junctions of the conversation. "I suppose my
greatest interest is music," said Muriel, and the Rabbi saw with a
quick flash of his mind's eye the dutiful cultivation of the piano; the
dreary practising; the yawned-through concerts in the quiet aquar-
ium light of the Wigmore Hall on Sunday afternoons. What could
one do for a Muriel Gould who had nothing but money? Who had
no taste, no style, no wit, no looks; whose fairish hair sat rigidly
about a pale, long-featured, vulnerable face?

It was, he saw, no use and as soon as he decently could he made
his get-away, leaving, though he did not know this, Levinson to
make good his "guarantee" with someone else.

This was the incident to which Leo's mind reverted on the evening
of Joel's visit. And, lying in bed, he was seized with sudden terror at
the idea which came to him that he might be the male equivalent of
a Muriel Gould. No one she might conceivably want would ever
want her. Did that apply with equal truth to him?

"Oh nonsense, nonsense," he muttered and thrusting the idea
from him turned over and tried determinedly to sleep. But all
through his dreams, when he eventually managed to fall off, the
thought persisted so that he woke with a lowered, sinking heart and
a feeling like a grey bruise, which haunted him throughout the day

# Chapter Two

## I

GIVING A LAST CURSORY GLANCE AT THE SMALL HALF-page of notes in front of him as the chairman drew his introductory remarks to a close, Leo silently counted five and rose slowly to his feet.

"My subject this evening, the fourth in our series on 'The Foundations of Jewish Thought', is 'European Jewry in the Twelfth Century'. This period was remarkable for two particularly interesting developments. The first was the extraordinary way in which Jewish thought as a whole escaped from the petrifying influence of medieval . . ."

His eyes wandered as his talk went on. He was experienced enough as a speaker and versed enough in his subject to be able both to take stock of his surroundings and hold his audience at the same time. He looked the latter over with some satisfaction. The room was crowded with members of the Guild, the group of young people—or mainly young—attached to his own Synagogue whom he himself had largely helped to form into what they were: an active, cohesive body.

Sitting right at the end of the front row was Doris Goldenbird, a not unhandsome girl, her large features, so like her mother's, softened by the colour and freshness of youth, her long, big-boned body with its promise of fat, still gawky, her tread heavy. She had come up to Leo before the lecture and introduced herself, but so simply and pleasantly, and so obviously without any guile in her head with its roughly cropped dark hair that, although he had seen at a glance that Doris Goldenbird would not do and the mystic syllables of her name had instantly resolved themselves into oblivion along with all the Rosalinds, Sandras and Carols of her generation, he had felt kindly disposed towards her. She had chatted away, before Leo rose to speak (her mother had been right there, she would obviously chat with anyone), to the nondescript young man sitting next to her who, after the fashion of many young men, did not seem to think it necessary to chat back. "I suppose she'll get on all right," thought Leo, "as long as she makes the running." And he felt annoyed as he often did with young men who never appeared to feel the necessity as *he* always had to pull their weight socially but just sat there sucking their pipes, not even looking thoughtful, only blank, while the girls, groomed and coloured and determinedly flogging their vivacity, worked away trying to evoke a responsive spark.

"For heaven's sake!" he suddenly said to himself looking towards the other end of the front row where, for the first time, he noticed, sitting at ease, old Boruch Gabriel. "What's he doing at a Guild meeting?" Then he noticed that the old man was sitting comfortably in a large armchair and, scattered in various places amongst the audience, were three of his daughters and that a fourth, the married one, was on guard at the door anxiously shooing the inevitable late-comers towards the most awkwardly placed seats which were, as usual, the only vacant ones.

"Good Lord! It's his house!" he suddenly realized and began talking a little faster, vexed with the annoying coincidence of his lecture and the Gabriels' turn to lend a house. Old Gabriel! That notorious interrupter of public meetings, the bane of every lecturer in London! Who didn't know that small, bouncing, wiry figure with its wide gestures, that thin, fanatical face and its peppery glance?

He came to the first of his illustrative anecdotes. Half way through, old Gabriel took his pipe out of his pocket and began hunting for his tobacco pouch. The Rabbi approached the climax of his story. Gabriel, searching frantically for his tobacco and fussing under his breath, became desperate and noisy. He went rapidly through his pockets again then lifted his head and gazed wildly round him. Even he could see it was hopeless, without open rude-ness, to leave his seat and struggle through to the door. "Serves him right for sitting right under my nose," thought Leo with some fury. He wanted to make his point with his accustomed lucidity and the old man's antics were disturbing him. He was now attempting to signal with violent gestures to the only one of his daughters within his range of vision but it was no use. She had her eyes fixed on the speaker himself, her tall, thin figure bent forward in concentrated attention. "Blow the girl," he thought. "Do take your eyes off me and get the old boy his tobacco."

31

Suddenly, from behind the old man and seated a little to the side of him where the Rabbi had not noticed her before, a girl leaned forward and offered Gabriel her cigarette case. He took one with a relieved smile and settled back again inhaling with huge appetite. It was obvious that tobacco was a raging necessity to him. The Rabbi, relieved, made a brilliant addition to his illustrative story, was greeted with applause and continued to talk with one half of his attention gratefully trying to see behind the high wing of the old-fashioned armchair in which the old man was sitting. From where he stood he could see only a slight, girlish shoulder clad in blue wool and a curl of pale brown hair.

He looked away and immediately caught Lillie Stiel's eye. It was annoying and amusing to reflect on her mother's tactics—as blatant in their way as Mrs Goldenbird's—when he had first become minister (received a "call" as they irritatingly put it when ninety-nine times out of a hundred the "call" was no more than the louder rustling of a greater quantity of pound notes) to the Ferne Road Synagogue. A single Rabbi was always a target. Never mind that he was almost fifty, was fat, grey haired, heavy-faced. Never mind that, compared with many of his congregants, he was a poor man, excellent though his stipend happened to be: neverthless he was an eligible bachelor with an assured place in the community. Inconvenient as this occasionally proved to him personally, calling for reserves of tact which it was often tiresome to maintain, he could not help nevertheless an occasional, affectionate smile to himself at his people's respect for the degrees after his name and the learning that his calling implied. What some of the mothers wouldn't give—and the fathers too!—to say: "My son-in-law, Rabbi Norberg, M.A., Ph.D."

"Only what has it all brought me . . . me, the prize?" his thought ended this time as it always did.

He started on his second anecdote, an illustration from the Talmud. Half way through he perceived that Mr Gabriel knew it also and not only knew it but was already muttering the phrase which capped and pointed it, bounding about in his chair, delighted at this opportunity to demonstrate his knowledge. Before Leo had finished, Mr Gabriel, unable to contain himself, jumped up and danced round to the bookcase which was behind the speaker's chair and was fumbling noisily amongst the huge, tattered volumes of Hebrew for the particular passage.

"The minute I've finished," thought Leo, "I'll remember another meeting I have to attend."

At that moment the girl with the cigarette case moved a little as she reached for her handbag and her whole face come into view. She struck a match for her cigarette and as she held it the light illuminated her round chin and the shape of her mouth. There was something about her face which puzzled him but he could not think what it was. The puzzle nagged him faintly as he went on speaking after coping, good-temperedly enough, with Gabriel's interruption. It was different from every other girl's face in the room but he couldn't say how. He wondered what kind of voice went with it.

Making a final joke he tidied up his subject, patted it on the head, looked at his watch and sat down. It had been an admirable performance and there was a great deal of applause. The chairman, an attractive, fortyish and entirely charming Viennese doctor, rose and complimented the Rabbi. "If zere are any questions Dr Norberg will be very pleased to answer zem," he said. "Lillie?"

Lillie Stiel, vice-chairman of the Guild, promptly stood up.

"I'd like, first of all, to thank Rabbi Norberg for his extremely interesting lecture," she said in her assured voice. "I'm sure we all enjoyed it tremendously. Er . . . there are one or two points about which I should be pleased to have his opinion. It seems to me . . ."

The Rabbi answered her a little self-consciously for all the old association between them. Lillie was thirty, rather older than most of the other girls. She was what he classified as a "possible": smart, efficient, could talk, dressed well, was good for all the duties of a minister's wife, pretty if one liked that small head of sleek, black hair and those coldly shining black eyes. "Money too! though to do myself justice I don't much care about that." He had to admit that when he looked at the credit side she seemed a likely candidate for office. It was when he looked at the debit side that his heart turned uneasily. Her family was comfortably off and harmless enough, but that was all that could reasonably be said for it. Her father manufactured furniture, her mother managed her father, and her brother, a business man, ran a good car.

33

"But that's not what I want," he said often to himself. He knew the difference between the Lillie Stiels and the real thing. The Stiels were nothing; a middle middle class, tasteless, moneyed clan, living in a dry, neat, well-polished home devoid of all signs of that intangible atmosphere which his bones could recognize as his. Sometimes he tried to imagine that rather stupid nonentity, her father, as his father-in-law. The effort defeated him. "Chill," he would think to himself of Lillie, "chill, calculating, fourth-rate. It's impossible." And yet he still kept her on his private list. Occasionally he recited her virtues over to himself. "She wouldn't be so bad," he told himself once or twice when loneliness lowered his spirit.

After Lillie a lot of other questions came popping at him. It was when he had disposed of these that the cigarette girl bent forward and, taking her cue from his own remarks in answer to a previous question, said in an unfamiliar accent: "But how did the Rabbis ever come to agree on anything?"

Everybody laughed and the girl smiled, her face tilted up to look at him. He laughed too.

"How indeed?" he said.

Mr Gabriel, who had been jigging about behind him, balancing a pile of books on one arm, again tugged at his elbow.

"I want to show you," he said, "in the Talmud it says like this——"

Leo nodded absently and contrived to signal to the chairman who promptly took the hint and called for a vote of thanks.

Tea and cake were immediately circulated by the four Gabriel sisters and Leo, hemmed in by the crowd and unable to escape as quickly as he had promised himself, sat down in an obscure and rather dark corner with his cup and plate, glad to escape from conversation for a few moments at least. He had just begun to relax and feel comfortable when a standard lamp he had not noticed beside him was suddenly switched on. With an exclamation of annoyance he half turned in his deep chair to see Sara, the second of the Gabriel daughters, kneeling on a footstool at the side of his chair, her back, which she was in the act of straightening, to the room. She had evidently been reaching down to the switch on the skirting board of the wall.

34

"I'm so sorry," she said quickly, noticing at once that he objected to the light, "I'll put it off again."

"No don't," he said, mollified by her quick apology. "I'm going in a few moments anyway."

"I am so annoyed with myself for disturbing you," she went on, still in her low, slightly hesitant voice which he had heard on occasion before but—perhaps because it came to him from a near and unusual angle (they were facing each other across the padded arm of his chair, her face a little lower than his)—he had never noticed to be of so pleasing a quality.

"Forget about it," he said, "I was just relaxing for a minute before throwing myself to the mob again."

"It is a crush," she agreed, turning her head to look over her shoulder at the room. The deep, amber light of the lamp glowed across her face and the effect caught the Rabbi's eye. He would never have thought Sara Gabriel could look so striking. Her face, contrary in effect to that of most people's, was one of those which look better when closer to the observer's eye. In some odd fashion her severe features softened, her pale complexion became delicate, at close quarters. The light illumined her smooth, pale-brown hair which was (though he did not realize this) with its ashy lights a very unusual colour, a kind of *brune cendrée*. Worn drawn up and away from her face and coiled in a bun at the nape of her neck, the style showed up the gentle, austere modelling of her profile. Her nose was too long and her chin too pointed but the line of her jaw and her slender neck, the turn and poise of her head, pleased him.

For some reason a line of verse he knew came to his mind and he quoted it aloud, not in English but in Russian. She looked at him inquiringly.

"You don't understand Russian?"

"About two words."

"Ah, that's a pity; those words are so beautiful. It is a song really, a song about a bird which sings only in winter when the other birds do not sing at all——" He broke off seeing her turn her head away as if uninterested. "Perhaps you do not care for poetry; only for music?"

"No. I *prefer* words," she said turning back and giving him a shy, quick, momentary glance from what he saw for the first time to be remarkable eyes. "I'm not musical. At least . . . I just like things like Italian opera which musical people don't think much of."

As this was precisely the kind of music which he himself liked (which had enabled him to regard the latest exploits of his cantor with a secretly sympathetic eye) he felt bound to defend it. "But that's music too. You needn't be ashamed of liking it."

"I'm not." She spoke with a kind of spirited gentleness as though surprised at her courage in arguing with him. "It's just that I'd like to have that authentic thrill down the spine from other kinds of music too. I feel I'm missing something, that I'm being cheated out of my rights."

This conversation with someone he had always thought of—if at all—as "one of the Gabriel girls" gave him a great deal of surprise. He would have gone on talking to her but at that moment he caught sight of her father pushing his way fussily through the crowd with a huge volume of Hebrew under his arm and—frightened of being pinned down to some interminable discussion—he heaved himself suddenly, almost rudely, to his feet saying with an abstracted smile: "I think I'd like another cup of tea."

"Oh, please let me——" she began also rising hastily and rather confusedly from the foot stool.

"No, no," he said, "I have to go in a few minutes anyway." And he made his way over to where her elder sister was still dispensing tea from the huge, aluminium teapot.

In another moment he found himself at the centre of a small group. It pleased him that, hovering on the very edge of this group, he saw again the cigarette girl. He made up his mind to speak to her and, reaching for another piece of cake, managed to collide his hand with hers.

"I beg you pardon," he said.

She smiled at him.

"No, take the sponge. Please do. It's much too sweet for me, anyway."

"I like sweet cake," she said biting with her small, irregular teeth into the cake's pink icing.

He looked closely at her face. He could see now what it was that had puzzled him about it. She was the only girl in the room without a scrap of make-up on. This was so unusual and surprising that,

36

without thinking, he helped himself to an excessively iced and decorated cake of a kind he much disliked.

"So you want to know how we Rabbis ever manage to agree on anything?"

"I didn't mean you personally, Dr Norberg," she said and the second puzzling thing about her cleared up.

"You're Welsh!" he said. "By the way, what's your name?"

"Sophie Olendorf. Did you guess from my accent?"

"I did."

"It's too bad! I think I've no accent at all but in London people are always pointing a finger at me in an accusing way and saying 'Wales!' as though it's the last place in the world anyone should come from. I don't go around here pointing at people and saying 'Cockney'!"

With one eye Norberg saw Mr Gabriel converging on him again. He said hurriedly: "I'm afraid I really must go now," and then, because she looked a little crestfallen and lost, and he felt he'd rather hurt her feelings by this abrupt end to their conversation, added: "Perhaps I could give you a lift if you live in this district?"

Her face brightened immediately. "I'm staying in a sort of hostel. It's quite near. But do you mind if my friend, Trudy, comes too? She lives there as well."

"Not at all."

"I'll just tell Trudy and get my coat," she said.

"Right."

She darted away. Leo was just raising his teacup to his lips to finish his tea when he saw Sara Gabriel across the room standing alone by the fireplace. The light there was quite different, white and harsh, and from the angle at which he now saw her she looked quite different too; drawn, fatigued, older. As he looked across wondering whether to speak to her again or not, Sophie Olendorf returning with her friend cut across his line of vision and he immediately went up to her. "Ready?"

"Yes. We're both ready." And she introduced him to her friend, Trudy Harris, a pretty, red-cheeked, dark-haired girl.

In the car he found out a little more about Sophie. She was twenty-three. Behind her in Wales she had left her parents and three young brothers. She had a job in the headquarters of a Jewish international charity organization. She and Trudy both hated the hostel.

"They're nearly all refugee girls who spend their time writing letters to America trying to get themselves sponsored. Trudy and I'd like to take a little flat together if we could only find one cheap enough."

"How do your parents like your living away from home?"

She said in surprise: "Oh but it was always understood that I'd have to earn my own living as soon as I could."

"But couldn't you have found a job in Wales?"

"No indeed, I couldn't have got nearly so good a job at home. Anyway, I don't want to live at home. I wouldn't go back there for anything."

"Neither would I," said Trudy cheerfully from the back seat.

"I must see what I can do about finding you somewhere else to live," he said avuncularly.

They whooped, then went on chattering. When they ran out of chatter they burst into song, unselfconsciously, like children.

"What do you do with yourselves—apart from work?" he asked.

"We knit, we sew . . ." said Sophie.

"We go to lots of theatres," said Trudy. "We've seen a lot of plays, only it's not easy to get down in time for a good seat. The queues start so early."

He made up his mind to take Sophie out, not in the cheap seats to which she was accustomed but properly, in comfort. He held her back while Trudy went into the hostel and asked her if she would like to go to the theatre one evening.

"Thank you. I would," she said with that faint, Welsh lilt.

"We'll make it next week," he said. "Any night except Thursday. And Friday of course!"

"Wednesday will be all right, I think."

"What would you like to see?"

She chose the ballet. He looked at her bemused. "All right. I'll book." He hated ballet.

As she came to meet him outside the theatre, smiling in greeting, he thought with surprise: What a lovely face! It seemed to him that he must surely have noticed her beauty the first time he met her but he couldn't remember having done so. He thought of her

38

friend, Trudy, whom he had immediately seen to be a pretty girl and—as he sat beside Sophie in the theatre—tried to define why Trudy seemed merely pretty while Sophie he now saw was beautiful. He tried (abstracting his mind completely from the boredom of the performance in front of him) to classify her features. Her hair was short and curled roughly all over her head. It was a nondescript, pale brown in colour where Trudy's had shone in a deep, rich, glossy chestnut. Her eyes were pale too, a light blue-grey and were none too large. Her skin, compared with Trudy's brilliant rose and cream, was colourless. Peering closer, even in the half-light he could see that it was roughened in texture, almost weatherbeaten. Her pale, wide lips looked roughened too. Only her nose was perfect; straight, charming, delicately dented at each nostril. And yet, the planes of her face, curving beneath a high and lovely forehead, were beautiful. There was a plenitude, a breadth and rounding to her features and yet a delicacy to make one catch one's breath. It was in direct contrast to her tall, childishly angular and even awkward body. The stray thought occurred to him suddenly that she was of exactly the same build and colouring as Sara Gabriel. And he asked himself vaguely, before promptly forgetting about Sara, how the result could be so ravishing in the one case and so austere in the other.

*Coppelia*, which would normally have bored him half under the row of seats in front, danced on before him, bearable, even made lovely, by the sheer accident of beauty in the line and bone of the face beside him.

In the intervals, listening to her talk about it, he wondered if she really liked it so much. He suspected her of following a fashion; she'd probably read herself into balletomania like so many others.

After the performance he took her for supper to a small restaurant.

"Tell me more about yourself," he said. "What are your parents like? Who do you like best, your father or your mother?"

"It's hard to say," she said looking surprised at the question which Leo had unconsciously put in his usual, authoritative tone. "Dad's not very . . . modern," (Leo surmised that what she really meant was "not very refined".) "Mum's the one at home. She likes reading and music . . ."

"Do you like reading?"

"Oh yes. Sometimes. Just now," she brought out rather grandly, "I'm reading *War and Peace*."

"Ah!" said Leo, pleased. "And what does your father do?"

"He travels round the Welsh villages selling drapery and clothing and that sort of thing. He's away a lot, he's only home for week-ends usually."

"What about your brothers?"

"Sam, that's the eldest, he goes round with Dad and Barry's just won a place at a Technical College. The other's just a kid."

"What's he going to do?"

"The little one? I don't know. He's good at figures. I think mum wants him to be an accountant but he's not sure yet."

It did not seem to occur to her to ask him any questions about himself and this slightly disappointed Leo. He rather enjoyed talking about himself and his work, about synagogue politics and the antics of some of his congregants but, afraid of boring her, he did not introduce any of this into the conversation.

On the way home he said: "I've got a surprise for you."

"What is it?"

"I think I've found you a little flat."

"Oh! Oh, Rabbi Norberg! Honestly? Are you joking?"

"No, honestly I'm not joking. I promised you I'd make in-quiries. Well I think—I'm almost sure—I can get this for you. The thing is . . . I'm not quite sure what you can afford, you know?" He waited in an odd state of anxiety for her answer. In some curious way it seemed to him as though to know how much money she earned would let him into her life, the mysterious, unknown details of which were beginning to take on in his mind a charged, magical quality.

"Oh quick! Tell me what they want for it? I'm sure Trudy and I can manage. Is it big enough for two? Is it furnished? Where is it?"

"It's in Egremont Road. D'you know where that is? At the top of Bollards Place, not far from where you are now. There's a living room, a bedroom and a kitchenette. You share the bath with the woman who owns the house. She has the ground floor. It's one of those small, modern houses and she's letting the first floor furnished. She want three guineas a week."

Sophie heaved a sigh of relief. "We can manage that all right. I get eight and Trudy seven fifteen. Hurray! No more of that awful hostel!"

"What do you do with all that money?" he asked teasingly.

"It doesn't go very far these days you know," she said seriously. "We like eating! Oh, won't it be marvellous to do our own cooking!"

"I hope you're going to ask me for supper," he said in a jocular tone.

"Of *course* we will. D'you like mushrooms? I have a wonderful recipe . . ." she said in a suddenly sophisticated voice which made him think of arty bed-sittingrooms in Swiss Cottage. He had noticed this manner in her once or twice before. "Oh this is wonderful! Thank you *so* much."

When they drew up outside the hostel she thanked him again. He put his arm round her shoulders; they felt very light and brittle. She moved away slightly but without embarrassment. He heard a small sound which might have been a smothered giggle and his arm jumped away from her as if electrified. "Good night," she said and sprang out of the car.

"I'll let you know about the flat," he said half-heartedly wishing he had never mentioned it but feeling committed now to a generosity he did not feel. Unwittingly perhaps—and he was prepared to give her the benefit of the doubt—she had done or appeared to have done the unforgivable thing: retreated at the first indication of Leo, the man, as a physical entity. Driving home, he was able to feel in his own flesh the piercing insult Joel's ex-wife, Irene, had inflicted on him. Again terror shook him with fear of such an end for himself. How little the outsider knows, he thought. "Get married," they said. "Get married." And there were always girls to marry. But where amongst them could be found the mutuality he longed for, the pull of moon and wave, the fused, galvanic crash of the leaping sea upon the spread-limbed, eager, drowsing shore?

2

The two young girls moved into their small flat, with the Rabbi's help, a fortnight later. He transported all their luggage for them in his car. They were enormously excited. Leo stayed with them all evening helping them to settle in. They ate scrambled eggs for supper and after it Sophie sat him down at the table and made him help her frame some photographs in *passe-partout*. She kept him at it, fumbling with his big fingers, till it was late. As last he got up and went home. He was surprised and even annoyed at his own reluctance to leave.

After that he often took to coming round in the evenings, half hoping, yet afraid, to catch Sophie by herself. He always had an excuse. Sometimes it was to take them both out to some Little Theatre in a distant suburb; sometimes he brought a new book which he wanted her to read. In the intervening days he found it difficult not to think about her. He was entranced by the curving delicacy of her face, her angular boy's body, her gawky, delicious way of standing with her toes turned in; and her wide, pale, roughened lips.

Just as he was dialling her telephone number one day, the thought flashed into his mind (between the numbers two and seven) how appropriate it was that she should have been reading *War and Peace*. He had fallen in love with Natasha when he was fifteen. And now, here was Sophie, the slender, lovely girl who could not (he thought as the ringing tone commenced at the other end) have been more like his conception of Tolstoy's heroine. Even her name, Sophie Olendorf, needed only the title "Countess" before it, it was so fitting, aristocratic, Russian. And, amusing himself with picturing her against that background which would have been most perfect, most fitting, her young beauty shining from sables, her face glowing against snow and stars, surrounded by authoritative men, French conversation, magnificent jewels, he lost almost completely (while the telephone rang in the empty room) his awareness of her real environment and was never quite able afterwards to dissociate this imagined setting from her real circumstance. When he recalled (as he replaced the telephone at last) that Pierre too was a heavy, fat man, his sudden uprush of identified delight was so keen that he exclaimed aloud with joy.

One evening he found himself at a reception held in Manor Green in honour of some visiting celebrity. At the end, while putting on

42

his coat in the hall before leaving, he stood chatting to Lillie Stiel and Dr Gildheim, the Chairman of the Synagogue Guild. John Gildheim was a tall, prematurely grey, distinguished looking man with a delightful Viennese accent; a charming, gaily eligible bachelor.

It has long been Leo's custom to give Lillie a lift home whenever it so fell out that way. They were such old friends that the habit excited no remark. This time, as Dr Gildheim turned away to speak to someone else, he said as usual: "Hurry up, Lillie, I'm ready." He found it pleasant not to have to stand on ceremony with her. To his surprise she said half-heartedly: "Will you wait a minute, Leo? I'm not sure whether John's giving me a lift or not."

He stared at her in some annoyance.

"Listen, Lillie, I'm not a chauffeur for you. If you want to hang about in case John wants to take you home, hang about. I'm not waiting."

He walked off angrily, his vanity a little hurt. Going down the front path he almost bumped into Sara Gabriel. "Hello, how are you?" he said. "Enjoy the evening?"

"It was all right," she said. "I quite liked the professor. He's got an enormous personality; but you know I think he's a bit of a mountebank underneath." As this was exactly what he himself had thought, priding himself on his penetration, Leo was rather struck by her remark.

"Come on, I'll give you a lift," he said.

On the way he set himself to talk entertainingly. Instinctively, without thinking about it, he felt that what might have bored Sophie would interest Sara and so talked about himself.

"There are three things in the world I refuse to do," he said, and paused fractionally, half expecting the automatic come-back "Only three?" which nearly every one of the "smart" girls he knew would have made. She said nothing however for (had he known it) the simple reason that she did not know the fashionable way of conversation making, so he continued: "Wait for a woman, stand in a queue or carry a parcel."

"Surely you have to do something you don't like doing sometimes?"

"As a matter of fact, never! For instance, if my housekeeper cooks

43

me a meal and I don't like it, I leave it. That's why I'm still a bachelor. A wife wouldn't stand for that, would she?"

"I don't know. If she loved you I suppose she'd stand for anything."

"Love?" he said, thinking of Sophie and for the first time coupling his feeling for her with the word. This describing, the giving of a name and form to his emotion, at once enlarged and solidified it, as though a weight had suddenly crystallized out of cloud and settled warmly within his heart. "Love, love," he said, "Do you believe in love, Sara? Do you think for instance that anyone could love me?"

Behind these words, even as he spoke them, he could feel a touch of lazy sprawling cruelty. To discuss love when he had just discovered his own, and with Sara Gabriel for whom the word must encompass an empty, tender, anguished place, was cruel. But she was there, an innocent and willing ear, and he could not refrain from the luxury of self-examination.

"Yes of course I do," she said surprised. It was on the tip of her tongue to say "You know very well just how many girls would be pleased to fall in love with you with any encouragement". She looked at his thick, solid hands on the steering wheel and then at his profile with its large, curved nose and fleshy jowl. His eyes were small and set far back in his head. When he was concentrated, as now, upon his driving, the pupils contracted noticeably. It was a physical trick of his which she had noticed before. Her eyes stayed on his face, noting the broad, high forehead, the way he had of pushing his lips forward.

"The point is," she said, "could *you* love anyone?"

"Could *I*? What do you mean? Do you think me incapable of love?"

"No, no," she said and then, unexpectedly, as the phrase walked into her mind and out again on her tongue: "I think you *capable de tout*."

Leo turned his head quickly and looked at her with some amazement. Such phrases were not included in the conversational small talk of Manor Green and he was not quite sure that he approved of them. Was she being intellectual at him and pretentious? He was prepared to answer somewhat stiffly when she turned her austerely

44

modelled head towards him and, in the light of passing headlamps, he saw her smile hesitantly with an almost beseeching look in her grey eyes. It gave him a strange irritated pang to see the uncertain, defenceless creature which momentarily looked out from behind her strong, remote features.

"At least . . ." she said. Centring back on himself again he pounced on her hesitation.

"So you think I *can* love? Can but won't perhaps? Is that it?"

"In a way. In a way perhaps."

"Oh! And why?" he demanded. "What makes you think that?"

"I think . . . I think perhaps that, like many men, you have very little sentiment really. You have only a collection of appetites and fancies; romanticism without emotion."

Leo was struck into silence. He tried to remember other girls in his life before Sophie. He could remember nothing of those loves beyond their bondage. Three times in his life he had proposed marriage; each time to some frail and lovely girl; each time to someone fresh and brutal who didn't want him.

"Are you annoyed?" she said at last with an evasive, sideways glance at him. She was frowning with shyness.

"No, of course not. I'm surprised! You seem to know me—or men!—very well."

"The onlooker," she said looking down at her finger nails with a sad half-smile, "with the seeing eye."

"Yes you have! Yes you have, Sara. I think you're seeing too much. Let's talk about something else. What else does your seeing eye see? Let's gossip! What do you think about the other members of the Guild? What do you think of John? Our Don Juan? Every girl in the world, I understand, is ready to run the minute he beckons with his little finger." There was a touch of jealousy in the way he spoke.

"He's a very attractive man," she said. "He doesn't appeal to me personally but I can quite see it with other people. I think Lillie likes him."

"Lillie! Lillie'd like anything in trousers."

He was still annoyed with Lillie over the earlier incident.

She laughed. "Well, I wouldn't have said it, knowing you're a friend of hers, but you're quite right. I've been watching her for a long time."

45

"I'm not such a close friend of hers as you might think. Of course people have been coupling our names together for years but there's nothing in it. She did some work for me at one time when I found myself without a secretary and I know her people fairly well. But go on, tell me what else you've noticed about her? D'you think she'd make a good wife?"

"No I don't," she said forcefully. "I detest the girl if you must know. She...I've known her to ignore repeatedly anyone she thinks she can't make use of, anyone she thinks doesn't matter. She's got no standards of her own. She's got no principles. Oh, I know she's efficient and she's got a cold sort of intelligence, but fundamentally she's nothing but a fake. She's a sham. She doesn't know anything about anything."

"I don't think she's as bad as all that," he said, "but in some things I agree with you. She *is* cold. Cold and calculating. Her mother's just the same. She's going to find it a hard job to get married, you know," he said thoughtfully. "She's been out with literally dozens of men and not one of them have stuck."

"I'm not worrying about her. She'll marry a nonentity with a lot of money."

He turned and looked at her curiously. They had been parked for some time outside her house which was a rather shabby Victorian villa in a long, second-rate street, not quite in the purely artisan part of Manor Green East but not an integral part of the Garden Suburb either.

"What an observant person you are! I had no idea you were like this. How long have I known you? On and off?"

"Oh—h . . . years—on and off," she said laughing. "I suppose all this time I've been just 'one of the Gabriel sisters'?"

"Yes. Yes, you were but that's really no excuse."

"It's usually like that," she said pensively. "I'm 'one of the Gabriel girls'. I'm 'old Gabriel's daughter'—with all that that implies," she said with a touch of bitterness. "You know my father. It's lucky we've got Monty. At least he keeps the shop together. If we left it to father he wouldn't have a customer worth speaking of."

The Rabbi looked tactfully noncommittal. He knew very well that to go into Mr Gabriel's shop which though devoted primarily to Jewish books, praying shawls and candlesticks served also as a meeting place for the old man's friends, old men like himself full of confused rags of ideas, was to become involved immediately in lengthy discussions lasting hours and leading nowhere, on Jewish politics, ethics, half-digested, passionately advocated philosophical notions.

"Monty? Oh, you mean Monty Halpern. Your brother-in-law?'

"Yes. He married my eldest sister, Rebecca; brave boy!"

"Why do you say that? Your sister's a very nice girl," said Leo, somewhat mendaciously.

"Oh . . . to marry into our family . . ."

"Nonsense," he said vigorously. Then: "Look, I must go. It's after twelve. We'll continue our gossip again I hope. We've only done the chairman and the vice-chairman! Next time we'll do the secretary and committee! Sorry I've kept you so late. Will I see you in *Shool* this *Shabbos*? No sermon this week, I'm giving myself a holiday! Good night."

3

Sara let herself into her home. Going into the kitchen to make herself a hot drink she was surprised to find her younger sister, Esther whom they called Essie, there before her, sitting at the kitchen table with a book propped up in front of her, drinking cocoa.

Essie, the third Gabriel daughter, was as tall as Sara but her bones were smaller and she gave an impression of vividness as against the gaunt quietude of her sister. Her whole physical self was more feminine than her sister's for though her nose was as sharp her face was rounder, square of jaw, her hair darker and wavy, her eyes a warm, bright hazel. She was, too, more volatile in manner, quicker and more alive in speech. It was possible to see in her what the young Mr Gabriel must have been like forty years before, though she was without that particular, brooding part of his nature which had been Sara's inheritance from her father. These two middle daughters both took after him in one way or another where the oldest, Rebecca, and the youngest, Fay, commonly called Fagy, took after their mother, dead now for many years and who had been small, plump and not at all clever.

47

"What are you doing up so late," she said to Essie. "Surely you haven't just come in?"

"Yes I have."

"But your class must have been over hours ago!"

"Oh . . . some of us went on to a coffee bar and . . . we just sat there talking."

"For three hours!"

"For heaven's sake, Sos . . . you've just come in yourself."

"Yes, but I went to the Silverberg reception. It didn't finish till after eleven."

"Enjoy it?"

"I . . . it was very interesting," said Sara, trying to bring herself to mention Leo and failing.

"Good," said Essie and draining her cocoa she stood up, went into the scullery and rapidly washed her cup and saucer at the sink.

"Why don't *you* come to the Guild affairs these days?" said Sara following her.

"You know very well why. We've had all this out before—to the point of nausea," said Essie, a note of quick temper rising in her voice.

"Because I'm sick and tired of these lousy Jewish meetings and their stupid propaganda and their idiotic audiences; and I'm fed to the teeth with the 'nice' girls all hoping to meet the right man and most of all I'm sick of the 'nice' Jewish young men and their sublime conceit of themselves. It's a wonder some of them don't charge half-a-crown a time to speak to you. Would if they could get away with it, I suppose."

"Oh, they're not as bad as all that," said Sara laughing.

"*You* think they're not so bad! First because generally you're too tolerant by half; and second because you've never lifted your head up and taken a look at the world outside Manor Green. But I have. And I can tell you this. I prefer any of the students in my class to all your Godalmighty lawyers and doctors . . . all clutching their degrees in one hand and holding out the other for five thousand pounds and a freehold house."

Both her voice and her colour had risen and Sara look anxiously at the door. "For heaven's sake don't wake father up," she said, "and *don't* let him hear you about the class. You know what he'll say!"

"A lot of ignorant *Goyyim*," Essie chanted gravely and the two sisters began to laugh.

"Nevertheless——" began Sara.

"Nevertheless," broke in Essie, "I've got to be up for work in the morning. Good night." And with suspicious haste she flew out of the kitchen and up to her room. Fagy was fast asleep in the other bed and Essie undressed herself cautiously in the dark. It wasn't until she was lying in her own bed that, stretched and taut between the sheets, she allowed herself to think undisturbedly of Kenneth Groby.

# Chapter Three

## I

ESSIE GABRIEL WAS TWENTY-SEVEN; TWO YEARS younger than Sara and eight years older than Fagy. A few days after her birth (there was a story that when she, his third child, was delivered, her father, told it was yet another girl, had refused to see both child and mother) Mr Gabriel, whose finances were in a bad way at the time, had been obliged to take a job teaching in a Talmudic seminary abroad which had kept him away from home for nearly two years. When he came back he came as a stranger to the toddling, talking child who was equally a stranger to her father, he who had missed the first growth of her nature, her first stumbling steps, her infant gropings towards speech.

What had been begun was not afterwards undone. Boruch Gabriel, no psychologist at the best of times, both a fanatically devoted and an incredibly stupid father, was not the man to put aside himself or the incessant demands of his own nature in order to try to understand the needs of another. Essie, the quality of whose temperament, warm, obstinate, romantic, he completely failed to grasp, grew up the only one of his children who consistently flouted him. His eldest child, Rebecca, was a shy, plain girl who had, without ado, married the young man he had encouraged for her. Sara was reasonable and her taste was for quietness. Fagy, the baby, the only really pretty one, was his darling. Left with these three he could, as was his demand from life, have been lord, patriarch and master of his personal kingdom. The thorn, the immovable block, the wanton obstacle to this which he conceived of as his right, was Essie.

"You'll do what I *say*," he would scream at her in his strong, rasping voice, his hot, brown, sunken eyes flaming, his fists clenched in the air. But she wouldn't. Her temper, blind as his, fed itself on his injustices.

"If you can't be like me," said Sara to her on one occasion, "if you can't resign yourself to taking him as he is, then for heaven's sake be like Fagy; don't rise every time. Don't listen."

"I can't help it," she said through clenched teeth. "He's got to be told what he is; unjust, tyrannical, a left-over Mr Barrett. He doesn't even know what century this is. How you and Fagy can listen to him without going off your heads I don't know."

"Oh he's not so bad," said Fagy in a careless tone. She was giving herself a new hair style, sitting at the living room table with a mirror propped against a pile of books in front of her. Her curling brown hair hung damply about her white neck. She was a very pretty girl with Essie's bright, hazel eyes and a creamy, oval face, just a little spoilt by the too-long Gabriel nose but not enough to matter. Perhaps it was her looks which gave her a serene assurance no one else in her family possessed. Sweet, bland, apparently pliant, the youngest by some years, she nevertheless in some odd way exercised a kind of unwritten authority in the family. Her father himself drew back with a curious caution from too-open argument with her. Seldom exercising her will she usually got her own way in a manner difficult to pin down. The only one of them likely to inspire romantic love, she was of an unromantic, even temperament; intelligent though not in the least intellectual; very clever with her hands; good at mathematics; bored and not bored by quite different things from the rest of them. They were all very proud and slightly wary of her. They also loved her in a way quite apart from their feeling for one another. Placed by some odd accident of birth in a family stamped with eccentricity, she was their only real link with the outside, ordinary world; she was their claim to normality.

"It's no good shouting, Essie," she continued, winding a strand of hair with quick expertise round a curler, "you only make him worse. And it makes everything so awful . . . Howard was walking me home from the Tube the other night and I had to stop him on the corner and make some excuse for leaving him. I could hear the shouting right up the street."

"If you're really going out with him seriously he'll have to hear one of our family rows sooner or later," said Sara somewhat drily.

"Oh, I couldn't," said Fagy with a shocked look. "I'd be too ashamed."

"Anyway these rows'll be nothing compared to the one when father gets to know about Howard," said Essie. "He's just about as un-Jewish as he *can* be without actually being a Goy. Everybody knows his family don't keep up a thing."

"I'll worry about that when the time comes," said Fagy nonchalantly fitting a hair net with careless precision over her head.

Essie, from the armchair in which she was sprawling, her head bent forward, her arms slack, looked up and gazed with a puzzled, ironical expression at Fagy, and Sara who was ironing also looked up, held her head sideways for a moment, smiled suddenly, a small, vulnerable smile, and bent to the iron again. To neither of the two older girls had anyone resembling Howard Gerzow, handsome in his rich, fleshy way, come as wooer. Both, apart from the natural drawbacks of their temperaments and lack of commonplace appeal, had suffered from their father's early mistake over Rebecca.

Monty Halpern, Rebecca's husband, came from the kind of family which can be found almost anywhere but in proportionately much larger numbers amongst Jews. The Halperns were numerous, vulgarly bred, poor to the point of squalor; but they had thrown up in the person of Monty's eldest brother a brilliant classicist of the first rank, Professor at one of the older universities and already an international name. The rest of his brothers and sisters, though slightly enlarged by his stature and of recent years more comfortably off, remained what they had always been; insignificant, talkative, somewhat absurd; certainly of no account.

All this Mr Gabriel, in the first flush of intoxication at the thought of relationship to the great Professor Halpern, made nothing of when Monty was suggested as a possible husband for Rebecca. He had not rested till the two had been brought together under the wedding canopy. His snobbish delight at the professor's presence at *his* daughter's wedding—as the bridegroom's brother no less!—had gone beyond all bounds. It was not till some time afterwards that, even to Mr Gabriel, contradictorily obsessed as always, by appearances, it began to dawn that a professor's brother was not a professor. Monty, like many brothers of shortish, thick-set, successful men, was tall, gangling, a weak, narrow-shouldered young man. He wore spectacles. His face, which was pale and should have looked scholarly, looked vacuous, accurately reflecting the mind within. His virtues were many and negative. He was honest, trustworthy, a good and faithful husband, a pleasant babbler in conversation, genuinely orthodox in the observance of his religion, blindly partisan to his people. He was also unimaginative, occasionally petulant and quite spectacularly dull. The professor, fifty miles removed from his family, showed no inclination towards any closer contact with them. In the twelve years of Rebecca's marriage, the Gabriels had seen him scarcely half a dozen times.

As his expectation of searching philosophical discussions, the kind of acute, Talmudic analysis in which, however muddled his own thought, he delighted, became less and less; as Monty's lacunae in every intellectual direction became more and more apparent, Mr Gabriel's disappointment, like his earlier glee, knew no bounds. Disgusted, disappointed to his bones, under, moreover, constant obligation to his son-in-law who showed some mild talent for salesmanship and on whom the book-shop business had begun to depend, the old man, to whom self-accusation was an impossibility, had taken out his rage on his daughters.

Like some violent adolescent, rocketing between utterly opposed conceptions, he would at one moment urge both Sara and Essie to agree to meet some utterly impossible young man with a view to marriage—the disgrace of spinster daughters appalled him—regardless of the fact that this was a form of social torture inexpressibly distasteful to both girls or, veering to the other extreme, talked largely of his high expectations in the quality of husbands he fully expected them to marry. In the very face of the Monty fiasco his demands for the other two to redeem *his* status rose insanely. Could he have married one daughter to a Vice-Chancellor and another to a Lord Rothschild it would, he felt, have been scarcely his due.

Making the situation still more raw was the comparative failure of both girls in that crucial period of social life, the late teens and early twenties, to attract young men. The Jewish religion is not one which encourages monasticism; nor does it deny the importance of the world. Mr Gabriel, in his own eccentric way, was fully aware of worldly values. And it galled him inexpressibly that his two middle daughters did not attract popular attention.

Only one painful episode had relieved the blank, emotional pattern of either Sara or Essie's earlier years.

Sara had given up the struggle sooner than her sister. Faced with a calamitous inequality of talent, an utter unfittedness for competition in the sexual scramble, she had opted out as soon and as unobtrusively as possible though, being lecture-minded, she continued to go to meetings such as were held by the Guild.

Essie, at nineteen, just as her rough, edgy personality was beginning to make a place of sorts for itself in their suburban Manor Green circle, had had the misfortune to fall into what she thought was love with an irreligious, somewhat older man of nondescript background and mysterious sexual attraction: mysterious because, though many girls fancied him and competed for his attention, no one, not even the girls themselves, could quite say why. He had a long, lined face, a prominent bony nose, a grey complexion, a lank figure. There was no accounting for his popularity save perhaps for the weary expression of his sardonic eyes. To the respectable Jewish girls of Manor Green just the suspicion of disillusioned roué was enough to make them mad about him.

There was more than one "Oh!" of rather jealous astonishment when he was seen to be seriously attracted to Essie Gabriel.

They need not have worried. After a short period of nerve-cracking struggle to gain her father's consent—or at least his good behaviour—towards her proposed engagement ("Who is he? What is he?" Mr Gabriel had shouted and kept on shouting: "A nobody! A nothing she wants to marry!") she had been obliged to look on at the quick fading of her suitor's interest in the face of the loud boredom of perpetual scenes. At the peak of her father's violence she had run to the man for strength and found instead an ebbing away of solicitude so sudden and shocking that she had released him at once. This defection she could have borne. The first despair of ever finding love again might have faded; a natural resilience would have lifted up her hope again on the crest of the wave. But the man, with a swift alacrity she could not deny to be wounding, had got himself engaged to someone else almost immediately (though his taste remained, it seemed, odd; the girl he married being also slightly off-key to the general run).

Out of this her father had made instant and gleeful capital. He loved his children fanatically. But, in the midst of forcing beaten egg and brandy down Essie's throat to improve her paleness which he instantly and loudly suspected to be physical illness; in the act of shouting down the telephone to the butcher for expensive calves' liver to be sent *every day*, he could not forbear to exult in his own cleverness. His vanity, his delight at his own judgment being vindicated, overbore completely his minuscule understanding. The house had rung with his triumph, his trumpetings of: "What did I tell you! *Now* will you listen to me!"

That his own behaviour had largely contributed to the way in which the situation had worked out did not occur to him. Had anyone pointed out the innumerable joints in any love affair which must be delicately circumvented, given a chance to knit solidly before being made to bear intolerable pressures, he would have clung blindly to the one incontrovertible fact of the man's rapid consolation and to this there was no answer in terms unsubtle enough for him to understand. As usual, he was half right.

Meanwhile irreparable damage had been done to Essie. It was after this episode that she had defiantly gone to work for a non-Jewish firm of stock-brokers, made friends with the various Gentile young women she met there, and filled up the non-family part of her life with theatres, bachelor-girl evenings, and a general disregard, as far as she dared, of the Jewish life of Manor Green.

2

Like all the Gabriels, save possibly Fay, Essie was a voracious reader and until fairly recently had welcomed Saturdays for the opportunity of burying herself for undisturbed hours in print. One Saturday afternoon however, about twelve months previously, she had looked up from her book with a curious sense of malaise, something like the indefinable strangeness of feeling which precedes a severe migraine.

She and her two sisters were all reading comfortably at ease in armchairs and the rather battered sofa grouped round the unpleasing, green-tiled hearth in the living room. The fire, built up after lunch by the Gentile woman who was paid to do this every Sabbath, roared softly under its high bank of mixed coal and slack, almost to the chimney. Though spring, the weather was chilly. Mr Gabriel, who did not feel the cold—and could never believe that anyone else did—was sitting in what they always called the "front room", the word "lounge" seeming inapposite and rather pretentious to them while "drawing room" was a term never used in their strata of Manor Green at all. He had ensconced himself as was his habit on the faded, grey velvet settee in the bay window of the ugly, square room with its Victorian china cabinet and marble fireplace, its upright, never-used piano and general air of musty, lower middle class best. A cold, grey light filled the room. Piled before him, on a round, lace-covered table, were many of his huge volumes of Hebrew learning, their stiff backs broken and dusty, their pages tattered. In all the week this was his finest hour; the quiet house, the Sabbath calm, the philosophic Word before him to feed upon with joy. Later, his cronies, the three or four ageing men who shared his tastes, would come in and discuss with passionate interest some minute textual interpretation in the writings of the great Hebrew law-makers and commentators of the past.

But for Essie, that Saturday afternoon, on that curiously momentous instant as she looked up from her book, roused as by some muffled, warning bell, there suddenly crystallized a huge, grey distaste for every circumstance surrounding her. Over the hideous house (which none of them had been able to persuade their father to improve), over the entire neighbourhood there seemed, to her newly awakened consciousness, to have fallen a deadening, choking quiet, spreading out and on, flat, tideless, suffocating, with a quality of hopelessness which dragged at her heart. With an effort she bent to her book again, but from thenceforward the malaise persisted, bringing with it from Wednesday on of each week a sense of intolerable strain against the shadow of the coming Saturday.

At first, while the days were yet short and the Sabbath ended at sunset, it had not been quite so bad. But then came the summer and a succession of hot, yellow, drawn-out Sabbath days when an actual nauseated, physical protest invaded her, when her nostrils became dry and painful, her ears throbbed, her head ached, a stiff, trembling lassitude invaded her limbs. So violent and irrational a distaste, sprung up it seemed from nowhere for a day of the week she had not particularly disliked before, at first appalled her. When it continued she made strong attempts to fight it, breaking up the long, caged-in, summer day as much as she could. In the morning she went to the synagogue, inadvertently pleasing her father and Sara (who always went) with such unexpected signs of conformity. They had no idea of the reasons behind it and she did not enlighten them.

Lunch, if good-humoured, was bearable with Mr Gabriel picking Leo's sermon to pieces and threatening darkly to leave his congregation and go to another. Though usually shy and abrupt in their social contacts with the outside world, within their family circle both Sara and Essie were often lively and humorous. Fagy, in her serene, unimaginative way, was almost always pleasant; and their father when by chance nothing had occurred to thwart or aggravate him, in those moments when he was not stung by vanity or gripped in the fever of power, was good company, in his own peculiar way.

At lunch one Saturday, in tremendous high spirits (he had been paid a compliment), he interrupted his daughters at the mention of some name:

"That one! Oh, a fine gentleman! Did you see him making a fool of himself at the girl Abraham's wedding? A *tanzer*! At his age!" And jumping up from the table in the middle of his soup he gave an imitation of the "*tanzer*", doing a quickstep, singing his own jazz accompaniment in a loud, stentorian voice. "If your *moth*-er and your *broth*-er——" he sang, skipping expertly round the table, his knees shooting rhythmically up and down, his small feet swinging out. "There! there!" he shouted excitedly, enjoying himself. "You see! You see!" he said, sitting down again at last still humming with energy. "Is that a behaviour for a grown-up, middle-aged man?"

He reached over and pinched the back of Fagy's neck. "*Meinë tirë Fagelë*," he said fondly. "Did I tell you what Ascher said to me this morning?" He looked round the table. "First of all . . . before I tell you . . ." he jerked the small pointed beard on his chin upwards, inquiringly, "what did you think of Norberg's sermon?"

"It was all right," said Essie casually.

He spread out his hand in her direction with a lofty, holding-off gesture. "Not you! Fagy?"

"I thought it was jolly interesting," said Fagy with her full, red-lipped smile.

"'I thought it was jolly interesting,' she says! Jolly . . . interesting," said Mr Gabriel meaningly. "How . . . jolly interesting? Excuse me! Excuse me!——" as Sara started to say something. "Well?"

"I think it was jolly clever the way Dr Norberg drew those parallels between the prophets and the politicians," said Fagy.

"It was 'interesting'?" he said.

Fagy nodded.

"It was . . . clever?" he pursued.

"Mm," she said taking up a forkful of chicken.

He gave a quick, satisfied nod.

"*Now* . . . I'll tell you! This morning I was sitting next to Mr Ascher. At the end of the sermon, Mr Ascher he turned to me and said——" he nodded his head slowly and impressively several times: "He said: 'Mr Gabriel! that was a good sermon. Norberg's a clever man'—just like *you* said, Fagy—'but I'll tell you something, Mr Gabriel; his ideas don't come up to yours. I've heard you give a better expounding in your own home than I've ever heard here from the pulpit.' Ascher to say that! An educated man! I remember Ascher when he came from Germany before the first war. In those days an education at a German university . . . *that* was an education. 'I'll tell you something,' he said, 'his ideas don't come up to yours.' The minute Norberg had finished—I'm telling you—he's hardly said the last word and Ascher turns round to me and says that."

Essie risked a look at Sara and muttered: "That old dodderer!" under her breath. Unnoticing, Mr Gabriel, his vitality and vanity flaming out together, continued to repeat to the end of the meal what Ascher—that educated German thinker—had said to him, to his daughters' slightly irritated amusement.

Saturday luncheons, then, were bearable. It was as the long afternoons set in that for Essie the appalling, ashen restlessness came down. It was then that the drab, fusty melancholy, made worse by sunlight, the terrible essence of suburban Saturdays falling, falling on the long, long afternoon sickened and terrified her. Sometimes she tried taking extended after-lunch walks with, as often as she could persuade her, Fay as company. She preferred her younger sister at these times because she seemed far more than Sara to resist or rather to be ignorant of melancholy, to be infinitely less vulnerable than any of them to the sense of waste and uselessness which dusts over with sadness the desolate afternoons of suburban summer. Usually they walked the streets, getting away as far as possible from the ugly, yellow-brick terraces of Manor Green East, through the petty, genteel uniformity of the Garden Suburb and on into the wide, handsome, mansion district of Manor Green West. Here it was at least possible to sense the existence of some richer, fuller life which had once been lived there in the golden years of the early century; when the rich Jewish merchants and the cultivated, Gentile upper classes had come together to form a community of stylish, luxurious living.

Occasionally, when it was too hot to walk further, they went—though Essie detested it—through their local park, surrounded by its fringe of pre-fabs, and walked up the hilly path which ran through its centre to the big country house set on a knoll over-looking what had once been its own private acres of meadow and garden. Its former stables had been turned into a cafeteria and there a constant, straggling queue stood awaiting their turn to buy raspberryade, cups of stewed tea, leathery buttered buns and revolt-ing, crab-shaped cakes. Children from the surrounding artisan-level neighbourhood sucked lethargically at their ice-cream. The few better-dressed people about were always Jews; smart, well-corseted women, their feet bulging from high-heeled shoes. With their stocky, well-tailored men they strolled desultorily in the heavy, hazy-gold air or stood in groups, loudly banal, clinging, thankful for the safety of each other in the alien, English grass. Separated they would stroll again, bored, smart, muted, the unformulated question: Is this what we are living for? looking always from their shrewd, unsatisfied, Oriental eyes.

As tea time approached it was with almost tangible relief that—the sunny air taken advantage of—they returned to the enclosed, congenial bricks and mortar of their homes. It is as if that great alien, Nature, holds a subtle terror for the bourgeois Jews of the Diaspora. Even in park-tamed, city meadows she is too wide and lonely for them. They dare not trust themselves to her, dare not trust themselves to retain their identity away from the crowded street.

Once or twice on these walks Essie was reminded of a conversa-tion she had once overheard outside her synagogue between Sir Robert Bart-Grune and the vastly wealthy industrialist, Abraham Feld, both of whom had country houses within a few miles of each other.

59

"We'll be down at 'Fairdenes' next week," said Sir Robert, "you come over to us on Saturday afternoon, Feld. My wife likes company."

"Delighted of course. If I can," said Feld, "But we're not down there much. Too busy to take advantage of the place." He shook his head. "Wonderful to get away to peace and quiet. Wish I could do it oftener."

"Course you can," said Sir Robert stoutly, looking very English, white-moustached and walrus-like. "If I can do it you can."

"That's all very well," said Feld, his voice becoming more Jewish as he became argumentative. "That's all very well. But" (he poked his forefinger quickly in the air) "you're practically retired, my friend. No more worries. No problems about markets, Stock Issues, personnel . . ."

"I still go in twice a week," said Sir Robert, hunching his shoulders, "sometimes oftener. We still live here, you know. Fairdenes is all right for a week-end. Tell me . . . I hear reports of a merger . . ." And they had walked off together to Feld's enormous, pale-blue Rolls Royce, parked in Veryan Square, talking earnestly of business.

Essie had smiled to herself at a mental picture of both men, bored stiff away from their offices, playing at country gentlemen, a faintly artificial air surrounding their best efforts.

And so she walked the dragging Sabbath hours away, holding to Fagy's presence and serene chatter as if to a lifeline.

3

Months later, the Sabbath afternoon after the Rabbi had brought Sara home, the three sisters were reading and lazing in the shabby, warm living room. An occasional spatter of icy, spring rain fell against the window panes. Sara, who was re-reading *Swann's Way*, found herself for once unable to concentrate on the page before her. Her attention wandering in spite of herself, she kept looking up and across at Essie—apparently sunk in her reading—with an expression of speculative unease. The evening before had seen such an explosion between her father and sister as to drive even thoughts of

Leo from her head; this time because Essie—and even she had never gone so far before—had insisted on going out the previous evening and had remained out from before supper till nearly midnight.

In the mythology of Jewish life in the Diaspora a peculiar sweetness and reverence attaches itself to Friday night—which, at sunset, is the actual beginning of the Sabbath. More, far more than the attendance at Synagogue on Saturday morning, is the gathering together of the family round the supper table on Friday evening a ceremony of holy participation. It is then, when the candles on the table are lit and blessed, when Grace has been said over the big, plaited loaves and the silver goblet, filled with dark red wine, stands on the starched, gleaming tablecloth . . . it is then, while the candles flame, that all which is most purely exemplar, most wholesome, most filled with loving warmth in the Hebrew spirit, flames too. It is then that the Jewish family can be seen, if only in a second's vision, as a symbol of God's sane, ordered wish for the human kind; that the concept of "The Family" can be strongly felt as part of the natural, human order. Tired after labour, there is in the exclamation of every observing Jew as Friday evening approaches: "Thank God for the Sabbath when we *may* not work", a tribute to the divine common sense of a God who has ordained that "on the Seventh Day ye shall rest". Like God, if the Sabbath did not exist it would be necessary to invent it. To observe a Sabbath is to fall into the harmonious rhythm of the universe.

For Essie, therefore, flagrantly to defy tradition was shocking even to Sara who in her greater forbearance as opposed to Essie's intractability often reminded herself of Charlotte as opposed to Emily Brontë. She had once pointed this out to Essie who had rather gloomily observed that there was nothing in common between Manor Green and Haworth except that their father would probably have been much more at home in the latter.

She glanced over again at Essie, who at that moment looked up and said irritably: "It beats me how people can bring themselves to write such nonsense."

"What?"

"That Gilson! Professional letter-writer, self-appointed, for the Jews." She waved a copy of an Anglo-Jewish periodical. "Letter

here from Gilson . . . this time even dafter than usual." She began
to read aloud in a sardonic tone:

"Dear Sir,

I have happened to notice in the Furniture Exhibition opened
last week a new fabric exhibited, scattered over with a Shield of
David design. Could this pattern carried tastefully out in the
Jewish national colours of blue and white perhaps be the fore-
runner of a large scale influx of Jewish colour into the Gentile
home? Will—is it too much to hope?—those interlocked triangles
henceforth seeping into the British living room act as homely
ambassadors for our wonderful traditions and way of life? It is to
devoutly be hoped that, if this idea 'catches on' as well it may do,
that other manufacturers will follow suit, weaving perhaps dainty
motifs of Jewish significance into curtain material or fashioning
ash trays, pouffes etc. in Shield of David shape. I am sure that
apart from being commercially profitable it would bring a burst
of gladness to every Jewish heart to see some of its own traditional 'colour' and joyous 'glamour' enlivening this colder Northern clime. Yours, etc. . . ."

Sara could not restrain a laugh.

"I don't know," said Essie, dropping the paper and looking
reflectively up at the ceiling, "which I admire more. The grammar
or the imagery. I can just see those triangles seeping under the
door . . ."

"What kinds of dainty motifs does he have in mind I wonder?"
said Sara.

"*Lockshen* puddings," said Fagy, looking up from her magazine
and chuckling.

"*Lockshen* puddings; a pickled herring, rampant; a *baigel*——"

"A Beth Din certificate . . ."

"You are speaking," said Essie primly, "of the Law Court I love."

"I only wish father didn't love it so much," said Sara smiling and
sighing. "A good half of the telephone bill every quarter must be
made up of father's calls to the Beth Din. What business is it of his
if he saw Tomashel the butcher out in his car on *Shabbos*? He's not
even our butcher. But of course father has to ring up the Beth Din
and tell them if Tomashel can do that his meat can't be kosher and
they ought to take away his licence."

"But this 'colourful' tripe," exclaimed Essie in a vexed, contentious voice. "All right! Gilson's an idiot. But how many more idiots have we got like him? And how many people *not* idiots but not Jews have exactly the same idea? How in the world did we get ourselves this reputation in the Gentile mind for 'colour'? Even the people I know . . . You know, I went to Margaret's for tea the other week. She had some other people from the office there and we were playing some game they have of matching people with flowers. And what do you think they matched *me* with? A peony!" (In fact, with her strong features and vivid colouring she did look not unlike a peony. It was only her own inside knowledge of herself as shy, brusque, touchily sensitive on occasion, which gave her to her own fancy a picture of her personality as violet-like and retiring.)

"Well Jewish people *are* much brighter than others, aren't they?" said Fagy with a kind of placid, earnest pride which made both her sisters smile fondly at her.

"Oh, we *look* colourful enough," said Essie, "a damn sight too much so. That's the trouble. That's where the Goyyim go wrong. We lead such 'colourful' lives they always say. What utter bloody nonsense when you come to think of it."

"Oh but——" began Sara.

"Now admit it, Sos! Look at the neighbours for instance. Look at them! The Goldbergs at Thirty-three with those two fat kids of theirs and holidays at Westcliff (they haven't even got the guts to call it Southend!). The Wittstein's at Thirty-seven . . . did you ever see a duller couple in your life? They work in that shop of theirs all week, go to the pictures on Saturday night, visit Ethel and the grandchildren for Sunday tea . . . and that's all, week after week, year after year. That's all they'll ever do till they die. I suppose if either of them did, the other would at last have something to talk about!"

"Like old Mrs Lankowitz . . . 'since my trouble'," said Sara, laughing in spite of herself. "But Ess . . . what do you want of them? They're no different from millions of others——"

"They're supposed to be," said Essie vigorously, "*that's* the point. The Jews; so alive, so vital, so exotic, so 'cultured', God help us. How in the world did such misconceptions ever arise?"

"I suppose in the old days," said Sara tentatively, "it really was so."

63

"Never! never from the inside. Those 'old days' we're so senti-mental about—like the Western intellectuals today with their Mexi-can peasants—in the little villages of Eastern Europe or the slums of East End London (or East Side New York for that matter) . . . what were they, those days, those lives? I'll tell you. That they were lives of struggle and poverty—that's nothing. The dirt, the smells, the discomfort; the tiny, freezing, hideously ugly bedrooms with tattered lino on the floors if you were lucky, the bugs in the walls, the lack of privacy . . . I don't condemn them for all that. Even the quarrels, the noise—call that 'colourful' if you like!—the bargain-price ostentation and wholesale clothing . . . But it was the ignor-ance, the confusion, the appalling narrowness, so coarse, so stifling . . . and, above all, the fear. The constant presence of fear. 'Colour' they call it, those spiritual tourists walking round the bazaars . . . Colour! All the virtues of that so-picturesque society so lovingly cherished in our nostalgia," said Essie, her voice deepened with sarcasm, "were the exact reverse of colourful. As a people we have —and had—all the drab virtues of the drabbest and dunnest of poor Scottish villagers; family pride; racial pride; good housekeeping; ambition; brains; thrift; and a talent for money."

"What's wrong with all that?" cried Sara heatedly. "I should think that any race that can maintain those virtues *in the air*, in face of persecution, without a resting place for their backs, without a country of their own to lean on . . ."

"There's nothing wrong with it," said Essie exasperated. "It's wonderful. I admit it——"

"You needn't sneer——"

"I'm not sneering. But in heaven's name where's this wonderfully *colourful* life we're supposed to have? So far as I can see, today it's non-existent and if we had any in the past it was all concentrated between 10 a.m. and 2 p.m. every Sunday morning in Petticoat Lane."

"You're being unfair——" said Sara.

". . . and the reputation for intellect," said Essie rushing on indignantly. "There's no more intellect proportionately in the Jews than there is in the Scots or the Welsh. Where *are* these great Jewish audiences for culture? I don't see them. If I go to a concert I don't see rows of Jews from Manor Green lapping up music.

64

Oh—h—h, yes," she held out a flat, protesting hand, "I know! If it's Menuhin or Heifetz they'll go. But not because they're fond of music——"

"*What* a sweeping statement——" said Sara crossly.

"Do they read . . .? or buy books for pure love of literature? Not that the non-Jews are much better!"

"It's the same . . ."

"All right! Western culture's going down the drain anyway. Do we do anything to stop it?"

"But . . ."

"*What we're fond of*," said Essie in a loud, determined voice, "is *success*. Give us a 'name' and we're there all right. I tell you I see red, I could scream——"

"You are!" said Fagy from where she was curled up in a corner of the sofa no longer taking much notice of the argument. Essie gave her a half smile and lowered her voice.

"I feel absolutely wild," she continued, "when I read about 'famous orchestras owing so much to Jewish support' and 'great newspapers backed by the liberal, Jewish intelligentzia'. It's all a cock-eyed myth. Oh, there are always Jewish geniuses around— that the rest of the world have to acclaim before the Jews wake up to their achievements. That saying about prophets being without honour in their own country . . . it couldn't apply more closely to anyone than it does to us. Every Jew who's got anywhere has had to be an expatriate so to speak before he could get there. In time as well as place. Whom do we venerate now? The great figures of the past. Our glorious past we're always paying plenty of lip-service to. But who, I ask you, gets honour among us today . . .? leaving aside for the moment our greatest Gods—the ones with the money. But to leave money out of it for once—if we can! Who? I'll tell you," she said hotly, laying down the law in a way which, had she known it, closely resembled her father's, "*Chairmen*! Chairmen of committees, chairmen of charity organizations, of synagogue congregations, of old people's aid societies; chairmen of Lodges, chairmen of ball committees, chairmen of education groups . . . *that's* our aristocracy! Plus a few Zionist leaders—chairmen again!—and a couple of Rabbis. In every other field you can think of the Jews have had to go outside their own community to find recognition, to be respected, to be sought after. We're so uncertain, so distrustful of our own judgments, we've got such bloody great inferiority complexes that we don't know and don't recognize and don't believe in our own great till someone else tells us about them. The red-tape, petty official, the worthy, the jack-in-office, the whole, middle-class set-up . . . they're the ones——"

"They've done more for other people than you've ever done," said Sara. "You've only got to look around you to see the quickest, most warm-hearted response to every need . . ."

"I know what they *do*!" cried Essie, making the gesture of tearing her hair. "I *know*. I know they're always working for someone or something. But to make their *position*, their status as executive a kind of badge of all merit . . . what could be more stupid? Yes, there is something more stupid! the idiotic game with names . . . pluming ourselves on our celebrities. Greatest mathematician in the world . . . a Jew. Greatest sculptor . . . great historians, musicians and— most important of all, naturally—" she said satirically, "great names in entertainment; comedians, crooners . . ."

"*And* doctors!" said Sara, "*and* justice! *We are entitled to our pride.*"

"I suppose if we threw up a Shakespeare," said Essie bad-temperedly, not listening, "we might get around to being proud of him after the rest of the world discovers his genius. But do we care two-pence about literature, for example, or about any Jewish, living artist—for the value of his work? All *we* want to know is—is he still one of us? In other words, is he on one of those dreary committees? Yes, do look around you. Do, I implore you! Look around Manor Green particularly. What do you see? Come now . . . be honest. What do you see? A restless, bored, for the most part materialist society; a good-natured, maddeningly prestige-ridden lumpen-bourgeoisie divided into two parts. On the one side there's the Jews who are miserable in their Jaguars and burdened with their mink-wrapped ennui; and on the other side the Jews who are just plain bored in their beaver lamb and unhappy in their second-hand Fords. And that's about all the bloody difference there is. The fact is there's no zest in us any more. We've gone soft. Our 'life', our 'vitality', our 'culture'; where is it? Drained out over the card table and the business deal and those never-ending committees. Who invented this colossal fiction about Jewish culture anyway?"

"You're a Jewish anti-Semite," said Fagy from her corner.

Essie gave her a quick look and subsided. Against any other opposition she would have continued but Fagy's bland ordinariness often flattened out the lawless, oblique enjoyment the rest of the family found in argument.

"Oh, blow," Fagy continued, getting up and stretching, "it's getting too dark to read." She looked at her watch, straining to see the time in the light of the fire. "It's not even tea time yet. Surely it's too dark too early for this time of the year?"

"There's heavy rain coming up. The sky's like lead," said Sara.

"Think I'll go round to Hilda's for tea," said Fagy, yawning.

After she had gone out Sara said: "I don't mind if you want to talk like that, Essie. Say what you like, you're entitled to your own opinions; though I don't agree with you. That is . . . everything you say is right; but it's only half the picture. I won't defend today; though in literature at least we're bounding, absolutely bounding with talent, Jewish writers popping up all over the place. My goodness!" she said, her austere face sunlit with pleasure, "think what a lot in the last ten years! You mightn't find creation in Manor Green but there's revolt going on somewhere. I tell you there's a new kind of Elizabethan Age setting in for us.

"It's true," she went on uncertainly but with the fairness of judgment which characterized her, "you don't find Jewish greatness here, in this place, at this moment. Not in the social strata we're familiar with. It is strange . . . there are so many talented, sparkling Jews, genius Jews—and yet we never seem to come near any of them. Oh, I agree with you, Essie, the attractive, wonderful, fabulous Jews aren't here in Manor Green. They are always somewhere else, at some other place or time, never here. The gay Jew . . . once, perhaps, in Vienna or Warsaw. The adventurer Jew . . . in China. The statesman Jew . . . somewhere between Africa, Washington, Whitehall . . .'"

"And here," said Essie, "*nothing*. No richness. No gaiety. No intellect . . ."

'You are being unfair. Your outlook is too narrow. You accuse *me* of never raising my head and looking beyond Manor Green. But that is just what you are failing to do. You are blaming our particular luck in being born to our particular circumstances. And you are really grossly unfair about the past. Why, even I can remember as a child—surely you can too?—the stories of Friday nights at grandfather's house when people used to come in, the talk, the ideas, the *glow* of Jewish life. And for the generation before it was still more wonderful. Have you never listened to Aunt Leah's stories about the Judaism of the old days? A kind of marvellous, liberal opening out towards European thought without losing its own identity. Good heavens! half the people who used to come into grandfather's home are international figures today.

"Sometimes," she continued in a softer voice as Essie made no reply, "I find myself thinking about that time before we were born and envying the generation who had it with all my heart. I can imagine grandfather's great long kitchen with the colossal black stove; that stove held a hundredweight of fuel at a time. And the great big buttoned-leather sofa; and the red twill curtains; and the book-cases full of the most extraordinary collection of books, Turgenev, the *Talmud*, Victorian romances . . . And the talk that went on there round the big table, science, politics, philosophy, gossip about Europe over glasses of mead and Russian tea with spoonfuls of jam in it, and talk, talk; the Czar, the Kaiser; and the barrels of pickled cucumbers in a corner of the scullery . . . It was a *wonderful* life. Oh, I envy them: I envy them. And all that gone. Gone for ever now. Now the pattern of our culture, as a race, isn't with us, here, any more; if it lies anywhere it lies in Israel. But quite apart from that," she went on, ignoring Essie's muttered "Same old Zionist propaganda", "I do beg of you *not* to risk talking like that in front of father. If you say anything more to inflame him after last night's business there'll be murder."

She stopped short as she saw the sullen look settle on Essie's face, flushed in the firelight, then (she had her own obstinacy) she went on determinedly: "How could you have been so silly, Essie?"

Essie said nothing, only sat with her bent head poked forward, watching a little, yellow tongue of flame licking out unexpectedly at one side of the black, high-banked coal.

"You knew very well," Sara continued, "that going out on a Friday night was just asking for trouble. You knew very well father would see red."

"That's just it! What *right* has he to see red?" said Essie straightening herself in her chair, the flush still on her high, broad cheekbones, her dark hair curling wildly. Had her features been modelled on a just slightly smaller scale, her jaw less square, her nose less aggressive, she would have been a pretty girl just as, had Sara's features been smaller and less prominent, she would have been beautiful. "At twenty-seven years of age I'm old enough to decide for myself when I want to go out and when I don't. What business is it of his?"

"He thinks you took a bus somewhere."

"Indeed!" She got up from her chair in one quick movement. "And even supposing for one moment that I did," she said biting the words out, "whose business would that be may I ask?"

"Oh, Essie *don't*," said Sara showing in her turn a flash of temper. "Aren't things difficult enough? Why provoke him? You know very well if you *were* seen getting on a bus last night——"

"Well I couldn't have been because I didn't," Essie said defiantly and terminated the discussion by walking out of the room.

Sara looked anxiously at the door as it closed. She was half inclined to go after her sister and warn her again but just then there was a knock at the front door and she was obliged to let in several of her father's cronies and, hard on their heels, her sister Rebecca and her husband who both followed her into the living room.

"Well," said Monty bursting into the rapid, slurred speech which was habitual to him: "Doing all right, eh?"

"What is?"

"The new shop!"

"What shop?" said Sara absently. She was wishing he would join the men in the front room but Monty, no scholar and a great gossip, much preferred women and kitchens. Rebecca sat down in the space Fagy had vacated but Monty, restless and loose-jointed—the backs of his long legs always looked curiously adolescent—hovered at the door leading into the kitchen and talked to Sara as she fumbled in almost complete darkness for cups and saucers.

"Wha' shop!" he said in his slurred, shrill voice. "Manor Green Delicatessen Stores. Y'haven't noticed?"

"Oh yes, of course, I'd forgotten. It looks rather nice."

"About time they brightened up the High Street," said Rebecca.

69

"There wasn't a decent Jewish grocers between here and Green West."

"Wha'r'y' mean?" he said, his eyes opening behind his glasses, "And what's wrong with Balbergs?"

"My husband," said Rebecca largely, 'My husband, bless him, he likes what he likes. But to *get* what he likes, the fact is I have to go right over to Green West. Every Thursday, rain or shine." Even in the firelight, as Sara came in carrying a tray she could see the flirtatious look on her eldest sister's face.

Rebecca's character had taken a curious turn after her marriage some twelve years previously. Although the oldest of the four girls, she was or had been in many ways the shyest. By no means unintelligent, she had never mastered the knack, even in the family circle, of direct or forceful speech and this, the possession of force and the inability to express it plus her undeniably plain looks (like Fagy she took after her mother but where Fagy was short but small-boned and delicately rounded, she was short and fat with heavy-lidded, black eyes, a double chin and a sallow complexion) had given her both a profound conceit of her own ideas and a large scale difficulty in expressing them. Marriage—after a year or two—had changed all that. Complexes, inhibitions . . . nothing like that could flourish by the side of Monty's continuous babble. As the years went on and neither Sara nor Essie showed signs of serious attachment, the sense of superiority conferred by the gold ring on her left hand solidified into a pleased complacency. Completely secure of her husband's fidelity—absorbed with all the petty detail of life it would never have occurred to him to look at another woman—she was never happier than when combating some imaginary rival from whom she was forever wresting him away with a whole armoury of wiles. She was lying now with her head tilted right back to show her short, full throat, looking with rolled-back eyes at her husband who stood behind her. He was talking now, though how he had begun it was difficult to say (no one ever quite knew how Monty *started* a conversation, he always seemed to be in the middle of one) about a pupil of his. He taught Hebrew to a few private pupils during the week.

"That gang!" he said referring to the boy's relatives. "Spend money like water. Make it like water," he said with a grin and

70

a blink (he rather enjoyed mild, lavatory jokes), "and spend it——"

"Monty!" said Rebecca.

"Well . . . if you've got a bad mind . . ." he said laughing up-roariously.

"Well I don't know!" she said helplessly. "What am I going to do with you?" she said reaching backwards and taking his hand.

"Shall I tell you?" he said working his eyebrows up and down like a stage comedian.

"You can take him into the front room for *Havdalah*," said Sara and switched on the light. "*Shabbos* is out." And she led the way into the other room where her father and his friends were still arguing. Mr Gabriel poured out a glass of wine and they all stood up while Sara, lighting two candles, held them up before her father and he recited the *Havdalah*, the prayer for the ending of the Sabbath. Then he drank off the wine, Sara extinguished the candles and she and Rebecca served tea.

4

Though Essie had escaped from the living room before Sara could question her further, she could not so easily escape from the sense of guilt which accompanied her. The fact was, though it was perfectly true that she had not taken a bus on the Sabbath, that was only because she had committed the equal sin of allowing herself to be driven in a private car.

One rainy evening about the middle of the previous September, Essie Gabriel had entered a large, many-windowed building near the Strand, taken one ravished look at the brilliant entrance hall, alive with bustle and movement, and fallen in love with the London Evening College.

For some years Essie had been saying periodically that she would like to study something in the evenings. When, having at last made up her mind, she incautiously voiced her plan to her father, he instantly, in his erratic, obstinate way, decided to oppose it. No one ever quite knew *why* Mr Gabriel either defended or opposed any-thing. Even his reasons were, when given, suspect, being often smoke screens before his own eyes. His decisions, his appraisals of men or events were always unpredictable, often capricious to the point of fantasy.

As soon as Essie had broached the subject he had looked up with a kind of sharp, simulated amazement.

"Evening classes!" he said in his loud, tearing voice. "What for?"

"To study."

"Hah!" Mr Gabriel gave a sarcastic bark to the air. "And what do you think you can study at a Gentile college?"

"A thousand things," she said shortly.

"Ah!" said Mr Gabriel dramatically, beginning to enjoy himself. He jumped up from the table and struck an attitude. Nervous strength drummed through his short, wiry body. "Ah! these thousand things . . . name them! Is it a university *so big*?" he ended on a rising, artificial note.

"No, it isn't a university," said Essie, tightly trying not to say the words which came red-hot to her lips. Both she and Sara had longed for a university education but their father, though both the girls were clever, had refused them their chances, pleading poverty. They had had to waste themselves, Sara half at home and half in the shop and Essie in an office knowing very well that this was their father's revenge on them for not being sons. To educate a son he would have seen them all starve.

"Look, father," said Essie controlling herself, "there's nothing wrong with my wanting to go to classes in the evening——"

"What class? What is it you're in such a rush to learn?"

"There are several things I might . . . history, economics, a language perhaps . . ."

"Language! D'you know English even?" He held out his small hands with a quick, jerky movement, cupped them in front of him and, shortening his neck, pushed his head forward. "What's the meaning of 'tautology'?" he demanded.

"Tautology?"

"Yes, Yes. You don't know!" he cried triumphantly. "My clever student, so clever she doesn't know English . . . *she* goes to study Economics!"

"I do know," said Essie with the greatest possible tactlessness. "It means repetition."

There was a pause.

"Oh," he said in a jealous voice.

"I don't see why she shouldn't go," said Sara mildly. "The classes aren't expensive; they're harmless; what's wrong with her going?"

"To mix with a lot of *Goyyim* . . . Gentiles . . . there's nothing wrong with that?"

"Good God in heaven!" Essie cried, exploding, "we're not living in a little Jewish village in the heart of Russia; and we're not living in Israel either. We're living in England, London, *England*," she said, her voice rising to an angry scream as she saw the well-known mulish look settle on her father's narrow, red-veined face with its long nose and staring, hot eyes.

"What's wrong with Jewish classes? Go and learn Modern Hebrew, that'll do you more good."

"*I don't want to learn Hebrew.* I want to study what *I* want to study."

"Oh—h—h," he said waving his head contemptuously from side to side, "she wants to study! A daughter of mine wants to study . . . what? How to cook bacon? How to believe in Christmas?"

"Father!" said Sara sharply seeing the colour of passionate, aggrieved fury flying into Essie's face. "Don't be so ridiculous. Why shouldn't Essie go? What crime is she committing? Would you stop all Jewish young people from studying medicine for instance, or law, at a university?"

"A university's one thing. An evening class . . . pooh! What is it? Can you take a degree at an evening class?"

"You can as a matter of fact——"

"An excuse," he shouted, "an excuse that's all it is to mix with a lot of *Goyyim*. Jewish boys aren't good enough, my daughters want to marry road-sweepers, brick-layers——"

"You're crazy," said Essie in the biting, controlled voice of extreme temper and with a last effort of self-control lurched, half blind with anger, to the door. "I'm going anyway," she said and walked out.

"Aie, aie," groaned Mr Gabriel instantly giving way to self-pity. "My ungrateful children. What have I done that I should be punished like this?" And the tears of thwarted power rose in his eyes. Sara, with the mixture of pity and repugnance which had for so long

73

been a familiar companion to every scene she witnessed involving her father, set herself to soothing him, not so much for his sake as for the sake of the whole family. Mr Gabriel in one of his moods could make life intolerable for everyone.

"Leave her alone, father. Leave her alone. Let her try it if she wants to," she said over and over again, rejecting even as they sprang to her mind such phrases as "you've no right . . ." Any questioning of his "rights" as a father would only inflame him further. "Good heavens," she started, then stopped short, overcome by a sense of shame and fantasy that in a modern world where girls ten years younger than Essie were rushing about the globe, the Gabriels should be living in this eccentric, nineteenth-century corner. "It'll serve him right if she walks out of the house," she thought.

"Goyyim!" he said nodding his head heavily. "To mix with *Goyyim* brings nothing but trouble. First it's classes and then it's going out and then it's entangled and then it's marriage. Do we know where it'll end?"

Sara stood up and said impatiently: "For heaven's sake don't be so *damn* silly," and in her turn left the room.

Mr Gabriel sprang up and with quick, darting movements raked out the fire, muttering: "Spend. Spend. Fires already! Is it winter already? Ruin me! Ruin me!"

Essie had dismissed this scene by the time she was studying the Syllabus in the big library at London College. Like many another student at the beginning of the autumn term the lists of classes, dozens of them, had an effect on her as of strong drink. The sheer breadth of prospect, the amount of possible knowledge there for her to gorge on produced a kind of intoxication. She wanted to register for everything; World Affairs: An Outline of Philosophy: Appreciation of Modern Art: Elizabethan Drama . . .

The passionate longing for scholarship surging up, she enrolled for several courses only to find that in many cases the tutor's personality was not strong enough to hold her interest in the subject. By Christmas, as happened with many students, her attendance had dwindled and concentrated to one: European Social History, a large, intelligent class under an exceptionally able tutor. Her acute pleasure in the College itself however remained undiminished. Even

74

the somewhat risible sight of over-earnest students taking endless notes which they would obviously never look at again did not detract from the over-all excitement and anticipation with which each week she entered the lively, purposeful, resounding place. Her able mind, rotating for so long in emptiness, gripped on to knowledge with a zest which surprised herself. Her romantic curiosity about life, stifled by long years of imperious instruction from her father on what she *ought* to know, her good taste continually offended both by the gross, bourgeois quality of the strata of society by which she was surrounded and the confused, violent brand of thought which her father and his friends claimed as 'intellect", she took to the pleasant, invigorating, rational atmosphere of Mr Marchant's class with a kind of vivid delight, gradually finding herself during the first term coming to live only for her Tuesday evenings, hastening to the College as if to a lover.

By the end of the winter term she was so engrossed into the life of the class that she joined eagerly in with the plan of several of her fellow students to attend the usual Christmas Party given by the College. This she kept secret from her family, even Sara, knowing well their reaction. That she, who shunned all part of Manor Green social life, should engage herself with enthusiasm in a Gentile occasion could not cause less than a doubtful wonder on the part of her sisters; the effect on her father was not even to be imagined. Resolutely refusing all thought of it, she arranged to meet the others for a preliminary drink at a nearby pub before going to on the party. It was the last Saturday night before Christmas.

The "Duke of Albion", a large, rather gloomy public-house, almost directly faced the London Evening College from which it drew a great deal of its trade. When Essie pushed open the swing door of the Saloon Bar she found most of her group already there. Mrs Pickering, the class secretary, waved at her from the far end of the bar and Essie made her way over and joined them.

"What'll you have?" said Mr Coombes, a stout, heavy-featured man, rising to his feet as Essie sat down beside him, "Sherry? Gin? Beer?"

"Sherry please," she said wondering if she ought to offer to pay for herself. When Mr Coombes handed her her drink she held it embarrassedly for a moment wondering if there was some correct pub formula before drinking it. "Cheers?" said Mr Coombes knocking his back and gratefully. "Cheers!" she replied taking a sip at hers. Though she would not have acknowledged it, Essie did not feel at ease. Jews by and large do not "drink". Whether this is because wine, from earliest childhood, forms a part of the ordinary ceremonial of every Sabbath and every sacred holiday, holding none of the charm of forbidden or unusual fruit, or whether in the Jewish temperament there is a lack of reserve already manifest, leaving nothing for alcohol to release, or whether it is the sensible, Hebrew calculation that wine may be wine but a good dinner (ah!) will do you more good, the fact of Jewish abstemiousness—one of the subtle, impalpable, social difficulties between Jew and Gentile —remains.

Mrs Pickering was telling Essie about her seventeen-year-old daughter who was already a professional actress in a repertory company in Kent. Mr Coombes was telling an involved story about a car accident to young Bingham, a bouncing, merry boy and his girl friend. Opposite Essie sat Frances Warren and Jess Liversidge, two Civil Servants of formidable knowledge and somewhat impressive character. They were, as usual, absorbed in some private discussion, Frances's deep, resonant voice which held a kind of lugubrious overtone contrasting with Jess's lightly fluttering voice-notes. Both women (they were each about forty), however, had the upper-grade Civil Service laugh which is made by opening the mouth very wide, puffing out the breath rhythmically like a steam-engine and nodding the head very fast. At the same time the eyes must be crinkled as if with amusement. Though intimidated by this laugh—which can be very frightening indeed—Essie was rather anxious to be friends with them. Frances Warren's tongue was barbed but witty and her friend, softer and more feminine with her pale blue eyes and dark hair, was both widely read and somewhat elegant in personality.

Though a chilly December evening outside it was very warm in the pub and Essie unbuttoned her big coat and slid it off. Beneath it she wore a navy blue silk suit, simple enough by Manor Green standards but it became her very well, bringing out the brilliant, natural colour in her cheeks. The dim light of the bar softening her strong features she looked at her glowing best. Unconsciously the others' manner towards her altered. Without wishing to be different, indeed, wishing most ardently to be one with them, she could not help impressing her companions with a sense of her richer nervous life as compared with their thinner and more phlegmatic temperaments. Amongst the British, elegant or sturdy, sweet or sensible, she stood out, plainly dressed, modest in manner, English-accented as they, yet strangely foreign, an indefinable, alien stamp all over her.

"Have you enjoyed the term?" said Mr Coombes to her.

"I think it's been wonderful! I can't imagine why I didn't go to evening classes years ago."

"Well," he said jovially. "Why didn't you? There isn't anyone who won't tell you what a grand institution they are."

"Ah! you should hear my father's views," she said laughing.

"Do you live at home, Miss Gabriel?" said Jess Liversidge leaning forward.

"Yes," she said in a somewhat nervous tone. "I do." She had been long enough in the class to know that hardly any single students did anything so odd as to live at home with their families, though this state of affairs was less the matter of choice she thought it, most of them coming from provincial homes they had left behind them.

"Poor you!" said Jess lightly. Essie laughed in acquiescence. "Poor me indeed," she said glancing round at the party of students, some twenty of them by now who had collected there.

"What part of London do you live in?" she said, anxious to maintain contact between herself and the other.

"I have a tiny flat in Holland Park with some charming landlords I never see: that being the greater part of their charm."

At the mention of the word "landlord" the conversation immediately became general, this topic being of the most burning interest to a company largely composed of bed-sitting room dwellers. Essie listened and laughed with genuine amusement as Frances Warren finished an account of one of her experiences with the words, uttered in her dry, lugubrious way: "Of course the ideal from their point of view is that you should never be there at all: just pay the rent!" At the same time she became aware of an increasing discomfort, a widening divergence between herself and the others.

77

The fact was that, though the Gabriels were far from well off, something about the structure of the society in which they moved was inimical to that in which she now found herself. The Jews are the natural rentiers of society. They are suppliers rather than consumers. Try as she would, Essie could not but feel a kind of sympathy for the landlords at that very moment being alluded to in a way taken absolutely for granted by everyone as natural enemies, Even Mr Coombes, who was buying his small house on mortgage, looked disapproving though slightly guilty (as a property owner) at the same time.

She received another uncomfortable prick a little later when Ida Pickering said: "No, we're not having turkey. My husband doesn't like it. But of course we're having a bird. A chicken probably. Must have a proper do; after all, it's Christmas!"

For one split second Essie gazed at her astonished. Nothing would at that moment have dragged from her the information that the Gabriels, like all Jewish households, however poor, automatically bought a chicken every Friday for the Sabbath. She felt guilty and —irresistibly—lofty, at the same time. Depising as she did the standards of Manor Green, she yet carried within her a kind of natural acceptance of ampler, richer living. She was unprepared for the mincing quality, the budgeted economy, the peculiarly genteel smell of the English middle class way of life. Curiously enough she had not encountered this problem with her office friends, both the girls with whom she worked being products of the upper middle class, the background of the one being industrial, Surrey rich, of the other, genuine County. Each of them were used to a higher, gayer standard of living, a lavishness in the way of luncheons and taxis far greater than Essie ever allowed herself. But they were also imbued with the idea of "property" in much the same subconscious way as she was. She got on excellently with both of them.

Mr Redfern, a Government official of some sort, was telling her about an encounter he'd had when on holiday in Spain. "Charming people," he said, "charming people. We exchanged addresses at the end but somehow we never got around to visiting each other in London."

"Oh but what a pity," said Essie warmly, "it's so seldom one meets one's own kind. You should have kept it up."

"Oh, I know," he said, "but—well, after all . . . we don't move in their circles, you know."

"Good heavens!" she cried too emphatically. "Surely that wouldn't have mattered," she said seeing in her romantic mind's eye a kind of delightful meeting between kindred spirits, neither of them noticing in their pleased, urbane converse any disharmony of background.

"No . . . no . . . no, of course not," he muttered. "No, it shouldn't make any difference. . . . He's so well known in his field though . . ."

"What *is* his field?"

To her surprise Mr Redfern mentioned that in which Monty's brother was so pre-eminent.

"Oh," she said rather pleased to be able to contribute something of interest. "My sister's brother-in-law is *the* one in that world. Professor Halpern."

"Indeed," said Mr Redfern but instead of the wide-awake interest she would have shown had he confessed to such a relationship, he turned his head away and his nose up with a look at once glazed, indifferent, touchy.

"I suppose you've heard of him?" she pursued half in innocent tactlessness but with just a trace of longing for recognition of this interesting fact of her connection with scholarship.

"Oh, yes. Yes. Certainly," he said in a colourless tone and changed the subject.

Vexed by what seemed his denial of both her and his equality with his "charming people" Essie felt both snubbed and irritated. Never before had she encountered socially the wary, grumbling resignation of the English, lower middle class to their condition or the suspicious nose with which they sniffed for "side".

Caught on the wrong foot she found it difficult to respond when others of the party spoke to her. In looks she still glowed, vivid, strong-jawed, her hazel eyes bright beneath her thick, black eyebrows and low, square forehead. But her manner (as she began to sense more strongly the divisions between herself and her company) in some way did not match the power of her appearance, becoming abrupt with shyness, diffident, over-emphatic, angular. The subtle discrepancy, bringing with it a kind of disappointment of expectation, affected the others unconsciously and their manner too changed.

At last, to her relief, Mr Coombes looked at his watch and started them all moving.

Crossing the road they entered the college, now almost unrecognizable draped in paper chains, holly, balloons, a huge, spangled, Christmas tree in the entrance hall. The sound of dance music filled the building. In the basement the canteen had been converted into a concert room where many of the older and staider students had already congregated waiting for the show. Essie deposited her coat and made her way with Frances and Jess upstairs to the dance. It was the first interval.

"Come on, come on," said Mr Coombes, genial and proprietary as they entered. "Piece of luck. I've got two tables together for our lot."

"That's very clever of you," said Jess in her brittle voice as they all sat down. She looked very poised and stylish in her white, black-striped, taffeta blouse and full black skirt, just how much smarter than everyone else Essie did not at first realize. Then, as she looked around more closely, again the feeling she had had in the pub of alienation, of apartness, overcame her. "Where on earth do they get them from?" she said to herself horrified, glancing hurriedly away from the shiny, coral taffetas, the droopy florals, the peculiarly tasteless, powder blue crepes she and Sara always called "working-class bridesmaid". Even Frances Warren was wearing an artificial satin dress heavily bunched at one hip. Involuntarily, before she could stop herself, a picture of similar functions in Manor Green flashed into her mind, the girls and women too red-lipped, too flashing-eyed perhaps, but dressed for the most part with a sense of style and fit and colour which could not help but please the eye.

There was a general reshuffle as their tutor and his wife, arriving late, joined them. They sat down almost opposite to Essie. Mr Marchant, lecturer by day at London University, was a slightly-built, twinkle-eyed, brown-haired young man in his middle thirties, good looking, clever-faced with an admirable, clear-cut brain. His wife was delicious; a tiny, sparkling girl with huge black eyes and an unmistakably upper-class, charming voice. She was, it transpired in conversation, half French and her clothes looked it. She wore a grey and white check silk frock with a tiny black bolero.

A perceptible, self-conscious change came over the whole party as soon as the Marchants joined them. Mr Coombes, normally hearty, became over-anxiously host-like; Mrs Pickering, like some Hollywood duchess, stiffened her voice and raised it two full tones. All separate conversations dithered, dwindled and came to a full stop while the attention of the entire class centred on whatever the Marchants were saying. Much as Essie herself wanted to listen to them, after some minutes of this the querying, satiric, independent spirit which lived somewhere inside her raised its head for a moment to sneer; her typically Jewish individualism reared itself in protest at such a cringing, social imbalance. "In a company of their equals," she said to herself angrily, "would everyone's attention be riveted on them in this absurd way?"

Somewhere behind her indignation lay a frustrating sense of displacement. She, Essie Gabriel, but for the narrowness of Manor Green Jewish life, but for her father's injustices (with relief she slipped into the old, raging blame), the stupidity of his poverty, his contempt for daughters, would have been on the Marchant side of the fence; an equal.

Meanwhile, thirsty for quality, she listened as charmed as the rest of them, to Mrs Marchant who was full of comic lamentations over their forthcoming Christmas, spoiled in advance by the irruption of one of Dick's (as she referred to her husband) professorial friends from Pretoria who had planted himself upon them for the vacation. Between them she and her husband gave a lively, funny imitation of his shortcomings as a house guest.

"He's one of these extremely thorough birds," said Mr Marchant. "Cam and I spend a lot of our time just reading, you know, peaceably in front of the fire. But there's just no peace with old Gerald around. You sit him down with a newspaper and he feels he's got to *catch up* with everything that's been happening in London since he went abroad."

"So he sits there," she chimed in bubbling and holding out an imaginary newspaper before her, "reads for five minutes, then he looks up——" she imitated the action, " 'What's this new play about?' We *tell* him——"

"Five minutes later," Mr Marchant broke in, " 'Who's this John Abbott?' We tell him about John Abbott and why he's hit the headlines. Then he tells us about the social significance of John

81

Abbott. And on. And on. He's got to talk, you see. And if we don't respond he thinks we're frivolous and tells us there's no conversation in England today . . ."

"Not," said Camilla, "that we don't feel a little sorry for him. To be obsessed with detail to the point of boring . . . To know—as he *does* know—that he is boring and not to be able to stop himself . . . this is very sad."

"I've got a friend just like that," cried Mrs Pickering and launched into a staggeringly dull report of her friend's conversation. The Marchants listened politely enough, though a certain concealed ennui floating between them was clearly apparent, at least to Essie.

Although she longed to speak to them she could not bring herself to do so, knowing with certainty that if she struck a note exactly within their idiom the others would bristle with unconscious resentment—even Frances Warren and Jess Liversidge, normally so sprightly, were subdued to the general deference—while anything less would leave her as anonymous as before.

The music started. Mr and Mrs Marchant got up to dance with each other, Bingham steered his Pat off, Mr Coombes, with a large, portly gesture, invited Mrs Pickering into the dance and, after one horrible moment of fearing herself unsought, Essie found herself taking the floor with a pleasant, mild-blue-eyed young man who worked at the Board of Trade. His dancing was circumspect, his conversation as mild as his eyes.

"Well, there!" she thought, making her way back to their table at the end. "Honour is satisfied. I've been on the floor!" She gave her partner a smile and sank down on her chair again. The conversation reverted back to food, Camilla Marchant describing with great style and comedy her attempts at a zabaglione which ended up as custard. Mr Haynes, a dentist, began lauding the virtues of chop suey which he had just discovered. "What's it like?" said Essie turning to her rather silent neighbour, a male student who, though possessed of a gritty, tearing voice, strongly Midland-accented, had given every indication in class of a clear, well-read, thinking mind.

"Never had it," he said belligerently, "and don't know that I want to. What I say is, a cut off the joint and two veg's good enough for me." And he tossed his head with a coarse, obstinate, offended shying away from any attempt at social grace.

"Well, yes," she said slowly, a little staggered by the cliché, "though I must say I prefer white meat to red."

"A good cut off the joint," he repeated, "roast potatoes and Brussels. Good enough for me. Don't believe in these fancy dishes," he ended up with a harsh, deprecating laugh. He scrubbed his handkerchief over his face, his eyes sliding sideway, nervously determined not to be put on by anything la-di-dah in the way of conversation.

With a pained, puzzled look Essie turned away, remembering with dull surprise a brilliant essay of his from which their tutor had read several passages earlier in the term. She looked round the floor on which dancing had started again, her shoulders sagging. Apart from the Marchants it was all so different, different from what she had expected; such a lack of excellence and charm. As the evening wore on Jess Liversidge disappeared from their table altogether, Frances Warren sat looking vulnerable and ill at ease in her bunchy dress, her clever tongue, for some reason, defeated by the occasion.

At the second interval it became obvious that the Marchants were weakening, their polished gaiety melting away under the strain of operating so to speak in mid-air with no one to bat the ball back in their own style. Twice Mr Marchant concealed a yawn.

Essie danced with Mr Coombes and Mr Redfern. By ten o'clock their party had dwindled to half. The Marchants had drifted to the other side of the room and were deep in conversation with another tutor and his wife. It was obvious that they would only return to say good night. Essie made some perfunctory remark to one of the men sitting across the table who had opened his mouth to no one during the entire evening. "Yes," he said, his broad face rather blank, "Oh yes. Yes. Yes."

She elaborated her remark.

"Oh, yes," he said. "Yes. Oh, yes. Yes."

Looking away she caught the gaze of Miss Fowler, with whom no one had danced, a tall, insipid-featured woman with a watery, grey eye. Her hair, which had pointedly been dressed for the occasion, fell in stiff, grey-brown ridges over her forehead. She wore a marocain dress and a string of steel beads. Leaning forward she smiled somewhat uncertainly at Essie and said: "Very nice, isn't it? They do it very well, don't they? The college, I mean."

"Very well indeed," said Essie, sitting forward as if to continue the conversation then suddenly could think of nothing else to say. She sat back, depressed, deflated, the evening's disappointment like a slow-sinking cloud heavy in her chest.

"I might as well be in Manor Green," she thought, and an even more profound depression overcame her. Her romantic conception of her fellow students, fostered by a lively term of classroom interchange (so skilfully, as she now realized, encouraged and enlivened by the tutor's carefully deployed personality), had been badly shaken. Naïvely forgetting (if she had ever known) that who and what we are can only be seen truly in our leisure, she had had—ridiculously—a pre-vision of the College dance as of some glorious Commem. ball minus only the champagne. The presence of the Marchants, so subtly different in style, idiom, polish from the ill at ease, shapeless social essence of the others had served only to point the enormous divergence between her imaginings and reality. It was impossible for Essie's natural Jewish instinct for the best quality not to see that socially and intellectually, in charm, life and culture the Marchants were fifty-five shillings a yard where her fellow students were twenty-nine and elevenpence. And she herself? Essie was no better and no better off than her companions. And yet . . . and yet . . . by some peculiar reckoning impossible to pin-point, she unquestionably came out somewhere along the forty-shilling line. It is this, this indefinable, forty-shilling strata which is at the root of one of the great vexed questions which so bedevil the position of the Jew in Anglo-Saxon society. He is always, mysteriously, one above his own economic and social level.

"Excuse me," she said getting up suddenly and pushing back her chair, "I must——" and she walked away across the dance floor and through the crowd milling round the door. Outside in the corridor knots of people clustered in talkative groups. A good-looking girl dressed in a cheap, white, backless evening dress stood arguing sullenly with a young man, darkly flash in appearance with a widow's peak in the exact middle of his narrow, flat forehead. They were almost certainly attached to a Drama Class. "It's no business of yours *who* I dance with," she was saying, her face ugly with temper. "If you don't like it you can do the other."

Essie pushed her way past them, climbed the stairs and, hardly knowing where she was, turned in through an open door and found herself on the balcony overlooking the dance floor. The concert in the lecture hall was over and the audience was now flooding in to the dance. A moment later the music blared out again and the floor crowded. She saw an empty seat in one corner of the balcony and sat down. From her place she could see some of her party almost directly below her. Mr Coombes, indefatigable, was taking the floor with Frances Warren. She was looking rather pleased as she danced by, a smile on her aquiline face which looked so incongruous with her deep-busted, Queen Mary figure. Jess Liversidge suddenly came into view dancing with the perfect stranger to whom she had stuck grimly all evening. Bingham and Pat were talking to Miss Fowler, Haynes and another couple. At one end of their table, with an empty chair on either side of her sat Miss Duboy, an ageing, would-be-fluffy blonde, notorious in class for such kittenish devices as asking, after the word had been in constant use for over two months, what pragmatism meant. She had a girlish giggle, used the word "love" wherever it could appropriately (or inappropriately) be dragged in, flirted her faded eyes constantly and teased her tired, dry hair into wisps of a desperate unbecomingness. Essie had been rather amused by her, repeated her sallies to Sara, over-dramatized her eccentricity. Now, looking down at her from the balcony, she saw, with a quick pang of pity, poor, kittenish, faded Miss Duboy drooping in isolation between the empty chairs, fatigue clamped on her narrow, pinched face, a tight mask of simulated interest fastened over her disappointment as she watched the dancers. "Oh, how cruel, how sad," she said to herself as Miss Duboy lifted one scraggy, waxen arm and adjusted the artificial violets in her hair, bracelets and bangles sliding back from her emaciated wrist. In an instant fired with pain she saw Miss Duboy dressing in excited anticipation of the party in her small, furnished room with its "cooking facilities" and gas meter somewhere in the long, drab streets of South London. What could be the end for such a one? And what, for that matter, would be her own? For a moment she stretched out mental arms to her family, to her home and to Manor Green, with all their drawbacks a solid wall behind her keeping at bay the loneliness and isolation of the bed-sitting-rooms and Miss Duboys. It was this image, occurring not for the first time, which had always been the most powerful deterrent against the constant, logical temptation, which so frequently assailed her, to leave home.

Then, still staring down at the crowded floor, she saw the Marchants dancing, Camilla with the other tutor to whom they had been talking, an exceedingly handsome art historian, and her husband with the other's wife. The two couples passed on the floor, swung gaily round each other, called out, laughed, exchanged a joke at someone else's expense, looked malicious, mock-wicked, mock-guilty, and danced on.

A heavy, powerful sadness came down over Essie, blanketing out the rosy, solid picture of Manor Green which had so sustained her a moment ago. In its place, narrow, iron-black bars seemed to rise from the ground, fencing her away from everything joyous, kindling, civilized. She shivered and looked away. At that moment all the lights in the hall were suddenly extinguished and a roving spotlight circulating through panes of different-coloured glass ranged over the dancers. There was an "Ooh!" from the floor, some laughter and the steady thump of the band as it continued playing in the dark.

"Quite a scrum," said a pleasant, masculine voice beside her.

"Yes, isn't it."

"I suppose you came up here for the same reason as I did; get away from the crowd for a bit?" the voice continued.

"More or less."

From the other corner of the balcony a certain, unexplained bustle suddenly resolved itself into a cascade of balloons descending on to the dance floor. Screams and loud popping noises began exploding into the dark. For a split second, caught in emerald light she saw Mr Coombes and Frances Warren struggling to keep a long, sausage-shaped balloon away from menacing hands. Then a large, red one floated across on to her own lap, lifted in the warm draught from the door and would have drifted off again if the owner of the voice had not caught it.

"Here," he said and Essie, putting out her hands, caught one end of the balloon between them. The lights went up and she saw the other end firmly clasped by a pair of masculine hands belonging to a fair-haired young man. "Saved!" he said laughing.

"Saved!" she repeated and laughed too.

"Well now," he said, "let's see if we can keep it alive for a bit."
And he was proceeding to tie the string of the balloon to one of the
railings of the balcony in front of them when she said: "Oh, but
that's not very brave. No one *could* get at it there. I think we ought
to release it and let it take its chance in the great, big world."

He paused, considered a moment, then said: "I tell you what.
How about our taking it on to the floor and defending it from there?
In fact——" he jerked his head towards the floor, "would you like
to dance?"

"Thank you," she said and they made their way downstairs, not
without a skirmish or two against marauding balloon-poppers.
Her spirits rising, she insisted on dancing with her right arm held
high in the air, the balloon waving above. Young Bingham made
a leap for it as they passed him and Pat on the floor but without
success, the fair-haired young man swinging her away in the nick
of time. "You wait!" she called after them. "You wait till next
term!"

"You go to the same class as those two?" said the young man,
dancing her into a comparatively quiet corner.

"Yes, I do," she said expecting him to say automatically,
"Which one?" but he said nothing, just danced on.

"Which one do you go to?" she said at last.

"Me!" he said. "Good Lord, I don't go to *classes* here. Not my
line of country at all. I use the gym. Come up for a spot of training
once a week."

"I see."

"He-ey," he shouted suddenly giving a lunge with one shoulder
in a very lithe, expert way at another would-be balloon-wrecker
who stepped back with such rapidity that he fell to the floor. Essie's
partner promptly bent down, swept up an armful of coloured paper
chains which were entangling everybody's feet by then and thrust
them over the recumbent young man's head and shoulders. Essie,
laughing, bonked her partner on the head with her balloon, still
miraculously intact, he bowed ceremoniously, and they danced off
again.

"I say," he said suddenly, "have you had your refreshments yet?
I didn't bother."

"No. I didn't either."

"Well——" he said. "Shall we?"

She hesitated. "Actually I'm supposed to be with a party."

"Oh," he said in a disappointed voice. "I suppose . . . d'you want to get back to them?"

She looked over at the tables where her group had been sitting but only Miss Duboy and the Board of Trade young man were there talking desultorily to each other. "They're not there anyway," she said. "I imagine they're having refreshments too."

"Good. Shall we go?"

"Are you here on your own?" she said as they settled themselves on the stairs with their cups and plates, the balloon safely tied to the banisters.

"I came here with a chap I know. Lost him as soon as we got in though. I suppose he's somewhere around," he said indifferently.

"So you keep fit?" she said taking a good look at him for the first time. He was of medium height, squarely muscular in build, with a round head on the top of which his very fine, light-brown hair was already thinning, though he could not have been more than twenty-six. His face was squarish in shape with a round, bulging, child-like forehead, but his features were finely cut, his nose delicately and tenderly chiselled, his lips very soft and pale, sculptured yet sweet. His complexion had the smoothness of a child's, very pale and clear, his only colouring coming from his eyes which were of a very dark yet milky blue like an opaque sapphire.

He nodded in answer to her question with a lift of his eyebrows, his eyes staring thoughtfully into space.

"Why?"

"Why do I keep fit, you mean? Jolly good thing to do, don't you think? What?" he said, the "what" coming out very clipped and Guards officer in tone.

"If you like that sort of thing, well yes," said Essie rather tepidly.

"Of course," he said, "we did get rather into the habit of it at school. Had to if we wanted a place in the rugger team and all that. Games master was fearfully strict. And my OCTU officer was worse!"

"Well, I'm sorry if this shocks you, but I do hate games."

"Oh!" he said lowering his chin. "That's a blow. Still, never mind. We're bound to hit on some mutual interest if we talk long enough. I say, d'you want this?" He held up a little paper cup of jelly with a blob of cream on top. "Come on, do have it. I really don't want it."

"Thank you," she said, "but only if you'll have one of my sandwiches. I've got far too many."

This was not quite true. Her real reason for not eating the sandwich was a sudden doubt as to whether it was filled with tinned salmon or tinned crab. If the latter it was—of course—forbidden. So, for that matter, strictly speaking, was the jelly, but in this Jewish emancipation has progressed. Making, automatically, the continual borderline adjustment so constant and wearying to her generation of young Jews of Orthodox background, Essie accepted the jelly and jettisoned the crab.

Accepting the sandwich, the young man began describing the routine of the gym class he attended. Nothing could have been further from her interest yet she found herself listening, interjecting, following whatever he said with great animation. Half way through a description of horse-vaulting however, she felt a tap on her shoulder and turning, saw Jess Liversidge and her partner descending the stairs from the floor above where they had retired for refreshments. "Meet Mr Clive-Jones," said Jess, "who tried to teach me the elements of Economics all last year."

"I think I succeeded" said the tutor shaking hands with Essie who said rather confusedly: "This is Mr——"

"Groby. Ken Groby," he said scrambling to his feet.

"Having fun?" said Jess smiling down on Essie who, feeling that her manners were somehow not quite right, also rose so that all four of them stood somewhat awkwardly on the stairs at varying levels.

"Yes," she said smiling with her eyes and wondering if that was true.

"Good," said Jess and with a cordial nod she and Clive-Jones passed on down the stairs.

"I rather thought he must be a tutor," said Essie watching his well-shaped head recede and thinking that she was not, after all, the only one to have renegued on the class party.

"Well: now you know my name," said Ken pleasantly, "What's yours?"

"Essie Gabriel."

"Right! Shall we dance, Essie?"

"Yes, rather," she said, her animation returning.

It was late and the floor was emptying. The hall began to look wan and greenish. Nearly all her original party had gone, their empty chairs set askew about the two tables.

"You know," she said to Ken as they finished a quickstep, "I'm afraid I must be going in a few minutes or I'll miss the last train as well as the last bus."

He hesitated, looked regretful, then said easily: "Don't worry about that. I've got my car here as a matter of fact. I can give you a lift if you'll allow me?"

One of those half unexpected, half uneasily anticipated abysses which open before the feet of the socially inexperienced confronted Essie at his words. Should she accept his offer? Was it, she wondered, "safe". Then . . . "idiot" she said to herself in the midst of the thought. Nevertheless the possibility of his trying to make love to her she found appalling. Not the thing in itself but the situation it might create frightened her. How would she know what to do, what to say?

"You'll be quite safe," he said as if echoing her thought. "If there's one thing I pride myself on it's my driving."

Oddly, this sentence reassured her and she accepted.

They separated to the cloakrooms.

When at last she got to the front steps of the college she found him waiting for her, a strange figure in a mackintosh, standing in the dark, his head bent as if in deep thought.

"Hello!" she said coming up to him in a bustling way as if in a great hurry.

He started, lifted his head and said warmly: "Ah! there you are! I've got the old bus round the corner. OK?" And with one hand under her elbow, not quite taking her arm, he steered her along the street and into a narrow alley. For one split second she hesitated. Then he said: "There she is," and to her surprise stopped beside a very large, handsome automobile.

"Is this yours?" she said in astonishment.

"It is," he said, fitting the key into the door. Helping her in he went round to the other side and got into the driving seat. With an expensive roar the engine came to life and with casual expertize he manoeuvred the car out of the alley and away.

"Manor Green, you said?"

"Yes. It's a bit further out beyond——"

"I know it," he said and rattled off the exact route, road by road.

"Good Heavens!" she said, "how d'you know it so well? I thought you said you'd nearly always lived south of the river?"

"So I have. But I know London like the back of my hand."

"You've made a hobby of it?" she asked curiously.

"Sort of."

She relapsed into a comfortable silence while the great car glided onwards through the dark streets. As they approached her own road she told him to stop at the corner. "My father's a bit strict." she told him with a laugh.

"That's all right," he said drawing in to the curb. "Mine was too when he was alive."

"Did he die a long time ago?"

"Nine years. Just a month after my mother."

"Oh," she said. "Oh, I am sorry. How awful for you, both together like that."

"Yes it was," he said. Then, rousingly: "But what are we talking about things like death for? Let's talk about something nice. Such as when am I going to see you again?"

"Oh," she said, at once uncertain and rigid. "Do you . . . do you want to?"

"Of course I do."

"Well I . . . perhaps . . . oh, I really don't know."

"I do want to, you know. What about Tuesday—or Wednesday?"

"Tuesday's my class night."

"*Is* it? That's my gym night too. We must have passed each other heaps of times without knowing. But you've forgotten; term's over, don't you know. No classes for the next four weeks."

"Oh, well then . . ."

"Pick you up on the Embankment outside Charing Cross Station," he said briskly. "About seven. All right?"

She nodded and fumbled at the door handle. He sprang out of the car, came round to her side and helped her out.

"You will come?" he said standing before her.

"Yes, I will."

"Promise?"

"Promise."

He took her hand, squeezed it hard and gave it back to her.

"Good night, Essie."

"Good night."

She went to meet him on the Tuesday rather reluctantly with a mixture of feelings which defied analysis. But as she came up into the open station from the platform below he hurried towards her his arms wide. Before she knew what had happened those arms were tightly around her and they had kissed.

"My car's in dock," he said immediately, "magneto's bust. I hope you don't mind."

"Why of course not," she said.

"There's a rather nice pub near here. Would you like to go there? Or a show? Whichever you like."

"There's nothing special I want to see . . . the pub I think."

"Good. I hoped you'd say that," he said blithely. He took her arm confidently and walked her off.

When she tried afterwards to recall what they had talked about she could not remember save that, like their conversation at the dance, it has been mostly technical, this time about the internal combustion engine and its many troubles. What she did recall, over and over again, each time with the same thrilling warmth and delight was the moment of their greeting; not the kiss but the thought of the eager, waiting heart at the top of the escalator. She could not get over it, the wonderful fact of having been looked for, awaited, with joy.

Motoring troubles apart, he was not particularly communicative. He had been born and bred and, she gathered, educated at Dulwich, though he did not seem very enthusiastic over the famous college. His father had been a director of a well-known automobile manufacturers and he himself was attached to the same firm though in what capacity he did not say. He did not seem in the least curious about her own background nor, when term started again and he took to waiting for her as a matter of course till her class ended half an hour after his gym, did he ever ask what she was studying or why. He seemed perfectly content, week after week, to take her home in the big car (when it wasn't suffering from one of its many breakdowns), stopping for longer and longer periods in some quiet road to kiss and hold her to him with passionate, murmured feeling. Quite early in their acquaintance he had told her that he loved her.

"How *can* you Kenneth? You've known me just a few weeks . . ."

"I've spent fifty-one hours with you——"

"Fifty-one? How d'you work that out?"

"I met you at twenty past ten the night of the dance and we were together till five to one. That makes two hours and thirty-five minutes. The next time we met we had three hours and forty minutes. That makes six and a quarter. The following Sunday I met you at three o'clock and we had——"

"All right, all right," she cried, laughing and flattered and clapping her hand over his mouth. "I give in. But even fifty-one hours is hardly enough time for anyone to fall in love. Properly, I mean."

"*One* hour was enough for me," he said in a voice dark with feeling and cupping her face between his hands he looked down into her eyes. "I love you," he said. "Never forget that. I love you, Essie."

He lifted his head and looked away from her, his chin jutting firmly, almost grimly, above her forehead. She looked up at his square, firm face with its pale, tender quality, at the turn of his head and the unfamiliar, youthful strongness of his shoulders and felt herself shaken and melted by the force of his emotion.

Putting up her own hands, in an excess of feeling, she caught his and bringing them down to her lips kissed them, burying her face in the two palms. As she did so she felt the scrape of exceptionally rough skin against her cheeks. Drawing away she glanced quickly down and saw, even in the chequered light of the street lamp near them, that the palms of his hands were extremely rough, cut about and scarred in places as with heavy manual work. She had noticed once or twice before that the nails were broken and not very clean, the skin discoloured as with ingrained dirt, but she had hitherto, with a kind of willed slackness of observation, refused comment even to herself. This time she was jolted involuntarily into remark.

"My goodness!" she said, "what on earth have you been doing?"

"Eh?" he said in a startled voice and snatched his hands away.

There was a moment of silence as Essie looked up at him with a

93

sudden, puzzled frown. It was not the gesture which had disturbed her so much as the extraordinary change of tone in his voice. The exclamation "eh" can be said in a variety of ways. But there is one particular tone, a kind of deep-bitten "Ay—y" shot out from the back of the throat with a quick snatch of the jaw, which is used only by the least-educated classes. It was this note, suddenly struck out of him, which had surprised her.

"I've been down at the plant several times the last week or two," he said casually. "Didn't I tell you:"

"Perhaps you did," she said still frowning slightly, "but I don't remember." She was almost sure, she thought vaguely before dismissing the matter, that he *hadn't* told her. For the last few weeks she had been steadily nearing that stage in a love affair where curiosity as to the other's slightest movements inflates beyond all bounds. All the trivial paraphernalia of his daily life had become enormously interesting. Though she was not in love with him, by the strength of his own feeling he had netted her into his orbit, opening up the vast, mysterious fields of another personality for her to explore. The secrets of his life, the brand of toothpaste he used, the name of his tailor . . . her curiosity ranged with ferocious interest about such matters, trying to bring into measurable compass this creature, this compact of enigmatic impulses, habits and desires which wished, so ardently, to give itself to her keeping.

"By the way," he went on, "I've got to go down to Beaconsfield this week-end. Darling . . . come with me!"

"For the whole week-end d'you mean?"

"Yes."

She did not answer him, only looked thoughtful. She had had not the slightest trouble in controlling him. Though he was ardent her slightest resistance was law. She had no objection to their becoming lovers. The moral issue did not even occur to her, so far, in spirit, had she already gone from Manor Green. What held her back from assenting was the enormous work of dissimulation to be done at home were she to agree. For a few moments she played with the scheme, sketching out the various tentative alibis she might offer her family for doing something so unheard of as going away for a week-end at so unlikely a time of year. Difficulties enough had arisen each year with her father when she and Sara had chosen such un-Jewish resorts as Edinburgh or Bruges for their summer holidays. "A place to go, I don't think," he would remark irritably. "A cathedral. A castle! Pooh!"

Reluctantly she shook her head. The thought of such a week-end, exciting in its strangeness, its toy-quality of playing at husbands and wives for a little time, the pleasures of sensuality which she did not underestimate; all these appealed with enormous force to her starved appetite for fun, experience, the warmness of life. But the price was too high. At thought of the lies, the rows, the careful primings of her friends, the semi-explanations and further lies to them, Sara's worried, unspoken questions . . . all these suddenly surrounded her as with a flurrying beat of wings.

She shook her head again.

His quick look of disappointment wounded her and she tried to explain.

"Yes, darling, of course I understand," he said but she could see that he did not.

"Anyway," she said with a smile, "it's just as well. After all, you never know. You might have had to make an honest woman of me afterwards!"

"That would suit me right down to the ground," he replied immediately with great earnestness.

She laughed, refusing to take the implication seriously.

"After all," she said, "you know very well that *that's* impossible."

"I don't see why," he said firing up.

"You know why."

"Because you're Jewish? Yes I know. But I don't see why that should be such an insuperable obstacle."

"Are you proposing to me?" she said lightly.

"You know darn well I am."

"Oh, Ken——" she said warmly in an access of gratitude so strong that almost it became love. She felt that she could not embrace him enough, show him tenderness enough, for his loving her. But as for marriage . . . for all her rebellious attitude at home, the idea of marrying a non-Jew was profoundly shocking to her.

"But why?" he said when she told him this. "Why? It just doesn't mean anything to you anyway. And you told me yourself you'd give anything to get away from home."

"Perhaps I did . . . but I couldn't get away from what's bred in my bones so easily."

"How d'you mean?"

She heaved a deep, tired sigh knowing in advance that he would not understand.

"Look, Ken, you mustn't confuse one thing with another. I'm not happy at home——"

"Specially with that old tyrant——"

"Oh," she said interrupting him quickly with a stab of annoyance. To her own surprise she found herself strongly resenting his criticism of her father, "leave that out of it. There are other things . . ."

"What, for instance?"

She hesitated, trying to put into words the Aryan smell to Jewish nostrils and the faint, inimical, guilty odour of their own disloyalty which affects them on too intimate fraternization.

"I wouldn't want to eat bacon," she said absurdly at last.

"You wouldn't have to, you silly sausage."

"Yes, but you would. Sooner or later."

"Would that matter?"

"It would if I had to cook it for you."

"But why?" he said, puzzled. "Everybody has different tastes in food."

She sighed again. How explain the complicated ritual of orthodox Jewish housekeeping where every utensil and every item of food must be kept in strictly segregated categories any violation of which must be judged upon by a Rabbi? How explain to Kenneth or any non-Jew, here, in the middle of the twentieth century, the rigid sense of commandment behind the great fish controversy which had not so long ago rocked Jewry to its foundations; the arguments over chocolate; the row about the tin-loaf versus the oven-bottom; the esoteric rules relating even to clothing to which the ultra-orthodox still cling; above all, the thousand prohibitions of the Sabbath?

"But what is this?" she all at once thought to herself. "If I married him I could throw over all this nonsense for ever." But—remarkably—at this idea, instead of the release it should have brought she felt instead a strangely desolate fall of the spirit.

What affected her, though she did not know it, was the momentary loss of the concept (so strong in the Jewish psyche) of Law.

"I wouldn't want to——" she cried out suddenly.

"You wouldn't have to do anything you didn't want to, darling," he said tenderly. "There's been too much dictatorship in your family——"

"Anyway, it's not only my family," she said interrupting him quickly, "what about yours? I don't suppose they'd be any keener on mixed marriages than mine."

"I haven't any to speak of," he said hastily. "My brother, the brigadier you know, died during the war. You know I've no parents. Good Lord, it's years since I've seen my only uncle . . . he's a country squire wrapped up in his estate down in Leicestershire, never comes up to London at all. So there's no difficulty on my side, you see! So what about it?" he said again with great, pleading earnestness in his deep, cloudy-blue eyes, his sculptured lips vulnerable.

To shake her head required enormous, painful effort.

"You have all the assets!" she cried attempting to lighten her refusal with teasing. "Handsome——"

"I'm not handsome," he interjected but with an unconcealably gratified smile.

"Yes you are. Very!"

"I'm not——"

"*Very* handsome," she insisted, "healthy, young, no mother-in-law in the offing! lots of money, a beautiful car——"

"It's getting late, darling," he said interrupting her and glancing anxiously at his watch. "I don't want to hurry you but you did say you had to be in early tonight."

"Yes, so I did," she said slowly. She had reached that stage of intimate conversation where women want to go on and men want to break off.

Though he was as lover-like as ever on the way home, she let herself in feeling that the evening had gone slightly out of joint though without knowing quite why. Perhaps, she thought to herself later that night, I expected him to press me further. How vain I am! I haven't the slightest intention of marrying him, yet I wanted him to beg me to!

Once or twice in the following weeks she asked herself just why —putting aside the question of religion—she felt no real temptation to marry him. Time and again the same obtrusive facts rose between her and the possibility.

The truth was, when he was not declaring his love for her, when she forgot the novelty of affection and the prestige of masculine company, she could not deny that he bored her. Were his conversation not frequently interlarded with "I love you, I love you," she would have found it intolerable. His social world, so far as she could discover from his talk, seemed to be one of automobile "deals" conducted in the smarter pubs of the West End, his associates large-moustachio-ed, duffle-coated ex-majors calling each other "old boy". He shared a flat, he told her, somewhere in Richmond, with one of these types, "bloke named Hartley," whom he seemed to admire immensely, but he had never suggested taking her there, a fact which she rather regretted. She longed to see where and how he lived but some shyness held her back from suggesting it herself. When she asked him to describe his friends more fully he could only say they were "damned good company". His opinions on politics were almost non-existent; on the colour-bar "lazy bastards". This had aroused her ire and she had attempted to argue with him only to be met with blank, uninterested incomprehension which she might not have minded perhaps, had he not become almost irritable at having to display his considerable ignorance on the subject.

On only two matters could he talk fluently, though not well, and these were motor-cars and money.

"For a well-off young man," she said to him teasingly one evening, "you seem to think an awful lot about money!"

"Eh!" he ejaculated with something of that same involuntary coarseness of tone which had startled her once before.

She changed the subject.

A few days later he telephoned her at her office. "Darling," he said excitedly, "I've got a surprise for you. Meet me tonight?"

"Ken! It's Friday! You know, I told you, it's impossible for me ever to get out on Friday night."

There was a crestfallen pause. Then he said: "I forgot. But can't you, darling? Just for once? I'm longing to show you——"

"Show me what?"

"No, I'm not telling you on the phone. I want you to see it. Can't you, Essie?"

98

"I c——"

"Please," he said with such a loving pleading in his voice that her heart melted.

"All right," she said reluctantly.

"I'll come straight up after work. About seven. Outside Manor Green Tube."

"*No!*" she said raising her voice but he had already rung off.

Not daring to go inside the well-lit station lest anyone saw her, she hung about outside, thanking heaven it was still early enough in the year for it to be dark by seven. Absorbed in watching out for the big, black limousine he habitually drove, she did not notice the long, pale-blue sports model which drew up beside her till she saw that Kenneth was waving to her from the driving seat and leaning over to open the door. She hurried over to the car. "What's this?" she said.

"*This* is the surprise," he said grinning widely. "Like it?"

"My *goodness*," she said looking at its impressive length and gleaming chromium. "But how . . . I mean, what's happened to the other?"

"Turned it in," he said airily. "It was always going wrong anyway. You know yourself, darling. Half the time I couldn't use it. Get in, sweetheart, and I'll let you see how she goes."

For a moment she hesitated. But it was impossible to start a whole discussion at that moment about the things forbidden to her to do on the Sabbath. And she could not bear the thought of his disappointment were she to refuse. She stepped into the car and shut the door.

It was for this meeting that she had walked out of her home on the Friday evening, precipitated her father's rage, Sara's reproach, and made her first overt transgression against the ancient laws of her people.

# Chapter Four

## I

A T THE NEXT MEETING OF THE GUILD THE RABBI noticed Sara in the audience but the memory of their frank talk embarrassed him a little and he avoided her, leaving early. He was feeling disturbed and frenetic and, although he had been surprised and pleased by the unexpected blossoming from what had seemed so drab a plant, he was low-spirited and wanted reassuring with the scent of prosperity and success.

Sophie was avoiding him. She didn't come to the Guild meetings any more. When he called round in the evenings, walking up her street with the light, slight, melancholy grey of the spring evenings overlaid by the magic of her living there, she was never at home. Only Trudy was in and sometimes he would sit and talk to her, looking at her with passionate envy because she lived in that mean little flat with Sophie. She was able to dress with her and eat with her and talk to her in the middle of the night. He tried to imagine them chattering to each other, lying each in her narrow bed inadequately covered with the worn, thin blankets. He imagined them getting up in the mornings, treading gingerly on the cold, shabby lino which covered the floor. The cocky, romantic way of their living thus, on their own, tickled him and pricked his heart. As time went on, once or twice in Sophie's absence, out of savagery and yearning to come nearer to her, he made desultory advances to Trudy in a heavy, half-hearted way but she was without mystery There was no magic in her, only red cheeks and a round, young body. He gave it up.

To distract his mind he decided to accept Joel Fredlander's repeated invitation to spend a week-end with him at the Hebrew Academic Institute where he was resident lecturer, placed, as he put it, "in the middle of a Kentish marsh". The building in fact was a converted farm-house, rather hideous architectually (it had been built in the eighteen-seventies) but impressively set in its own extensive acres. As it was the last week-end of the Easter holidays and just after the eight days of the Jewish Passover, hardly anyone was in residence apart from Joel and the principal himself, Solomon Tarsch, lately back from South America, and his family.

Rabbi Tarsch, characteristically beating Joel to it as host, came out on to the wide terrace to welcome Leo as he drove up to the front entrance of the Institute on Friday afternoon. He was a remarkably handsome man after the middle-European model with broad cheeks and bright blue eyes under slanted lids. Although of barely medium height his magnificent shoulders gave him an appearance of great power. Beside him Leo looked lumbering and swarthy.

"My dear Rabbi Norberg! I was delighted when Joel told me he had persuaded you to come down to us." His voice was strong but sibilant with a husky foreign timbre to it.

The two men walked into the large entrance hall together. Joel came out from a door at the back of it and greeted Leo, his manner in the presence of his Principal muted but satirical. He was followed by the younger of Tarsch's two little girls.

"This is my Deborah," said Tarsch fondling, but with an automatic gesture, the child's head. "Say 'How d'you do' to Rabbi Norberg."

The little girl strolled up to Leo and with bland good manners shook hands with him. She was about seven years old, a pretty child with absent, doe-like eyes and a dreamy expression. The cast of her features was not in the least Semitic nor was that of Alexandra her older sister who followed a few moments later, a ten-year-old with small features in a delicate, neat face and casual, polite eyes. She helped to serve tea in the absence of her mother who had not yet appeared, with an off-hand, social aplomb Leo found almost terrifying.

He was making inquiries about one of Tarsch's students, the son of one of his own congregants, when Mrs Tarsch entered, a slender, beautifully dressed woman with her younger daughter's remotely absent eyes. Leo received an impression of tough, light-weight fragility, like aluminium. She did not apologize for her late appearance and after an indifferent greeting sat quietly and abstractedly while the others talked, though twice she interrupted her husband with scant ceremony, in the middle of his somewhat florid sentences, about minor domestic matters.

Tea was almost over and Mrs Tarsch had brought in the eleven-months-old baby boy to be admired—it was easy to see that he was the only thing which aroused real feeling in her—when there was the sound of a taxi arriving at the front door followed by the appearance at the entrance of a middle-aged man and a young boy.

Rabbi Tarsch pushed back his chair, stood up and, moving rapidly towards them, called out: "Gotthelf! You are here at last. Come in. Come in. Just in time for tea. How are you? How are you?" He led the two forward and sat them down making a quick gesture to Alexandra, or Sandy as they called her, to bring round more chairs. "You know everyone, I think. Evelyn, can we have more tea?" His wife stood up and unceremoniously planking the baby on her husband's lap went off towards the kitchens.

"But this is a pleasant surprise," said Leo. "Did you come by train? Why didn't you tell me, Joel?" he said turning to his friend who made an "I didn't know myself" gesture. "I could have driven you down."

"Thank you. Thank you," said Mr Gotthelf in a quick, mumbling voice. "That would have been very nice. Well. Never mind. Never mind. We got here. This is my young son, Gedaliah."

The young boy, he was about eleven years of age, shuffled his feet nervously and with visible effort raised his eyes from his toecaps.

"And how are things with you, my friend?" said Tarsch.

"It goes. It goes," said Mr Gotthelf with a sideways half-nod and raised eyebrows, a characteristically Jewish mannerism. He was a man of medium height who managed to appear much smaller, partly on account of his emaciated appearance, partly because he held himself so badly, his very narrow shoulders humped and stooping, his head poked forward as if permanently deaf and humble. His face was wax-pale and deeply lined down the flabby cheeks though his mouth was very full, the lips thick like pale, chapped cushions. He wore a shabby, brown, pin-striped suit, the waistcoat loose across his meagre chest. Beneath his worn, brown, felt hat which, after a time he took off, substituting a black skull-cap, his hair escaped in faded, springy, brown tufts, the same colour as his almost invisible eyebrows. The boy was dark. He had a small, olive face, too small for his big, cushiony mouth, fleshy vulnerable nose and his black, protuberant, heavy-lustrous eyes. He held his cup and saucer rigidly.

"How is your wife?" said Leo.

"Better. Thank God, better. The news is better. I see her every day. It's a long way but I go. Maybe I could get her to a nearer hospital but it's not worth it now. Soon she comes out, please God. And the Sister is very good. Every day she allows me to come after visiting hours. I explained. An hour and a half to get there, every day. And my work not finished till so late in the evenings many times."

Mr Gotthelf worked in some obscure, not very well paid capacity for a Jewish educational organization. Though not a member of Ferne Road Synagogue, he lived in a suburb to the east of Manor Green, Leo had known him in a desultory way for years. Mr Gotthelf had a reputation for a rather narrow and old-fashioned but nonetheless much respected Hebrew scholarship and they had often met at the study circles organized by many synagogues on Saturday evenings.

"I told her of your kind invitation, Rabbi Tarsch, for me and for Gedaliah. She sends you her thanks."

"For what?" said Tarsch with an expansive shrug opening his hands out. "The staff is here. The house is here. Why shouldn't you have a week-end in the country, you and the boy? Only too pleased. And when your wife comes out, please God, she will come also, I hope. How far is it? Thirty miles! You know, in South America, in North America, in Canada, Africa, they drive that far to go to a movie—or a bioscope as they say in South Africa. You know, to travel four days there to get to another town . . . it's nothing! I fly now of course. On my last trip to South America I spoke in sixteen different cities in three weeks. In *their* summer, not in ours! It was, as they say, a sweat."

"I gather it was worth it," said Leo.

Joel was having a lumbering flirtation with Deborah who, dreamily dark-eyed, was not paying much attention.

"Ach!" said Tarsch with sudden energy. "We know nothing in this country. Nothing. The synagogues there—palaces! The communal halls, the clubs, every amenity under the sun laid on, sports, concerts, cinemas . . . In South Africa the same." His voice rose

103

ecstatically. "You've seen nothing like it, believe me. Our Yidden, bless them, when they do a thing . . ."

"A pity they can't lay on orthodoxy with all the other amenities," said Joel drily.

"I don't deny," said Tarsch, putting his finger tips together and shifting easily into his pulpit manner, "that that is something which causes me the greatest unease. I don't deny it. I'll even go so far as to tell you this. In the midst of the luxury—and in the homes too there's living on a scale we don't dream of over here—in the midst of the luxury I find myself longing for England. This happens every time. Every time I go abroad I think . . . nowhere is so good as England. We think our spiritual values faltering, inadequate here? Let me tell you, with *all* the money, all the luxury, all the organization—and don't let us deceive ourselves, in the colonies, in the States, the organization of our communities is marvellous, as efficient a machine as *anyone* could desire; with everything . . . the spirit isn't there. Holiness," he said raising a pious stare to the ceiling, "isn't there."

Mrs Tarsch, who had taken the baby and disappeared some time before, appeared briefly at the door, called the two little girls away and disappeared again. "Go. Go with the other children," said Tarsch interrupting himself, to the little Gotthelf boy. "Go my child," said his father. The boy got off his chair and went hesitantly after them.

"I tell you," said Tarsch, his voice rising again, "it makes me shudder, *shudder* when I see abroad—at home too to a certain extent, I'm not denying it, but more abroad, the shocking gap between our aims—and our achievements. We are dealing (I am speaking now as a teacher amongst teachers) every day of the week with people who are being overpowered by the outside influences of the modern world; on the one hand the power of wealth, position, prestige, on the other, the overthrow of all disciplines." There was a swift, blue flash from his eyes as he glanced round the well furnished hall.

"Everything combines to swamp, to destroy, the all-important moral framework," he continued. "Everywhere one looks one sees the retreat from moral principles. They think that if good behaviour cannot prevent unhappiness then good behaviour is no good.

Rewards, rewards, they ask for. A platitude! I know! But a tragedy can still be expressed by a platitude. We make colossal efforts in every direction to restore holiness, observance, the old religious spirit to our people. And what happens? Despite our efforts we seem to be getting nowhere. We make superhuman attempts to pump into our children, at least, a true Judaism . . . and what happens? Before they've finished their education, the little that stuck has become unstuck. The doors have closed. The mental attitudes resist and resist." His voice and whole bearing seemed to swell with real power and sincerity.

Leo gave a quick, sideways look at Joel but he was sitting heavily in his chair gazing upwards with a blank, torpid eye. He looked away again, wondering, as always, why Tarsch's diatribes, with which he was in complete accord, should affect him with unease. Was it the pulpit manner which gave them so unconvincing an accent? Was it his handsome, well-fed, well-tailored self? He looked again at Tarsch, at his narrow forehead widening out suddenly at the check bones to the square jaw and massive neck. His dark suit beautifully, expertly tailored, fitted across his imposing stomach, his shirt was lily-white. His cuff links and wrist watch were of heavy chased gold. His slanting blue eyes glittered in his smooth, full face.

Tarsch clenched his fists, put one over the other and shot them out dramatically before him. "We are suffering," he said in his strongly resonant voice, "from cultural schizophrenia. The meanest, poorest, least observing Jew is conscious of his heritage. But how many will accept the responsibility that goes with it? Leave it to someone else, he says. Leave it to the Rabbis: it's their job not mine. If he has any qualms he looks to see what his neighbour has given to the last appeal for charity—and tops it." He sank his head backwards into his shoulders and gazed upwards consideringly. "Keeping up with the Cohenses," he said at last. "That's what Judaism amounts to today."

"Nevertheless," said Gotthelf in his quick, nervous mumble, "you'd be surprised—oh, I'm not contradicting you, Rabbi Tarsch, what you say is correct—but there is also a turn. There is definitely a turn in some places. I have seen it in my own district. Many of the children for instance; they are educating their own parents! A neighbour of mine, her son goes with my Gedaliah to the children's services in my shool . . . she told me herself, her *jungë* Michael insists that she light the candles on Friday night. She even has to buy from a kosher butcher or he won't eat! And he's not the only one. I assure you, there's a turn."

"Excuse me, my friend," said Tarsch, "I am going to correct you. There is a *half* turn. Towards Judaism in its full sense, in its full spiritual glory, there is no turn to speak of. We have here, in what you describe, no passionate acceptance of a higher ideal. What *have* we? I will tell you. We have in your neighbour that peculiar hybrid the *Liberal* Jew, the *Reform* Jew . . . let them call themselves what they like, to me they are all the same: *Separatists*. A half observance," he hunched his massive shoulders, "is no observance at all. Religion with all the richness, all the meaning taken out of it. Such people as you describe—and I do not, believe me, question their well-meaning for a moment—are taking what I can only describe as the road *out* of Judaism, not into it."

"Between ourselves," said Leo, "when I think of the Shabbos morning automobile show in Veryan Square, I sometimes wonder whether it wouldn't be better after all to have less stringency and so less hypocrisy."

"That certain points of the law," said Tarsch hastily, "need amending, I admit. We are living in a modern world, a world so completely different from ancient times as to put an unprecedented strain on the psyche."

"I don't know about the psyche," said Joel breaking in, "but it's damned hard on the feet. Veryan Square doesn't surprise me. Maybe that's what induced our friend, Rabbi Tauber (you've heard?), to go over to the Reform. That long walk on Shabbos morning. I wasn't surprised mind you. It was on the cards. I expected it. As soon as a ministry became available . . . Well, I don't know that I blame him —or anyone," he said lazily. "Who'd be an orthodox Jew today? Comes Shabbos, you can't do this, you can't do that. You can't touch fire, can't strike a match and you can't smoke. You can't use transport, you can't use money, so you can't go any place—unless you walk. You can't take a bath, you can't play cards or the gramophone or switch on the television. If you've got a garden you can't pick a flower. You can't cut your nails. You can't open a letter (or write one) because you can't tear paper. That genius, by the way . . . its just struck me!—that genius who invented the interleaved toilet roll . . . he must have been a Jew!"

Gotthelf, after a quick look at Tarsch, burst out laughing with the others.

"Ah well," said Tarsch, getting up. "That reminds me—did you hear the joke about . . ." He told them, rather well, a mildly improper story after which they dispersed to get ready for the Sabbath.

## 2

The Hebrew Academic and Agricultural Institute of which Rabbi Tarsch had now been head for some time was a fairly recent creation started originally by a group of rich, orthodox, philanthropically-minded Jews as a kind of farm school where intending immigrants to Israel could receive training in agriculture and dairy farming. To this, as the scope of the thing had enlarged, had been added the rambling farm on whose land the original house stood (which was still kept as a hostel for the students), and what was virtually a campus established. Resident tutors taught Jewish philosophy and history, science and mathematics to the students. The aim—an admirable one—was to create and send off to Israel specially selected and trained young men and women to serve as orthodox and stabilizing influences in the tiny new country. As time went on, however, under Tarsch's commanding personality the agricultural basis from which all this had sprung had greatly diminished. By now there was an overwhelming bias in favour of academic learning. The tone of the place remained uncompromisingly orthodox.

Leo strolled round the grounds the following day after a very expansive Sabbath lunch. As at dinner the night before, Tarsch had been in great form, his massive vitality infectious. Even his wife had smiled, disturbing her usual, unresponsive, porcelain repose. At one point during the previous evening Leo had found himself looking at her peacock-blue dress, the County air with which she wore it, the huge diamond ring on her wedding finger and found his imagination, roaming round both the Tarschs, suddenly astounded. "What on earth . . .?" he said to himself and, "But really!" What a journey to make, from the Scottish slum and the provincial drapery shop to this yeoman squire and his lady, this master and mistress of the manor and the English fields outside! And he was contrasting Mrs Tarsch in his mind's eye with her mother-in-law as she must have been—the old, Yiddish-speaking, long-skirted, foreign woman in the grimy Gorbals tenement—when Evelyn stirred and spoke and the immense disparity was somehow diminished. Some impalpable element in her voice, her manner, perhaps it was only her glance, at once removed her distinction.

After their walk on Saturday afternoon Joel went off to his room, and Leo, the April day being sunny and warm, sat down on one of the two deck chairs which had been put out on the terrace. The other was occupied by Mr Gotthelf who was immersed in a book. No one else was about. Gotthelf had looked up at his approach, waited to see if Leo wanted to talk and then, seeing him lie back and close his eyes, turned to his book again.

Leo had lain for some minutes, half dozing, half thinking of Sophie whom the April day had conjured to his mind with a vivid, loving hopefulness, when a French window was opened behind him and struggling through it came Gotthelf's young son, Gedaliah, burdened by a biggish, fireside chair he was endeavouring to heave out of the room where it belonged in order to sit on it in the sun.

"Gedaliah!" exclaimed Mr Gotthelf, he and Leo both looking round. "What? What's this you are doing? Put it back. Put the chair back. What would Rabbi Tarsch say?" His voice twittered with shocked nervousness.

"It's all right, it's all right, pappa," said the child. "Mrs Tarsch *said* I could. The deck chairs are all being repaired. She *said*."

"Are you sure?" said Gotthelf. "You are telling me the truth?" The alarmed expression had not left his face.

"She *told* me. She *allows* me," the boy said, still heaving at the chair. He planked it down on the terrace just outside the window. His father subsided though not without an anxious look back at the house.

Leo too relaxed though not altogether. He had been disturbed by the fussed note of fear in Gotthelf's voice, disturbed and irritated.

He glanced sideways at the man, noting his unhealthy pallor in the sunlight, his faded hair under the tiny, black skull cap, the unmistakable Ghetto stoop of his narrow back; all, all of him appallingly incongruous against the green sweep of English landscape which surrounded them. A sudden enraged gust of temper shook him at the man's grovelling respect for authority and power, his sense of obligation, the humble readiness to *be allowed*. How often had he not come up against this same abasing attitude amongst his people, even to each other; this same, disgusting inheritance of centuries. He could have forgiven Gotthelf if the man had been stupid or ill-educated. But he was nothing of the kind. His field, though narrow, was deep, his learning respected, his papers, in the learned journals, thought much of. Only the ignorant, he thought, can sustain subjection with dignity. All other long-subjected peoples have been ignorant, their ignorance a condition of their servitude. In proportion, as they throw off their ignorance so also do they enlarge their status as men. But the Jews have never been ignorant. They know, they know—and *still* they are bogged down in indignity, thrust into positions of false humility. "A false position!" he exclaimed angrily, half aloud. Gotthelf stirred and looked up then turned to his book again. It is this false position, he muttered crossly to himself, at once despising and despised, the carrying of superiority on suppliant, bent backs, which gives that peculiar, enemy-making twist to our personalities which makes us both cringing and stiff-necked, the despair of well-meaners, patronizers, ruling classes everywhere.

It was with a pleased sense of distraction that Leo saw Tarsch's two small daughters come out on to the terrace each carrying a cushion from the hall which they placed on the ground and sat on, near the little boy sitting uneasily (his confidence shaken by his father's tremors) in the long chair.

Leo turned his thoughts inwards again, his eyes focused unseeingly on the lawns and shrubberies before him, the image of Sophie, of beauty, superseding the ugly un-grace of Jewish perplexities. He fell into a shimmering, erotic dream of her.

The sun grew brighter and more dazzling. After a time, Mr Gotthelf, his weak eyes unable to stand the excessive glitter, rose and went indoors. The small stir woke Leo from his reverie. Though he did not move, his senses became once more aware of his surroundings. On his left the children were chattering. He turned his head and looked at them. Sandy was sitting neatly composed on her cushion, her knees up, her feet crossed at the ankles. She was a most compact and graceful child. Deborah was leaning languidly against one of the wooden struts of the chair in which Gedaliah shifted uneasily. His olive face, like a small, full, dusky damson, wore a vulnerable, agonized smile.

"I don't know what it means," he was saying, shrugging his shoulders uneasily.

"I know what mine means," said Deborah in her slow way. "Deborah means 'a bee'. A *humming* bee, a *honey* bee," she repeated with drowsy pleasure.

"And Alexandra means 'a queen'," said Sandy. "Fancy you not knowing what Gedaliah means." Her voice was very clear and well bred and slightly contemptuous.

The boy, sitting on the very edge of his chair, twisted his legs and said, flushing more darkly than ever: "Are you sure about Alexandra?"

"Of course I'm sure," she said coolly. "I've just told you, haven't I?"

"Yes of course. Only . . . well, Alexandra is the *name* of a queen. I didn't know it *meant* 'a queen', that's all."

A quick, almost imperceptible look of uncertainty crossed Sandy's well-bred, so English-looking small face. Then she said sharply: "It *means* 'queen'."

She scrambled to her feet.

"You'd better come and tidy up before tea, Deb."

Gedaliah untwisted his legs and half stood up. "Shall I tidy up too?" he asked embarrassedly, obviously anxious to conform.

"If you need to," she said indifferently moving away with Deborah in tow. The boy hesitated, not knowing whether he was expected to need tidying or not. He almost sat down again then stood up and called after them: "I'll come too." They glanced back, giggled, and walked on, Gedaliah looking uncomfortable trailing in their wake, a clumsy-mannered, unhappy, socially maladroit little boy.

Perhaps it was this scene, filling Leo with anger, irritation and pity in equal parts, which sent him down into the neighbouring seaside town the next morning where, though it was Sunday, he managed to find a shop which sold toys, open. Buying for Deborah was simple, an attractive woollen animal, for Alexandra not so simple, she was too self-possessed a child to be easy to buy presents for; he finally settled for a book. The real difficulty came when he tried to choose something for Gedaliah. Nothing mechanical was suitable; he was not that kind of child. Nor would an ordinary story book do for the sensitive, jerky intelligence behind those coal-coloured eyes. He finally decided on a very large and elaborate jig-saw puzzle, much more expensive (and this gave him a peculiar, almost vindictive pleasure) than the other two presents put together.

He caught the three children in the hall where everyone was assembling before lunch and presented the two little girls with their presents for which, without prompting, they thanked him very politely.

Gedaliah, with the self-conscious look one assumes at other people's luck, was looking over Sandy's shoulder as she opened her book when Leo called him across, produced the jigsaw and handed it over. To his and everyone else's acute embarrassment, Gedaliah, flushing to a dark crimson and with wild, awkward gestures, immediately attempted to hand it back to him.

"No, no, Gedaliah," said Leo, caught on the wrong foot. "It's for *you*."

"But why *me*?" stammered the child, his face flaming. "Why me? Why should you buy *me* a present?" he repeated in a high voice, trying to thrust it back into Leo's hands.

For once at a loss, Leo remained silent. For a moment, hurt, he was extremely angry with the little boy. Then, as he sensed the boy's inarticulate mixture of profoundly felt inferiority and obscure, stiff-necked pride, the idea already ingrained in his head that he was not one of those born to receive, an extreme and painful pity overcame him.

"Why shouldn't I buy a present for you?" he said placing the puzzle firmly in the boy's arms. "I buy presents for everybody's children. I *like* buying presents."

"Of course, of course," said Mr Gotthelf rapidly. "Why don't you thank Rabbi Norberg, Gedaliah? So kind, How kind. Thank the Rabbi, he'll think you've got no manners. He was surprised to get a present, that's all. And such a big one! Thank the Rabbi, Gedaliah."

Powerless to help him further, Norberg listened to the few stammered words the child, his face still burning, managed to get out, then, with thankfulness followed the others in to lunch.

"By the way," said Rabbi Tarsch half-way through the meal, "I hope my dear Norberg, that you are going to be available for the whole of the last week in June. You have not forgotten the International Judean Council conference which opens in London on the twenty-third?"

Leo nodded.

"We are expecting representatives, both Rabbis and lay leaders, of communities from forty-two countries; three hundred delegates in all. And this time, *this time*, we are going to see results. The American contingent in particular is very strong. By the way . . . they have asked me if I can provide them with a temporary secretary for a few hours each evening, possibly Sunday also. Do you perhaps know of somebody? They'll pay well of course."

"I think I can find you someone," said Leo. He had thought at once of Sophie. It would be a good excuse to see and talk to her. "I'll let you know," he said.

"Good. Good."

Before he went back to London that evening Joel said to him: "Leo, what are you doing about holidays this year?"

He shrugged.

"Believe me, Joel, I haven't even thought."

"What about a week at Whytecliffe Sands later on?"

"There? Ach, Joel, I've had enough of Whytecliffe Sands. Leave me alone."

"No, no, Come down with me for a week. Come on. Come on. What have you got to lose?"

"About forty pounds!"

Joel wagged his head impatiently.

"If I can afford it you can! It'll do us both good."

"I'll see. I'll think about it," he said reluctantly at last and Joel was obliged to leave it at that.

As soon as he got back he telephoned Sophie, teased her with a story of a mysterious offer he had to make and drew a promise from her to go for a drive with him the following Sunday. To his disappointment the day was one of fitful sun and heavy rain and he had to abandon his plan of taking her right out of London. The best he could do was take her to an obscure café in Hampstead for tea. Afterwards he drove her, the rain by then lashing down, on to a high part of the heath where he finally stopped the car in a wet, deserted road.

"*Now* then, will you tell me?" she said immediately, taking out a cigarette. The immediacy, which seemed to him to carry a deliberate hint of coolness and detachment, affected his confidence. He slapped his pockets for matches, pulled the box out clumsily and gave her a light.

"I am *most* intrigued. What *is* this mysterious offer?"

With a feeling of anti-climax Leo muttered: "Oh well, it's nothing very much really. I thought you might like to earn some extra money. There's a temporary job going, just for a week. Secretarial work. It would be well paid though."

"But how can I?" she said with one of her mannered gestures somewhat constricted by the narrow confines of the car. It irritated him a little as all her more sophisticated poses, rapidly becoming more frequent, did. He preferred to think of her always as his imagination saw her; spontaneous, child-like and lovely. Even her clothes had altered, as he noted with an ever-suspicious eye. She had taken to slightly unconventional, wide-falling sleeves and long, flowing skirts and her soft, brown hair was brought sharply, even severely back to a tight, small bun on the very top of her head. It was a style only her particular beauty could have got away with. She still, however, used no make-up at all and her hands and wrists, red, youthfully bony, the nails small and bitten, were still the same.

"How can I possibly?" she said again. "I'm still working at the same job, you know."

"This would be only in the evenings. Just for a week." And he explained to her about the forthcoming conference. She looked thoughtful.

"Would they want me every evening?"

"I imagine so."

"Well," she said looking away through the car window. "I . . . really I don't know. I'd rather not give up a whole week of evenings just now . . ."

"It's not till the end of June," he interjected, a violent, jealous curiosity stabbing him.

She gave a faint shake of her head.

"I'll have to think about it. Can I let you know?"

A big sports car hooted behind them in the narrow road, then passed them with a roar.

A hopeless feeling dragged at his shoulders and down his arms.

"What a busy young lady you are," he said stiffly feeling the old-fashionedness of the phrase "young lady" damning him still further.

"It's very kind of you to think of me," she said, stilted in her turn. "I must say I could do with the money. Like everybody else I know I'm chronically hard up."

She so obviously did not include him in the category of "everybody else I know", so obviously and unconsciously left him out of her circle of friends, that a stronger pain than ever pierced him. He felt, like a valve opening and shutting in the top of his head, a sudden desire to cry, to weep tears upon that blithe indifference, to claim, absurdly, that he too was hard-up for money. He would have given anything to be young and poor and hungry.

"I'd better take you back," he said at last, adding with rough spite, "seeing you're so anxious, as you said, to keep an appointment this evening."

She did not reply.

He let in the clutch and drove off.

The big, pale blue convertible which had passed Leo as he sat talking to Sophie drove on up the road for another quarter of a mile. Then it drew up. Inside it Kenneth Groby pulled back the hand-brake, switched off the engine then turned and gathered Essie Gabriel, with this customary, ardent tenderness into his arms. They kissed.

"Happy?" he asked, as he always did.

"Yes."

"Really?"

"Really," she said gazing across his shoulder and out on to the heath which fell away on the left, wild, green and secret under the pouring rain. It was twilight. Across the narrow, uphill road, branches from tall trees reached out, touching and tossing. Bushes growing out from the grassy banks shook their wet leaves against the windscreen. The grey, spring rain fell steadily in the mysterious dusk.

Kenneth was kissing her again but she gently put aside his head, holding it with a turned back hand against her shoulder while she gazed with an intense, fierce joy out into the deep, rain-green, twilit tunnel which the trees and the gloom made of the road. Within the car there was a smell of petrol and leather and Kenneth's hair cream, warmth from the engine, a firm-sprung comfort in the seat holding her, and Kenneth's body close-wrapped to hers, and still. The sense of being enclosed and cherished by a lover, secure and warm, safe in a safe and private cave in the heart of the green, splashing world caught her with enormous joy. Every rain-drop drumming on the canvas roof above them increased her delight. Kenneth's kiss fell softly upon her throat. With the smallest movement of her hand she stilled him. In this marvellous pleasure there was no room for passion. It was the deep, aching joy of her *situation* which moved her.

After a time she stirred and, lifting her hand, stroked back the baby-soft, thinning fair hair from his round forehead. She looked down at the tender, delicately rounded angle of his cheek and caught, not for the first time, an impression of a curious, soft, shifting grace.

"How very soft and fine your hair is," she said, "not at all like mine."

He reached up and pulled at hers.

"Stop! you're hurting," she said. "And anyway you don't have to pull so hard. I know it's as strong as horsehair."

"I wish mine were," he said. "Another two years and I'll be as bald as a coot. Will you still love me, darling, even without any hair?"

"I guess so," she said without emphasis.

"You'd *better*," he said fiercely.

"If I still know you," she added.

"What makes you think you might not?" he said sitting up straight with a jerk.

"Nothing, nothing," she said shaking her head.

He stared into her eyes without speaking, then laid his head back against her collar bone. Absently she traced with her finger the line of his nose and his pale, Greek lips.

"When are you going to marry me?" he said.

"Oh Ken. Don't ask me that sort of question. I can't answer it. Don't."

"It's your father, isn't it? No one else would mind, only him."

"No. That is not true, darling. Many people would. My sisters, my relations, my whole *background* would . . . rise up and . . ."

"Background," he said in a quiet voice. Then, rousing: "Oh, Essie. You know it's only your father really. I know how you feel about him," he said in a reasonable voice. "I remember what I felt when I knew dad was dying. Never going down to see him unless I wanted something—money usually. I felt guilty about that. I made it up to him though. I spent the last weeks of his life with him; right to the end. I made it up to him. I made it up to him," he repeated several times.

"What was he like?" said Essie idly.

There was a short pause.

"The old man? Oh—h—. Quite a sport really," he said in his most drawling voice. "Fond of hunting. Leicestershire's great hunting country, don't you know. My father bred horses, actually."

"What with breeding horses and manufacturing cars your family seems to have had a corner in transport," said Essie laughing.

He turned and gathering her hard against him kissed her violently.

"Let's go and have some food," he said.

They were sitting in a small restaurant on Haverstock Hill waiting to give their order when Ken, who had been fidgeting a little, said: "Darling, will you order when the girl comes? I've got a feeling I shouldn't have parked the car where I did. I'll just take her round the corner where she'll be out of harm's way. Shan't be long. Here's something to read while I'm gone." He drew an evening paper out of his coat pocket and dropped it on the table, kissed her quickly and went out.

Essie undid her coat and unwinding her scarf took it off. She looked at the menu again then put it down and picked up the newspaper. As she unfolded it another paper which had been folded in with it fell out. She straightened it out on the table. From the front page of the *Saturday Illustrated*, a very low class, fourpenny weekly produced for an almost illiterate readership, a gaudy, cheesecake illustration hit her eye.

When Ken came back she said looking up at him and laughing: "*Now* I know your real taste, Ken Groby! Women like these!" And she held the paper up before him.

"Oh yes," he said with a gay air. He sat down.

It was on the tip of Essie's tongue to say: "Where on earth did you pick it up?" when he said in his most cultured drawl: "Haven't you seen it before? It's quite good. Rather amusing don't you know."

"This!" said Essie in a horrified tone before she could stop herself.

He looked away from her. "Oh, I don't buy it every week. Just occasionally you know. The jokes are rather good."

"And what Sunday paper do you buy?" she said uncertainly.

"I buy several," he said animatedly. He rattled off a string of names. "Can't get me out of bed on a Sunday morning till I've read the lot. All the dirt! I'm warning you, darling. You'll have to bring me my breakfast on Sundays when we're married. I'll bring you yours the rest of the week."

The waitress came up and they gave their orders. When she went away he laid his hand on hers and said gaily: "Don't forget! That's how it'll be when we're married, darling."

Essie raised her eyes from the fork she was playing with and gave him an absent, gentle, puzzled smile.

4

After an interval of several days during which he waited in vain to hear from Sophie, Leo at length decided to call round one evening without warning. If she were out he could at least try to pump Trudy about her movements and what was occupying her evenings so fully.

For once, however, Trudy was out and she was in alone. This

seemed to him a lucky omen and he sat back on their cheaply inadequate, little settee feeling cheerful while Sophie fluttered in and out to the kitchen.

"What on earth are you so busy with in there?" he called out good-humouredly through the connecting door.

"I'm making a *coss*-tard," she called back in one of her high, artificial voices, reappearing and draping her arms with gawky grace against the jamb of the door.

"Bother your custard. Come and sit down."

"I *couldn't*. Oh! the milk's boiling over!" And she flew back, her wide balloon sleeves flapping. She brought the empty pan back in with her however and, dropping to the floor beside the gas fire, proceeded to scrape it out and lick the spoon, looking so entrancing with that absurd bun screwed on top of her head that Leo could not take his eyes off her.

She leaned back to deposit the pan on the floor behind her and he looked with resentful hunger at her bony chest and under-developed breasts and then at her waist which, in its excessively narrow fragility, appealed overwhelmingly to the nerves of his hands. He noticed that the cuff of her picturesque sleeve was torn, that her shoes were unpolished and needed mending; her legs, stuck out on the floor before him, were like two sticks. He noted again that her eyes were small and pale in colour. Sara's are beautiful, he thought to himself unexpectedly. The thought of her for some reason made him shiver. Feelings of coldness and cruelty, boastfulness and anger towards her caused him suddenly to compress his lips.

The delicate, marvellously modelled tip of Sophie's nose suddenly presented itself to his eye and, unable to resist the desire, he leaned forward and, playfully at first, pinched it; then, as she jerked her head back, an almost murderously passionate impulse made him tighten his fingers so that she cried out in real pain. He let her go immediately, sitting back and laughing and apologizing.

"Such a pretty nose. It was really too tempting," he said.

She frowned, cupping her nose tenderly in her hand, then laughed good-naturedly.

"Well? What are you going to do about this job?" he said forcing himself to speak casually.

"The conference thing, you mean? Oh dear. I simply haven't been

118

able to make up my mind yet. P'raps you'd better get someone else."

"No rush," said Leo. "You can let me know in a few days time. But seriously, I think you ought to do it if you can. First of all there's the money! And secondly, you never know, you might find it interesting working with a number of Rabbis at close quarters. Remember the first thing you ever said to me? 'How do the Rabbis ever come to agree about anything?' Those were the first words you said to me."

"So they were," she cried. "Fancy you remembering."

"I remember everything about you," he said, then, seeing a closed, rather mulish look about to settle on her face, added quickly: "Well, now's your chance to find out. Come to the Savoy Hotel and you'll see Rabbis agreeing and disagreeing—mostly disagreeing! —every evening for a week."

"The Savoy!" she said. "My! they do themselves well, don't they?"

"They're not all staying there. Some."

"Well I don't know that I approve at all," she said primly. "It's purely unjustifiable capitalist expenditure."

Leo raised his eyebrows and satirically nodded his head forwards and back. "You don't approve?" he said.

"Well it's not right, is it? Nearly all the troubles in the world," she said, reciting, "can be traced back to that kind of outdated, economic privilege. People who stay at luxury hotels are just survivors from the old, private-profits system. Parasites on the body politic," she rolled out solemnly in obvious quotation.

"Now that's an admirable phrase!" cried Leo, unable to keep a laugh out of his voice. "You won't mind if I borrow it for one of my sermons?"

She looked at him uncertainly, colouring slightly and rather annoyed and he was reminded suddenly of the many pretty girls he had known in his youth, all ardently attending Socialist meetings as long as their boy friends did so too. Wondering, all at once, from whom she had picked up these catch-phrases he said in a mollifying tone: "I agree with you in many ways, you know. Really I do. Some of those delegates who are staying at the Savoy certainly have no right to do so."

"Do you think *any* of them have?" she said.

The Rabbi hesitated. It was a point he felt some delicacy about. The American delegation whose expenses were paid by the wealthy organization behind them, had automatically booked at the hotel, their excuse, if they wanted one, being that the opening meeting of the conference was being held there.

"Between you and me," he said at last, seriously, "no, I don't think it quite right. But any attempt to say so would be futile. As well protest against these appalling charity functions where so much time and energy and money are laid out to get back a fraction in return. The fact is," he said crossly, diverging from the main point, "people can't give to charity without getting *something* back: a ball to dance at, social advantage, or just plain something to do. They use charity to ward off boredom; that's all it comes to nine times out of ten. Yes, that more than anything else. But whatever the benefit there always *is* a benefit. In other words they have to be bribed to be good. Nothing for nothing's our motto. Even when there's nothing else they at least settle for the comfortable feeling that they've paid another instalment on their seat in heaven. This too much calculation, calculation . . ."

He got up and strode restlessly about the small, poorly furnished room, unbearable in the twilight had she not been there, dwarfing it still further with his powerful well-cared-for presence. "Always this forcing the note, this *too-much* of things. Too much charity of money, too much self-consciousness, too much arrogance, too much humility . . . Whenever I hear that bitter Orwell joke, "All animals are equal; but some are more equal than others', I think of the old Jewish chestnut, 'Jews are just like everybody else—only more so'."

"I thought," said Sophie, "that all the Ghettos being destroyed . . . and now we've got Israel . . . at least we're not so humble any more. The Israelis aren't, anyway," she said emphatically.

"We still have the humiliations of the centuries on our backs," said Leo grimly. And sitting down again he started to tell her about the incident with young Gedaliah and the jig-saw puzzle.

"The poor little boy," she cried when he'd finished. "What a shame. I can just see him. But I blame his parents. *They've* taught him to be like that. They ought to send him to Israel. He'd be all right there."

"Socialism! Zionism! You are educating yourself very quickly! I had no idea you were such a pro-Zionist," he said quizzically.

"Aren't you?" she promptly rapped back at him.

"I don't know," said Leo slowly with raised eyebrows and an inward look. "If you'd asked me that question even three years ago I could have answered you without a moment's hesitation. I've been a staunch Zionist now for——" he was about to say thirty years then hastily amended it, "the best part of my life. But that was before I went there, to Israel, myself."

"What made you change your mind?" she said rather coldly.

Leo frowned and sighed.

"I haven't 'changed my mind' as you put it," he said. "It's not that exactly. I can't call myself anything but a Zionist even now. But . . . but . . ." he made a groping, weighing movement with his hand, "it is somehow an emphasis which has been changed. Before you see Israel, you see it as an image of the heart. Afterwards . . . well, it has become a necessity of the head. You know," he said, unconsciously echoing Essie Gabriel's outburst, "not only have non-Jews (the pro-Semites I mean. I'm not talking about the anti's at the moment) got a strange, be-glamoured notion about the Jews into their heads. The Jews have it too. We are always expecting more—despite what our own Torah tells us to expect—from our own people than perhaps we have a right to. We're taken in by our own propaganda. So when we of the Diaspora go to Israel we expect—what? A united, heroic, *loving* people, larger than life size, shriven by suffering, intellectual, practical, tolerant; God knows what more in the way of virtues. And we find—all those things, yes it is true; but also . . . yet more human nature, all our faults still rampant, brassiness, vulgarity, self-congratulation, pig-headedness, dissension, acquisitiveness . . . only more so, more so. Perhaps I am too old," he said forgetting this time that it was Sophie to whom he was speaking, "the European sadness has penetrated too deep. Though they have it there too—what Koestler calls Jerusalem melancholy. Rightly so, since Jerusalem is nearer in atmosphere to the European spirit than anywhere else in Israel: full of misfits, psychological and spiritual. It is the only place where the intellectual, Western exile really feels at home. Everywhere else in Israel, unless he is very young," he said not looking at Sophie, "the

121

European intellectual is lost really, though he doesn't know it, lost without his melancholy, his outsidership, that familiar dress of history. It is not,"he continued, "that I undervalue the marvel which we have brought about. I *see* the wonder. Imagine!" he said in an astonished voice. "A collection of Jews who *don't* ask to be loved! Who don't ask for pity. Who don't wait, eager with self-justification, trembling and anxious, for other people's approval. This is a great miracle. But even miracles have to be paid for. And the Jews —never the spoiled darlings of the human family—usually have to pay more heavily than anyone else. It seems," he said with a frown, "to be decidedly God's will that we should never have anything without high price. And Israel is paying her price all right. She is buying her toughness, her immunity from European nerves, at the cost of—what shall I call it?—that strange, flexible, melancholy intelligence which was our special quality. We have exchanged our sad, aged wisdom for an intransigent and thrusting ability."

"Well I think that's a jolly good thing," said Sophie in a practical and unimaginative voice which clashed so strongly with his Natasha image of her that he gave her an irritable glance of surprise. But her profile, between him and the gas fire, glowed in a fiery, pure innocence of perfect line, and he sank back into illusion.

"This *is* a good thing," he said. "My head tells me it is good. But in my heart—I cannot help it—there is a shrinking from this chromium assurance, so able, so suitable to its task. I find myself longing for the old, soft, vulnerable gold. I ache for the *neurotic* strength."

"You're talking," said Sophie, "as though you admire being neurotic."

"I don't know that I don't," he said with unexpected brusqueness. "I don't know that to be smoothly enamelled with self-confidence is such a good thing. I think of little Gedaliah, the child's uncertainty, unhappiness, pride. I compare him with Tarsch's children, so calm, arrogant in their indifference, so on top of their world . . . and I think of the Jews and their enemies down the ages, the Romans, the Spaniards, the Nazis; and I wonder. Look at us; hurt easily, open to insult, confused and nervous in action. Yet it sometimes seems to me that it is in the Gotthelfs and not the Tarschs that our strengths reside, that it is those very qualities for which we are despised which are the flexible element within us which permits us to survive, our very humiliations which enable us to twist and turn, to burrow a way, some kind of way—on our hands and knees—through to survival."

"I don't see that it's worth surviving just for more suffering," said Sophie, leaning forward and turning the gas fire full on. "We might as well not be here at all."

"You think religion is a private concern," said Leo angrily. "That Judaism as a whole has nothing to offer the world as a whole. That we might as well not be here?"

"Well I can't see any good reason why we *should*," she said obstinately. "As a matter of fact I don't believe much in religion anyway," she added so naïvely that Leo could not help smiling, "but if you must have one, why Judaism more than any other? After all, being a good Jew isn't any different to being a good Christian or a good anything. Judaism's no better than anything else."

"*No!*" said Leo so suddenly and violently that she gave a start. "You are wrong. You are completely wrong. Judaism *is* more than Christianity or any other religion. It is more in this: it is more in that the precepts of Judaism form a pattern for life exactly *fitting* for life. It is meant for *man* in his relation to the universe, not the other way about so that he must torment himself for ever, trying to approximate to an ideal which will never fit, to extremes which go beyond nature. Judaism is *not like that*. It is, far more than the Greek, the religion of the great, golden mean, the perfect balance (could we achieve it) between Caesar and God. That is why we have no saints, hermits, convents, flagellants; why our patriarchs and psalmists speak of fruits and wine, of physical love, of friendship, of banquets and music, the beauty of the world, the whole good of the earth which we relate always to God and which, being His creation, we must not refuse or we refuse Him too. Judaism is round, whole, complete. It is the perfect compound, the perfect fusion, the one perfect medium between Man and God. All other faiths are in some way biased, they are off-centre, weighted too much to one side or the other. But in Judaism we have the exact and central heart. It is the great nub, the crossing point between the world and God. Only *we* possess this wise and tender balance, this joyous realism, this marvellous *sense* in the use of life."

He sat back, making the little settee creak on its rickety legs and smiled. "I am sermonizing. On a Wednesday night, too! You really must forgive me."

"Oh it was very interesting," she said politely, springing quickly however to her feet. "Now I'm going to make you some coffee."

When she brought in the coffee she brought in a plate of biscuits too. "They're not kosher ones I'm afraid," she said doubtfully.

He hesitated but only for an instant. "That's all right. I'm broad-minded," he said and took one.

When he went home at last it was with a feeling of lightheartedness. He liked the way in which she remained composed against his sudden outbursts. Her sudden political enthusiasms, her naïve comments he interpreted as the stirrings of a youthful but inquiring mind. He had a singing feeling that perhaps it might work, if she would have him. What had seemed a fantastic unsuitability dwindled, the more he thought about it, to a manageable disproportion.

He decided to propose.

Thinking it over it seemed to him wiser to do so by letter. It would be easier to touch her heart perhaps if he himself (and his bigness, his age) were not there. He wrote the letter over and over again but in the end, tired of trying to find the right, charmed words, he sent her but a few lines:

"My dearest Sophie,

You must know by now that I have fallen very deeply in love with you. I want to ask you to marry me and let me look after you always. That would be the greatest joy I should ever ask in life, to have you to cherish and care for. Please say you will. I love you very much.

Leo."

As he posted it the thought flashed through his mind: Me, the wary, cautious bachelor to post this letter, to commit myself on paper!

She kept him waiting three days for his answer.

"Dear Rabbi Norberg,

I received your letter for which I wish to thank you. I appreciate very much the honour you have done me and you have been so

124

kind that I wish I could say yes. Unfortunately I can't. It wouldn't be suitable anyway because as you know I'm not a bit religious and I'd have to be if I married you. I hope you won't be very hurt and that we will always be friends. With best wishes.

Yours sincerely,

Sophie.

P.S. I'm afraid I won't be able to do that temporary job you suggested for the Conference but I'm sure you'll get someone else quite easily. S."

He made no attempt to see her again.

# Chapter Five

SEVERAL TIMES DURING THE WEEKS THAT FOLLOWED Leo took Sara Gabriel home from the Guild and other meetings. He never actually asked her and she never approached him in public but on several occasions he contrived to walk out of a house or hall at the same time as she did and once or twice he passed her in his car as she was waiting at a bus stop and picked her up there. He found her increasingly easy to talk to. There was a kind of quiet, wry acceptance about her and, when she criticized, it was without bitterness.

The problem of whom to approach for the temporary conference job had still to be attended to and deciding, as he had often done before, to ask Lillie Stiel, he accordingly took her home one evening after a meeting, passing Sara on the way. He saw that she had seen them and, angry with himself and with her for the unreasonable feelings of guilt which seemed to be imposing themselves upon him, took pains to be pleasant to Lillie.

She was lively enough in return, but at one point in their conversation she made some slighting reference to Mr Gabriel.

"Not at all," he said firmly. "My dear Lillie, you have the wrong end of the stick. I assure you you are making a big mistake when you dismiss him like that. It's a pity we haven't a few more like that man."

She looked down her straight nose with a rather contemptuous smile which so annoyed him that he said warmly: "I don't expect to find a present-day saint amongst my congregation, but if I did Mr Gabriel is the nearest approach to one that I can think of." To his great surprise he found that he really meant what he had just said.

"Really, Leo, I'm not all that interested in him—or his family," she said in a light, bored voice but giving him a quick glance from her sharp, black eyes.

To change the subject, a move which some cautious instinct

warned him was imperative, he broached the matter of the conference work.

"I rather think I'll be away for part of that week," she said.

"Don't you know for sure?" he said impatiently, beginning to feel fed up with Tarsch for having bothered him about the whole matter.

"Some of us are thinking of going to the Jewish Society's weekend school at Folkestone."

"Oh!" he said taken aback. "I didn't know. Who's going?"

"John. Cyril and Rose. Franz . . . several more. Would you like to join us?"

"I haven't been asked," he said trying to sound jocular. He was, in fact, both hurt and jealous that he had not been included in their plans.

"Well I'm asking you now!" she said but added to the words so cool a laugh that his pride and his temper both rose.

"Left it a bit late, haven't you?" he said. "Anyway, I couldn't even if I wanted to—which I don't much. I *have* to attend the conference. I'll rule you out then, as far as the secretarial work is concerned, shall I? I'll get someone else."

"Why don't you ask one of the Gabriels?" she said.

"Which one would you recommend?" he retorted promptly, aware that he was being baited. She had probably, despite his precautions, seen Sara in his car.

"I'm sure they're all equally *saintly*," she said.

Refusing, with some effort, to be drawn, he said: "D'you know, Lillie, that's an idea. That's quite an idea. Perhaps the younger one, Fagy, is it? might do it. You know, she's a very pretty kid. I noticed her only last Saturday, in *shool*."

He saw with some satisfaction that this idea did not please her at all and, further that if he did ask Sara which he immediately made up his mind to do, Lillie would be forced back on to blaming her own suggestion rather than his inclination.

At the first possible opportunity he waited for Sara to come out of a meeting and, taking her arm, pushed her firmly into the car before, as he had known instinctively she would, she could refuse the lift.

"This is really not necessary at all," she said rather stiffly as he quickly drove off "It's a lovely evening; and really . . . I would like to have *walked* home."

"Nonsense! It's much too far."

She said nothing, only sat with that rigidity which betrays an inner trembling.

He debated with himself whether to explain why Lillie had been with him on the previous occasion but the very thought of being obliged to explain anything set up an acute, disliking restlessness. It was strange, this trick she had of making him feel responsible to her while never demanding anything at all from him. At last he said brusquely: "By the way, I'm sorry I couldn't take you home last week, I——"

"Good Heavens," she said quickly, "you don't have to take *me* home every time we meet anywhere. I hope you don't think that I——"

"But I *prefer* to ask you rather than——"

"Rabbi Norberg," she said, turning to him with a straight look, "you really must—if we have to continue talking about this—choose your words rather better. You know as well as I do——" she stopped short.

"What do I know as well as you do?"

She hesitated, then, speaking in the direct and personal manner very shy people sometimes adopt, she said: "You have *never* 'asked' me as you put it, if you can take me home. Only picked me up outside or at the bus stop. And not even that if any of the others are around. If they are you take someone else. It is not that it matters," she went on rather desperately. "Whether you drop me or not it is of absolutely no importance . . ."

"But you have got me all wrong," he said not looking at her. "I don't deliberately 'not take' you. It just happens. Sometimes I take one home, sometimes another. It isn't that I pick and choose. I like to be free to follow whatever whim takes me. Tonight it's you and tomorrow I'll take home someone else and the next day it might be you again. But get it out of your head that I 'drop' you."

"I wouldn't mind if you'd drop me and leave me," she said, "I don't like being dropped and picked up, dropped and picked up again all the time."

"I don't," he said but he knew very well that he did. The fact

128

was, he had known all along (and disliked the thought of) what Lillie or the charming Dr Gildheim or any of their circle would think; that he had gone raving mad to associate himself in any way socially with the Gabriels.

"Now to change the subject," he said hurriedly as he drew up outside her house, "can you do me a favour?" And he explained to her about the week's work required for the conference.

"My shorthand and typing are both very rusty," she said doubtfully.

"That doesn't matter. Long-hand notes will do for most of it. And you can take your time over the typing."

"All right then," she said at last.

Nothing had been settled on the personal level between them, yet, as they parted, both felt curiously lighter of heart than before.

The conception of Mr Gabriel as a near-saintly figure, formulated as it were almost by accident, a by-product of his annoyance with Lillie, took on with growing strength in Leo's imagination. Though he liked to think of himself as holding, in all aspects save perhaps love for women, a satirical-realist view of life, he was in fact almost wholly at the mercy of the romantic vision. Once this had been orientated towards Mr Gabriel all he had hitherto known about the old man, his absurdities, unselfconsciousness, fanaticism, began to appear to him as strengths. "If I had half his . . ." he would sometimes think to himself though he never finished the thought for fear that it would involve him in choice.

About Sophie too he did not allow himself to think. Her refusal had left him curiously becalmed. He ate and slept well, mixed rather more than usual socially, enjoyed company and work. The only strange thing about his life just then was this growing preoccupation with the Gabriels. He could not rid himself of the idea that in Mr Gabriel there lay some gigantic strength of conviction which, could he but reach it, would make some tremendous difference to his own life. Once or twice he tried to get Sara to talk about her father, half fearfully wanting to see what his own fascination sprang from. He wanted to hear some assertions of nobility concerning the old man, some information about goodness and some tangible description of it by someone who lived with it. Had

129

Sara known of this misconception, this fantastic misreading of her father's nature, with its vast, blinkered vanities, its wilful, senseless careerings from pole to pole of unbridled emotion, she might have attempted to disabuse with gentleness and loyalty such illusions.

But she had no idea. Beneath Leo's urbane surface she sensed, with the minutely observant eye of feeling, that he was disturbed and groping, but she was afraid, with her long-frozen delicacy, to lead their talk into serious, personal channels. The only time she had tried to do so of her own accord he had taken fright and said with severity: "Now don't get sentimental about life. It's no use being sentimental with a hardened old realist like me," allowing himself the luxury of speaking exactly as he pleased because he knew that there would never be from her a petty taking of umbrage.

He made no move to seek out Mr Gabriel himself. But often on a Sabbath morning he would look up at the Ladies' Gallery of his synagogue to make sure Sara was there. He was always pleased when she was and would try to put more into his sermons knowing that there was at least one critical, listening ear, and was much put out by her occasional absence as if she had deliberately slighted him by not coming.

2

Through some manipulation of her office holidays Essie discovered that she had a day off due to her which she decided to take advantage of one sunny morning towards the end of May.

The bright sparkle of the day was irresistible and on a sudden impulse she decided to telephone Ken on the off-chance that he would be free to spend it with her, perhaps somewhere out of London. She dialled the number he had once rather reluctantly given her; something she had never done before as he had got into the habit of ringing her every day at her office, sometimes only to murmur "I love you".

Now, as she stood in the telephone booth, the crisp sunlight dancing in the street, she felt a certain expectancy as the instrument at the other end burr-burred within a place which held him in all the strange otherness of his daily life.

There was a click and a masculine voice said: "Hullo, Silver Globe Motors."

"Could I speak to Mr Groby?" she said and realized that it was the first time she had ever called him that. A breach had been made in the private enclosure of their relationship.

"Sorry, he's not here," said the voice.

"Oh!" she said. "D'you think he''ll be in soon?"

"Well I don't think so. Is it urgent?"

"Well . . . it is rather."

"I'm *afraid* he's out on a job. Shouldn't think he'll get through much before three."

"Oh dear," she said in such a disappointed voice that the man at the other end said again: "Is it very urgent? Perhaps I could send someone else?"

"No I wanted Mr Groby particularly."

"I see," said the voice doubtfully.

"Could I possibly get him anywhere else?" she said.

"Well now . . . let me see . . . seeing you want him to do the job personally . . . the only thing I can suggest is—I know he's working pretty near his own place and he'll probably, it's not certain mind, go home for his lunch. You might catch him there. Would you like the number?"

"Is he on the phone?" she said in surprise. He had told her several times that he was waiting for a telephone to be installed in his flat.

"Yes. Hold on a minute and I'll find it."

She held on, her heart beating with an inexplicable tension.

"Are you there?"

"Yes, I'm still here."

"It's—have you a pencil?"

"Yes, yes," she said, opening her bag with one hand and scrabbling for her diary. The voice gave her a Chiswick number.

"Chiswick?" she said unguardedly, "I thought it was Richmond?"

"Could be, he's moved from round here. D'you want his new address?"

"Yes please." With shaking fingers she wrote it down. "Thank you very much. I'm most obliged," she said.

"Pleasure. Glad to help," said the voice. They both rang off.

She came out of the telephone booth with a peculiarly guilty feeling as though she had been making a criminally anonymous call. Her limbs weak, she loitered along the sunny street undecided what to do next, the uneasy, unformulated questions she had for some time now been suppressing from her consciousness before they could be defined stirring inside her. She reached the main road and walked along it aimlessly. When she came to a bus stop she halted. "What shall I do?" she said to herself confusedly. "Such a lovely morning. Perhaps I'll go to the West End? Or should I go to Kew?" She stood by the kerb unable to decide what to do with herself. "The first bus that comes along I'll take," she thought at last.

It wasn't till she was sitting on the top deck on the way to Kew and had even bought her ticket that she realized that the bus route went through Chiswick. As she entered the borough her heart beat violently. For a few stops more she sat on as the vehicle lurched its way through the crowded shopping streets. Then, with a sudden movement, she jumped up, scrambled down the stairs, and swung herself off just as the bus began to move off from the main stop. "Watch yerself!" the conductor called after her sharply but she did not even hear him.

Redditch Place was a short thoroughfare in a maze of smallish roads a good ten minutes walk from the High Street. The houses were large, in bad repair with crumbling porticos and flights of broken stone steps and very ugly. Number Fourteen was a corner house, a story higher than its neighbours and it had a large overgrown piece of ground, too derelict to be called a garden, round three sides.

Although it was not yet noon and Kenneth could not possibly be there, Essie nevertheless approached the house with a nervous, almost furtive manner. She hesitated at the gateless entrance to the cracked, black-and-white-tiled path, then, walking quickly in, ran up the broken steps and stood hesitating in the grubby vestibule. A double line of cards slotted into the wall beside the bell-push caught her eye. "Mr K. Groby" was written messily in ink on the card opposite Number Three. Also on the card was written "One long and one short ring".

Her heart thumping, she reached out a finger and pressed his bell as instructed. Two muffled, tinny peals came from inside; then silence. Swept by a panic of curiosity she caught suddenly at the handle of the big front door which immediately swung open. She stepped into a very large, square, extremely dirty entrance hall. Though the day outside was still brilliantly sunny, such light as penetrated the hall came diffused by dust, into a thin, quiet, yellow haze. A huge, dusty mirror across one wall seemed to reflect nothing but shadow. Circulars in filthy envelopes littered the floor. Apart from the guilty thumping of blood in her head, the quiet loomed round her like a tremendous presence.

She looked at the numbers on the doors nearest to her. One and Two were on either side of the front door. Number Three then was obviously towards the far end. Stepping quietly she took a few paces towards the rear of the hall where it gave on to a small passage. At the end of this passage she found Number Three. She stood gazing at the door with its chipped and scarred black-brown paint, then with a quick movement bent down and applied her eye to the keyhole. It was blocked. Straightening up she stood cogitating for a moment. It was obvious that the room faced the back garden. With a sudden abrupt gesture of her head indicating decision, she turned and made her way out. As she passed the slotted cards beside the bell one at the bottom opposite Number Eleven caught her eye. The name on it was Hartley. For a moment she stayed there puzzled by a connection she could not recall. Then it came back to her. Hartley was the name of "the bloke I share my flat with. Jolly good sort."

Running quickly down the steps she turned right and made her way down the remains of what had once been a neatly gravelled path which, together with a wooden fence now broken to pieces, separated Number Fourteen from its neighbour. Kenneth's window, as she had guessed, looked out over a squalid travesty of a back garden. His window, though a big one, was very grimy, the net curtain grey with age and dust. Sun was dazzling into the room making it difficult for her to see what it was like. She lifted up her handbag which was large and square and interposed it between herself and the light. At once the room leaped into focus.

The first thing she saw, proving that it was indeed his room and that she was not dreaming it all, was a silver grey tie with black and red stripes which he had bought specially to go with his new, grey suit and for which he had insistently demanded her admiration and

133

approval. So much indeed had he demanded that she had laughed and accused him of being a great dandy which he had taken as a most pleasing compliment.

The tie was hanging over the back of a chair looking, there was not a crease in it, as though it had just been carefully ironed. And indeed, as she looked at the table in the window to which the chair was set sideways, she saw a collection of ironed clothes, pyjamas, shirts, socks, all lying there in a neat pile. The sight of them suddenly struck at her heart with such a feeling of forlorn sadness that tears came to her eyes. Looking, with an effort, further round the room she saw up-ended on the harshly-black fender before the grim, Victorian fireplace, an electric iron. A divan covered with a cheap counterpane stood against the wall to her left, facing the hearth. Opposite her a huge, old-fashioned, three-part wardrobe with a full-length, outside mirror faced the table and window. An indescribable what-not and two shabby armchairs, one large and one small, stood on either side of the fender and a combined griller and gas-ring stood on what looked like a marble-topped washstand in one corner. The wallpaper, cracked in streaks across the walls, was a soiled buff with faded, purple flowers strewn here and there.

There was a sound behind her and she turned quickly but it was only a bird landing untidily on a bush. She turned back to the window, pressing her face against it, looking and looking at the room which held Kenneth's life, his getting up and going to bed, his sleepings and dressings and eatings, the mysterious, secret whole of another's person's existence. And as she stood, again the strange, sad pang, dry and searing, shot through her. For long minutes she stood there trying to grapple with, to absorb the raw elements of anguish, bewilderment, puzzle which swept through her in an endless tide. Then, hurriedly, terrified lest he should suddenly appear, she walked away down past the broken fence, through the gateless entrance and away, rapidly, to the High Street.

It was lunch time and, turning into the first self-service teashop she saw, she bought herself a meal and carrying her tray upstairs sat down at a table overlooking the busy street. Essie had a fondness for this chain of teashops and had once or twice defended them hotly against Kenneth who had said in his most Mayfair voice that they were "not quite in my line, darling. All right for the odd cup of tea, don't you know." They had been having a meal at the time in—chosen by him—one of the rather depressing, pretentiously named restaurants on the wrong side of Oxford Street and she had not been able to resist a rather puzzled glance at his portion of heaven-knew-what meat over which he was at that instant pouring a great amount of bottled sauce.

Her neighbour at the next table, a hulking-size labourer in some sort of overalls, was just then doing the same thing. Her gaze fell on his hands . . . and she remembered Ken's so oddly cut and grimed. A hundred small, unexplained circumstances and incidents flashed through her mind which had for long deliberately avoided taking out and looking at them: the involuntary, peculiarly coarse-toned "Ay—y" whenever he was startled which had shocked her ear; his admiration of a flashy signet ring worn by a man in a pub; the occasional, unconscious use of quite the wrong kind of slang; a kind of affronted mulishness, a refusal to admit, when she had unthinkingly corrected his surprising mispronunciation of a word, that he had said it wrongly. How did all this square with Dulwich College, the expensive cars, the huntin' horse-breeding father?

She finished her meal and going downstairs and into the street made for the nearest telephone kiosk. "Silver Globe Motors" the voice at the other end had said when she telephoned that morning. She pulled out the blue-backed S–Z directory and looked it up. There was only one firm of that name and the number was the same. It was in Richmond. The mixture of truth and lie in everything he had told her became more bewildering than ever. With determination she set out for the garage.

3

Silver Globe Motors was a big, super-modern garage situated just off Richmond Hill, its name spelt out in huge, silver letters on a black background right scross the façade of the main entrance. At the topmost point of a kind of small, central tower a silver-coloured sphere slowly revolved in the sun. Its front courtyard was filled with cars, mostly expensive ones. Plate glass windows on the left revealed equally good but mostly second-hand automobiles priced ready for sale. Outside what were obviously offices on the right of the building large boards advertised the Silver Globe Driving School. A long row of petrol pumps occupied the centre between the two wings.

As soon as Essie caught sight of the place, the big, metal globe gleaming and turning high above it, she stopped short, paused for a second, then instantly retreated. Reaching the Hill she walked up it a little way trying to control her rushing confusion. After a time she turned and walked slowly down again, passed the street where the garage was situated and turned into the next one parallel to it. Two right-angles and she was approaching it from the other end. With great circumspection she walked, keeping one wary eye open, right up to the well-trimmed hedge which marked the furthest boundary of the garage. Two empty cars fitted with big Driving School L-plates stood just inside. As she hesitated there, half concealed by the trunk of a plane tree and wholly concealed from the petrol pumps by a sort of little, separate kiosk which stood on a patch of lawn not far from the pavement, another tuition car drove in through the wide side gates and drew up not more than a few yards away from where she stood. The driver got out and, going round to the other door, opened it and helped out a middle-aged woman. She was pale and looked rather shaken.

"Well now, Mrs Atkinson," said the instructor, "you're not doing at all badly you know. Just a bit more practice on that third gear . . ."

"I sometimes think I'll never learn, Major Beresford," she said. "And my husband gets so cross. Always telling me he learnt in a couple of hours."

"Don't you believe it," he said cheerily, glancing at his watch. "They all say that. Anyway, thirty years ago it was a very different proposition, don't you know. I'd like to see him tackle the traffic today, as a beginner. Ve—ry different now, you know."

"That's what I tell him," she said eagerly, "but—oh, I don't know. I sometimes think I'd better give up the whole idea."

"Give up now!" said Beresford in a tone of incredulity. "Not on your life, dear lady. I'm going to get you through that test if it's the last thing I do." He glanced at his watch again, more openly. "Now just you go right in to the office and make your next appointment."

He opened the car door again and bending down fiddled with one of the controls. Mrs Atkinson, with obvious reluctance, vanished in the direction of the office. Suddenly, so suddenly that Essie's heart gave a great, lurching bound, Kenneth appeared from, as she distraughtly thought for a moment, nowhere. Then she realized that the little kiosk must have hidden his approach. She gazed at him in astonishment. His face, that face so tenderly modelled, so palely fair of skin, was extremely dirty, a big smudge on his forehead. He wore blue dungarees stiff with grease and stains. His hands were black.

"Take her in for you, Major?" he said with a gesture towards the car. His tone was unmistakably that of a subordinate.

"Thanks, Ken," said Major Beresford with a weary look. "Lord! I'm beat." He leaned back against the bonnet and lit a cigarette. He was a short, bulldoggishly built man, dressed in a baggy tweed suit. His face was pale brick in colour, his eyes glazed and red-veined. His rich-brown, military moustache was overgrown and ragged.

"You having trouble?" said Kenneth nodding towards where Mrs Atkinson had disappeared.

"Trouble!" said the Major. "Give me the war, old boy. Every time. Nearly had me head through the blooming roof at one point. 'Sorry,' she said! 'Oh dear, I'm not very good am I?'" He gave an imitation, falsetto giggle.

Kenneth laughed with a ready, eager-to-please laugh. "What did you say to that?"

"What *can* you say?" said Beresford with a shrug. "Can't say 'What the flipping hell d'you think you're playing at?' No, no. Customer is always right. Besides . . . toujours la polytechnique, old boy. Always remember," he said slurring his words a little, "toujours la bloody old polytechnique. 'Not at all, Mrs Atkinson. It was really that bounder in the green Riley. Tut, tut. Cut in far too close . . .' Ah well," he said standing himself up straight with an effort, "only another three hours till they're open. By the way, she's pinking a bit. Might take a look if you've got time, Ken." And he rolled off; hard-up, glad-of-any-job, ex-officer, failure written all over him. Not, however in letters prominent enough to reach Ken's eye. Even as she watched, Essie saw him direct a glance

137

of admiration touched with respect at the Major's back before getting into the car and driving it round to the back.

One more glimpse she caught of him that afternoon as she cautiously walked past the front of the garage. He was filling petrol into a beautiful Aston Martin. Essie saw the driver tip him and heard him say "Thank you, sir," in a clipped, cultured, military voice strongly modelled on Major Beresford's, as the car drove off. He stood still for a moment in the bright sunshine and, shading his eyes, looked after the automobile, standing there, pliant, boyish, fair-haired, the dirt in which he was smothered adding some strange, heart-breaking quality to his bold, soft, physical grace. He dropped his hand and Essie saw him, as she had seen a hundred times, give several small blinks with his eyelids, his expression sweet and rueful. The total effect, accidental perhaps, was one of uncomplaining, passionate longing which pierced her to the bone with pity.

Shivering with nervous tension but determined, her square jaw set, Essie gave his bell one long ring and one short about eight o'clock that evening. There was an appreciable time lag during which she did not know whether to be thankful or not that he was out, then she heard his light, unmistakable tread in the hall, a click as he switched on the light and then the front door swung open as silently as it had done that morning and he stood before her. His jacket was off and he had half rolled up his shirt-sleeves.

"Hallo!" she said.

He looked at her, at first blankly, then an expression of slow pleasure gradually crept over his face and reaching out one arm he pulled her in. "Darling!" he said halting her under the central light in the hall. "How on earth did you . . . oh! *you're* the 'lady' who rang up this morning. Well I'll be blowed! Well!" He put his arm round her and kissed her cheek.

"Aren't you going to ask me in any further than this?" she said.

"Of course," he said and, his arm still round her shoulders, he ushered her into his room. It was badly lit by one small bulb half obscured by an enormous, dusty, yellow-pleated shade, like a drum. On the table lay the remains of his supper, a meat pie of some sort, the inevitable bottle of sauce, a loaf of chalky whiteness, butter still

138

in its wrapping paper and a banana. An evening newspaper was propped against a packet of sugar.

"Sit down, darling," he said, shifting about the bigger armchair. "Well I never! So you were the lady who 'wanted me personally'," he said, laughing.

"You see," she said, loosening her jacket and gabbling a little with nervousness, "I had the whole day off——"

"How was that? You never told me——"

"No, well I . . ." and she explained about the day due to her. "So I thought if you happened to be off or going out of town some-where or . . ."

"Darling, I wish you'd told me. I *might* have arranged something."

"And I thought if you could . . . as it was . . . I thought you lived in Richmond," she said suddenly in a plain, strong voice.

"So I did, darling. Lived there for years. But—oh, I don't know —old Hartley and I didn't seem to hit it off after a time . . . always getting in each other's hair. You know how it is. So we decided to break it up. I didn't want to tell you darling till I'd found another place. Of course this is just temporary. *Rather* a dump, don't you know. But it'll do for now. Matter of fact I saw a very charming little flat the other day that I've got my eye on. Rather expensive but just the job."

"Are you taking it?" she said quietly.

"Depends on the present tenants, dear. If they're willing to move out soon, well and good. If not, well I'll just have to look around for something else. I certainly don't want to stay here for longer than I can help. Though I must say it looks a different room with you sitting there!" He got up from the other armchair and coming over sat on the arm of her chair, gathered her against him and kissed her hard.

"Is Hartley's room similar to this?" she said after the kiss.

He gave a very slight start. "Oh! you saw his name by the bell did you? You *are* observant, my precious. Yes, he followed me more or less here. He's the *dependent* type, old Hartley. Needs a nurse or a mother or something I always say. Darling let me make you some coffee or tea. Are you hungry?"

"No, no, not a bit. Well all right then, just some coffee."

She watched as he picked up a tall, white enamel jug and went

139

out saying, looking back as he opened the door: "I'll just go and get some more water. There's a tap on the landing. Won't be a minute." Then he added anxiously: "You won't have disappeared when I come back? You are real, my dearest?"

"I'm real," she said.

"You know," he said a little later pausing in front of her, saucepan in hand, "I can't believe it. I've dreamt so often of having you here . . . all to myself . . . dearest . . ." His lips quivered. Putting down the pan he went up to her as she sat in the armchair, bent down and looked deeply into her eyes, tears welling into his. Then with a quick movement he flung himself down on his knees before her and pressed his face into her lap. She looked down on his young, round head, the ivory scalp showing through the soft, chicken-down hair. Then, with an effort breaking through the frozen cloud of still unresolved suspicions, questions, uncertainties, she put her arms around him and raised his head to her throat. His wet lashes moved against her skin. A tear ran down her breast.

"What about that coffee?" she said after a time. He gave her a vast, convulsive hug and sprang to his feet. Then he said desolately: "Essie, sweetheart, I'm terribly sorry but I've got *no milk*."

"Well that's all right," she said cheerfully, "make it black."

He made it, quickly and badly, sitting at her feet and not taking his eyes off her face as she drank.

"If you knew, if you *knew* what it means to me to have you here——" he began several times only to break off and kiss her hands or her instep.

"I love you so much. I love you so much," he repeated again and again. And, as she had often done before—"Why?" she asked. "But why should you love me?"

"I just do. I just do." It was no answer. But she knew. The answer lay in the instinctive caresses between them, the fit of his head to her throat, the warmth and timing of each kiss, the unstrained, perfect harmony, so rare, inexplicable and moving, of their physical selves.

"More, sweetheart?" he said when she'd finished. She shook her head and gave him the cup. Without moving his gaze or his position before her, he deposited it on the floor.

She gave a deep sigh and leaned back. "Ken," she said.

"What darling?"

"I want to talk to you."

"Fire away," he said gaily. "What about?"

"You."

"Well? what about me?"

"Kenneth darling, I want you to tell me something."

"Ready ma'am," he said sitting back on his heels and saluting. "Anything you want to know."

"Ken," she said leaning forward, "just what is your job?"

"I've told you—heaps of times. I work for the Silver Globe Automobile Company. You ought to know! You rang me there this morning!"

"What as?"

"What as? Well . . . general representative, supervising, interviewing, sales . . . that sort of thing. Why do you ask me again?"

"This company . . . I thought you said your father was one of the directors——"

"So he was," he cried, "when he was alive, that is."

"Then how d'you come to be working the petrol pump—in dungarees?"

He stared at her, completely taken aback. "How d'you know I do?" he said at last.

"I just know, that's all," she said with a shrug.

"Well I'm damned," he said slowly. "How d'you find out?"

"Oh what does that matter? Anyway, I did."

"You . . ." he said struggling for words, "you—*witch*!" He swayed forward then flung himself against her. "*You—clever—witch*, you!"

"Sure you don't mean bitch?" she said laughing even while she noticed that he had not answered her question.

"My clever darling," he said kissing her all over her face. "My *clever* darling."

With an effort she pushed him away. Holding his face above hers between her two hands she looked earnestly into his eyes and said: "Ken. Don't pretend. You're not to pretend. I know anyway, so what's the use? You're a garage hand aren't you?"

Gazing back at her with equal steadiness he nodded his head.

"You've lived here all the time, haven't you? Hartley's just another lodger."

He nodded.

"You never went to Dulwich College. And your father——"

"My father *was* a director of an automobile company. He lost all his money when I was about eighteen——" he began insistently.

"You were well off till then?"

"We certainly were."

"Ken! Where were you educated?"

He was silent, the mulish look she had seen once or twice before appearing on his face and in the set of his shoulders.

"It wasn't Dulwich was it?" she said at last getting out the words with such a feeling of shame for him that she could hardly speak above a whisper.

"If you want to know I went to a jolly good school near Leicester. Dash it," he said, "you can tell that from the way I speak I should think."

She turned her head away quite unable to say another word. Thinking he had gained his point he took her hand and said: "Remind me to introduce you to old Hartley some time darling, will you? You'd like him. He's got some corking stories when he's had a pint. Came out of the Air Force a Wingco, don't you know. He hasn't had much luck lately but he'll be OK when the big deal pays off. Great pals he and I. Staked him to a meal many a time."

"Has he ever returned the compliment?"

"Ay—y!" he said. "Well of course he would if I wanted it. He's all right, old Hartley. Jolly good company."

Fantasies! Fantasies! All his attitudes pathetic adumbrations of all the Hartleys and Major Beresfords and Aston Martin owners and who knew who else against whom he brushed in his working life. Thought of the Aston Martin reminded her that there was one more thing that she had to ask.

"And the cars?" she said. "The big Daimler? The convertible? Oh, I see," she said, the light dawning as she spoke. "You 'borrowed' them from the garage."

"We—ell," he said nonchalantly, "we all do it you know. All the staff. The brutes are sitting there doing nothing, rusting up half the time, while the owners are abroad. Does the engines good having a bit of a shakeover."

She looked at him sadly but it was not his nature to ask why.

Instead he said quite lightheartedly: "Anyway, when we're married I'm going to buy a little runabout. You won't object to that will you?"

"Marry you!"

"You are. Aren't you?"

She looked at him in great astonishment. He smiled back at her lovingly.

"Ken! You're not really serious are you?"

"Well if I haven't convinced you of that by now I don't know what will."

"But . . . Ken . . . look darling, even if I want to believe you, and I honestly don't know whether I do or I don't, I don't see how I *can*."

"Why can't you? I love you. You *know* I do."

"Then . . . if you love me . . ." she hesitated, the words refusing to come out of her mouth, "why did you . . ." she heaved a great sigh, "—— deceive me?" she said at last in a rush. "Surely you must have known I'd find out sooner or later? How could you hope to keep everything from me?"

"I didn't want to lose you, Essie," he said hardly waiting for her to finish. "I was terrified of losing you. I suppose that's why I didn't tell you the truth—about my job."

*And* your background, *and* your education, *and* your whole life, she added silently and suddenly felt extremely cross that he had been so naïve as to think she would have swallowed his inconsistencies all this time without question. For a moment she was inclined to say this to him but one glance at his soft, loving, blind eyes told her at once and irremediably that it would be no use. He would only swerve from and avoid the issue, not because of any vicious element in his nature but because some opening of the eyes had never taken place. He was not so much a liar as a somnambulist, walking across the moral sense with no idea of danger.

"But I haven't lost you, have I?" he was saying triumphantly.

With a feeling of enormous weariness she let her gaze wander round the appalling room.

"That's the only reason why I ever lied," he said. "Just to keep you."

Yes? she said to herself. What about that first time—at the College dance? You were lying practically before you saw me. And she remembered that cultured-sounding voice coming out of the dark.

"You're not going to leave me now you've found out? I haven't lost you? Have I, Essie?" he said again in an alarmed voice. "Say it! Say I haven't, Essie. *Say it*!" He shook her shoulders in terror. "I won't always be at the garage. I can get an executive job any time I like. I just didn't want to be shut up in an office all day, that's all. I can get a different job dead easy." In his agitation he had lost control of his voice which now came out with a strong Midlands accent, the "easy" pronounced "oisy".

She saw that he would always lie; that indeed life would be intolerable for him if he didn't: that he was one of the dreaming misfits thrown up by the heaving, billowing ferments of society. His situation, tragically absurd as are all struggles against class, was really the same as hers; in a word, "misplacement". He should have been born a peer's son just as she should have been a professor's daughter. It would have suited him so well, been in such deep accord with his talents. He should have been gay, wealthy, carefree, unthinkingly at home and decent in his proper place. He should have driven an ancient, sporting Rolls-Royce to Ascot, become roaring drunk on Boat Race night; a bowler-hatted young banker by day and a favoured deb's escort at night.

("Just say I haven't lost you. *Say it*.")

He would never see himself as Ken Groby, garage hand. He would always lie. But he would also always love her. The huge, strange responsibility of being another person's happiness presented itself before her. "But at least," she thought, "I shall be loved. I shall have a use for myself."

Her eye fell on the half open door of the hideous wardrobe. Inside on a shelf she saw two chipped cups and a beaker; one saucer; two plates of different sizes and patterns; some bottled coffee; an unopened bottle of sauce; one tin of sardines; two knives, a fork and three teaspoons, of cheapest metal. A wrench of deep, tearful pity gripped her heart. As the paroxysm died down she felt, for the first time, a small flame leaping from the angry, anguished spark of pity into love.

"No, you haven't lost me," she said.

# Chapter Six

## I

THE OPENING MEETING OF THE INTERNATIONAL JUDEAN Council conference, convened annually to discuss problems of world Jewry, was starting. Up on the platform behind the long table draped in the blue and white national colours of Israel, Rabbi Tarsch, as urbane, self-assured and stoutly handsome as ever, was in the chair. To either side of him spread a row of delegates from countries all over the world representing every force in Jewish social organization. Approximately sixty per cent of these were Rabbis or ministers, of all shades of the faith from the heavily-bearded, patriarchal, fanatically orthodox to the pink-skinned, frog-faced, stockbroker-like American Advanced Reform—ministers who claimed to be Jewish religious leaders while not even fasting on the Day of Atonement.

Though Tarsch was in the chair the visiting guest of honour for this opening meeting was a well-known Church of England ecclesiastic of high repute, famous for his liberal humanitarianism, courage and sincerity. He sat now on Tarsch's right, a very tall, lean, hawk-faced, handsome man listening, at ease and attentive, to Tarsch's well-delivered, opening remarks. Once or twice he made a quick note on the pad before him.

Tarsch was working, with meticulous care, through the long list of organizations represented by the delegates, extending to each a brief welcome appendaged to a short list of its aims and achievements. God would have had to help him—and his secretary—had any of these been left out. But with Tarsch they never were.

Finished with the list he went on to glance lightly at the Council's financial position—which was good but, he implied, could or should be even rosier. Leo's attention had wandered but occasional phrases fell on his ear. "... finance our great work ..." "... further emolument ..." "... increment ..." "... budgetary arrangements ..."

Leo, in the body of the hall, was watching the guest of honour whom he had himself met and on whom he had once had occasion to call in his own home. For some reason he had never forgotten this incident though it had occurred years ago. Dean Mitchell had received him with the greatest courtesy. He had discussed the joint Christian-Jewish manifesto which was then being prepared in a manner which held not the faintest suggestion of patronage. So far from feeling himself requesting help and favour, Leo had had the sensation of being deferred to in the most sensible and flexible way. Something all the same had troubled him as he sat there in Mitchell's study, something which had afflicted him as soon as he had entered the house with a sense of being alien. Perhaps it was the faint ghost of fried bacon and larded Sunday joint which, together with the aroma of furniture polish and fresh roses, had combined into a curiously Gentile smell—rather like waiting rooms in Harley Street. It was certainly something to do with the outer trappings of the Dean's life. His own home was almost as well furnished, though in a heavier, foreign way, but he had been unable to avoid being impressed by the atmosphere, the lovely, dark, polished woods, the bowl of rich-coloured roses, the whole taste and flavour of the tall, Kensington house. There had been in this ambience of English, upper-class culture an essence compounded of some secret quality to which he could not quite put a name. The only clue he got to it was when Mitchell, screwing up a sheet of paper, looked around for his wastepaper basket, found it standing rather away from his desk and, stretching out one long leg with a casual, athletic movement which somehow disturbed Leo still further, hooked it towards him. It was a large, comic sort of affair made of raffia with huge, vulgar flowers embroidered on it.

"What d'you think of this?" said the Dean with a smile, breaking off what he was saying. "My young daughter made it at school. She's only nine, you know."

"Very clever indeed," said Leo, but a puzzled frown settled in his eyes. He was trying to make out why the basket in the midst of so much elegance was an obvious, family joke and did not jar, whereas in so many carefully, expensively furnished Jewish homes it would not have appeared, to a stranger's eye, as a joke at all, only as half-expected bad taste. Perhaps it was, he thought, that, once firmly

146

set at a particular level, you could have as much bad taste as you liked and it would still appear as good; or rather there would be no danger of any deviation being misunderstood. The alchemy worked outwards from the person not, as the Jews tried so hard to make it, inwards from the trappings.

So that it was, in the end, not the elegance, not the roses which floored him, sending him home from Mitchell and Kensington with a sense of dissatisfied inadequacy, but the mysterious, waste-paper-basket element; some peculiar essential to easy dignity in life which neither he nor hardly any Jew possessed.

"There must be a definition of aims . . ." Tarsch was saying, and Leo's thoughts ran away with him again, nagging him to explain Mitchell's secret. Everything, in the end, depends on the quality of the human material, he thought. How right the British are to elevate character above all else. The character to be oneself—how difficult a feat for a Jew in middle-class, Anglo-Saxon society. And he fell to musing on the odd paradox of the so easily recognizable, bourgeois Jew with all his blatant, self-assertive characteristics, in reality so hollow and coreless, so bereft of identity; a victim of wrong instinct, cloudy with self-consciousness. For the fact is, he said to himself, unlike people whose instincts are at one with the pattern of their culture, for whom in fact the one has shaped the other, the Jew dares not rely on instinct for the regulation of behaviour. His instinct, while he is living in western society, is always wrong; too fervent, too throbbing with feeling, self-righteousness, injury; too emotional by half. If he is to live in the western world he must acquire therefore, as soon as possible, the cooler, western mask.

It is this necessity, this contant check to his temperament, thought Leo (as Tarsch, after a floridly welcoming introduction, sat down and Dean Mitchell, twinkle-eyed, hawk-profiled, rose to his feet), which has led to his ultra self-consciousness—that least endearing of traits. That—and his obsession with, his dependence on "personality". Well, that's easily enough explained he thought with a mental shrug. How often has our fate depended on personality; the personality of the people who have so often decided it.

"My friends," began Mitchell in his extremely pleasant, cultivated voice, "It has been said——"

The bourgeois Jew, split between his nature and his environment, has no character, Leo thought. It is *that* not lack of brains or power or money which gives him his particular unease in society, that which accounts for the sense of strain felt by others when in Jewish company. But it is not only the lack; that would be forgiven us. It is the constant, pitiful attempt to fill it, to *assume* a character, which makes us so irritating to others. The Jew is never content to be nothing, even a rich nothing. So he borrows any old fashionable or contemporary or desirable way of living he sees, and puts it on, regardless.

Mitchell's rhetorical style was delicate, neat, easy.

A Jew, for instance, Leo proceeded with his mental argument, can't depersonalize himself into a generic type and rest in that type —as an English country gentleman *is* an English country gentleman, not just puts on the appropriate tweeds. What such an Englishman follows is a way of life not a romantic idea of one. How he dresses, what he does, arises from what he *is*.

"You are all familiar," said Dean Mitchell, "—to desperation point one imagines—with the non-Jew who says: 'Some of my best friends are Jews'. Well, I am going to reverse that intolerable, patronizing phrase and say this: Some of my best enemies are Jews. They are the best enemies I know to such things as injustice, ignorance, intolerance . . ."

Our women too, thought Leo. However smart and slender, there is always an essential elegance they miss, a "style" they do not have.

". . . those great philosophical ideas, the depth of Jewish thought from Maimonides to Spinoza . . ."

Yes, but what happens to Jewish thought today? Hash! Hash and rehash, reflected Leo. And if a Jew did produce some concept of value how much better advised would we all be, for the theory's sake, to keep our enthusiasm for it secret. Our support might well be its ruin. Nothing is so dangerous to the Jew as his partisanship; so somehow absurd in its expression as his chauvinism.

"To those of you who hail from across the Atlantic I would go further and say . . ."

Not perhaps so much in America where a whole people want to be loved and publicized: where a whole nation adopts attitudes. But here, in Europe, where there is still, broken but breathing, an inborn sense of identity . . . Again Leo's mind reverted to the symbolic, outdated perhaps, figure of the country squire and the Jewish imitation, like a fake Elizabethan tea shoppe, of integration.

Mitchell quoted a text in its original Hebrew and made a great hit.

Yes, yes, I know, said Leo to himself as the Dean continued. He frowned at the pleased smiles all round him. Oh I know you admire us, you sympathize with your head and with your heart. But there is some third organ—I do not know what or where it is—with which you should but do not feel. Humiliation! You do not know humiliation. You live in a state of innocence, my friend.

Mitchell sat down to a great ovation and Tarsch, in tones of great respect, called upon the next speaker. This was a very old, very frail Rabbi who announced, with a somewhat perfunctory apology to the Dean, that he preferred to speak in Yiddish. Mitchell laughed with great good-humour and made a charming "But of course" gesture.

The old Rabbi, who looked as if a brisk wind would kill him off altogether, began his speech. Not much of his white face could be seen between the wide-brimmed, black hat and the huge, black-grey beard but the power behind his oratory was unmistakable. The big hall shook with it. Leo's satiric, grumbling, half-somnolent mood was shattered. The small figure in the long, black coat gesticulated. A stabbing forefinger pierced the air. The old, powerful voice roared with fire. A new element, *conviction*, blind, furious, real, suddenly galvanized the atmosphere. The quick, hissing, foreign syllables shot out at the audience.

Reverend Bolman (of the unfortunate syntax but good heart), who was sitting next to Leo, turned and signalled to him admiringly with his eyebrows. "This is it!" he whispered.

And—"This is it," Leo said to himself with a half-ironic smile. "This is it! Integration!" And he fell to contemplating yet another paradox: how it was that the least free, the most rigorously disciplined within the cramped, harsh frame of dogma, the least emancipated of all Jews enjoyed a special, extraordinary and powerful liberty—the freedom of the self. It was in this true product of the Ghetto with his pale face and curious, stooped back (there are no shoulders like Jewish shoulders, no feature, not even nose, more unmistakably of the race) and his undersized, meagre body, that there could be found the nearest approach to a Gentile conception of identity. His sublimely unselfconscious ignoring of other systems of behaviour, his lack of the sense of the necessity to conform, his insular scorn and impatience with other cultures, his passion for tradition . . . all these characteristics are like nothing so much as they are like the traits of ancient, hidebound, rooted aristocracies everywhere. Monarchies are built on such attitudes. Ruling classes lean on them. And here, in the end, of all the Jews there were, the most strange, the most different, was, after all, the most like.

"Sara," said Rabbi Makin, leader of the American contingent, in a soft, wheedling voice, "can you come down to the hotel? Now?"

"It's rather early. I've hardly finished breakfast," she said doubtfully.

"Oh I didn't wish to disturb you. Forgive me. I just didn't think. But——" the voice through the earpiece took on an even more coaxing note, "I sure need you pretty badly. However, if you can't . . ."

"I have such a lot to do, Rabbi Makin. Really. I've hardly been at home for the last four days . . ."

"Of course. Of course. But perhaps—may I ask you then to do me a little letter at home? Just one or two little letters. I can tell you right now what I want——"

"I'm awfully sorry but you know I haven't a typewriter——"

"Yes of course. I am forgetting. Then you can come this morning a little later on perhaps?"

Sara sighed, slightly exasperated. Then her usual obligingness took over and she said: "All right. I'll come down as soon as I possibly can. About eleven thirty if I can make it."

"You are always so kind," said Rabbi Makin and hung up immediately.

"In case I change my mind" she thought half annoyed but she hurried through her work nevertheless in order to get down to the hotel some time that morning. By twelve o'clock she was sitting in the private sitting room, nominally Makin's but actually used by all the American delegates, typing away at the "little letters" to which Makin had referred. "Little" as she had discovered (and not for the first time that week) was a pretty exact description. There was one to his New York dentist for an appointment in six weeks time; another to a tailor; a short note to his wife concerning mainly their refrigerator; and a letter to a Zionist organization in the north of England regretting his inability to lecture to their group on "Israel—now", as he would have no time.

Makin came in with two other Rabbis, Rutger and Fertlestone, as she was finishing the last of these.

"Good. Fine," he said as she handed them over to him to sign.

"What would we do without Sara?" said Rutger sinking expansively into an armchair and lighting a cigar. All three men had Americanized but guttural accents and broad, fleshy features but where Makin was smooth and baby-faced with thick, greying hair, Rutger was bulging and swarthy and Fertlestone short and pinkly bald.

She smiled rather uncertainly and remained poised over the typewriter at the small table waiting for further instruction.

Fertlestone said, tugging a sheaf of manuscript out of his pocket: "Now I just wonder if you've got time to do this for me before lunch? It's the script of the address I gave last night to that woman's club—the name escapes me right now . . ."

"The Hebrew Ladies' Circle," she said.

"That's right. Now if you could just do me a transcript of my speech—you went along there, didn't you?—putting in anything you think ought to go in the Press Report and leaving out what's not so important . . ."

"How's this poor girl gonna know what *you* think important?" said Rabbi Rutger with a wink at Sara. "There's only one rule for a Press Report," he continued. "Take out the gags and leave in the uplift."

"I guess you're right at that," said Fertlestone. "Say! did you hear the laugh I got with that 'wouldn't be seen dead with 'em' crack?" Sara nodded and smiled.

"That old——" began Rutger.

"Maybe it's old to you," said Fertlestone, "but by golly it's new to Britain. Say, about the script, Sara . . ."

"Yes?"

"There's only one part of it I'm anxious to have you plug and that's the bit at the end about Japan."

"Oh yes. But—well actually it's not quite at the end."

"Japan?" said Rabbi Makin in a dreamy, questioning tone.

"Well I'm not aiming to boost my own speeches," said Rabbi Fertlestone, "but I can tell you here and now that when I gave 'em Japan you sure shouldda seen the faces of those women in that vast audience. You boys sure shouldda seen 'em. Yeah, sure it's at the end, Sara. *You* know. When I brought in about that hymn and all . . ."

Sara looked at him undecidedly for a moment, raised her eyebrows, then nodded as if in resignation.

She had indeed been present on the previous evening when Rabbi Fertlestone had addressed a private drawing room meeting of some thirty women on "Israel's position in the Middle East".

Fertlestone, looking small, pink and paunchy, had started his lecture with an outline of his academic position, the number of American universities which had been graced with his residence during the past fifteen years, the titles, dates and content of each of his printed pamphlets, the production (he held it up dramatically before his audience) of his one hard-cover volume, a book of essays, and a lengthy account of its reception in various important centres and the information, repeated several times, about its English publication, name and address of publisher and price. He then told his audience that there was a growing demand for books in Israel where there was a cultured peasantry—as opposed to the other countries of the Middle East where most of the population was illiterate. Israel, he said, sure had a tough spot for itself right there in the middle of the Middle East, but, make no mistake about it . . . she could handle it. Yes sir!

He had then gone on to extol the British hospitality he had received while in London and denied the reputation of English cooking . . . "which wouldn't affect me anyway because I say, ladies, that *Jewish* cooking is not only the best in the world; it reaches the same standard of excellence *all over* the world." (Great applause.) "In fact, I may say that during my recent visit to the Jewish communities of Japan—in which I had the great anna of being the first representative from the International Judean Council to visit them over a pirriod of many years—my only regret was that these have now shrunk to such small numbers that a kosher meal—a *kosher* meal, ladies—is very difficult to obtain there."

Rabbi Fertlestone had then spoken for three quarters of an hour about his trip to Japan. "I think I can safely say," he said at last, "that, though small in number, our far-flung co-religionists are truly Jewish in heart. Just to finish up with, I must just tell you just this one small anecdote. I was visiting a small town in northern Japan where a few scattered remnants of our people had found themselves a small, let us say, sanctu-airy. Well, these few scattered remnants somehow got to hear that I was coming. How? I don't know. But what I do know is just how they got busy! A meeting place was found, everyone for miles around notified that a great American Rabbi" (he allowed himself a deprecatory smile) "was coming. And will you believe me, ladies, those far-away Jews in that lil corner of Asia got together and put on a reception for me—*with* a welcoming committee—as good as anything I've experienced anywhere. They met my train. They put on a banquet. They escorted me in state to the meeting. And when I entered that hall where the meeting was to take place and when I took my seat . . . what, ladies, do you think was the first sound I heard?"

The Hebrew Ladies looked expectant.

"I heard" he said impressively, "the sound of singing. Yes! The sound of singing! And what do you think they were singing?"

All the Hebrew ladies guessed immediately but continued politely to look expectant.

"They were singing a hymn!" he said raising his voice.

"And what do you think that hymn was?" His voice rose still higher. "*Hatikvah!*, ladies. Hatikvah! Our own great national anthem!"

All the ladies released their breaths and applauded and Fertlestone sat down well satisfied with his lecture on "Israel's position in the Middle East".

Sara was still wrestling with a precis of this exposition, the three men talking round her when Rabbi Makin interrupted her to say in his silky, foreign-American voice: "Sara."

She looked up.

"Sara. A leetle favour please. I wish to make a telephone call to a Mr Niremberg."

"Yes?" she said holding her pencil ready. "What's the number?"

He shrugged with slow helplessness. "Tha—a—at," he said, "you will have to please discover for me."

"Yes? What's the address?"

He shrugged again, rubbed the end of his nose with his forefinger and said: "You see, it is a leetle difficult. This Mr Niremberg is our representative in Buenos Aires. I suggest therefore that you find out first the address of the Council headquarters there—I regret I cannot help you there but no doubt the central London office . . ."

"You mean you want to telephone Buenos Aires?" she said rather taken aback.

He nodded slowly. "I can leave it to you," he said with absent-minded confidence and turned to his conversation with the others.

It took her the better part of two hours to discover the number he wanted. Hungry, for she had had no lunch, she waited for Rabbi Makin to return from his. It was after three o'clock when he did so. A little annoyed she refused rather brusquely his immediate, soft-spoken request to put through the call, but when she pointed out that she had had nothing to eat his apologies were so profuse that she relented. She sat at her table wrestling with long distance while Makin sat in his armchair looking drowsily through some papers for fifty minutes till the call came through.

Rabbi Makin took the receiver from her. "Hello!" he said, his voice suddenly sounding much stronger and more American. "Niremberg? Good, How are you? You are? Good. Good. Listen, my dear fellow—oh, I can't complain. Not so bad considering the English weather. Say—what's it like over there? Yes? Yes? Well we could certainly do with some of that sunshine right here. You know we've got Saretsky over here with us. You met him in Cincinnati last year, remember? Suffers with his sinus. Yeah. He says it's worse for him over here in London than it is back home. I guess it's the damp. Well now, I just wanted to tell you that this conference is going on fine. I'm sure sorry you couldn't make the trip this time. What's that? Oh. Yeah. Next year maybe. You what? Oh, your *wife*. You must give her my very best regards. Everything this end is going on fine. Sure I'll tell him. He was talking with me over lunch today. Well, I guess I'll have to hang up now. Back to work! We have an evening session commencing shortly. Shalom!"

With yet more apologies but without even the offer of a cup of tea he finally let Sara go. She had just time to swallow a quick meal before the evening meeting began.

2

"Would you," said Leo later that evening as he was driving her home, "do me a favour?"

"Of course. If I can."

"Would you—if you can spare the time?—come home with me now and type out a rather urgent memorandum which I must have first thing tomorrow morning? It will only take a few minutes; no more, I promise you."

"Of course," she said again. "It's not very late."

"You are my guardian angel," he said, "my angel Gabriel!"

She looked around her with some curiosity on entering his home. She had never been there before. Leo's house, of which he was secretly very proud, impressed her with its old-fashioned, comfortable opulence. He ushered her into his study and sitting her down before the big, leather topped desk gave her his typewriter and a small sheaf of notes.

"It really won't take you long," he said. "Just copy exactly as it stands. Are you comfortable? I shall go and make some coffee. It is my one talent. I make wonderful coffee!"

When he came back a quarter of an hour later, pushing the door open with one foot and bearing a tray triumphantly on high, he saw her bent concentratedly over his notes.

"Just another five minutes," she said.

"Right."

He bustled about the room, switched on the fire and put the coffee pot near it to keep warm, then sat down. His chair was set sideways to the desk and as he leaned back he found himself looking intently at her in full profile view. She was re-writing or punctuating some words in the manuscript he had given her and her unconscious pose, correcting his notes, her left elbow on his desk, the hand clenched against her jaw, her head bent, her attention absorbed, suddenly struck him with a profound and stirring sense of intimacy. It seemed, all at once, to be entirely natural, right and familiar for her to be there.

"As a matter of curiosity," said Sara when she had finished typing and was sitting in the armchair opposite him with her coffee, "would you mind telling me who pays the expenses of all these delegates?"

Leo looked up sharply, not recalling immediately that Sophie had once made a similar remark, but with a feeling that Sara had stabbed some raw and painful place of experience. By way of sub-conscious reprisal he immediately felt an inclination to contradict, even browbeat her for whatever opinion she might be going to express.

"The organization," he said rather shortly. "That is, each branch pays its own whack. Why?"

When she told him with a mixture of rage and amusement of Makin's telephone call to Buenos Aires he said, laughing and irrit-able at once: "I know, I know. It's typical. But what can you do? D'you think there isn't exactly the same sort of thing going on in non-Jewish organizations? The same waste—of time and money? The Council is a kind of Government department, a Civil Service if you like of international Jewry. And a Government employee is a Government employee all over the world."

"That's not a very good excuse," said Sara in that judging-from-high-standards manner of hers which irritated still further the mood he was in. She was aware of this effect (which she often made on others besides Leo) but there was an evangelical strain in her nature, a streak of Old Testament attitude towards unrighteousness, which she found impossible to restrain. "Such gross lack of conscience——"

"My dear girl, you are being naïve," said Leo testily, feeling, amongst other things, that she had taken his place in the pulpit. "You do not know how life arranges itself, by what paradoxical arrangements the whole thing works. You see this wrongness, that absurdity—and you judge the whole. You think in terms of straight lines. You forget or rather you don't realize that we Jews proceed like the rest of humanity, tortuously: that, by a series of back steps we somehow, miraculously, move forward."

"Somewhere along the line choices are made," she said obstinately. "*Someone* has to choose; *some* time. To see plainly, to see a choice in simple terms . . . is that always so difficult?"

"You are trying to lead me on in order to catch me on the old argument between principle and expediency," he cried but only to feel a little ashamed as she turned a surprised and puzzled look at him. He knew very well by this time that she was incapable either of trying to catch him on anything or of proffering a second-hand argument. Her ideas, however naïve, however blinkered, were her own.

"Let's put it another way," he said. "You over-estimate the quality of human nature. People see only what they want to see. Rabbi Makin does not think of himself as wasting public money. But *you* do not see that Rabbi Makin *does not see himself*. You think that plain truth is bound to be recognized. Nothing could be *further* from the truth! You yourself are blind to the peculiar structure of the moral vision which allows us only to see what we wish to see— and no more."

"Morality is imposed only by expediency, then? Is that what you are saying?"

The Rabbi paused. Her question, overshooting his thought, had penetrated depths of uncertainty in himself which he seldom dared approach.

"You cannot expect *me*—a Rabbi!" he said at last, "to discount the element of the Divine in man's nature. It is that—and *experience* rather than expediency which ultimately builds up moral law." Then he added hastily: "However, we are getting away from our original argument."

"Yes, yes," she agreed quickly, misinterpreting his lack of further courage as boredom.

"Anyway," he said, "you are really too young to perplex yourself over these philosophical problems. In ten years time perhaps I will allow you to approach them!"

"I'm not so young," she said turning her head away.

"Oh dear, dear!" he said playfully. "How old are you?" he added rather curious to know exactly.

To his surprise she muttered, "I'm not telling you," and continued to refuse the information, sounding very touchy indeed.

Leo was delighted as he always was at her rare exhibitions of femininity and continued to tease her with an affectionate scoffing until she turned and looking straight at him said defiantly: "I was thirty exactly two weeks ago."

"Thirty!" he said in a voice of mock doom. "Well, well." Then with a change of tone he said: "Why didn't you tell me? I would have bought you a present.

She looked up quickly in surprise, giving him what he rarely saw, the full beauty of her remarkable eyes, grey-green and shining, filled with some quality—hard to name—of spirit. "A present?" she said astonished and confused as much as little Gedaliah had been by such an idea. He laughed, his sense of tenderness towards her increasing. He felt, in the muscles of his arm, an impulse to place it round her shoulders. But before he could take this surprising feeling further she had turned her face away again and he saw only her austere profile, the long, narrow angle of her jaw and the severe delicacy of her lips.

"D'you think the English delegates would be so indifferent and extravagant with public money?" she asked with a nervous, hurried change of subject.

"Maybe not," he said. "I doubt if Tarsch, for instance, would be so blatant. And Shaffer certainly wouldn't."

"Now I am looking forward to hearing him speak," said Sara enthusiastically.

Leo gave a sideways nod.

"Yes. Shaffer is—there is no getting away from it—Shaffer is an ornament. The one Rabbinical figure we have whom we can put up against the best in other worlds. The only one, I should say, who has managed to bridge the gap between Jewish and non-Jewish culture and kept his balance."

Listening to Rabbi Shaffer the following evening Sara wholeheartedly agreed. It would have been difficult to fault him. His physical presence was handsome and commanding, his sense of humour European and delightful. He made small concessions to the more foreign element in his audience but did not attempt to exclude the many references to Western culture, literature, the arts from his address. There was, too, a quality in his manner of speaking, a way of forming his sentences perhaps, a habit of mind possibly,

158

liberal, intellectual and at the same time profoundly Jewish, which delighted Sara. She came away with a sense of pride.

"You were right," she said to Leo on the way home. "The only one we have—present company excepted!" she added rather shyly but determined to say it, "who has managed to combine two cultures perfectly."

"You can except me too," said Leo though he looked pleased.

"I certainly won't," she said indignantly.

"Oh yes, yes. I'm no Shaffer. Perhaps I could have been, I don't know. But Shaffer is Shaffer; a successful human being. He has a brilliant daughter too, did you know? At Somerville. Ah well," he said looking depressed. Then he said looking livelier: "Have you heard what happened with Spender and Auberbach? The non-clergy part of the American delegation. This is what happens when you let big business men into an organization like ours. Those two big idiots (luckily they weren't staying at the Savoy, we found them rooms at the Regal) picked up a couple of girls from heaven knows where and tried to smuggle them into their rooms last night. Not only that, they couldn't even do it efficiently, the hotel detective got on to them and they only got out of it by the skin of their teeth. Bloody idiots. That's all the organizations needs, a juicy scandal in the newspapers. 'Delegates to Jewish International Conference . . .' I can see the headlines!"

"They should have brought their wives with them," said Sara with an unconcerned practicality which surprised him.

He turned to her with a slightly astonished, quizzical look.

"You're not shocked?"

Sara, who was not without a slight starchiness regarding sexual morality, hesitated. Then she said: "I can't say I *approve*, any more than you do. But 'shocked'? Oh no. It is not that kind of behaviour which shocks me."

"What does then?" he said.

She turned her head away. Then with an air of bracing herself she said very quickly: "Untruthfulness," and, flushing deep red cried immediately: "Now you will think me a prig!"

He propped his arm on the steering wheel, held his cheek and chin against the inside of his hand and said consideringly: "No. Why should I?"

"Well you should," she said crossly, "because I am."

"No," he said again. "I should not say that that was your particular deficiency."

There was a pause.

"What is then?" she said at last in a subdued tone.

He put a bent forefinger to his mouth and pondered. "I should say," he said at last, "that you have too great a fondness for *order*, for *reality;* and this makes you . . . not light. You sort of *drive* at truth and forget or ignore the charms of fancy . . . fantasy . . . embroidery . . . I can't think of quite the right word. There is no . . . running free . . ."

"It's all right," she said in a low voice. "I know what you mean. I know exactly what you mean," she said again. "I . . . deplore it myself. But there are reasons. There are reasons, facts in my life. You see, at home . . ." She came to a standstill. "You see, when you are always with . . ." she tried again and stopped again. ". . . my father," she got out and then could say no more. The habit of loyalty caught her by the throat and forbade her to go on. "When you live with someone like my father," she wanted to say, "when you are caught up every hour of your life in eccentric unpredictability, unreasonableness, wild swervings from truth and sense, absurdity, vanity, self-delusion, when you have to cope with all this every day of your life—then you can't help but swing too far the other way. Fantasy! I have to cope with fantasy too often to have any taste for it. Embroidery! my whole life is scribbled over with mad-patterned embroideries."

But none of this could she bring herself to say before they parted. And Leo, thinking her reference to her father implied a lofty standard of truth in Mr Gabriel, was only too glad not to pursue a probing comparison in which he felt he might not himself show up too well.

At the end of the week the Conference was over, for which Sara was not sorry. She had worked for far longer hours than had been agreed upon but her only acknowledgment of this was Rabbi Makin's best thanks and a copy of Rabbi Fertlestone's essays presented by him with much pomp and a signed inscription on the title page.

One outcome of her week's work, however, was that one of the Hebrew Women asked if she would like to put in a few hours helping Mrs Davies, wife of a well-known and enormously rich Jewish industrial magnate, with her work for a charity concert. The terms of this temporary engagement were left rather vaguely "according to how much we need you" but Sara accepted nevertheless, more from a spirit of curiosity than for gain. The life of the Jewish rich was as much a closed book to her as it would have been to any Gentile.

The Davies lived in a cream-painted house near Park Lane. All four floors of it had been "done over" a few years before; it had to be admitted that the net result was impressive. From the big square hall, its glass-fronted alcoves holding small pieces of china and bibelots under special diffused lighting, Sara was shown into Mrs Davies' own private sitting room by a uniformed maid. The room itself was in excellent taste with mushroom-coloured walls, printed linen curtains and covers in subdued, pleasant colours, a walnut writing desk and some good modern paintings. It was not the furnishings, however, which gave the room its distinctive smell or opulence. Sara, waiting for Mrs Davies to come in (with some curiosity as she had not yet met her, only spoken by telephone), tried to locate the source of this impression. It was, she finally decided, made up of a number of small things; not the fact that scattered about were a number of solid silver cigarette boxes but that they were all filled with expensive brands of cigarettes and obviously kept filled. A portable typewriter of the newest and most gadgeted kind was perched carelessly on a pouffe. *Vogue, Harper's Bazaar* and no fewer than five different morning papers all of that day's date (only one of which, however, had been opened) were stuffed into a hand-painted paper-rack. And everywhere, flowers, huge, fabulous, massed clusters of them in marvellous glass and crystal vases.

The door opened and she rose to her feet as Mrs Davies came in tearing off her hat. "How are you, Miss Gabriel?" she said, not looking at Sara and going swiftly over to her desk. "So glad you could come," she said picking up the ivory telephone with her left hand and scuffling amongst some papers with her right. She gave

Sara a swift, absent-minded smile, then began to dial a number. "Speak-to-you-in-a-minute-do-sit-down," she mouthed and gave her a swift flick of a smile.

"Hello? Mirry? Listen, darling, you're to drop absolutely *everything* and come right over. Yes. Tell you when I see you. Oh! You did? Well, I told you, didn't I? Darling, I *can't* come to you. For one thing I've got someone here who's promised to be an absolute angel and help me with The Society function." She flashed Sara another smile over the telephone. "Yes. Yes. *There's* an angel. Quick as you can. Bye."

She put down the receiver and came forward. "Now let's see. Mrs Bray did tell you about our work, didn't she?"

"I understand you're having a Celebrity Concert at the end of the month?"

"Oh it's not just a *concert*. Didn't Mrs Bray tell you? You see, The Society—you do understand that that's actually the *name* of our group . . . rather chic we think, all the others have those long titles reduced to those *dreary* initials so much alike and very confusing when you're selling tickets you know . . . No! We've had what I really think the most stunningly original idea. We're not having *just* a concert or *just* a dance or just any old *one* function at all! This is going to be absolutely *the* . . . You see we're having *two*!"

"Two?"

"My dear, I can see the idea bowls you over just like the rest of us. Yes. A terrific Celebrity Concert in the evening *followed by* an All Night Ball! Cabaret, of course. Tombola. Raffles. The lot! Imagine the money we're going to raise for those *poor* things . . . So you can see why I'm so *swamped* with work I don't know where to turn. I swear I'll turn over the Chair to someone else after this year. Now you *can type*, sweetie, can't you?"

Sara nodded. "I'm not very fast I'm afraid——"

Mrs Davies was rummaging in a cupboard and not listening. She brought out several large files, opened them and said: "Look! Every one of these firms contributed advertisements to our special Concert Programme last year and *every one* has simply got to be made to take space again this year or my name will be mud. Letters to each and a slip like this one——" she held up a printed form, "enclosed".

She caught up the typewriter and almost threw it on to a small table. Then she picked up a chair, the seat of it covered in petit point and put it at the table. "Can you manage on this?"

"Yes, I'm sure I can," said Sara.

"You won't forget to put the price slip into each envelope, will you? Oh dear!" She stood beside Sara, scanning the advertisement rates. "You don't think we're asking too much, do you?"

Sara picked up one of the slips which offered "A full page in our grand Concert Programme" for one hundred guineas, a half-page for fifty and so on *pro rata* down to a miserable two line box for only five guineas.

"Well, if you can get it then you're not," she said reasonably.

Mrs Davies contemplated the list of prices rather moodily and Sara took the opportunity of having a good look at her. She was a young woman of thirty-three or four, of middle height with a slender, very good figure which she held badly. Her hair was black and sleek and cut very short in a serrated, "careless" style which must have cost a fortune to maintain, her complexion was smoothly ivory and she had fine, green eyes. Her nose was thin in her long, almond-shaped face. There was about her the faintly snake-like, sophisticated elegance of certain types of mannequins though something, perhaps her jerky angularity of movement spoilt her style. She was one of those women who have very long and slender legs but do not know how to manage their knees. She wore a fine cashmere jumper on a plain skirt and a string of real pearls. On her wedding finger she wore an immense, square diamond.

Sara was just beginning to type when the door opened and a small, blonde woman came in dressed in a pale-blue suit of finest tweed (the June day was chilly), tiny, coloured hat and wearing two diamond rings.

"Mirry!" said Mrs Davies jerking across to her and the two women burst into immediate and non-stop conversation, circulating restlessly about the table where Sara was trying to work.

"So you will *help* me, darling?" said Mrs Davies. "I *daren't* approach Clarisse. She's never forgiven me for——"

"I don't know that I can do anything with her either," said Mirry. "I'll have a try if you like. But don't expect anything. Have you done Harper Bros.?"

"Not a sausage. They've exhausted their charity allocation this year. I spoke to Chris Harper myself."

"Leonie, if *you* can't . . ." said Mirry with an admiring smile.

"Perhaps we might just try another letter," said Mrs Davies frowning. "Perhaps," she said turning to Sara, "you might—oh, Mirry, this is Miss Er . . . who's helping us with all the . . ."

Sara raised her eyes and smiled at Mrs Vincent who gave her a casual glance and a sharper one at the typewriter. She leaned over to see what had already been written. "Oh, you're trying Cohen & Phillimore?" she said to Leonie Davies. "They ought to be good for fifty at least."

"Fifty! They took a full page last year."

"Yes, darling, but Flora Levy swiped a full page off them only a month ago for their do."

"It's pure poaching," said Mrs Davies petulantly. "I'm getting absolutely fed up with Flora. She had no right to approach Phillimore's for her lot. I do think our Cause ought to have priority. After all, The Society was founded ages before her old Care Committee."

"She only started it because she lost the Chair to you."

"Well anyway ring Clarisse *now*, sweetie."

Mrs Vincent went over to the telephone and began to dial just as the door opened yet again and a huge doll dressed in Spanish costume complete with mantilla appeared with behind it a tall, blonde girl whom the two women greeted with squeals of "Bab!" Sara continued to type while the three women twittered round each other, Mirry interrupting her remarks to speak to an, it appeared, somewhat reluctant Clarisse at the other end who eventually promised to take a quarter page.

"She could hardly take less," said Mirry when she finally put down the receiver. "I spent over a hundred and fifty there this year."

"Is that one of hers?" said Mrs Davies eyeing Mirry's multi-coloured, tiny hat.

"Yes dear. I still say she does more for one than Martine, Leonie, though I know you don't agree."

"It's *sweet*, sweetie. Absolutely sweet. Don't you agree, Bab?"

"Gorgeous, Mirry," said Bab. "Now you haven't told me what you think of Conchita." She picked up the Spanish doll and displayed her costume with a practised hand. "For the Tombola. My husband had it made at the factory."

She waved it towards the two women and then towards Sara, giving her a charming smile at the same time. "What do you think of it?" she said to her.

"She's a beauty," said Sara, desisting from her typing.

"Oh I forgot. This is Miss Er . . ."

"Gabriel."

"Miss Gabriel who is going to do *all* the work for us till the concert," said Mrs Davies.

"How nice of her," said Bab warmly. She was a very attractive girl indeed, tall with rounded breasts and very slender waist and one of those oval, rounded faces which so often goes with cream and honey colouring. Although Mrs Vincent was also blonde there was a world of difference between the two women.

Sara bent to her work again, trying to concentrate in the babble and constant telephoning which filled the room.

Mirry Vincent was sitting on the arm of a chair smoking a cigarette and looking blonde and sharp with hard, shrewd eyes beneath blue lids. She was saying: "I'll just phone Nanny if you don't mind, Leonie, and remind her to take Neville to have his shoes fitted."

"How is he?" said Bab.

"Much better now. We took him to Garmisch for a month after he came out and Dr Warne's thrilled with him. He is *the* man for throats of course if you should ever need him."

"Grand et Cie!" said Mrs Davies suddenly. "Are they on the list?"

"No good," said Mirry with a rather vulgar "turned down" gesture. Her whole manner, it suddenly struck Sara, had a hard, common quality.

"They always give to Associated Charities." Then, with a kind of sycophantish air as if suddenly remembering that she was on a still slightly unaccepted level *vis-à-vis* Mrs Davies she added: "But I'm sure if *you* try, Leonie . . ."

It occurred to Sara that Mrs Vincent's husband's money had only been made during and since the war. In the ranks of old-established industrialists such as Mr Davies he was still considered very much a parvenu. Mirry Vincent was still working her way up.

"They're pretty tough," said Leonie doubtfully.

"You can do it," said Mirry Vincent as ardently as her hard, nasal voice could manage.

Mrs Davies went to the telephone again. "Grand et Cie? *Could* I speak to Mr Paul?" She waited, sitting on the edge of the desk, one foot idly moving up and down, her buckled, crocodile shoe half off. She must have paid at least fifteen guineas for her shoes. "Mr Paul? This is Mrs Davies. Oh very well thank you. And you? Look, Mr Paul, sweetie," she said in a coaxing voice, "we're just getting out the programme for our special charity concert and ball on the thirtieth. We're combining the two; don't you think that's clever? I felt sure you wouldn't want to be left out of it. Now what would you like? a full page?"

Bab Garrentz wandered over to Sara and murmured confidentially: "Isn't she a worker? I feel absolutely useless in comparison you know."

"I'm sure you do a great deal," said Sara politely.

"Nothing like Leonie. Just manage to sell a few raffle tickets and so on. Which reminds me——"

She was interrupted by Mrs Davies who hung up and squealed triumphantly: "Got a five guinea box! Hurray!"

"You're marvellous, Leonie," said Mirry Vincent excitedly. "No one else could have . . ."

"Hooray!" said Bab. And all three women whirled excitedly about the room almost capering with triumph.

"That'll put Associated Charities nose out of joint," said Mirry putting into words in her sharp, crude way the core of the achievement.

There was an infinitesimal pause long enough to tell her she had put a foot wrong but not noticing she went on: "Now you just have a go at Blettsworthy's."

Mrs Davies was silent for a moment then a moody look fell on her face and she answered pettishly: "Oh no. That's your pigeon, Mirry."

"Me! I couldn't possibly, sweetie. You're the one."

But Leonie Davies in her lightning changed mood said, so snappishly that even Mirry Vincent noticed: "No. I'm not doing any more. Anyway, I'm going to see about tea." And she disappeared

166

from the room. Mrs Vincent looked frightened and Bab Garrentz said she must go. "I'll go with you," Mirry said as Leonie came back into the room and, without too much attempt on her part to stop them, they went. Mrs Davies went out again then, reappearing for a moment, told Sara that she had to go out herself but she was sending tea in. "You can come tomorrow, can't you?" she said. Sara assented and they made arrangements regarding hours. Then she too disappeared and Sara was left at last to get on with her work in peace and to have a cup of tea and an undistinguished biscuit from the meagre assortment brought in by the exceedingly superior parlour maid.

She arrived at the house the following morning to find Mrs Davies out but a note awaiting her saying would she mind taking a bundle of the raffle books which had just arrived round to Mrs Garrentz who lived, it transpired, in the semi-basement flat of a huge luxury block in Kensington.

The blonde, graceful girl opened the door herself, smiled warmly at Sara and ushered her in enthusiastically to a rather handsome, chintzy room, installed her, before she knew what was happening, in a deep armchair and was standing at a miniature bar with strip-lighting asking her what she would have to drink.

"But I really couldn't," said Sara laughing and uneasily conscious of the work waiting for her at Mrs Davies'.

"Of course you can," said Bab.

"But isn't it rather early?"

"Never too early for pleasure," she said taking out two glasses.

"I really should be getting back to all those letters."

"Oh come on now! Have a sherry. Yes?" She poured out two and bringing them over gave Sara hers and sat down opposite, crossing her long legs. "Cheers," she said and they both sipped. Then she sprang up again and picking up a bundle of silk continued with the nightdress she was working on, catching a fine lace edging on to the hem with delicate, tiny stitches and plunging into animated talk in her light, charming voice about the artists appearing at the concert, the evening dress she was going to wear, the huge basket of fruit she was preparing as one of the prizes to be raffled. "That's the only sort of thing I *can* do really for The Society," she said.

"There's the raffle tickets," said Sara.

"Oh well actually Sidney takes care of those. He has what he calls his 'connection'. He sells them to his business associates and all those kind of people you know and they sell him theirs. They've been taking in each other's washing like that for years, I believe. "

She looked up and caught Sara's slightly questioning look.

"We've only been married three years," she said, "though I do look an old hag."

Sara attempted a disclaimer but she said: "Darling, I'm *twenty-eight*!"

"You don't look it!" Sara exclaimed spontaneously.

Her fingers working delicately along the silk, Bab said: "It's sweet of you. But my dear, in terms of experience I sometimes feel I'm fifty. Sidney's not my first husband you know."

Sara, looking non-committal, took another sip of sherry.

"My first marriage only lasted two years. Mike wasn't the kind of man to stay married. Wonderful to be with . . . heaven . . . but not to marry. I *adored* him—still do. Oh, only in a way, of course! We're still friends. He often rings me," she said, her voice tense and light, "between assignments, that is. He's foreign correspondent on the *Daily Wire*. But of course I daren't mention it to Sidney. Although there's absolutely nothing *to* it; just being civilized that's all. But Sidney can't bear to hear his name even. Well you can understand it really. Mike's such a handsome, massive, toughie you could hardly expect a little Jew not to be jea——" She caught Sara's eye again and said: "Of course you know *I'm* not Jewish."

"Oh I see," said Sara. For some reason this had not occurred to her, obvious as it now seemed.

"Two wonderful, heart-breaking, marvellous years," Bab went on in her flowing, engaging voice so easy to listen to. "I tried so hard to make it work," she said. "I even tried a baby but that didn't work either. They had to take it away from me in bits. In bits," she repeated with a sort of pride. "All that hell for nothing. Nearly put paid to my career as well. I was a model. That's how Sidney met me. He's in the rag trade himself, Garrentz Models. I expect you've seen them. He's terribly good to me. I met Mike in a restaurant. I'd just flown in from Paris and dropped in at the Lugano for a late dinner and there I was cold and starving and thinking of

168

nothing—but absolutely nothing—but a large plate of spaghetti and bed, and not looking at anyone, and Mike was there too watching me sitting on my own, *eating* away . . ." she put down her sewing and demonstrated eating spaghetti rapidly with an imaginary knife and fork, delicately and vivaciously acting it out with immense style, ". . . and Mike just left his table and came over to mine (he'd been watching me *all the time*) and said: 'I'd like to buy you!' Just like that! And we were married inside the month."

She bent to her sewing again.

Sara looked at the pretty, graceful, long-legged creature ruffling lace on to the ninon nightdress and felt a curious pang, half of pity, half of amazement, her imagination reaching out to apprehend a life composed of elements of which she could scarcely conceive; a rippling, stylish gaiety in a world of fast cars, restaurants and perfume, dashing, tough men and sweet, fashionable, golden girls such as Bab had been. A magazine-story world which really existed at certain points of time. Was it possible that that existed side by side with Manor Green suburbanism, stifling and narrow, with Rabbi Fertlestone, the Synagogue Guild, her brother-in-law, Monty, Jewish guilt and rawness, blatancy and melancholy? A dizzying sense of the teeming, crowded variousness of life overcame her, bringing with it a kind of oppression and she made a movement as of leaving but Bab, hastily jumping up, fetched a large box of chocolates from the sideboard and put them down beside her.

"Have some chocolate, do," she begged. "We've got masses. Sidney brings me home a box every night. Now don't worry about getting back to Leonie. I'll tell her you were doing some committee work for me. Don't go," she said in a forlorn, persuading voice. "It's so delightful to have a visitor. The days are so long. I really haven't very much to do. Sidney won't let me put my finger in cold water. If I asked for the moon he'd buy it for me. But what fun could you have with a moon? Can you imagine?" she said more brightly, "I didn't want him at first! He must have asked me twenty times. But I'd been through so much with Mike . . ."

"What made you change your mind?" asked Sara rather hesitantly though it was obvious that Bab was one of those charming, open talkers who never mind personal questions.

"I guess he just wore me down in the end. Besides—he was so

*mad* about me. D'you know what he did? He locked himself into his room at home and swore he wouldn't come out till I accepted him! His mother was so crazy with worry she actually came to see me and beg me to marry her son! She's a sweet, little old Jewish lady."

Sara blinked, her imagination for once stymied by this picture.

"She absolutely adores me—almost as much as Sidney! He's terribly generous. I'm very happy, really. Only there's always so much *time* to fill . . ."

"Wouldn't you like to do some modelling again?"

"Oh my dear, I long to."

"Then why not——?"

"Sidney won't let me," she said quickly. "I daren't even mention it."

"But why not?"

She shook her head. "He won't hear of it. He likes to think of me at home. He likes to know where I am, you see." She glanced at the clock. "He'll be phoning any minute now just so he can know I'm here. He's a wonderful husband really; terribly devoted."

The telephone rang and with a "what did I tell you?" glance at Sara she picked it up and answered, telling her husband at some length what she had been doing during the morning. While she was speaking Sara was quietly getting herself ready to go but Bab motioned to her to stay seated saying involuntarily: "No, not yet." A sharp exclamation came from the telephone and she turned back to it laughing and saying: "It's just Miss Gabriel, darling, who's working for Leonie over The Society function. She's brought the raffle tickets, by the way. Yes. All right, I won't keep you if you're busy, darling. Bye."

With an insistence she could not disregard, Bab made Sara sit down again, forcing another sherry on her, a cigarette, more chocolate, and all the time talking, talking in her light, extraordinarily attractive way until, suddenly, the door opened and Sidney Garrentz came into the room with a sidling, nervous, rapid step.

"Had to go through to Hammersmith anyway, darling, so I thought I might as well come home for lunch," he said to his wife who rose quickly and introduced him to Sara. She was a good three inches taller than her husband who had to stretch upwards to kiss her.

"Don't work my wife too hard," he said to Sara, sitting down on the arm of Bab's chair as she settled herself again.

"Darling! I'm doing absolutely *nothing*," she said.

"What's this?" he said fingering the silk on her lap.

"Just a nightie."

"What d'you want to spend your time on that for?" he said. "Go out and buy yourself one."

He bent over her and, slipping his arm round her head, caught her chin in his hand, fondling it, his small, swarthy, plain face with its little, black moustache almost touching her lovely, shining, gold hair. She tilted back her face trying to loosen her chin and milk-white throat from his small fingers and smiling at him with a sweet, pearly, blind smile. With an abrupt movement he got up and lit himself a cigarette standing uncertainly in the middle of the room, sallow, unequal, his narrow shoulders sloping, conveying—un-bearably—the imprint of deep, humiliated pain.

Sara determinedly got to her feet and at last made her escape.

She told Essie about the Garrentz a few days later, on one of the rare evenings her sister was in these days.

"Serves him right," said Mr Gabriel, coming in and catching the tail end of their conversation. "If a man's such a fool as to marry out he deserves to be miserable for the rest of his life. For the rest of his life," he repeated with relish.

"Oh for goodness sake, father," said Sara, exasperated, "I'm not talking about the rights and wrongs of it. I'm talking about the suffering."

"That's it! The suffering's a punishment. A punishment! The Almighty has punished him," he declared in tones of great satis-faction. "And you wait! God hasn't finished with him! He'll suffer more! You mark my words."

Used as they were to his striking of melodramatic, noisy, senseless attitudes, both his daughters found themselves curiously shocked at the absurd vindictiveness, the wallowing enjoyment in his own self-righteousness with which he spoke.

There was a pause before Essie said casually: "There are lots of mixed marriages which aren't unhappy. It's not a crime.'

"Excuse me!" cried Mr Gabriel, flying into argument with

passionate enjoyment. "If that's not a crime . . . to marry *Goyim* . . . *to marry Goyim!*" he bit out, his eyes glittering fanatically, "then what is? It's not only a *crime*," he said lowering his voice theatrically to a note of doom (and inadvertently saving the situation for both Sara and Essie flashed a helpless laugh between them) "it's the *greatest* crime a Jew can commit!" He sat back with a righteous nod and produced his pipe.

"Some people think smoking's a crime," said Essie.

"I have it on the highest authority, the highest authority that pipe-smoking is harmless. I'll tell you something else. Did you know that tobacco is better than all the disinfectants? A germ can't live in tobacco smoke. One of the highest specialists in Harley Street says so. I saw it in the paper."

He absorbed himself with great fuss in the lighting of his pipe.

"If you could have seen her, Essie," said Sara, seeing it was safe for her to continue. "That lovely girl, caged, wasted, beating out her life . . . and he . . . so *beaten* . . ."

"Yes, yes, I know," said Essie impatiently, "but that's nothing to do with it being a mixed marriage. Exactly the same could have happened—it's happening every day—if it hadn't been. Marriages work or don't work for quite different reasons. Religion's got nothing to do with it."

"I wouldn't quite say that——" began Sara doubtfully but Essie interrupted her saying roughly, "Well I would." Then, changing the subject abruptly, she asked how the charity committee was getting on.

Sara began to laugh. "Oh dear! did you see the paper this week? Our rivals, Associated Charities, have had the unmitigated nerve to pinch our idea of two functions at once. *They're* advertising a combined theatre premiere *and* champagne dinner three weeks after ours. *We* are livid!"

"That's nothing," said Essie. "Did you read the correspondence column? No, I thought not. There's a letter—really heartbreaking I must say—from the London Appeals Organization, complaining that they really can't compete with the richer charity committees in organizing *their* functions and—wait for it!—*appealing for funds!*"

Even Mr Gabriel, on whom irony was lost and who seldom saw a joke, burst out laughing.

"So the charity committee's asking for charity!" he said and, well pleased with his scintillating wit, repeated his remark at intervals for the rest of the week.

# Chapter Seven

## I

SARA'S WORK FOR THE SOCIETY COMMITTEE ENDED with the famous double function itself. She was given free tickets for the concert but not for the ball which had been a great relief to her as she knew no one whom she could conceivably have taken with her as partner save possibly Monty, her brother-in-law, who would have gone anywhere but had no evening suit or, just possibly, Leo, though the idea of asking him terrified her. She had in any case scarcely seen him, except in his pulpit on Saturday mornings, for some weeks. The lecture season at the Guild had finished as had nearly all other meetings at the onset of full summer, and without the constant expectation of meeting him, the days dragged heavily for her. A flu epidemic was raging across the country and her father caught it, though lightly. The main part of the nursing fell on her, both Essie and Fagy being out all day and equally elusive in the evenings, though she could not altogether blame them. Mr Gabriel was a fiendishly bad patient and she was the only one able to deal with him. She heaved a sigh of relief when he was about again.

Then one morning in the shop she heard a customer say that Leo was down with flu also, and rather badly. The news threw her into a state of acute tension. Her immediate instinct was to go to him—an instinct she at once checked but which returned again and again. To a temperament like hers, even to telephone his house, which she did once asking how he was but leaving no name, left her racked and shaken. The years she had spent crushing down spontaneity, cultivating her particular brand of independent resignation left her totally unfitted for such an act. She longed to go, made detailed plans . . . and did nothing. Finally, after a wretched few days she spoke, longing for some pointer however slight as to what she should do, to Essie one evening saying casually: "I believe Leo Norberg's been quite ill. Don't you think one of us might go round . . . ask if we can do anything? It was decent of him to get me that job with the Conference, after all."

"But of course," said Essie absently. "You know him better than I do. You go, Sos."

"Do you really think I should?" she said, looking down and up with an agitation she could not for the life of her quite control.

Essie, shaken from her own preoccupations, looked over at her with some concern. The sisters had never discussed their private emotions with any degree of intimacy even when they were younger, and for years now there had been none to discuss save Fagy's changing boy friends. Nevertheless she was not entirely unaware of Leo's increasing friendship with her sister. Of Sara's feelings, her occasional quotations of Leo's opinions, her animation when she had been in his company, the more frequent appearance of those moments of rare, austere beauty which occasionally gleamed out like starlight on her sister's face, all combined to tell.

"Of course go," she said vigorously. 'It's the least you can do I should think. Go now!"

"Now? I don't see how I can. Father says he wants me to do something for him. He's on the rampage about something or other." And in fact Mr Gabriel entered at that moment. "Sara," he said commandingly, "as soon as you've finished clearing away I want you in the front room."

"What for?"

"I want you to write a letter for me to Mr Fremsl."

"Sara's going out," said Essie swiftly. "She'll do it tomorrow."

"Tomorrow's too late. Fremsl's going away. As soon as you've finished, Sara."

Essie hesitated; she had been about to go out herself. "I'll write it for you," she said at last.

"Am I asking you, miss?" said her father impatiently. "So good-natured all of a sudden! But thank you for nothing. If you'd taken the trouble to learn to write in Yiddish instead of your fancy evening classes with the *Goyim* . . ."

It was true, Sara was the only one of them who was able to write in Yiddish. Essie turned and gave her a "Give in if you dare" scowl and Sara said mildly, the opposition unexpectedly strengthening her resolve to go: "I really can't tonight. Surely it'll do in the morning?"

"And I tell you it *won't* do in the morning," said Mr Gabriel obstinately. "Tonight it has to be written."

"Why don't you write it yourself, anyway?" said Essie.

Mr Gabriel raised his voice and shouted, "Do I have to give explanations every time I want to blow my nose? I'll tell you why I can't do it myself. Because I'm too ill. Look! look at my hand, my arm! In an agony with rheumatism." He held out his arm, moving it stiffly and wincing exaggeratedly. Both the girls frowned, trying to remember if he'd been holding it like that earlier. He had had his supper before any of them were in.

"Oy—y!" he said moving his fingers feebly in front of them. "Agony! Later on," he said to Sara, "you can rub it with liniment."

"I'll do it now," she said putting down the tray she was holding.

"Na! na! later on when I go to bed. So meanwhile you'll come in to the other room as soon as you've finished."

"You're just damn well going," said Essie as soon as he'd gone out. "I don't believe he can't write. He's play-acting. Anything to get his own way."

"P'raps he's really in pain," said Sara looking worried.

"Not on your life. Now you're to go, d'you hear! I'll finish the dishes—I've just got to make a phone call first—and then you slip out. If he starts creating I'll hold him at bay. Now go and wash your face!"

Sara laughed and with the rarest of gestures, the sisters were never demonstrative to each other, gave Essie a hug before going upstairs. In order, however, that her father shouldn't see her through the window she was obliged to go out the back way and this gave her her first twinge of uneasiness. She was incurably law-abiding and the evasive action worried her where it might have stimulated others. The walk through the empty, suburban streets in the long, summer twilight increased her qualms. As she approached Leo's road the whole idea of visiting him seemed impossible, the very act an emotional stripping like an open declaration of love. She slowed down, turned into his street with lagging steps and stopped. She looked at the number nearest to her and seeing with fright that Leo's house was only two doors away she almost ran along the pavement, passing his door with a hunted, sideways glance and did not pause till she was fifty yards past it. Panting, she leaned against a tree. Then she pulled herself together and walking back was about to open his gate when a light suddenly flashing on in the front bedroom, like a warning, startled her. Her acute self-consciousness came back and she began to think, "What shall I say to him? Or is he in bed and I shall just see his housekeeper? Or—" (and this was even worse) "perhaps some of his congregants are with him?"

"Oh this simply won't do," she said to herself distractedly and resolved firmly to go in. "Only not just yet. In a minute. When I've calmed down." And fixing her mind firmly on the fact that he had been ill, perhaps still was, she found herself building up a scene in her mind of herself sitting talking to him, making him laugh about the absurdities of The Society and the story of the row on the night of the famous "double function" itself when *all* the young daughters of the committee women (to say nothing of their mothers) had insisted that *they* would only sell programmes in the stalls and someone else should be sent to the circle, the balcony and the gallery; an impasse solved only by a hastily improvised ballot and the formation of several brittle enmities. It was while she was thinking and smiling about this that she happened to glance at her watch. It was nearly half-past nine. With a shock she realized that her father must long since have been taking it out of Essie, that if she went in to see Leo now she might not get home till late, that that letter had to be written and her father's hand and arm seen to. She hesitated, torn between fulfilling the delightful dream in which she had been indulging and going back before her father worked himself into one of those fuming passions when life was impossible for weeks. She put one foot forward then drew it back. All her uncertainties came rushing at her once again. Then suddenly she thought of a new idea. Opening her bag she took out her diary, tore a leaf out of it and, standing beneath a street lamp which had just come on, scribbled a note.

"Terribly sorry to hear you've been ill. Is there anything at all I can do for you? I am so worried but I didn't want to call in case I disturbed you. Please, please let me know if you would like me to come and see you."

She signed the note with her initial S. and slipping stealthily up his path pushed it through the letter box.

"Well?" said Essie as she came in, "did you see him?"

"No. I left a note," she said adding anxiously, "Where's father?"

"Gone to bed," said Essie grimly. "*Why* didn't you actually call——?"

"Oh Essie, I couldn't. It was getting late and I knew what must be happening here. Is he furious?"

"What does it matter what was happening here? Yes he is. So you see you haven't avoided anything. You might just as well have stayed out."

"I'd better go up," said Sara.

"Oh no you don't!" And Essie barred her way to the stairs, folding her arms and with a look of thunder on her face.

"What on earth are you playing at?" said Sara and she made to ascend.

"Go in the living room. I want to talk to you," said Essie, her eyes flaming. Sara stood for a moment looking up at her then, shrugging, gave in and went into the living room. Essie followed.

"Well, what is it?" she said sitting down wearily at the table in the middle of the room. Essie sat down facing her. The centre light, with its ugly, flakestone bowl, cast its glaring yet curiously dull, white light over them. The shabby room with its soiled, buff paper, worn carpet, appalling furniture in the brown tastelessness of thirty years ago, held them suspended in its drab, harsh-lighted heart. Outside, the chill, summer night, deepened to a forlorn, despairing dark, spread itself across the boxed, deadened lives of the suburb.

"Would you like to know what happened tonight?" said Essie, her voice and manner grim and rigid.

"Well?"

"*Not* well, Not well at all. He wanted to know where you were. Went rampaging about as usual. How dare you go out when *he* wanted you. The usual. So just to shut him up I made the first excuse that came into my head." (Both of them knew without saying that Sara's expedition must at all costs be hidden from their father's meddling hands.)

"What did you tell him?"

"I said that John Gildheim wanted you to do a little job for him, something to do with the Guild, so you'd gone round there. He knows he's Chairman. I thought that might hold him."

"Yes?"

"I blame myself for being such a fool," said Essie in a heavy voice. "I ought to have known. Don't I know him? Don't I know what he's capable of doing? Only . . . you sometimes tell me I'm hard, Sara, that I *look* for faults in him. That isn't true. I *don't* bear resentment in my heart from one time to the next. On the contrary. The fact is—you can believe this or not—I forget! Each time I forget and expect him—against all my experience!—to be normal and ordinary and reasonable like everybody else. You won't believe me but I swear to you that each time he commits some fresh enormity I am . . . surprised. I *don't* expect the eccentric, crazy thing . . . though God knows I should have learnt to by now." She sighed. "Well. To get back. As soon as I mentioned Gildheim his eyes began to blaze and he walked straight out into the hall. I thought he'd gone upstairs but what he was actually doing was looking up John's number in the telephone directory.'

Sara raised her head sharply. "He rang him up?"

"I came out into the hall just in time to hear him say, 'Is that Dr Gildheim?' I suppose John asked who was speaking and then father started. You know what happens when he's consumed with rage and wants to *punish*. He doesn't even shout. He said in that peculiar, high, soft, affected voice which . . . when I hear it I want to commit murder . . . 'This is Boruch Gabriel,' he said with that . . . vicious politeness . . . 'Will you please tell my daughter, Sara to come home *at once*. Tell her *I-am-waiting*.' John must have been absolutely dumbfounded. If I'd said anything at all he'd have begun to scream —with John at the other end; so I said nothing. He went on: 'She can come and do your work for you another time.' I think John tried to say something then but father was working himself into that sort of silky fury of outraged *will* of his. You know. You've seen it as often as I have. 'After all,' he said, 'after all, Dr Gildheim, a father comes before a guild, before a committee, before a *grossartige* doctor. Even if you are a doctor that doesn't mean you can insult a father and steal a child away from her duty. Find someone else to lick your stamps.' "

Sara put up her hand and rubbed it with a hard movement across her eyes. Essie took out her cigarettes and lighting one gave it to her. Then she lit one for herself.

179

"There was a good bit more of this, with John not getting a word in, then after he'd talked himself out he just put the receiver down and—with that guilty, smirking dignity of his when he's done something outrageous—stalked up to his room."

She made a hopeless gesture.

"Sara," she said pleadingly. "How much longer is this going to go on? This tyranny. Worse . . . this—madness. Can't you see he's draining the blood from us both? Rebecca is out of it and Fagy— well you know Fagy always gets out of everything. But you and I? How much longer can we stand it? What is the rest of our life going to be?"

"What do you expect me to do? What do you *want* me to do? You're his child as much as I am."

"We can make a stand. Present him with an ultimatum. Either he treats us with sense and common decency, so that we can lead ordinary, normal lives, have a chance of happiness, or——"

"Or . . .?" said Sara.

Essie sat silent. "Or he'll get more than he's bargained for," she muttered at last.

"I suppose you mean you'll leave home," said Sara sharply.

"That, maybe," Essie muttered.

"I suppose you'll go and live with Margaret or one of your other English friends you spend so much time with,"

Essie gave a non-committal jerk of her head.

"Well that might solve your problem," said Sara, "but it wouldn't solve mine. Even if I got a job d'you think I could rest easily wondering what's going on here? Who'd look after the house —and him? Who'd smooth over the thousand difficulties he creates around himself every day? Rebecca? Fagy? You know they wouldn't."

"Supposing . . . we were both married? He'd have to learn how to live, how to manage life, then."

"Supposing, supposing," said Sara impatiently. "Everybody says the same and it's a stupid argument. Supposing we weren't us, supposing we'd been born in China or another century? Meanwhile there's no marriage in sight for either of us——" She stopped abruptly.

"And never will be if we go on like this," Essie flared in sudden, bitter anger. "Who do you suppose will look at us once he starts on them? Can you even go to the Guild any more after what happened tonight? There must be something *we can do*." She brought her fist down hard, on the table, the expression on her face drawn and desperate.

Sara put her elbow on the table and leaned her forehead on her hand. "I don't know what to say, I don't know what to do," she said. "If you're looking for solutions, Essie, I can't give you any. So far as I can see there aren't any. You still think there are answers, don't you? Do this . . . do that . . . Anything less than happiness is outrageous behaviour on the part of life, and must be corrected. Don't you understand? Some problems can't be solved, you just have to live with them."

"To live like this? Until we die?" cried Essie in a strangled violent voice. "*No . . . No . . .* and *No!*" She put her two clenched fists together and pressed them on the table before her. "There are limits," she said in a rigid, controlled voice. "Do not push me beyond . . . I don't want . . ." she said piteously. "God knows I . . . Help me! Sara! For God's sake help me, help both of us. Look . . . you are being dishonest anyway. Supposing——" Leo's name was on her lips but desperate as she was some delicacy of feeling forbade her to use it, "supposing someone . . . entirely suitable asked you to marry him next week. What would you say? 'I'm very sorry, I've got to look after my crazy, selfish father.'"

Sara hesitated, flushed and looked away. She was too honest to try to evade the question but her reply nevertheless sounded evasive. "I think," she said carefully, "that if it were right—and *meant*—that events would somehow work rightly. I don't know . . . but I would not pit my will against Fate. I have not the strength—or arrogance . . ."

"You think it's right then never to fight, only accept, accept?"

"For me. Perhaps you are different," said Sara simply.

Essie with a giving-up gesture suddenly slackened her shoulders and nodded her head slowly backwards and forwards. "Yes," she said. "I'm different." And she sat on still nodding her head slowly, backwards and forwards, backwards and forwards, hypnotizing herself with the rhythm into not thinking, till long after Sara had gone out of the room and up to bed.

Leo, who was feeling exceedingly depressed and seedy on his first day down and would have welcomed Sara, had gone up to bed early that night (it was his light flashing on which had startled her and put her off from opening his gate) but was unable to sleep. After a time he got up and went downstairs for a book. As he switched on the light in the hall he caught sight of Sara's note lying on the floor. Picking it up—such notes were not uncommon through his letter box—he put it in his dressing gown pocket and went upstairs again where he read it standing beside his bed. As soon as his eye fell on the S. of the signature his head seemed to expand and become full of a light, singing sound. He took several paces about the room while waves of prickling, nervous joy flooded through him. He held out his hand towards the telephone beside the bed then stopped, looked at his watch, calculating how long it would take Sophie to get home, realized that he did not know exactly when the note had been delivered, and set himself a time limit of thirty minutes.

After thirty-five minutes (an exercise in will-power) he dialled her number. Trudy answered. "Why, hallo!" she said with surprise.

"How are you, Trudy? How are you getting on?" he said and prolonged the conversation with her for as long as he could from sheer, delighted expectation. At length he said casually: "By the way, I'd rather like a word with Sophie, if I may. Is she there?"

"I'm afraid she isn't. Didn't you know? She's on holiday."

"On holiday?"

"Yes. She went home—to Wales—about a week ago. I'm not expecting her back for about five or six days."

"Are you sure?"

"Sure?" she said. "Yes of course I'm sure. I had a card from her only this morning."

"I see. I see. You're sure she's not in London, then?"

"Positive."

"Oh well, never mind. It's nothing important," he said and as soon as he could rang off.

He sat down on the edge of his bed and looked at the note again, realizing this time that it came from Sara. Try as he would he could not prevent a burning, sinking, regretful bitterness against her and the curious way in which she seemed, like some stern angel, always to come between himself and his weakness: a mood which settled so heavily upon him that the only refuge was vacancy. So that by the following day he had relapsed into a vacuum of no-thought which, while protecting him from his own disappointed misery, prevented him from even the most meagrely polite answer which would have relieved hers.

It was in this frame of mind that, a week later, he yielded to Joel Fredlander's pressing insistence that they go together to Whytecliffe Sands for a short holiday.

3

The South Coast seaside resort of Whytecliffe Sands is approximately a two and a half hour motor run from London, though Jaguars do it in less. Its great pride and boast is its promenade, the famous Whytecliffe Front which curves in a great sweep from the headland called Great Rock on the western side of the bay to the smaller promontory known as Little Rock, to the east. Between these two points stretches a wide, pink-waved promenade with, on the landward side of the road facing the sea, a tree-lined shopping centre laid out as a boulevard. Along this boulevard, fronting hand-some shops, with its rock gardens, coloured chairs and open-air café and bandstand, stroll the better off, better dressed, consider-ably classier of Whytecliffe's residents and visitors, shopping, meet-ing, chatting; leaving the other side of the Front, which runs along the edge of the beach, to the *hoi polloi* of whom, coaches not being admitted and trippers rather inadequately catered for—no fairs, no stall, no Bingo—there are comparatively few.

At the western end of the Front, as the shops peter out, the hotels begin to take over, interspersed with some blocks of glass and con-crete many-windowed flats. The road here takes a sudden upward rise, then flattens for several hundred yards, then rises rather steeply upwards again, finally disappearing round the curve of Great Rock. It is on the flattened out bit that the three, great, Jewish hotels, one pink, one black and white, one cream, are situated. All three are of almost equal size, impressiveness and luxury. Across the sweep of

183

the bay, on Little Rock, stand the four Jewish hotels of slightly lower rank than the big three, and scattered through the town lying between these two points are some thirty or so boarding and guest houses.

Though the prices of the three big hotels, the Grosvenor, the Dorchester and the Berkeley, are as high as practically any five star hotel in Britain they are full to bursting point all the year round and it was only by a stroke of luck plus Joel's unscrupulous use of Rabbi Tarsch's name that he and Leo were able to secure a last minute cancelled booking at the Berkeley. This was the pink palace in the middle position between the Grosvenor and the Dorchester.

The two men, Leo driving, arrived on Friday afternoon.

Like eighty per cent of the Jewish population of Great Britain, both of them had stayed at Whytecliffe several times before. For any Jew with any pretensions whatever to better living not to have spent at least a week-end "on the Rock" was unthinkable, even if—as the old joke had it—they were on the rocks by the time they had paid their bill.

Leo, who was still rather washed out after the flu, elected to lie down almost as soon as they arrived and he did not get up until it was almost time to go in to the Friday night Service held in the little synagogue attached to the hotel.

The first person he saw as he entered the lift to go down that evening was Mrs Goldenbird.

"Well I never!" she exclaimed excitedly. "Well I never. Now isn't that strange! Doris and I were only talking about you the other day. We heard you weren't well—flu was it? It does pull you down, doesn't it, we've managed to escape it so far thank God, and I said 'I wonder how Rabbi Norberg's getting on, p'raps I ought to ring up and find out.'"

"That's very kind of you. I'm much better now though, as you say, it——"

"Yes, Doris was quite worried. She kept saying 'I do think we ought to ring up and . . .' but you know how it is, the days fly past and all the shopping before we came down here, it takes it out of you, you know I was so exhausted by the time we got here all I could do was just flop. I just flopped!" she said as she stepped out with the briskest energy on to the ground floor, Leo following. "Well this is

184

really fine! What a surprise! Oh, you're going to the synagogue. Well, I'll see you later. I must tell Doris you're here. She'll be so surprised." And she walked on into the brilliantly lighted lounge with her ungraceful, heavy tread, her large figure robed in elaborate black and topped with a sapphire mink cape.

To his relief he saw, when he and Joel sat down later on in the huge, silver-grey panelled dining room, that her table was some distance from theirs but a moment later recognized that he had under-rated her. Mrs Goldenbird, who would have done well in the '49 gold rush, noting with one practised glance that *two* obviously unattached men were at the table, sent Doris over to ask the Rabbi about his flu. He answered the girl pleasantly and introduced her to Joel, Mrs Goldenbird straining and looking and smiling as he did so and beaming with satisfaction as Doris returned to her seat.

The candles in silver candlesticks on every table flickered their pale, orange flames like butterflies in the great, hot, silvery, chandeliered room. Huge portions of magnificent food flashed from silver serving dishes to loaded plates. Diamonds glittered on the women's fingers.

Looking around Leo saw a great many people, some provincial, some from London, whom he already knew. Looking over to a distant corner Joel said: "Hallo! Manton's here!"

"Which Manton?"

"You know! *That* Manton. The Brain."

"Him!" said Leo. "Where? Oh yes, I see. One of the great financial geniuses of the century. And look at him!"

Both men gazed curiously at Manton who sat silent, motionless and alone at his secluded corner table, his vast, scored, ravaged face with its loose jowls expressionless, the hooded eyes torpid. It was impossible to guess his thoughts as he gazed out over the soft, brilliant luxury of the Berkeley dining room. Whether they were of the contrast between this place and others he had known, or whether, lost in the strange, calculating cells of his extraordinary mind, he hardly noticed the difference, no one knew. At no time during his stay did he speak to anyone save his waiter.

Half way through dinner, Mr Loeb, the proprietor of the hotel, came up to their table and said: "Dr Norberg. And Dr Fredlander. A Brains Trust this evening. I insist we have you on the panel.'

Both men attempted to refuse but he merely walked away leaving them laughing and shrugging helplessly. They knew Loeb of old. Almost penniless in the 'thirties he was now sole owner of this great hotel, diplomatic and amusing and efficient, ready for anything which would please his guests from crooning through the microphone with the resident dance orchestra to taking the chair at the Brains Trust later that evening.

This he did with an aplomb which Leo could not but admire. For some reason, perhaps his recent illness, disappointment, heartache, he did not enjoy being a panellist as much as he sometimes did. Facing the crowded, hot lounge after dinner, a wave of resentful futility swept him. He had to exert all his control to answer without irritability the usual questions. The other members of the improvised panel were a stockbroker, a smooth, black and white man, named, appropriately, Silky; a Polish woman lawyer, broad-featured and shrewd; another lawyer, Bresco, a pleasant young man; and—the only one listened to with respectful interest every time he opened his mouth—Dr Ellenberg, an American sociologist touring Europe with his mother.

A noticeable air of unrestraint pervaded the big, bright room. Here, surrounded only by each other, without so much as a waiter intruding his Gentile presence, well fed, entertained in an idiom uniquely and unmistakably their own, the peculiar, coarse, shrewd, restless yet curiously child-like Jewish vitality let itself go. Here, on this Friday evening, they could be themselves at last. For here, in a sense, was the womb. Here they were safe. Comfortably they called out from their easy chairs, interrupted the panel in the impatient, unceremonious Jewish way, got up, walked round, called across to each other, started private arguments, broke into Yiddish, exchanged dressmakers, wished each other Mazeltov, shouted "Shah!" to quieten their neighbours and disagreed with violent naïvety on the political questions.

The Panel, to all of whom this was familiar, remained imperturbable.

On the stroke of ten Loeb, who knew his customers, ended the session and they all dispersed to the next lounge where tea, coffee, chocolate and soft drinks, cheesecake, strudel and a dozen other cakes, and, above all, sandwiches and rolls with fillings ranging from smoked salmon to cream cheese were being taken round by the night waiters. The guests, who had all eaten their way through a whopping, six course dinner three hours before, with an immediate unanimity seldom observed in other aspects of Jewish behaviour, fell on the food with a magnificent abandon which reduced all conversation to a low hum. Leo, tired out and still for some reason he didn't himself understand, disgruntled, went off to bed almost immediately and so, to the chagrin of every mother and daughter in the room, did the American eligible, Dr Ellenberg. Joel, who rather enjoyed hotels, stayed up talking to Silky and one or two more till late.

"Has it ever occurred to you," said Joel over lunch the following day, "has it ever occurred to you, Leo, that a hotel like the Berkeley is just about the purest expression of democracy we could hope to find in an imperfect world?"

"I can't say that it has exactly," said Leo taking a spoonful of soup.

"Then consider. Consider first of all that everyone here is bound together in a particular, homogeneous mass in a way that no collection of guests in a non-Jewish hotel can ever be. In a way this is more like an ocean liner than a hotel. But a liner with only one class of cabin, that's the difference. Here, we all eat together, we are all entertained together, we all *pray* together. This morning, in *shool*, I had on one side of me a Mr Freiwinkel who told me—with pride mark you—(and why not?) that he has a good, little green-grocery business in Paddington. On my other side, saying his prayers with a sort of slick dignity—but I suppose that we ought to be grateful that he says them at all—was Mr Edward Silky, stock-broker to His Majesty, Carl Morris, our happiest millionaire (who, by the way, is also in Whytecliffe, staying at the Dorchester)."

"If it's millionaires you're after you won't have far to go," said Leo nodding towards the door as an elderly, dapper man came in followed by a nineteen year old boy. "Here's our ration. Leave it to Loeb to hook at least one. Wonder if he travelled down on Shabbos? —shame on him."

"No, do Rosenthal justice, he wouldn't do that. He's been in bed since Thursday. They told me last night he was here. But to go back to what I was saying . . . duckling please," he said to the waiter, "what could be more democratic than Mr Freiwinkel rubbing shoulders and exchanging a Yiddish crack with, let's say, Rosenthal. Granted that one's a Jew and the other's a Jew, there is after all a considerable difference between them. Our Mr Freiwinkel, prosperous enough to afford Loeb's prices once a year, nevertheless still lives over the shop and spends his life weighing carrots. Men like Rosenthal, to say nothing of Carl Morris, occupy positions, let us acknowledge it, of enormous power in the community. It's not just the millions, the mansions in Millionaires Row, the portraits in the Royal Academy, the Rolls-Bentleys and chauffeurs . . . It's the psychological grip they exert on the imagination. I assure you, when Silky told me (quite gratuitously, I didn't ask him) last night that he operates for Carl Morris, the great C.M., he blushed with pride. And yet I wouldn't mind betting that we see young Rosenthal doing the hokey-cokey or whatever they call it with Freiwinkel's daughter tonight. She's a pretty kid."

"Is she?" said Leo turning to look and turning back hurriedly as Mrs Goldenbird caught his eye and smiled largely.

Joel's theory may have been right but it soon became evident when the two men went out for the ritual after-tea walk (everyone was always too stupefied after a Berkeley Sabbath lunch to do more than sit about the garden till tea time) along the "diamond strip", as the flat stretch of road where the three main hotels were situated was only half-satirically nicknamed, that millionaires of a feather flock together. Up and down the few hundred yards (which closely resembled as was often pointed out, the Corniche) strolled Carl Morris, ruddy-cheeked, whitehaired, surprisingly aesthetic and gentle-looking for a tycoon, deep in conversation with the dapper Rosenthal, closely followed as they passed by the breeze of a thousand, sharply-turning heads and the puffing out of a thousand breaths of awe.

"Oy—oy—*oy*!" said the Whytecliffe visitors more to themselves than each other as outwardly, at least, a more ironic attitude (mid-twentieth century mores having made their mark) towards wealth was now the form.

All along the "strip" the Jewish holiday makers were greeting each other with the words: "Where are you staying?" The salt air

was filled with little puffs of shamefaced declarations, defiant assertions and, here and there, casual, name-dropping admissions by
guests of the Big Three. "Gone over," said some of the challenged
breezily "to Little Rock for a change." "Stayed on The Rock
hundreds of times," they hastened to add. The bedrooms at the
Grosvenor, they asserted, were too small. It was *too much*, they said,
all that food. "What's the good of it?" they asked with belligerent
common sense. "You pay all that and eat yourself ill trying to get
your money's worth." This year they were being sensible. How
much can you eat? What's wrong with the Southern? After all,
how much can you eat? Very comfortable. Very nice. Who wants
the Rock?

Visitors at the minor boarding houses crept about trying to look
invisible or went down into the town.

Leo and Joel had reached the Boulevard and were turning back
when Leo, exclaiming, detached himself suddenly from Joel and
went over to speak to an elderly woman sitting alone. Sitting down
beside her he turned and beckoned. When Joel came up he introduced him to Miss Wilmark.

"Wilmark?" said Joel as he lumberingly lowered himself on to
the bench. "That's a familiar name. Where have I heard it recently?"

"Last night, of course," said Leo. "During the discussion. Over
that question on Zionist leaders."

"*Of* course," said Joel. "We were actually discussing your . . .
brother?" Miss Wilmark gave a deprecating nod, " . . . for several
minutes. A very fine man."

"Thank you," she said in a faint, refined, wispy voice. Everything
about her save her eyes, which had that indefinably Semitic curve of
the lids, looked almost comically English spinster. She could have
walked straight on to the stage in any country house comedy, bony
figure, droopy clothes and anxious air; faded, refined and pathetic.

Leo was talking to her, asking (automatically) where she was
staying, had she recovered from her operation and how the hospital
where he had last seen her, in a public ward, had treated her.

"Oh very well, very well," she said in her faint voice, "and you
know, my own doctor was so kind, so kind. He came in twice to
see me. A personal visit, you know. Such a busy man. I was very
touched."

"Now why shouldn't he come and see his favourite patient?" said Leo gallantly.

"Oh, Dr Norberg," she said, her voice pink and fluttering, "I'm sure I'm not that. Though of course he's known me for many, many years. I remember my brother being one of his very first patients. He was very grateful—oh I remember it so well—to have the opportunity of attending such a famous man. It quite made him, he used to say."

"You don't take much part in Zionist affairs these days, Miss Wilmark?" said Joel.

"Not very much I'm afraid since my dear brother died. It hasn't been quite the same since, you see. Of course, *before* that," she said, her voice becoming stronger, "Zionism was my life. My whole life. I was my brother's secretary you know, and oh, I did have a full life of it. I travelled everywhere with him. They were great days, great days you know. Of course now we have Israel it isn't quite the same, is it? I mean, there isn't the same need for men like him is there?"

"There's still the same need," said Leo, "the trouble is we don't breed men like him any more." And he spent the next ten minutes talking to Miss Wilmark about her brother, to her enormous pleasure.

"Poor, pathetic old thing," he said after they had left her. "It's enough to break your heart, meeting these ghosts. Did you ever see Wilmark? What a remarkable man." And they spent the rest of their walk discussing with admiration and envy the early founders of Zionism, those legendary, towering figures of the movement's golden age when, with the spread of the "Haskalah", the "enlightenment" or Jewish renaissance running like a flame through Europe, there had emerged those marvellous men with their fiery intellect and juice and vigour, the great, rounded personalities flowering from the Ghettos of Eastern Europe and the universities of the West, to bear, like oaks, the enormous weight of the first foundations of modern Israel.

"What a time to have lived. What a cause to have lived for!" said Leo in a tone of passionate envy.

"And what luck," added Joel, "not to have the dreary aftermath of consolidation in this broken, shifting world. I suppose we have a few heroes still . . . but no giants. No giants left now. Only squabble and endurance."

"And recent millionaires," added Leo as they came in sight of Morris and Rosenthal again.

"They're not so bad. Not so bad," said Joel. "They have their own dignity. Hang it all, C.M.'s not someone we need be ashamed of."

And indeed, as they came abreast of the two millionaires, now halted and talking to an extremely elegant and well dressed couple, they heard Carl Morris speaking in a very excellent German with a most pure and lucid diction. Neither he nor Rosenthal looked anything like the popular conception of tycoonery, let alone the Jewish brand. Both men were quietly dressed and small featured but Morris's complexion was pink, he had been blond in his youth, and Rosenthal's was ivory, his hair black.

Arriving outside the Berkeley, Leo and Joel went in to prepare for dinner, as nearly everyone else was doing. Within half an hour the diamond strip was empty, the dying, pastel day left, deserted and beautiful, to wane to evening alone beside the soft, pearl-violet sea.

4

That evening, the Jewish Sabbath not being over till nearly ten o'clock, the regular Saturday night dance could not be begun until something like ten thirty. After dinner, therefore, Leo ensconced himself in a remote corner of the lounge and attempted to read. Almost immediately he found himself obliged to give up this idea, the noise making it impossible. Still holding his newspaper before him as protective cover, he let his eyes rove round the room, watching, with the clear, disengaged detachment which sometimes comes with depression of spirit, the antics of his fellows.

"What an impossible lot we are really," he thought looking at the young, business-men husbands with their stocky figures and wavy hair and well cut suits talking to each other in what looked like vivid conversations till one overheard the content, their wives talking to other wives with flourishes of jewelled fingers about their homes and children, always with the peculiarly used, emphasized, possessive "my" attached to everything. *My* cooker, *my* child, *my* refrigerator, *my* husband, *my* carpet. "God knows, the men are bad enough," he thought crossly, "but the women . . . !" And he said to Joel who had just sat down beside him: "Don't look now, but did you ever notice the faces of some of our women?"

Even as he spoke, a young woman, heavily made up with a fat face and yellow hair, beautifully dressed and wearing some magnificent rings, who was sitting near them, gave a wide yawn without bothering to cover her mouth. With one fat hand she tapped boredly on the arm of her chair.

"The men are decidedly better," said Joel, looking round with interest. "At least they wear better." In this he was correct. Jewish masculine faces, especially as they grow older, often appear to have great character. How interesting they look, those heavy-lidded eyes, those furrowed, swarthy cheeks, those bold, hawked noses and sensual lips. All this till they open their mouths. And then, what commonplaces of the mind are revealed behind those fascinating, wrecked features. At that moment, a Mr Berg, an older man with a dark, sardonic face, could be heard saying: "I'll tell y'. I used to hev a fency for a glass of water after me dinner, h'either with limmon or with h'orange. For years I hed it. Then one day I says to my doctor, 'Look 'ere,' I says . . ."

"Where they mostly fall down is the legs," said Leo, looking at some of the men standing about, their short legs bent in the typical, Jewish stance, with its cringing, yet vaunting element, their very trousers, so expertly tailored, looking deprecating, paid-for, defensive.

Mr Freiwinkel, behind Leo's shoulder, said heatedly to a man on the settee beside him: "Your son, 'e's a bloomin' liberty-taker, that's what 'e is. 'E comes knocking at my door eleven o'clock at night, takes ten quid off me for 'is bloomin' committee an' on toppa that I hass to give 'im a cuppa coffee!"

Leo yawned involuntarily.

"Bored already?" said Joel. "Snap out of it, my friend."

"Show me someone—apart, just possibly, from the three honeymoon couples we also have with us—someone who isn't bored."

Joel shrugged. "It's a matter of comparison. Are they more bored here than they are at home?"

"Yes," said Leo, "And I'll tell you why. Because ninety per cent of the people here don't know how to use time. They want to, you know. They are not beasts in the field. They want to *live*: but they don't know how. At first they think making money and spending it is the answer. They think having children is the answer. They think getting together in large crowds is the answer. As if a collection of bores ever succeed in doing anything but boring each other. This 'holiday' to them is one long, inward yawn. You think they want to get away from business worries? Or housekeeping and cooking? You couldn't be more mistaken. Why do so many spend so much time on making money? Because they don't know what else to do with themselves. It's a way of passing the time. We are a people racing with vitality and spinning in a vacuum. We are too efficient. We wrench, with a kind of frenzied eclecticism, the best out of everything and race on crying: 'Next! Next!' And there is no next, no ultimate perfection on which to rest in happiness. We —and when I say *we* I mean this particular slice of the bourgeoisie we see before us—are all rushing in the wrong direction towards a sated, frightened ennui. Like the rest of our society, of course . . . only, as usual, more so. Bored, bored. My dear Joel, you must take boredom seriously. It is the great, twentieth century problem. Boredom is important. You, for instance, happen to be lucky enough to be actively unhappy. The same, with minor reservations perhaps, applies to me. We are, therefore, in a sense, fortunate. We each have an occupation to keep us going. The majority of people in this room are not unhappy enough to really keep them busy. Oh yes, I know what you are going to say. We are all—to use that, by now, somewhat overworked phrase of Emerson's—'leading lives of quiet desperation'. I suppose even Silky (do look! he is talking so eagerly to Rosenthal, who isn't listening) has times when both bulls and bears momentarily lose their charm.

"What we lack," he continued, "is self-sufficiency. That hard core which endures the loneliness of thought, the responsibility of individual living. So . . . when there is so much not knowing what to do with ourselves, is it any wonder we lay stress on material things? After all, prices, qualities, manoeuvres (business or professional) they all help to fill the huge gap of being alive. This attitude, it is true, is certainly not confined to us. But with our people, bless them, even

193

their emptiness is spectacular. We can't even be bored quietly, like other people. We have to make a noise round it. Oh for an ounce of quiet contemplation! However," he added yawning again, "I heard lately of a Jewish Angling Society, which gives me some hope . . . though not for the fish who are now in for stirring times! Talking of fish——!" he said ducking his head suddenly . . .

Through the door sailed Mrs Goldenbird, magnificent in kingfisher blue. Leo hastily held his newspaper up before him but, fighting to keep Joel from rather meanly trying to grab it for the same purpose, divided they fell and Mrs Goldenbird marched formidably over, bared her slabs of teeth at them and sat down. "So that's where you two men are hiding!" she cried archly. "What's the matter with a little *female* company?"

"They won't any of them speak to us," said Leo solemnly.

"The girls won't speak to you!" she cried horrified. "What's the matter with them? Two nice men and the girls won't . . . You stay here," she said rising purposefully. "Now keep my chair. I'll soon get you some nice company." And she swung off to where Doris was sitting with two other young girls. "Come on!" they saw her say, "come with me. I've got a nice corner over here." And with an almost physical impression of pushing and pulling, she manoeuvred the girls across to where the two men were sitting, miraculously conjured up chairs in the packed lounge and sat herself down at last saying: "Now we're a nice little circle, aren't we? We can all stay together when the dancing starts."

A thought struck her. Turning to her daughter she said "We need another man! Doris, go and see where that American man is. Tell him to join us. D'you happen to know where that American professor is, Dr Norberg?"

Leo shook his head.

"Look in the other lounge," she said to Doris who went off and came back empty handed.

"Now where can I find you young people an extra man?" she said distracted, half stood up to peer round, sat down again, then stood right up saying: "I'll be back in a minute," and disappeared.

One of the girls spoke across the circle to Joel who, not hearing in the din, made a helpless "can't hear" gesture. "Sorry," he bellowed over to her, "you're sitting too far away."

"Then I'll come and sit nearer," she said promptly with a kind of acquired sprightliness which jarred on him, and moved with a bounce into Mrs Goldenbird's seat.

Joel, usually more taciturn than Leo, exerted himself to talk to her. This was not difficult to do, she chattered loudly with defiant, head-thrown-back laughs and many oddly middle-aged gestures, jerking about in her chair. Something, perhaps Leo's previous monologue, had affected Joel's critical faculty so that he found himself analysing the girl and her companions far more sharply than usual. They had, he saw, a curious and somehow tiring similarity. All three were simultaneously bouncy and stodgy. Their vitality was without style. Behind their fresh faces, their firm necks and expensive dresses, he could detect no glimmer of real ambition beyond a good marriage; for them there were no horizons, no sense of the marvellous, no rebellion even, nothing beyond the immediate and measureable. Yet two of them were university students, one doing science and the other law. Joel had come across this not infrequent phenomenon before: the Jewish student who passes through university life without apparently acquiring to the slightest degree either intellectual curiosity, academic polish, or the stamp of taste on his personality.

Mrs Goldenbird bore down on them again bearing in tow a young man she had somehow managed to winkle out of the television room. She proceeded to introduce him all round as Gerhard Ziegen, a refugee from the latest troubles in Central Europe. The young man, bewildered but polite, was drawn immediately into reciting his story of flight and danger and kind English relatives, speaking simply in his charming, broken, fluent English and punctuated with horrified Ohs and Ahs from Mrs Goldenbird. At one or two points Leo detected signs of genuine emotion, even moisture, in her bulging, cow-lidded eyes and decided that for all her absurdities she was not heartless. Indeed, considering that she had not hesitated to bring in the two other girls to what she called their "nice little circle" and exerted herself to make the numbers even, it seemed to him that she was both generous and kind.

As the evening wore on he found himself positively liking her and when, the Sabbath at last over and the dance begun in the white and gold ballroom, he good-naturedly gave her and all three of the girls a dance each before retiring to the same corner of the lounge. This was now completely empty, everyone, even the oldest of the old, Jewish women and doddering, throaty-voiced old men having made eagerly for the ballroom as soon as the music started, hardly able to wait till the manufactured entertainment began and they were relieved from one boredom into another. There they sat, silently lining the floor, watching the dancers, holding on, sleepy but determined not to miss anything, till the cabaret was due. Occasionally, when a teenage couple swung past they stirred, nodding towards the pair and whispering proudly to each other: "The future generation!": a phrase they clung to. "The future generation," said the old Jewish women again and again, the words relieving their inarticulateness, giving them comfort and the promise of their own immortality.

Apart from Leo, the only guests not in the ballroom were some of the richer men who had retired to a high-stake poker game in the sun lounge from which they did not emerge till the small hours of the morning.

Leo was thinking again of himself and his mood. It was unlike him not to enjoy a dance or the proximity of a pretty girl such as the little Freiwinkel who just then came in to retrieve the handbag she had left on a chair near where he was sitting. She smiled at him as she went past but he only nodded from where he sat, slumped and immovable in his deep chair, his chin on his chest, facing with dismay the knowledge that he had not the faintest desire to flirt with her. Once, he thought, every journey, every public event, every encounter had been attended by a hopeful magic which had transformed it. Now, sitting there in the brilliant, empty room, he faced for the first time the fact that that springing, charmed hope had gone for ever and that much of his persistent sadness and melancholy was for its end. Suddenly, for no reason, the image of Sara came before his mind's eye and with it, as it were, a switched-on light in a dark corner and he knew why his mood and temper had been so uncertain since he had arrived at Whytecliffe Sands. "I should have answered her," he said to himself, his face flushing. And he was deciding to go up to his room and do so there and then when Joel came in saying with exasperation: "Ach, there you are!

196

What is the matter with you, Leo? Usually it is you who drags *me* in to the dance. Anyway . . . you are to come immediately. The cabaret is starting. Well? Don't sit here by yourself. Come!"

With a resigned heave Leo lifted himself out of his easy chair and followed Joel back to the ballroom, Mrs Goldenbird greeting him with her large smile and patting the chair beside her. He sat down.

All the ballroom lights had been turned down, save for those over the orchestra platform and a half moon of empty floor in front. A young woman was crooning strongly through the microphone against a considerable background noise of chairs being shifted about and loud conversation at the back. She sang two numbers, announced the next turn, called for the lights to be turned up and disappeared. With a roll of drums four athletic men with bulging muscles and a young woman scarcely less bulging, all dressed in brief, rather tawdry, spangled costumes, sprang on to the floor and commenced a balancing act.

They had hardly been on three minutes before the background chatter had risen in volume to such an extent that the accompanying orchestra could hardly be heard. Loeb, who should have known better, had made a serious mistake in hiring that kind of turn for his clients. There are few emotional overtones discernible about feats of muscular strength and, unless truly prodigious and performed by a co-religionist from Stamford Hill, Jews bore rapidly at such entertainment. The din increased.

The girl acrobat hastily conferred with her partners and then with the bandleader. A crashing roll of drums reverberated through the room. In the momentary silence the girl stepped forward and asked in a rousing tone for a member of the audience to help with the next feat.

"Just one gentleman with a strong, right arm," she boomed. "Come along, gentlemen. Just one volunteer. Who's going to offer? You, sir? No? There is absolutely no danger, I assure you. *Come* along, ladies and gentlemen. Would any lady like to nominate her husband as being the possessor of a str—r—rong right arm?"

There were a few sporadic titters from the audience. Then, from somewhere near the back a smallish, oldish, thick-set, little man stood up and somewhat self-consciously waved his arm.

"*You*, sir? Now that's what I call sporting. Let's give him a hand, ladies and gentlemen."

The little man picked his way to the floor to the accompaniment of noisily ironic applause mingled with: "Didn't know you was a h'athlete, Sammy-boy."

"Now, sir," boomed the girl flexing his arm for him, "I'm going to ask you to do one very simple little thing. I'm going to ask you to stand in line with these two partners of mine, your right hand on Ted's left shoulder and your arm stretched *right* out and held firm. Got it?"

Sammy-boy nodded, grinning weakly at the audience, looking strangely incongruous standing there, his respectable, bourgeois world momentarily contiguous with the precarious, rackety, spangled world of the troupe. She got him into place on the right of the other two men standing in similar positions then, with a nod from her, the two remaining men jumped lightly on to the base of the pyramid of which Sammy made the bottom right-hand corner, remained poised for a moment, then the girl, leaping lightly from shoulder to shoulder stood at the apex, grasped the two hands held up to her on either side and slowly raised herself till she was balanced head down and feet up, holding herself straight as an arrow in the air. She had disengaged one hand and was rising, supported only by her right arm, Sammy-boy gritting his plastic teeth in the effort to keep his arm from wobbling when, into the comparative quiet there was a sudden violent eruption of sound and Sammy's wife, of whose absence he had evidently taken advantage, came rushing through the audience and on to the floor shouting: "Sammy! Sammy! What you doing? 'Im with 'is bed beck. Come out from there immediate. What you think you doing? 'E'll kill 'imself!"

There was a second's pause. The girl, balanced on one hand high above, wavered slightly. Sammy stood frozen with fright. Then there was a great roar of laughter over which Sammy's wife, taking not the slightest notice, continued to upbraid him in a voice which cut through the noise like a hatchet. Mr Loeb, quickly coming on to the floor, took her arm and tried to lead her off, speaking soothing words, not one of which could be heard. Defiantly she stood in front of the pyramid, her face, with its small nose and heavy chin, red, her grey hair frizzy, a dumpy, little woman screeching above

198

the screams of laughter: "Sammy! You want to kill yourself? What for the doctor give you treatment? You gone med?"

With two quick movements the girl swung herself down and on to the floor and the pyramid broke up, bowed and ran off to loud cheers. Blushing till he almost came out in flames, Sammy allowed himself to be pulled off the floor protesting, in vain, that: "It was nothing, mama. What for you want to make a fuss? Embarrassing me like I don't know what."

The entire audience had collapsed to such an extent that Loeb had to signal the next turn not to come on until, minutes later, something like order had been restored.

Leo, restless, took advantage of the pause to leave.

At last, with a tremendous roll of drums, Mr Micky Spivitz, that well-known, chubby-faced comedian, bounced on to the floor, took a bow at the applause which geeted him, rolled his hips at the microphone and, grasping it, began his act.

It was perhaps bad luck for him that none of his jokes could compete with the devastating turn which had just preceded him. In vain he told the one about the Jew and the packet of margarine, in vain he produced the ribald version of the Jewish little boy and the bus conductor . . . the house, normally delighted with Micky (though known to have married "out" to a blonde who'd been stooge to a conjuring act when he'd met her), remained sticky.

In desperation he decided at last to do what bitter experience should have warned him against. He tried to get them to sing.

"Now, folks," he shouted, "this is what I wan' y' to do. I'm going to sing the chorus of this new and very, very beautiful, romantic, new number which I have the honour of presenting for the first time to any audience and which I'm sure you're all gonna like— because, folks, this song is, believe me, the most fabulous, new number . . . I'm gonna sing it through once myself and then I want all those people in the first three rows to sing the *first* four lines, the people in the next three to sing the *middle* four lines, and all you loafers in the back—yah!—to sing the *last* four lines. Got it? Right. Take it away, Sid."

He began to sing.

The audience, temporarily exhausted perhaps, listened with no more than the average amount of background clamour till he had finished. It was when he rashly attempted to force the concerted effort that Mickly suddenly realized—too late—what he was up against.

"C'mon, c'mon," he roared at them. "First four lines, first three rows. Nah then! 'I *want* to *tell* you I love *you*'," he crooned swaying around the microphone. " 'The very *birds* could say the *words*, Which *I* can't *do*.' Come on you lazy *mamzers* . . . *again*! 'I *want*——' *Concentrate!*" he yelled. " 'My *heart* is *wit*-ness *that* it's true—ue—ue!' Na, na, na." He made a downwards, flapping gesture with his hands. The band paused.

"What's the madder wid yeh? Again, Sid!"

He burst out once more. " 'I *want* to *tell* you *I*—' ach! a bunch of no-goods . . . 'But-what-my-heart-would-say-my-lips-refuse-to-do'," he gabbled. "All right. Next four lines, next three rows. *Now!*"

He swung his hands up.

" 'Though *I* have *wan*dered *far* I *still*, Believe it's *you* and only *you* who'll *fit* the *bill*.' Cor! Stop it! You're breaking my 'eart. Worse than the first lot! I ought to know better at my time of life," he added bitterly. "The Yidden, God bless 'em. Worst audience in the world."

He was quite right. Not counting those who weren't listening, or holding private conversations or just walking about, his audience, in matters of this kind individualists to a man, were going their own way. A few of the younger people were making a half-hearted effort to keep the melody going, though even there deviationists among them were rocking it but, defeated by the middle-aged isolationists, they were gradually subsiding to a low, ground murmur. A well-known cantor, annoyed that Loeb hadn't asked *him* to perform, gave out a few trills from Tosca, stopped and waited for someone to beg him to go on. Nobody did. He started again with Pagliacci. "A word . . . allow me . . ." he sang on a deep chest note. Some original humorist started the Soldiers' Chorus from Faust. "Da . . . da da . . . dardiddy, dar . . . diddee!"

" 'If I could *find* some other *girl* to *whom* I'd *thrill*'," Micky belted into the microphone only to be drowned out, together with Pagliacci and Faust, by a group near the door who, suddenly catching a chance resemblance in a couple of notes to a Sabbath morning hymn, now chanted it out in Hebrew in something resembling unison.

"And Shalom Aleichem to you!" yelled Micky mopping his face. "*Last four lines.*" The band blared into the melody.

" 'I'll *look* into your *eyes* of *blue*'," he was bellowing when, unobtrusively at first, a new noise was joined to the general pandemonium.

Brought into the adjacent lounge too early by an inexperienced new waiter, the rattle of cups on the evening trolleys was heard, at first, only by a few at the back. With that fine community of impulse Micky had so far been begging for in vain, those within earshot at once dived rapidly for the next room. Within seconds, the news spreading, Micky found himself singing to scurrying backs. A swell like an ocean wave swept across the ballroom. Mrs Freiwinkel dropped her mink cape and was nearly trodden underfoot herself. Three chairs overturned. Sammy-boy, struggling against the tide to retrieve his wife's spectacle case, got swept out to sea again.

" 'Ere!" said Micky, his eyes popping at the rows of tables emptying at breakneck speed. Automatically coming in on the beat, he was just beginning the next line: "Your smile so sweet and tender too," when with good, Jewish, practical sense it occurred to him that it was no use going on to an almost vanished audience. He had half turned to signal the band to stop, his voice fading on "smile" had in fact almost ceased, when some deep-buried romanticism suddenly pushed up into Micky's consciousness the phrase "The show must go on" followed at once by so confusing a multitude of other attitudes that, involuntarily, he continued singing.

" '. . . so *sweet* and *ten*der too'," sang Micky, counting the house.

"Barmy! I must be barmy!" he thought, only to hear "good trouper" faintly chiming at him from another corner of his mind.

With a bang the two predominating strains in the Jewish character, common sense and the idealistic principle, collided in the soul of the chubby comedian from Stepney Green as he continued to sing.

"Stark crackers!" he said to himself. " 'Ere, pack it in!"

His voice wavered for a second time, then, as he felt the nuisance of spiritual pressure, strengthened again, and he gamely sang on. When it came to ultimate choice, Micky, true to his race, wobbled towards expediency but, in the last resort, settled for principle.

" 'Like *tur*tle *dov*es we'll *bill* and *coo*'," sang Micky, choosing, even after years of Tin Pan Alley, the ideal, the romantic and the moral way.

" 'Till in the *end* we'll *both* win through —oo—oo . . . '," he ended on a last, high sob.

The room was empty.

The cabaret was over.


Meanwhile Leo had found sanctuary in a corner of the television room occupied solely by one other refugee from the ballroom, a certain Mr Harmon. He settled down in the dark to watch in rather morose silence a fleshy-jawed, very self-assured, political commentator lecturing at the camera. Leo looked at him with some hostility; he was known principally amongst Jews (who too often used this one and only criterion about public faces) for his on-again off-again attitude towards Israel. As soon as the commentator had finished, stars exploded on to the screen and the advertisements began. With an exclamation of impatience Leo went over to the set and lowered the volume till it was inaudible.

"You don't mind?" he said with belated courtesy as he went back to his seat.

Mr Harmon gave what even in the semi-darkness could be discerned as the characteristic Jewish shrug and half lift of the hands.

"Not at all, Dr Norberg. Not at all. So long as you don't turn it down when my product appears."

"You use this medium?"

"Certainly. Why not? It gets results. Besides . . . I can't help myself. My rivals use it. If Harmon-y Clothes didn't advertise in every possible way what would become of my business? You've heard of them? Live in Harmon-y . . . you must have heard of our slogan surely?"

"Who hasn't?" said Leo.

"That's right," said Mr Harmon, highly pleased. "Ah! here it is!"

He went over to the set and turned up the sound and the two men sat watching the large screen where a tailored, wavy-haired young man in a dashing overcoat was talking to a tailored, smooth-haired young woman in an equally dashing sports coat.

"Do *you* want to live—IN HARMONY?" demanded an unseen inquirer. "Is everything between you—IN HARMONY? When you go out together—ARE YOU IN HARMONY? If not, why not go to the nearest HARMONY dealer—best shops everywhere stock them—NOW. Buy HARMONY—the clever, lovely clothes which make you feel so good—and make sure of a life filled with HARMONY. *Remember*— buy HARMONY clothes."

In rapid succession pictures of the young couple on a golf course, in a night club, round the fireside, moved across the screen. There was a rush of moronic voices up the scale and the advertisement vanished.

"Cost me two thousand," said Mr Harmon proudly, lowering the volume on the set again. Leo said nothing and, after moving restlessly in his chair for a few seconds, the manufacturer burst out: "I suppose, Dr Norberg, you are one of those who condemn advertising."

"Condemn?" said Leo startled. "Not at all."

"Ah, you say not to me perhaps. After all, I am a self-confessed sinner. A hard-headed business man. But tell the truth, Rabbi! In your heart of hearts you, a professional, learned man, despise business and everything to do with it."

"I assure you," said Leo thinking of certain Rabbis he knew who ran the "perks" side of their profession with the most business-like methods, "I assure you that a Rabbi is no more free of the instinct to make money and plenty of it, than any of your business col-leagues."

"You say that, Dr Norberg," cried Mr Harmon, the blue illumination from the television screen flickering light and dark shadow across his spectacled, round face as the pictures changed. "You say that, but . . . between you and me . . . you know very well that things are not *like* that. No. There are two worlds. Let's face it. Two worlds. Yours and mine."

Leo attempted a disclaimer but it was apparent that Mr Harmon was well away on his permanent hobby horse and it would have been a shame to take his argument away from him.

"But there is another way of putting it too. Oh yes! There is also, if you like," said Mr Harmon, not without a hearty laugh at such a preposterous idea, "there is also 'Ours' (yours and mine) and 'Theirs'. Now you take our world, Dr Norberg. Oh, I'm not speak- ing about the brainy side you understand," he threw in hurriedly, "excuse me, when I say 'our' world I am now speaking with regards to income; the two thousand a year and upwards people. Now take marmalade."

"Marmalade?" said Leo, taken aback by this new element in the class war.

"Marmalade," repeated Mr Harmon, nodding his head. His glasses flashed in the dark room. "Now tell me . . . what marmalade do you like for breakfast?"

When Leo told him he said, pouncing: "Exactly. I had an idea you'd say Keswick marmalade. And very good too. I like it myself. *Now*—tell me . . . *why* did you choose that particular one?"

"I don't know," said Leo shrugging. "I suppose my housekeeper tried it out on me and I told her to stick to it."

"And why did she try it?"

"I suppose she saw it ad——" said Leo without thinking.

"*Ex*—actly. There you have it, my friend. *Now*. Consider! Supposing your marmalade had not been advertised. Not that it wasn't being made! Oh no! Will you believe me, Rabbi, when I tell you that Keswick marmalade has been available for years. Where? I will tell you. At a few specialized shops up and down the country, Fortnum & Masons, a few others, who all got it from a little factory in Cumberland. And who knew about it up to two years ago?" he demanded rhetorically. "I'll tell you. The upper classes! That's who. This fine Keswick marmalade was the preserve—— ha, ha . . .!" He interrupted himself, laughing with great appreciation, "did you hear that? That wasn't bad though I say it myself. Ah well, they say punning is the lowest form of humour . . . was the *preserve*, the privilege we might say, of the few. And why? Because the others, even you and I in the upper income brackets as they say, *had never heard of it*! How should we? Do we go to Fortnum's for our groceries? There was no one to tell us. Who was to tell us? Who've our class of people got around to tell 'em where to go for the best? We only know each other. You get my meaning? You've got the money, I've got the money, come to that these days everybody's got the money. What we haven't got is the 'know-where'. See what I mean? Plenty of know-how about. Take my word for it, we all know how in this day and age. But to know *where* . . . A different story, Dr Norberg. A different story. To know where to look for the best . . . that's not so easy as it sounds. Easy for the upper classes with their Gleneagles and their clubs and posh restaurants . . . they've been eating Keswick marmalade all their lives most likely. But . . . granted we've got the money to buy it (double the price of an ordinary jar, don't forget) who's going to tell us about it? And now we come back to where we came in. *Advertising*, Rabbi! Advertising! Telling the world. Look! here's something good. Expensive—but good. And for two years people have been finding out about something good. Maybe if you're born upper class you can afford to despise advertising. Maybe if you get your suits from Savile Row—to take my own business as example—Harmony clothes don't matter. But to ordinary, comfortably off people, my advertisements telling them where to look for something good is doing a service. And my stuff's wonderful value, Dr Norberg," he said in a tone of such passionate sincerity as to remove the indulgent smile from Leo's face. "I don't put out nothing but the best. Pricey but good's my motto. Even the Yidden wear my clothes!" he said, bursting out laughing again. "Well anyway, who's going to know about the best if nobody tells them? That's my argument. I daresay to the cultured, high-falutin' high-ups, advertising *is* shocking, bringing everything down to this what you may call mass-level. I daresay the manufacturer of Keswick marmalade feels a bit ashamed of himself making so much money because he's made available a quality product to a large public. *He* may not think he's done a public service. But I do!"

Leo, who, like most intellectuals, automatically despised advertising, could not help seeing a certain sense and logic beneath Mr Harmon's fuzzy rhetoric. Being—unlike most of his colleagues—well read in English literature, he also was able to identify a certain Forsterian echo in the little business man's remarks. Nevertheless he felt a certain necessity to argue back.

"The point is," he said, "not that advertising but *over*-advertising is bad."

"Could you draw me a dividing line clearly showing exactly where the advertisers ought to stop?" demanded Mr Harmon. "Come now, Dr Norberg, you know as well as I do . . . people are thick-headed. If you want them to take notice you've got to drum it into their heads. And even then, if they don't want it they won't have it. In my experience you can plug a product just so far. And if it's no good it won't take, no matter what you tell 'em. Even if it's good—if they won't bite . . ." He made a thumbs down gesture.

"I still think," said Leo, rather haughtily enjoying a sense of superiority towards Mr Harmon, "that there is something in a way morally wrong about attempting to force a commodity on to someone who can do just as well without it."

"Ah," said Mr Harmon who was enjoying this argument with a learned Rabbi very much, "Ah! now without any disrespect, Dr Norberg, couldn't I equally say the same to you? What——" he raised an almost invisible forefinger in the semi-dark to where it stood out, a dark, stubby silhouette, against a line of chorus girls waggling the feathers on their behinds across the screen, "what are *you* doing every Shabbos morning from the pulpit? Selling something! Same as me! You believe in your product. I believe in mine. *You* say . . . do this, believe like that—and you'll feel better, live better, die better, maybe. And I say to you—I'm speaking metaphorically mind—I say to you . . . Why? I can live just as well without doing everything you're telling me to do. And you say, 'Ah, but you don't know what you're missing'. And I say . . . well, what I say is, whether it's the best marmalade or the best overcoats or the best religion—people have got to be told about it. People have to *know*," he said with real passion in his voice. "There shouldn't be any keeping it to themselves about what's good. That's my belief, Dr Norberg."

"Or what's bad?"

"You make the good, good value," he said chuckling. "You'll see. I'm a manufacturer. I *know*."

"It seems to me," said Leo, feeling a little ashamed of his private attempts to remain superior to Mr Harmon, "that you are as much philosopher as manufacturer."

Even in the faint, blue light it was possible to see that the little man's expression had changed.

"Now, Dr Norberg," he began, all the beam and animation gone from his face, "you mustn't laugh at me."

"Laugh at you! Nothing could be further——"

"I know very well that to a learned man like yourself I must

206

sound like an ignoramus. After all, what am I? A business man. No education, no learning . . . Excuse me, I talk too much."

"On the contrary," said Leo warmly, regretting more than ever his somewhat condescending, mental attitude to Mr Harmon which the man had been quite sensitive enough to be affected by, "I find what you say extraordinarily interesting. You over-rate the academic approach I think——" He stopped abruptly, sensing, though he could not properly see, that Mr Harmon was made even more uneasy by the very words in which he was expressing himself. Something in his very slightly "educated" response had immediately and regrettably lowered the temperature. This was not a new problem to him. He had found it indeed almost impossible to discover a way of getting on with the Mr Harmons of his congregation. If he spoke to them strictly in their own idiom they slightly despised *him*, wondered if the community was getting value for its money and felt uneasily that they were overpaying for what could have been picked up cheap in the January sales. If, on the other hand, he attempted as now to speak in a slightly more cultivated language of ideas, he was invariably brought up sharp by hurried disclaimers.

"I'm afraid I don't know much about philosophy, Dr Norberg. Always been too busy earning a living to read much."

"We—ell! that doesn't matter," said Leo with exaggerated heartiness. "Books aren't all that imp——"

"I used to, mind you! My father, God rest his soul, was always in a book. I used to read quite a bit myself when I was younger. Don't seem to get the time for it these days."

Leo restrained a somewhat impatient sigh. Often as he heard this remark it never failed to irritate him. Then, still determined to try to restore to Mr Harmon his *amour propre*, he said: "I must tell you that what you have been telling me just now bears far more directly on to *real* philosophy and allied subjects than many of the books which are supposed to have been written about them. Indeed, it is people like you Mr Harmon, who know far more about, say, sociological trends . . ." he stopped again, seeing himself once more on the edge of linguistic difficulties. Mr Harmon had removed himself into a kind of bristling inattentiveness. Suddenly he burst out with: "To tell you the truth, Rabbi, I can't make head or tail of these 'ologies'."

"Oh now," said Leo impatiently. "A man who can talk so sens——"

"In my own field," cried Mr Harmon stubbornly, "I can tell you a thing or two. I won't deny it. But the minute you bring in all these learned words, the minute you make a thing . . . make a thing . . ." he groped for the phrase. "Abstract?" said Leo. "Yes, Abstract! Y'see! I can't even express myself!"

"I repeat. A man as intelligent as yourself . . ."

But it was no use. Mr Harmon, successful, round-faced, merrily talkative, would not be praised. A deep sense of *lack*, of falling short, reacted with terror to the responsibility of living up to praise and long words. It was a relief to Leo when, glancing at his watch in the dim light, the man said: "Time for evening tea, I think. I could do with a sandwich. One thing you've gotta say for Loeb— he gives good value!" And he went off, leaving Leo, who was deeply vexed with himself—and not for the first time—for his failure with the common touch, to follow.

5

Joel jumped to his feet. "Well I never!" he said and, moving with unusual haste, made for the door of the lounge and disappeared into the entrance hall. He did not reappear again for nearly twenty minutes. Leo sat on, listening idly to the conversation going on around him. Even in Whytecliffe Sands the weather, which had been uniformly nasty all over the country that summer, was bad. He and Joel had been there a week and were due to leave in two days time . . . for which he was neither glad nor sorry, having sunk into a state of apathy (helped by the Berkeley's enormous meals) where almost any effort seemed not worth the trouble. Even Mrs Golden- bird had practically ceased trying to entice him into corners "with our little lot" as she put it. She had failed with the American pro- fessor too but had managed to retain the refugee, Gerhard Ziegen, and had collared the young lawyer who had been on the Brains Trust, together with an old bachelor from Hull.

She was sitting near Leo now, not with her "little lot" whom she had sent out to play clock golf on this damp, Friday afternoon, but with some older people. Every now and then she gave him a bright smile though he had politely refused her invitation to "join our circle".

Mr Freiwinkel and his wife were telling her and another couple about an afternoon trip they had made during the week to a stately home near Whytecliffe Sands. "Fine place," he was saying with a knowing, sideways jerk of his head. "Fine place. No denying—it's a fine place. Wouldn't like to pay the rates on it though!"

"Very intrisstin'," said his wife. "Only Hymie would leave his pullover in the car. I told him he'd feel the damp, all them stone passages."

"You know what?" he said. "We saw the owner! Lord La-di dah, himself. Fine looking chap. Saw him face to face!" A note of vast respect came into his voice. "Very old family that. Good class." He shook his head. "No getting away from it. Good class."

"Oh you and your class, Hymie. Got a bee in his bonnet about good class."

"We—e—ell," he said self-consciously, "y'know, sometimes it's good to see how the other half lives."

"For an afternoon he likes to see how the other half lives! Any longer than that and he's screaming to get back to Yiddish people again. Your own's your own, after all. Here! Tell them about that place in Devon, Hymie. Last year my Hymie decides he wants to go all posh and go motoring for an 'oliday staying where we felt like each night, y'see. Went all over Devon and Cornwall. D'you think he enjoyed it! Past Torquay not a kosher meal to be had for love nor money. We don't eat no *treifa* you know. I didn't mind it you know . . . but my husband! He wasn't so thrilled. He likes his Jewish food, bless him. *Anyway*: in the wilds, what can you do? So we had to eat vegetarian wherever we went. And did we find ourselves in some places . . .! Hymie! tell them about that place we went to. You know. This was a *real* vegetarian place," she said to Mrs Goldenbird and Mr and Mrs Brinkman with an anticipatory smile. "Just listen to this!"

"You never seen nothing like it," said her husband excitedly, leaning forward in his chair. "In the ordinary hotels so if we didn't eat meat or poultry we had fish, we had eggs, we had omelettes . . . you can't starve. But when we gets to this village out on the open moor, not another place in sight, right off the map I'm tellin' y' . . .

and it's coming on night . . . So then we see this sign up saying Vegetarian Guest House and Florrie she says to me, Let's try it. So . . . what can you lose? For one night? So I said O.K. let's try it. But if I'd known what we was in for!" He clapped his hand dramatically to his head.

"Wasn't it strictly vegetarian then?" said Mrs Brinkman. She had dark hair and a big, handsome face with square, clean-cut features, but wore a permanently depressed expression. She and her husband were both fairly young and obviously well off—she wore a beautiful diamond and emerald brooch on her blue, cashmere cardigan—but he too had this same gloomy, distrustful look, as if he didn't trust life an inch.

"Not strictly! *That's* a joke," said Mr Freiwinkel.

"It was that strict," broke in his wife hardly able to contain herself, "it was *that strict* they didn't even eat eggs! I'm telling you, a Chief Rabbi could've eaten there!"

"You've never seen anything like it," said her husband. "No fish! No eggs! I'll tell you something better still! I come down for breakfast in the morning——" he paused for full dramatic effect, "and what d'you think I get?" he said nodding his head up and down with an expression of ironic patience. "Greengages!"

"Greengages?" cried out Mrs Goldenbird aghast.

"By my life. Greengages! *Oy gewalt!*" he said with an appalled lifting of his hand which he again clapped to his forehead.

"I told you!" said Mrs Freiwinkel. "A Chief Rabbi could've eaten there! I tell y' . . . we had some experiences . . .!"

"Listen," said Mr Brinkman bending his gloomy face nearer. "Nothing worse should happen to you. If that's all you have to suffer in life . . . a few greengages . . . say Thank God and leave it like that."

"Thank God I say also," said Mr Freiwinkel. "Believe me, I don't complain. I've got a nice business in the greengrocery line, I've got a good wife, a nice daughter . . . Please God, some day I have grandchildren . . . I'm satisfied," he said with a prolonged shrug right up to his ears. "And if sometimes a little thing don' go right, well . . . there's others worse off I say to myself."

"Yes," said Mrs Brinkman with a profound sigh, "life's a funny thing. Some have all the luck and some have all the kicks. Have y' noticed how some people are so made they get just what they want? You take my sister-in-law. She so lucky; whatever she wants comes to her. I should live so. She on'y has to ask—she don' have to *ask* even—and it falls into her hands. And other people . . . whatever they do don' come right. She wants a big Jaguar car (a Vauxhall's not good enough awready) she gets a Jaguar. 'Er little boy, he's so clever awready, at ten years of age 'e's top of everything. 'E carn go no higher where he is. 'E *won* everything. And the daughter! Married at eighteen to a fella 'is father owns thirty-eight shops! All over the country! That's a luck for you? And my sister-in-law's *sister* . . . just the opposite! That poor soul struggling along, an ailing husband . . ." she swayed her head heavily from side to side, "and *she* has to lose a child. A beauty, I'm tellin' you. You never seen in your life a child like that boy. Well? Can you ask questions? I'm asking you? Can you ask questions?"

"You can ask questions," said Mrs Goldenbird who had been listening with sorrowful, head-shaking attention, "you can ask questions." And then she added with that peculiar, mournful poetry which so disconcertingly crops up from time to time in even the coarsest-fibred Jew: "But who's going to answer them? We ask questions from God. But God doesn't answer."

A young married woman came up and joined their group. "You haven't seen my husband?" she said sitting down.

"You lost him awready?" said Mr Freiwinkel with a guffaw. "You on'y been married two year! An' awready he's run off from you?"

"Oh, 'ush, Hymie," said his wife, worried lest he should be taken seriously.

"A pretty girl like you don' have no need to worry," he added hastily at once, beset by the same fear.

"If my husband wants to run off he can," said the young woman tossing her head. "Two can play at that game you know."

They all screamed with laughter.

"Well all I know," said Mrs Goldenbird in her forceful, nasal voice, "if you want to play games like that then it's no good coming to Whytecliffe. It's not Brighton."

"That's what I like about here," said Mrs Brinkman, looking more miserable than ever, "it's very select."

"Ah, now there you got something. I've said the same to my wife many a time. You can keep your Sarthends and your Waistcliffs. I like a place that's refined."

"Now Eastbourne," said Mrs Freiwinkel, "that's all right. If you go to the right part that is. There's a little bit not so . . . but Hymie and me, we always say, after Whytecliffe—then Eastbourne. Qui—et, refined; it's a pleasure."

"A real pleasure," he concurred.

Leo, who was still listening, and who had heard Mr Freiwinkel at an impromptu concert the night before start singing a song which began: "It's a secret between me an' my laundry . . ." before his wife had hurriedly checked him, smiled to himself.

". . . and fitted carpets in every room. Right to the wall," said Mrs Brinkman who was back on her sister-in-law. "I know for a fact she was paying sixteen pounds a week for that flat. And what about the thousand she paid goin' in? For nothing, I give you my word. Bare walls. They even cut the electric wires off at the ceilin'."

Mr Harmon who was making his way past the group paused and hit Mr Freiwinkel on the shoulder. "Well! how's the world treating you?" he said.

"It's not treatin' me at all," said Mr Freiwinkel. "No one's treatin' me. I'm payin' for meself."

This exchange evoked a great wheezy "heh-heh" from everyone.

"You met my daughter?" said Mr Harmon, pushing forward a fat little girl in a ruby velvet frock.

"Is this *your* daughter? Ah! bless her!" The women fell on her with loud cries of praise. "A lovely child, *ke nein hora*. Come here, sweetheart. That's right, darlin'. How old are yer?"

An elderly, stooping, grey-faced man who had been working his way steadily round the room for the last half-hour now approached the group. In a low voice he asked them to donate a little something towards a Jewish old people's home which was finding itself new premises. Without a moment's hesitation the men dived into their pockets and the women into their handbags.

"You been to the Grosvenor yet?" said Mr Harmon, handing over a note.

"Next. Next," said the man. "I've just come from the Dorchester."

"How much d'you collect there?" said Mr Harmon alertly.

The man fumbled with his receipt book. "Nearly forty," he said at last.

"And how much here?"

"So far just over thirty."

"Wait a minute," said Mr Harmon pulling out his cheque book. "Here." And he handed over a cheque for another two guineas.

"I remember," he said after the collector had gone, "I remember," he repeated with a sigh and a rueful nodding of his head, "my father, God rest his soul. He died just when I started making my way. Never had a chance to make it up to him. Ach, the poverty he had to live through. Hard and bitter. Hard and bitter."

"Don't we all know," said Mrs Goldenbird. "That's one thing your little Freda there won't have to go through, Thank God."

Everyone gazed after the child with fond smiles when her father at last led her away.

Joel returned and cast himself back in his chair.

"Would you believe it," he said turning immediately to Leo. "You'll never guess who's arrived. I couldn't believe my eyes when I saw her through the door. Zella! Tarsch's sister! I didn't even know she was coming to England. He never told me. Of course I haven't seen him for nearly a month. She only arrived a week ago from New York. Well I never! You could have knocked me down with a ton of bricks! And as beautiful as ever. You'll see her at dinner tonight. She's gone up to unpack."

"What was she doing in the States?"

"Her second husband was an American. He died about a year ago. Poor girl. She's had a lousy time of it. Apparently she's not crazy about America. She wants to settle down over here again. I gather she's been left pretty comfortably off. But as she says, what's the good of money when you're lonely?"

"No children?"

"No. No luck there either. However, perhaps it's just as well. She was a bit restless at one time, Zella. But she says that's all over now. All she wants is peace and quiet."

Zella Harris may have wanted peace and quiet but her incessant conversation made no contribution towards that state. Leo was also disappointed in other directions when he met her that evening. How Joel could have thought her still beautiful mystified him. At one time perhaps those five proposals she had received—or so the legend went—at one week-end school, might conceivably have really taken place. But now . . . Leo looked searchingly at her discontented, pinched features, at the blue-lidded, hard-expressioned eyes and touched-up, blonde hair, tight and dry. By what stretch of the old magic could Joel still see in her the blonde, small-featured beauty he had once known?

Her talk was as dry and tight as her hair; full of factual, trite little statements about life in America: "They know how to live over there. Of course it's a pretty vast country you know. They got pretty vast resources. You wanna see some of the hotels down in Florida. Just out of this world. That whole set up they have over there, so luxurious it just isn't true. This place is nothing, just *nothing* in comparison."

When she talked about herself her voice became complaining and martyred. "I've spent too much of my life sacrificing myself for other people. From now on I'm decided on looking after Number One. If you don't look out for yourself nobody else will."

After a time, she stood up. She was still very slim with elegant feet and ankles. She wore a good deal of genuine jewellery. The two men also rose politely to their feet: a point of etiquette not always observed too rigorously amongst Jewish men. "Excuse me," she said, "but I guess I'll go to bed early my first evening. See you around in the morning. When're you two going back?"

"Sunday," said Joel.

"Too bad you're not staying on another week. Still, maybe I'll see something of you in town. Oh, I forgot," she said to Joel. "You're actually living at my brother's place. I'll be coming down to stay with him soon as they get back from their vacation. Be seeing you anyway. Good night."

"Good night," they said.

They sat down again.

"Poor old Zella," said Joel thoughtfully. "You can see she's had a hard time of it."

"She hasn't done so badly," said Leo in a rather sardonic voice.

Joel, failing to notice, shook his head compassionately several times, his lined features and pale blue eyes suffused with sympathy.

On the Sunday they went home.

# Chapter Eight

## I

"**I**-ORDER-YOU," SAID MR GABRIEL, GRINDING OUT the words with a wild ferocity, his eyes glittering and inflamed. "*No!*" said Sara.

He turned back to the bureau in the living room, every drawer of which he had pulled out to empty its contents—old letters and papers—in an enormous, confused heap on to the table. He rooted in the pigeon holes, dragged out some soiled envelopes and cast them on top of the heap. Then he sat himself down at the table and began, aimlessly, with trembling fingers to sort and tear up one letter after another, hardly able to see what he was doing, his eyes blind with rage.

Suddenly he sprang up again. "I do it myself," he said and running outside to the linen closet in the hall Sara heard him fumbling and gasping amongst the shelves. He came back with an armful of sheets. Dragging a chair to the fireplace he sprang on to it and proceeded to drape a sheet right across the mirror which hung over it, completely obscuring even the wooden frame. He jumped down and did the same to the old-fashioned, mirror back of their sideboard. Sara watched him in silence. Then he went out of the room carrying the rest of the sheets. Sinking down on to the settee she sat staring in front of her listening to the sounds of her father's progress from room to room of the house covering all the mirrors. This is a custom of the Jews during the week of mourning after a death.

When Mr Gabriel came back into the living room he had put on his slippers. Bringing a low stool with him he sat down on it and began reciting the *Kaddish*, the prayer for the dead. These too, the wearing of slippers, the sitting on low seats, are Jewish mourning customs.

But there had been no death in Boruch Gabriel's house: only what, to fanatically orthodox men like him, had to be treated as such. His daughter had run off and married a Gentile. For half an hour the old man sat, beating his breast from time to time and praying in angry, broken spurts of sound which rose and fell in the quiet room. Then he rose and went out again.

Sara sat, as she had sat or lain during the last twenty-four hours, rigid, numb, in a ceaseless confusion of meaningless thoughts and broken images dissolving into each other, mute cries breaking from her brain. "Essie. Essie. Essie," she called wordlessly. And again: "Essie. Essie. Essie."

She had left a note. "All I regret in this is *your* pain. Nothing else. Forgive me what I am doing to *you* my dearest sister. I was married today to a man called Kenneth Groby—not a Jew. We are flying in a few hours to Canada. I think I will be—perhaps happy, perhaps not. I don't know. But in any case there was nothing else to do—except grow old. I have left another letter for him so that you won't have to break the news yourself. That is the only thing I can do for you. Please don't worry about me. *Above all, don't worry about me.* I will write. Don't worry. Essie."

There was the noise of a door opening and she looked up to see her brother-in-law, Monty, who had come in by the back door, enter the room. For once he spoke directly to the point.

"I'm not letting Rebecca come," he said.

Sara moved her head sideways. "You're quite right," she said tonelessly.

"What I meantersay is," he said, "it's going too far. I'm not saying he's not justified. For Essie to——"

"I don't want to discuss Essie," she said in a precise voice.

"All right. If you don't want to you don't want to. Have it your own way. But Pa's taking it too far. It's crazy, that's what it is. After all, it's modern times. To sit *shiva* for a marriage out belongs in the dark ages."

He walked slackly about the room but his voice was decidedly and surprisingly firm. "Anyway, I won't let Rebecca do it. She's not too well anyway."

"What's the matter with her?" she asked but Monty was evasive. "Och just one of these . . . I dunno . . ." he mumbled.

"A diplomatic illness?" said Sara with a hint of sarcasm.

"Eh?" Not understanding he let it go. "Where's Fagy?"

Sara looked up and gave him a faintly bitter smile. "Fagy? As usual, the lucky one in our family. She left for France three hours before we found—— You knew she was going," she said impatiently.

"I forgot," he said looking vague.

"To the European-Israeli summer school; outside Paris."

"Yes, I remember now."

"Father wanted me to wire her to come back. That at least I stopped.

"So you're on your own with him?"

"Yes," she said. "I'm on my own with him."

"Well," he said moving unobtrusively towards the door, "let me know if there's anything I can do."

"Yes," she said again with a touch of sarcasm. "I'll let you know."

Mr Gabriel's footsteps were heard descending the stairs and Monty hastily went out, as he had come, by the back door. Mr Gabriel, entering, made again for the huge, disordered pile of papers on the table, sat down and began tearing, his motions regular, bitten, frenzied. There was no sound in that ugly room, only the old man's panting breath, the rustle of paper and the regular, tearing, violent r—r—rip, r—r—rip of destruction.

Suddenly he flung himself up again and, grabbing at a prayer book, thrust it before her eyes. "Say the *Kaddish*," he said. "Say the *Kaddish*. Mourn for the death of your sister."

She pushed the prayer book away with a movement as violent as his.

"*You too!*" he screamed. "You too will destroy me!"

"It is you——" she began and then stopped. "Father," she said more gently. "Do not make things worse. I am unhappy enough."

"*You* are unhappy! You! Then what I must say? I have brought into the world one sinner. Must I have *two*? Two children sinners? Say the *Kaddish*. Make amends to me, your father. And to God," he added as an afterthought.

An ironical laugh choked itself inside her.

"What have *I* done?" she said at last looking at him steadily.

"You could have stopped her. You are to blame. Oh, I know. I know! It was a conspiracy. You helped her. It was a conspiracy between you to defy me, your father."

"I knew nothing," she cried.

218

"You! You! You encouraged her to mix with *Goyyim*, to go to classes . . ."

She moved uneasily and he pounced. "You see! where else could she have met this . . . this . . . *devil?* You made her go. You knew everything. You could have stopped her. Make amends to God," he screamed at her and thrust the prayer book into her hands again.

This time she held it, her eyes looking blankly at the open page. "Could I have prevented what has happened?" she said to herself. "The night she asked me to help her. She was sitting . . . where was she sitting, this side of the table? No, the other side . . . or was it . . .? No, the other side. I sat this side facing her. 'Help me,' she said. What did I . . .? If I had *known*. How could I have known what was in her mind? She asked me for help. And I was dry, dry. Self-righteous. He is right. It *was* my fault. I encouraged her. I wanted her, at least, to break from this outmoded bondage. I wanted her escape. But to lead to this! No, that I never envisaged. There is no controlling the consequences of what we do. Wrong as he is he was right. I was too arrogant, too arrogant . . ."

"Say the *Kaddish*!" said her father again. He had been standing by the bookcase with his back to the room, but, swinging round on the words, he flung out his arm in an utterly absurd, theatrical gesture and pointed and shook his finger at her. She stared at him coldly through the melodramatics of the situation he was trying to contrive. Incensed by her gaze, foolish as ever, instead of withdrawing before it was too late, he went too far.

"Will you defy the Almighty . . ." he began in a lofty, sombre voice. But he advanced towards her at the same time with a kind of little, skipping step so badly at odds with his manner that a shiver of furious distaste swept over her.

"Stop enjoying yourself," she said in an icy, cutting tone.

He stopped dead and gave her a look of hatred.

"You're glad this has happened," she said, losing some of her habitual control. "You've got a made to measure grievance at long last. You've been looking for an excuse like this all your life. Haven't you? Haven't you? It is your delight to see life wretched, to see human beings unhappy and driven. It's the only time you feel equal, isn't it?"

"Mad! Mad!" he ground out at her, smashing his fist down on

219

the table between them. "One child bad. And the other one *mad* and bad."

"Stop play-acting!"

"Acting! Is my shame, my disgrace, *play-acting*? A daughter throws me and my religion in the gutter and spits on it! And you say I am *play-acting*!" He sank down on to a chair and, covering his face with his hands, began rocking backwards and forwards.

With an effort, steadying herself, she went over to him and tried to pull his hands away. "Father, father," she said to him, "this will not help. Do you think I *wanted* Essie to do this thing?"

Dragging one of his hands down she saw that he was weeping, the tears running down his sharp, red-veined features. With a kind of enormous, painful decision she threw herself into a belief in his real suffering.

"It is something which has happened," she said. "It has happened. We must learn to bear it; live with it; forgive it——"

"Forgive!" cried Mr Gabriel, who had begun to sob as soon as he saw that his genuine tears were having an effect. "Forgive! Forgive who? There is no one to forgive. Your sister is dead. In her grave. I have only mourning for the rest of my days." Carried away once more by the irresistible, dramatic angle, unable to refrain from over-doing it, he again managed to squander the capital of his genuine grief. Seizing the prayer book he tried to thrust it on to Sara. "Mourn! mourn!" he cried.

Oddly, he almost won.

An emotional exhaustion suddenly falling upon her, weakening her sense and balance, she began to feel a kind of superstitious soft-ness, a need for propitiation sweeping over her. It would have been a relief to have fallen, weeping and child-like, into the soft, con-soling sands of guilt. A sense of sin, the pull and mysterious force of race-memory, of dark Bible-fears, of thousands of years of Jewish crime and punishment and guilt, of repentance struck repeatedly by God out of the rock of their intransigence . . . all these sucked suddenly at her will.

Her father's hand clutched her shoulder. She shivered, once, with disgust. Then she pushed away the book and rose swiftly to her feet.

"*No!*" she said. "I will not call my sister dead." And going out left her father alone.

The weather at last was changing. With the best of summer half gone, the grey skies cleared, the persistent rain and chill hesitated, hovered in the air, then ceased. Within two days the temperature shot up to the seventies. By the time Leo's holiday was over it was hot with every prospect of getting hotter.

Early on the Sunday morning Leo drove himself and Joel back to London from Whytecliffe Sands and deposited the latter at Liverpool Street station. His housekeeper, who had also been on holiday, not being due back till the following day, he then went into a Jewish restaurant near Oxford Street for lunch. On the way out he stopped to speak to and congratulate two members of his Synagogue Guild who had just become engaged. Accepting his good wishes they told him, casually, that Sophie Olendorf, another member of the Guild —did he remember her?—had also become engaged that same week.

He knew the young man slightly. He was an Israeli, an uncompromising, rather poorly circumstanced student pushing himself ahead to an English law degree by sheer, blunt will-power.

For the first moment or two Leo couldn't believe his ears. For a while he had hardly thought of Sophie except to congratulate himself on not thinking of her. He had believed himself, after the final disappointment of the note he'd thought had come from her, to be over it. He was totally unprepared therefore for the swift, lashing panic which now took hold of him. Getting into his car he drove blindly home.

Once there he didn't know what to do with himself. His Sundays, winter and summer, were usually packed with meetings he had to attend, but on this particular day, as if in ironic preparation, he found he had the afternoon empty. Restless, pushing the pain away and trying not to think, he went upstairs and stood looking out of his bedroom window. It was a blazingly hot day. He looked out at the long, quiet street where he lived. Not a soul was about on this Sunday afternoon. The pretty, suburban, red and cream houses lay quiet in their green gardens. The heavy, yellow sunshine pressed flat over London. Everything drowsed and lay still, grave and quiet in the heat.

He moved away from the window and went downstairs again,

a lumbering fat man, descending with careful deliberation as if deep in thought. He paused for a moment in the hall. It too was filled with sunshine. He walked into his dining room and looked around it, at the old-fashioned foreign furniture his mother had brought with her from abroad and been so proud of. The dark, shining wood of the bow-fronted sideboard and the long, oval table and big, blue-leather armchairs were all suffused with yellow light reflected back from the cream walls. "What a lovely room it is," he thought as he always thought each day whenever he entered it. But as he looked he could feel none of his accustomed pleasure in the glowing blues and reds and creams of the room. It lay in its pool of silent, dusty, golden light, empty and still and dead.

"What is the good of this beauty?" he muttered to himself. "What good? It needs a family." And at once, caught up in fancy, he began to picture the figure of a woman leaning against the mantelpiece. She was dressed, by some unknown need of the imagination, in a long, clinging Edwardian gown and she was slim but not very young. And he pictured too an Edwardian family of sons and daughters grouped round the long table. Then he turned and opened the big double doors leading into the drawing room. The sun now streamed the length of the two rooms, lighting on the blue-satin, flowered brocade of the old-fashioned drawing room suite his parents had also brought from abroad. All was blue and cream and light and filled with the gold silence and the quiet. He walked through to the french windows at the far end of the drawing room and, opening them, let himself into the garden, baking in sunshine, at the back of the house.

Here the fancy still persisted of the family of Edwardian children. On the lawn he could see a schoolboy son lying on his stomach reading *King Solomon's Mines*. A makeshift, orange-box swing hung from the big, spreading pear tree and a little girl swung in it. Upstairs, in the back bedroom with its sloping ceiling under the eaves, an older son sat studying hard for his approaching Finals; absorbed, self-sufficient, and yet a part of them all. The illusion was so strong that he turned and faced the back of the house in order to locate the window of that particular room. Inside the house the slender, Edwardian woman was preparing tea while an older daughter sorted out her stockings.

Lonely, aching tears seethed in his heart. The terrible, thick, hot sunshine and the waiting, silent, golden rooms frightened him. He went back and into his study, a dark room long and narrow in shape at the side of the house, but even here, though it was usually darkened by the high, dividing wall which separated him from his neighbours, there was visible through the upper, left-hand pane of the window, the sharp-angled red-tiled gable of next door's roof shining full in the sun against a patch of deep-blue sky. He pulled the heavy hangings across the window and switched on the light but the room looked lemon-coloured and sickly. He switched it off again and sat down in the dark, hot gloom.

"Sophie! Sophie! Sophie!" he called inside him. And at last let himself go, floating away on the pain which rose and fell, swelled and shrank within and around him. After a while he became maudling, sobbing to himself: "My love, my pretty love, how could you, how could you?" And it seemed to him that because she had chosen another then he could be nothing; that everything he had ever achieved or valued, all his superiorities were worthless. Then, between washes of pain, his mind began to play with words, with images, choosing and discarding them, trying to define his suffering because while he was defining it and searching for the right words, he forgot it. And he thought how it was like a large hole with jagged edges in a sheet of paper. All round the jagged edges flames were burning fiercely: and the hole was there, being nothing, in the middle of the flames.

After a time he began to reason with himself. And he said: "After all, what I want is something very simple. I want to love and be loved." Then he said: "No, it's not so simple as that. I want to love and *be good* and be loved. Is that so difficult? It comes to so many, to love in the right place. Why not to me? But," he cried out, "it will never happen for me!" And as he said these words aloud to himself in the dark, hot room he realized that he was looking at naked fact, that what he was saying was true and happening and was not a literary description and that he had really lost without ever having known it, the whole living, natural warmth of life and there was nothing left but to grow old. A terrible, poignant regret flooded him. God, in whose service he spent his life, seemed nothing. Faith, belief . . . these were the idle concepts of tranquillity. Only life, life, was desirable. He thought suddenly of his parents and, in his hot loneliness, longed for them.

During the whole of his agony he had not given one thought to Sara Gabriel. Now, all at once, she appeared gently in his mind and he longed for her, longed for her presence opposite him in the dark room, made up conversations with the big leather chair in which she had once sat, bathed himself in her unpretentious quality, excused himself to her and received her luminous, benevolent sense like a gentle snow on his fever. Even imagined, her spirit soothed him till in the end the thought of Sophie no longer cut but only underlined what was after all an old statement.

Yet during the days that followed he did not attempt to communicate with Sara. He wanted to, she was hardly ever out of his thoughts; both she and her father, bathed in a kind of glowing light of goodness, appeared to him constantly in his mind, angels to whom he was being irresistibly drawn . . . and yet (as so often happens when we have only to lift an arm to the telephone, to rise from a chair, to walk up the stairs to get something we badly want, yet do nothing) a continual inertia affected him and he made no move.

Absorbed in the deadened, summer apathy both of his own mood and the suburb he did not hear about Essie's elopement till several days after, though it occasioned much gossip. Opinion in Manor Green was uneasily divided between general condemnation of what her father was doing and a secret, somewhat horrified respect for anyone who took religion so seriously.

The Rabbi, after he got to know, found his position difficult. The situation in fact caught him neatly speared upon the two horns of his usually deeply concealed dilemma. How far in fact (he was forced to ask himself) was he prepared to support the steely, fanatic element of his faith, and how far was he prepared to modify to suit the century?

What is the good he said to himself (as often before) of attempting to force a demanding spiritual condition on a people so nearly indifferent, who refuse thought, decline the struggle of the soul, who have been made slack and purposeless by the prevailing winds of the time? Attempt force, he concluded as always, on such apathies and we are lost. Coax, compromise, meet half-way, modify the stringent, relax the too difficult and too severe . . . *hold*, by any means: only *hold*.

So, outwardly condoning by his silence, he held with the moderates in condemning Mr Gabriel while at the same time finding himself increasingly aware of a strange feeling, a kind of distant love for the old man, springing from the bonds his own sloth tried to lay on it. Divided, irresolute, the existence of—as he imagined it—such unquestioning conviction, the pure, unanxious power of single-mindedness drew him with enormous force until, arriving at sudden decision, he turned on his heel in the street one day and walked with a rapid yet curiously trance-like determination towards their house.

He was half-way there when a car drew up beside him and Dr Gildheim put his head out and offered him a lift.

"Depending on where you are going, of course, my dear Leo," he said in his soft, Viennese accent. "If it is to somewhere like Battersea or Blackheath I shall have to withdraw my offer immediately."

"You won't have to," said Leo heaving himself into the car. "I'm only going up to the Gabriels."

"Ah! Yes. What a business. I know I shouldn't say it to you of all people, but I cannot bring myself to blame that girl. She was a nice girl you know, Leo. I didn't know her so well as Sara. But she was a nice girl. With a father like that it's a wonder the other daughters don't do the same."

"You too?" said Leo. "You also have this curious prejudice against the old man. I cannot understand it," he continued angrily. "Because a man is unconventional in his outward behaviour must every man's hand be turned against him?"

"It depends entirely on—not what is *conventional*, but on what is permissible," said John pulling up at a red light. "It is not Mr Gabriel's behaviour at public meetings to which I object so much— though heaven knows it is embarrassing enough. But his private behaviour must really be quite unspeakable——"

"You say that because you are so unused to seeing goodness in its rarest, undiluted form," said Leo excitedly.

John Gildheim turned and gave him one astonished glance before the lights turned green and he was obliged to drive on.

"You really can't see it?" said Leo in an exasperated voice.

"If that's goodness . . ." began John. Then, with determination: "Look here! I'll tell you what that terrible old man is capable of doing." And he narrated to Leo his conversation on the telephone with Mr Gabriel several weeks before.

"There's probably some explanation," said Leo impatiently.

"I don't know. What was actually going on there I don't know. I can only imagine he got me mixed up with someone else. But really, Leo, mistake or no mistake, a man who can talk like that to an acquaintance of his daughter—poor girl, I suppose she had one hell of a row when she came home . . . You have no idea, really . . . I have had some dealings with mental patients in my time. If ever I saw symptoms of imbalance . . . He's not mad. I'm not saying that. On the contrary he strikes me as being only too sane—for himself. In other words he's a howling neurotic. That's worse, believe me. Psychotics we can do something about. Neurotics . . . they are the real blood-drinkers. Well, I wish you luck in your parochial duties! Here we are."

He drew up a few yards past the Gabriels' house and Leo got out, then put his head back through the window. "You're the doctor! But I bet you you're wrong and I'm right. You medicos! You'd have all the angels in prison and all the saints in hospital if you had your way!"

"Rightly! Rightly!" said Dr Gildheim laughing as he engaged the gears. "How uncomfortable it would be if they were not!"

3

Sara let him in. Quickly, before she took him into the front room where her father was, he said: "I didn't answer your note. Forgive me. I went away almost immediately. Please forgive me. I have been disturbed . . . not well . . ."

"It's nothing, it doesn't matter, it is nothing . . ." she murmured, embarrassed. "I had no right to bother you even——"

"You have every right," he said before he walked in by himself to the room.

It was the last day of the self-imposed week of mourning. Mr Gabriel, in slippers, sat before the round table covered with books. The mirrors in the room were still shrouded. A shaft of glaring sunlight fell on one wall. The room, though clean, seemed full of dust. Leo sat down.

Mr Gabriel, looking up from the huge volume he was balancing in front of him, nodded his head slowly and portentously up and down several times.

"So," he said. "You have come, Rabbi Norberg? I expect you before this."

"I have been away," said Leo.

"You have been away," he said nodding his head again. "Well. You have been back long enough to have heard of my tragedy. You knew my . . .?"

"Yes of course. Not well. But I knew her."

"Tell me, Rabbi Norberg . . . you think it worth to bring children into the world?"

"You think it worth time even to ask a question like that?"

"We live, we sacrifice for our children. And then what? What is the result? Ingratitude! Heartache! Treachery!"

"Mr Gabriel, what Essie has done is a terrible thing. When I heard it I said to myself 'A tragedy'. Why do these things happen? Why? And why to so many? Believe me, Mr Gabriel, yours is not the only case. This year alone I have——"

"To *me*! To *me*!" the old man interrupted petulant at any diminution of his uniqueness.

Leo was silenced in mid-sentence.

"It is to defy me, to injure me, *her father*, that she has done this."

"No, no, that I do not believe for an instant," Leo said and, unable to avoid a touch of the pulpit, went on: "We must not blame too much any one individual when all around us we see such a loosening of controls."

Noticing, rather angrily, that he was talking exactly like Rabbi Tarsch, he made an effort to collect himself, only to fall still further into sermonese.

"In life, Mr Gabriel," he said, "each one of us has two conflicting aims . . . the one, to get what he wants from the world around him —and the other, to adjust his desires to what is *possible* to attain while still obeying a moral code. In other words," he said, trying to rally, "I believe in the moral *wish* in men. We aim, consciously or not, for goodness as much as for happiness——"

"Our aim must be *at all times* to obey God," said Mr Gabriel in a stiffly sententious voice.

"Do we always know what are the rules of God?"

"Certainly!" cried Mr Gabriel, beginning so much to be pleased by the prospect of a theological argument that the cause of it temporarily slipped his mind, "certainly we know. And we know because it's written. It has all been written! You want to know where?" he cried, quite carried away into forgetting that a Rabbi probably knew where, "Here! In these books!" And he gave a triumphant thump with his hand on the outsize volume of *Torah* commentary lying on the table before him. "It's all in there," he said glaring at Leo and raising one rhetorical finger at the ceiling. "All there. You don't have to go any further. *Hafoch ba va hafoch ba d'chola ba.* 'Turn it and turn it over again for everything is in it'," he translated from the Hebrew in case the Rabbi hadn't quite got it.

"Yes, yes, I am familiar . . . well, perhaps you are right," said Leo, finding himself a little shaken by Mr Gabriel's social absurdity. "But while the Word is eternal and remains, the re-interpretation is continually necessary. We must find modern answers to modern predicaments. In other words, a discipline which worked well enough in the past——"

Mr Gabriel, whose attention to any voice but his own was minuscule at the best of times and who was, now that he was not actually speaking and impressing the Rabbi, bored and itching to get back to his grievances, interrupted him.

"And with my children discipline was not necessary? Is that what you think? *I should have locked them up! Bread and water I should have given them.* Aie . . . aie . . . worked, worked always . . . and what for? To give them the best of everything. Everything. They like spring chickens? A fowl isn't good enough? They have spring chicken every week. Always the best butter. Always the best oranges. Everything for them. *Everything* I give for them. And for what? For what?" he said with one of the melodramatic gestures well known to his family as was also the strong sob of self-pity in his voice.

"All through my life I have struggled," continued Mr Gabriel, nodding and sighing, nodding and sighing.

Leo, slightly taken aback but still tolerant, said quickly before Mr

Gabriel could embark on another provisions list: "Who doesn't struggle? And against what forces! Pressures from our environment, pressures from within our own natures, from heredity——"

"Heredity!" said Mr Gabriel fiercely. "From where did my daughter's evil come? From heredity? Excuse me, Rabbi. Her badness comes from herself."

"No, no. But forgive me. I did not for one moment mean to imply——"

"Heredity!" Mr Gabriel interrupted, rising to his feet and speaking with passion. "Has she not had good example? A good home, an education, a fine Jewish background? What more did she want? Sin! Filth! To walk the streets like a prostitute. That is what she wanted. And for this you find excuses? Environment, pressures..."

"I did not speak particularly," said Leo, falling, as many equally intelligent people did who were unused to it, to Mr Gabriel's cunning—though largely unconscious—trick of deflecting an argument into some irrelevant exaggeration. "I spoke only in general, of human nature."

"*Human nature*," said Mr Gabriel with deep scorn. "I am not interested in human nature. Keep your human nature." He made a violent, throwing away gesture. "Excuses. Always excuses. Human nature! What *is* human nature? Human nature is badness. Human nature is behaving like an animal. To go away leaving a note! Even a dog in the street you don't humiliate before the world. Did she stop to think of *me*? Can I go out? Can I face people? If I go anywhere what will happen? The people nudging, whispering . . . 'You see him? Mr Gabriel? His daughter is married to a *Goy*. She ran away with a *Goy*.' Very interesting. To degrade a father . . . *that* is human nature."

"To love and forgive: that is also human nature," said Leo very stiffly indeed, shaken more than ever not only by the wilful egotism being revealed but by the curiously blind unashamedness with which it was being done. A recollection of what Dr Gildheim had been saying not half an hour before came back to him, causing a strange sinking of the heart. Resist as he would against the acknowledgment of his own fault of judgment, he could not prevent the cherished image of Mr Gabriel's holy single-mindedness beginning to slip from him.

"That a child of mine should go away from Judaism," said Mr Gabriel, this time on such a genuine note of grief that Leo's rapidly withering illusions sprang green again for a hopeful moment. He looked sadly at the small figure of the man standing before him, but he was wiping his eyes and blowing his nose with imperative, loud honks into his handkerchief, his gestures conveying somehow a kind of comic, stiff-necked intransigence which made it impossible to take him seriously. Indeed, as the little man started to talk again in a long, self-pitying tirade, Leo found himself utterly unable to shut from his mind an irresistible impression—enhanced by his sharp red nose—of *gobble* in his talk, a suggestion of ridiculous, turkey-cock strutting and wailing and baying at the impassive moon of fate. His grief and shame were undeniably real: but something naïve, violent, self-pitying and self-righteous in his modes of expression managed, fatally, to falsify his suffering.

"Meanwhile it is me, *me* that suffers," said Mr Gabriel, striking attitudes with his taut, little body as he moved about the room. "I should have joy from my children. And I get from them suffering. That is my reward from their cruel, hard natures. But God will punish them," he added with satisfaction. "The Almighty, blessed be He, will not allow them to escape."

"You *want* them to suffer?" said Leo suddenly in an incredulous voice.

Mr Gabriel, all at once looking childishly sly and pleased, gave a theatrical shrug.

"You will see. You will see," he cried. "They have disobeyed the Commandment. *Honour thy father and*——"

"They? Sara too? What has *she* done?"

"All of them. All."

"You must allow me to disagree with you," said Leo sharply.

Not understanding Mr Gabriel's dramatically sound choice of the word "all" rather than "some" to express his sense of injury, he took him literally.

"I know Sara very well," he said. "She has a pure nature——"

"Sara! As bad as the other one. A plotter, a deceiver . . ."

"No!"

Mr Gabriel laughed satirically. "You tell me about my own children? I know better."

Leo sat silent, Then he said: "Believe me, Mr Gabriel, when I say I would take an oath on Sara's goodness."

There was such a warmth of sincerity—and something more—in his voice that the old man (who was by no means without shrewdness) cast a suddenly watchful, startled look at him. At any other time he might have attempted a heavy-footed laudation of his daughter, more damaging than criticism, but forgivable. He did, in fact, hesitate. His father's heart, the twisted but profound love he felt for his children, for that which belonged to *him*, told him what to do. But against it reared a sudden complexity of revenge on life, unsated egotism, fear of further loss and loneliness and, most of all, a kind of jealousy of happiness.

"She has flouted me as deliberately, as wickedly as the other," he shouted.

The door opened and Sara came in quietly carrying a tray of tea.

"Are you quite better now?" she said with her head down, busy with the cups.

"More or less," said Leo. "Thank you," as she handed him a cup of tea.

"It has been such an awful summer till the last week or two," she said in a low, steady voice. "Nothing but rain. I hope it was better in Whytecliffe Sands."

"So-so," he said, stirring the spoon round and round in the cup. "Not very good really."

"Tell me," said Mr Gabriel suddenly with a kind of deliberate travesty of a conversational tone, "tell me, Rabbi Norberg, did you meet any more ungrateful children while you were away? Any more——"

"Father!"

He gave her a brief, blazing stare then switched on the deliberate, parodied joviality again, but overacting the overacting so that the effect was profoundly embarrassing. ". . . any other children wilfully shaming their parents physically, mentally, spiritually," he said rolling out the words with savage, childish enjoyment.

For all his experience of people in extremity, of the greatly enhanced raw-nerved tensions of crises, it seemed to Leo, listening with appalled distaste, that Mr Gabriel's attitude was revealing a

231

degree of spiteful unbalance which he found so increasingly shocking that he could not bring himself to look at either of them.

"A fine world to live in, isn't it, Rabbi? *A world of selfishness and treachery!*" he shouted suddenly. "Ask her! Ask her why she encouraged her sister to run away from Jewish life, to hob-nob with the Christians, *to go to church*, I wouldn't be surprised!"

"Father, you must not be so——" "foolish" she wished to say but, not wishing to point his absurdity, said, choosing a word which would at least lend him dignity, "unforgiving." She looked at Leo and said imploringly: "You must forgive being brought into this . . . this family affair . . ."

"If I could help . . ." said Leo uncertainly, looking down into his tea cup. He felt as though a heavy weight on the back of his neck was preventing him from raising his head.

"Family! Family!" broke in Mr Gabriel, set off by this word. "A word which should be sacred. A word which has been *violated* in this house. All my pride, my joy in my family, gone, destroyed."

She saw Leo give a slight, unbelieving shake of the head and half glance at his watch and every nerve in Sara's body seemed to her to scream. The impression her father was trying to convey was that of lacerated, sardonic bitterness. This she understood. But she also knew that, as always throughout his life, he was playing it wrong. He had not the correct pitch for such performance. The essential ingredient which gives dignity to misfortune, that mysterious sense of style, of timing, without which it is impossible to put over a cause, an attitude or a grievance, had been left out of him. Whatever happened to him he would always appear absurd. This sadness of the perpetually ineffectual suddenly struck her as being, in essence, almost wholly tragical. His struggle to match the demands of his nature with the limitations of his personality seemed all at once of such agonizing pathos, revealing such failure, that instinctively she tried to help him.

"Who would believe," her father was saying, bending his head towards Leo who still did not look at him, "who would believe that people we see around us every day can hold such feelings in their hearts? It makes you think. Doesn't it make you think, Rabbi Norberg? What are we to believe?" he said with a flash of his usual rhetoric. "What does the *Torah* tell us?"

"Dr Norberg must have seen a great deal of the worst of people," said Sara. "The underside of human nature is always terrible. My father," she said earnestly to Leo, who was hunched in his chair and studying his shoes, "has a character which does not comprehend evil. It is a kind of innocence he has. He does not really believe it exists. At least—outside, yes, but not here, around us. That is why, you see——"

"Oh I understand it now," interrupted Mr Gabriel, breaking up with blind, mulish stupidity the protective shield she was trying to make for him. He wagged his head pettishly. "See what examples I have to teach me all my life. Robbers and thieves I reared . . . to rob me of my good name, to steal my happiness . . ."

With a desperate gesture she stood up and said to Leo who also jumped up: "Please . . . I don't . . ." The lids came down over her eyes and on her face appeared a look of great, controlled suffering. A circular saw-edge seemed to him as he looked at her to cut into some dark fleshy core at the centre of himself and he could stand no more. Appalled by the old man's vicious, posturing absurdity and shrinking from the horrifying vision of pain and indignity they both presented to him, he could only make his escape as quickly as possible.

"You have had a bad week," he said hurriedly to Sara as she saw him off at the front door. "I'm sorry. I should have tried to come sooner."

"It doesn't matter," she said, then added: "You must not think . . . my father does not always express himself . . . and then he has taken this very badly. He is really very unhappy."

"You mustn't take it to heart," he said vaguely, his eyes passing over her face like a stranger's and gazing across the street.

She withdrew in manner immediately, saying, with a kind of gentle, inflexible remoteness: "Well, good-bye, Rabbi Norberg. Thank you for——"

"No, no," he said, confused and agitated, his apparent inattention disappearing. "What I mean to say . . ." but he had not the faintest idea of what he meant to say. Faced with her stern, painful composure, all the phrases which came to him seemed too small. Sympathy would be an insult. Nothing less than an effort to match her own would do; and this he felt a profound, dragging reluctance

233

to attempt. Underneath, smothered but there, there was also a kind of aggrieved feeling that such an effort there was no right to demand from him.

She should have made it easier for him but she did not know how to break, to show weakness, to display her need. For another moment he hesitated then, turning his back on the choice she presented, left her. She watched him striding down the path as though in a hurry to get away, his head under the wide-brimmed hat bent towards the ground.

"I gave him something to think about," her father observed in a self-satisfied yet furtive way as soon as she rejoined him.

"Something to think about," she repeated in a flat, dreary voice, automatically collecting the tea things.

"Well, what then? I should cover over such behaviour? I should tell everyone I am a bad father? *Is it my fault?*"

"How *could* you?" she cried suddenly, pausing, a cup and saucer trembling in her hand. "How can you not see how shaming, how stupid it is to have spoken like that in front of him?"

"Why not?" he said defiantly and weakly.

"Why not?" she said hopelessly. "Because you're ruining your own case, that's why not. Oh, for God's sake don't look like that. I'm not your enemy——"

"Aren't you?" he muttered.

Controlling herself she went on: "Father, don't you see that to *under*-state carries more conviction. It is more dignified——"

"Dignified!"

"Yes. Dignity, human dignity *counts*. It is what people judge us by in the long run. Not pride. I don't say be proud. But have respect for your own human dignity. What is the good of *abusing* the way you did just now? *Examine. Admit. Weigh.* To speak like that in front of Rabbi Norberg . . . Oh!" she exclaimed, putting down the tray and walking about the room, "it is not possible for anyone to have behaved with such . . . such absurdity."

"Criminal!" he cried, deliberately attacking on the easier flank though it was the word "absurdity" which had stung. "You use such a word to me!" he screamed rushing over to her. "So I am criminal now! Your sister has done nothing wrong——"

"Of course she has. I am not defending——"

"Oh no," he interrupted, "you are not defending! You are not finding excuses!"

He stood confronting her, a taut, narrow little hairpin of a man looking up at the thin, tall girl, his daughter.

"I . . ." she began austerely, holding up her wide-spread fingers stiffly before her, "I am trying to judge in terms of compassion. Not will. It is necessary to loosen the will; to . . . to judge in context. Essie is not bad. She is human. You can't *force* people, father. If you attempt to do so *their* will bursts out at some other seam, in some other and more terrible way. You should have left her alone. You are not God."

"*I am her father*." And falling back again on the Commandments he cried: "*Honour thy father and thy*——"

"Oh yes," said Sara half to herself. "But I can't help wondering, now and always, what God means by this. If a good child has a bad parent . . . must they still honour that parent?"

"So I am a bad parent!" said Mr Gabriel with such vastly exaggerated and deliberate misunderstanding that she was provoked into irritation again.

"No," she said after a struggling pause to control it. "You are not a bad parent; but an unwise one. Can't you see," she added in a gentle tone as she caught the look of real misery in his eyes, "what I am trying to say? You are my father and I love you. But your way of dealing with life, with people, is wrong." She reached out and took his two clenched hands between her own. "I cannot bear that anything should shame you——"

With a violent wrench he tore his hands out of hers. She had gone too far. She had behaved too well, spoken with too much reason, understood him too well: and he could not stand the effort she was forcing upon him. Like Leo, he was unable to face the moral compulsions, the choice of conduct which, by the very presence of her pure, moderate nature, she was bringing clearly before him.

"It is *you* who shame *me*. You! You! You!" he screamed and, flinging up his arm, hit her violently across the face. The blow caught her off-balance and she staggered then fell sideways. She could perhaps in other circumstances have saved herself from falling but the scene had unnerved her and she could not exert her will quickly enough to command her muscles. She fell, knocking her head against the side of a chair, down to the floor. She half-raised herself then pressed her face against the faded, grey velvet seat of the chair, tearless and powerless against the monstrous, perverted truths and half-truths of her father's argument with life. Then she became aware that he was pushing at her shoulder muttering, with frightened anger: "Get up. Get up. You tripped over. Get up. Stop lying there like that."

She raised her head, longing with weakened limbs to stay as she was, to rest there with covered eyes. But in her father's voice there was the terrified, panic bad-temper of extreme guilt and, unable to ignore his need, she dragged herself up again.

He stood fidgeting in front of her, unable to apologize, alarmed into love, virulent, pitiable.

"I . . ." he began, "I . . . am nothing. What I am counts for nothing . . . To fall down like that," he said trembling and accusing. "Where did you knock . . .? let me see. Show me."

Sinking down on the chair she touched her forehead. "It's nothing."

"Nothing!" he said. "How many times must I tell you? A knock can be dangerous." He darted out and was back with the butter dish before she could move. "Butter," he said. "Always remember, butter for a knock." He took some on his finger and rubbed it on her forehead. "Is it any wonder you fall?" he said belligerently, rubbing away. "Such high heels!"

"They're not very high," she said faintly.

"There," he said, not listening. He smeared on a little more butter then stepped back concentratedly wiping his fingers.

"D'you want a cup of tea?" he said at last, not looking at her.

"Yes. Yes," she said out of pity.

"I'll put the kettle on," he said and ran out of the room.

"I could have told you those rubbishy sandals were no good," he said when he came back. "But to nothing do my family ever listen to from me." He sighed very deeply, a genuine sigh. "Why can you not listen? I am older than you, I have more experience . . . Do I not know more?" he said looking up with one hand on the lid of the teapot, holding it as he poured.

236

"You don't always draw the right conclusions from what you know."

"Hah! that's what *you* say," he said with a flash of his usual intransigence. "Do you know what they used to call me when I was a boy, in the little village? *'Die kleine Rebbe.'* At ten years old I was a little Rabbi already! Such ideas as they had not heard from *grown men* they heard from me. From grown men! And my children say I know nothing!"

"There *are* things I don't know about," he flashed out suddenly with scornful fire. "Business! All right! For business I am not good. How should I be? What do I know of business? I have no taste for it, I am not clever for it. Ask me to be a man of culture, a philosopher . . . To sell an idea, yes. To sell a collar stud, no. Is that a crime? Yes," he answered himself, carried away as usual by his own drama. "To your mother's family it was a crime." (Sara in her turn heaved a sigh. All her life she had had to listen to her father's scornful diatribes against his wife's family.) "To your mother's family it was a crime. What were they, her family . . . ignorant, of no education . . . of no *respect* for education. When I was learning for twelve hours a day, what were they doing, your mother's brothers? Buying, selling, a little swindle here, a little business deal there . . . While I was getting poorer they were getting richer. Like they got rich from me! Not a penny dowry promised me do I ever see to this day. *Me*, a man of culture, a man of learning," his voice rose, "such a one as me they cheat."

"So I have never suffered in my life," he continued after a pause, in a mild and absent tone. "You think you know everything. You accuse, you blame; and what is it that you really know? Nothing. *Nothing*. Have I ever even told you . . . ? Or any of my children . . . ? Your Aunt Leah," he said unexpectedly, "*she* knows. She could tell you. Ach, she could tell you a story if you asked her. She knows what I have been through in my life. Before you were born *and* after. Aiee!" He heaved a deep sigh, and settled in his chair nodding his head with an expression of self-pitying patience.

"What was I when I came to England?" he said. "A pauper. A young boy. What did I know of life anywhere? All I knew was poverty at home and worse poverty here. At home, in the little village, what had I done but study? A student, a *clever* student," he

237

said proudly, dipping his head on the word, "a student from a long line of students. And suddenly I am flung here, no family, no home, nothing."

"This happened to thousands of Jews," she interjected.

"Maybe," he said with a shrug and a sideways nod, "but you think that makes easier? To think of others? To each his own misery. Then, then," he continued, "your mother's family get hold of me. She is the eldest of four daughters, she is six years older than me . . . but that you know . . . yes?"

"Yes."

"Well . . . I am married. As soon as we walk from under the canopy your mother's family want nothing to do with us. Hah! *That* you did not know!"

She did not answer.

"Well, happens like that sometimes. Well? what can you do? We live, I work, Rebecca comes, you come . . . and all the time poorer and poorer. What do I know about making a living? Comes a time you are—how old?—one? two? . . . and Essie is coming . . . and no bread to eat. And with a bitter heart I have to go and beg. From that family! You think I forget such a moment? But it was that morning that I buy two pound potatoes. And in them when I go to cook, I find one big potato is a stone! Looked exactly like, shape, colour . . . I take it back to the greengrocer's and show it. Must have weighed half a pound. Exactly the shape and with earth on it, you understand. So I take it back. And the greengrocer laughs. 'How do I know,' he says, 'you found it in my potatoes? Get away. Get out of my shop.' And he drives me out with the stone together. That is the day I have to go and beg from the rich family of your mother who spit on ideas, who think to be a student nothing, who despise me. Me!" he said his voice powerful again with outraged pride. Then he continued: "I ask for twenty pounds. To help till Essie is born. What was twenty pounds to them; even then? They send me home while they 'think about it'. Think about it! While we starve they 'think about it'. And when they have thought—what then? They make a collection between themselves and they send round . . . how much do you think? *Six pounds.* And a message that I should go to work! You think this unbelievable? That a Jewish family behave like that? If anyone else tell me I don't believe either.

238

And after that? Your sister is born. I am offered a position to teach; but where? In Russia. For two years away from my family, my children. I go, I send money, I come back. And still poverty. Poverty. Sometimes people were good. Your Aunt Leah . . . she was poor herself. What did she have? Also an ailing husband, children . . . but if she met your mother at the grocer's she would put into her basket a loaf, a piece of cheese . . . *She* was good. But others . . .! I live by selling Jewish books from door to door. I walk. All over London I walk. In the boiling heat, in the snow, in the rain—I walk. From rich Jew to rich Jew."

Sara stirred, a long-buried memory struggling to the surface of her consciousness. She was standing, a very small girl, holding on to her father's hand just inside the door of a huge, richly-furnished room. At the far end of the room a portly woman was shouting: "I don't like being bothered every five minutes, Mr Gabriel. I told you, I'll pay for the books soon. Come back next week." Her father, trembling, was saying in a shaken voice: "Of course. Of course. I am sorry, Mrs ——. I thought you would wish to settle this week." She had stared, terrified, at the fat, vicious, overdressed woman. Then they had gone away, creeping ashamed down the wide drive before the handsome house.

A spasm of anger shook her and she said hardly: "Why didn't you tell her you needed the money? Such stupid, false pride."

"Tell her? Who? What are you talking about?"

She shook her head and, never very interested in what anyone else was saying, he let it drop.

"Yes, yes," he continued, his voice beginning to sound very sleepy. He yawned. "Yes. Suffering, cold, hunger: and was that all? No! the worst of all was the shame. So much humiliation, so much contempt. And from whom? From a family so ignorant they could scarcely read. *They* despised *me!*" He sat up suddenly, his eyes burning. "*They* to *despise me!*" he said grinding the words out.

"Well," she thought as he paused to contemplate his wrongs. "This is no more than the common lot of many. Why pity him?" Yet, even as she thought this the thought also occurred to her how badly equipped was her father for such a lot, how unfit for lowliness. The whole stretch and range of his temperament was unsuited for what had happened to him. It was not, as she had judged for so long, a question merely of vanity or pride. It was the temperament producing the pride, with which he was obliged to battle; and for this he was not responsible any more than a frog for producing a croak instead of the note of a nightingale.

"And my children," said Mr Gabriel, coming with sudden violence out of his thoughts, "are they any better? Do this! Do that! Hitlers in my home. Like a concentration camp!"

With a jolt, the pitying understanding she had been with difficulty dredging from the depths of her will, cracked.

"How can you . . . how can you . . ." she got out the words half strangled in her throat. "To compare . . . To speak of *that* . . . Have you no conception of what we have been saved from? And why? Why should we have been saved? Those others . . . why weren't we among them? Why should we have escaped? What accident," she cried, the repressed, ceaseless, guilty question of all Jews who find themselves still safe, breaking out from her heart, "what accident of fate, geography, time, kept *us* from the gas chamber?"

He had been going to answer but that would have meant admitting a question to his consciousness which for years had managed to shut it out. Crumpling into a willed unhearing he reverted back to his earlier grievance. "*I* mustn't speak. *I* must say nothing. *I have a right to speak.* To Rabbi Norberg, to anyone. Who is Norberg that I should hold back for him? Norberg! He tells *me* what to think. Has he children? What does he know? Has he been married even? Norberg to dictate to me! When Rabbi Norberg is a father himself——"

"Stop it! Stop it!" she said softly, the obsessional repetition of Leo's name, with its reminder of an agony she had yet to face, more than she could bear.

"Who is Rabbi Norberg," he repeated with, what seemed to her in her disorder, deliberate spite, "that I should choose my words for him? Time I spoke out. It is time somebody knows the truth," he added fatally.

"*Truth!*" she said, the word suddenly producing such a great, tumbling landslide of feeling that she crossed her arms tightly across her body as if to prevent it being annihilated. "*Truth* you told him!" she said turning to her father a look so blazed with violence that he quailed. This time it was he who had gone too far. Even the exacerbation of her feelings in the situation regarding Leo was forgotten in this last, profound outrage which was being done to the very essence of her nature. What she had once told Leo had been no more than the real facts about herself. Lying affected her with a kind of agony. Where it had come from, how it had sprung from such parents, such environment, such a deadening, self-deceiving society, this adoration for *truth*, this deep, strong, flowing passion for clarity even at the cost of pain, which was so firm a strand of her spirit, it was impossible to say. But it was there. And Mr Gabriel's profane and dangerous, mischievous and idiotic use of the word was, all at once, too much. Already cracked, the shell of pity broke and fell away.

"I should show respect for him?" Mr Gabriel was saying. "Better that he should show respect for what *I* am."

"And what are you?" she said.

"What am I?" he said disconcerted.

"Yes," she said roughly. "What are you? *What are you?*" she said in a screaming whisper. "*Scholar* you call yourself," she said aiming directly to the heart. "*Learned*, you fancy yourself! *You* are not a scholar——"

"A thing to hear!" he said firing up but not at first taking her seriously. "From my own daughter! When have I not studied? For how many years? What do you know, in any case . . . a girl! Ask Mr Ascher. Ask Horowitz. Ask! Ask anyone. They will tell you. I am a scholar," he repeated in an annoyed but self-satisfied voice which inflamed her still further.

"Oh no you're not," she exclaimed giving him a look at once jarred, menacing, sad. "You," she burst out with despairing contempt, "you are only an admirer of scholars, not even of scholarship, only the title. You think because you admire you are."

"I do not think," he half shouted at her, twisting in his chair. "I know!"

"Delusions! What delusions always. Oh!" she cried raising her head and pressing it back towards her shoulder-blades. "Delusions!" she said between gritted teeth to the ceiling, clenching her hands as if to fight the word. She brought her head forward again, sinking her chin with a deliberate movement towards her chest, her eyes staring fierce and vacant before her.

241

Sullen, alarmed, obstinate, Mr Gabriel eyed her.

"Ah!" she said on a groan, "what sad, deceived monkeys do our values make of us.

He made to turn away with an insulting, impatient shrug.

"Tell me," she said harshly in revenge, "if you are so truly learned why did you not become a Rabbi?"

"Ah!" he said with a flounce, "I'm very glad you asked me that. I'm very glad. This gives me an opportunity. You want an explanation . . .? You will have one. All in good time. This you should have asked before. Years ago you should have asked. An important question like this has never occurred to you before? How is it——?"

"I'm asking you now," she interposed pitilessly.

He hesitated, his eyes red-veined, flickering, self-conscious, looking away from her.

"For the answer you should ask not me," he said at last, "but your mother's family. Yes, yes," he said, his excuses gathering momentum, "ask *them*. They stopped me. They were jealous. Always, like ignorant people everywhere, they were jealous of brains. Always they worked against me, plots, schemes, to get hold of your mother, to stop me. Was it my fault," he demanded self-righteously, "that I had my children's mouths to feed?"

"That should not have prevented you," she said intently. "There have been many in your circumstances—worse than yours!—who lifted themselves up, who found sponsors, help . . . *What stopped you?*"

"Jealousy!" he exclaimed. "Always jealousy. Was I given opportunity?"

"You know very well," she began, standing up, "that——"

Mr Gabriel also stood up and began walking rapidly about the room with small, nervous steps, as determined to avoid truth as she was to uncover it.

"I knew more than all the Rabbis put together," he shouted. "That is why they stopped me."

"Can it be that you are so deluded about yourself?" she asked, dimly realizing even as she spoke that this was a hopeless question. It was not exactly that he *would* not answer truly but that he *could* not; that there was in him not only an illusioned obstinacy but also a raw, untrained naïveté which did not know how to behave, how

242

to acknowledge, how to admit. But at that moment, all tolerance, all pity gone, this was something she would not herself admit.

"The truth," she said, unable to control the scorching release of the words. "For once you must hear it. The truth is that you are a stupid, blinkered man. You are ignorant. You know nothing, only the stale, chewed-over fragments of what you learnt as a boy. You have no ideas, only prejudices. You have no abilities, only vanity. In the world you count for nothing. You have achieved nothing. Who are your friends? Men of standing? Men of value? You *don't know*," she said cruelly, "that your friends are fools? Or that you are a failure? Didn't you know," she said in harsh, mock surprise, "that you are a failure?"

His hand, which he had been holding over his eyes in a gesture of ostentatious suffering, suddenly sprang away and he made for the door. With a movement quicker than his she put herself against it. "Oh no!" she said. "Oh no. You don't escape!"

"I will not stay here for you to torture me. Have I not had misery enough in my life? Let me out!"

"As soon as you speak to me in truth. Only speak truth. The truth. For once in your life, the truth!"

"I tell the truth. Always I tell the truth. The world lies; not me. *You* lie——"

"Why did you not become a Rabbi?"

"I told you," he said in a pettish, gritting voice.

"You weren't good enough, were you? You weren't clever enough? Admit it! Admit! For once in your life, *admit!*" she suddenly screamed out and, utterly distraught, sank to her knees before him.

"Get    up," she heard him say in so strange a voice that she raised her head and looked at him. "Get——up," he said again.

She rose.

He had crossed the room and was standing before the high, old-fashioned bookcase with a look so strange to his face—a kind of cool, hostile patience—that it frightened her. It was too sane an expression to be normal to him. She shivered as she sensed a degree of evasion so far advanced, so steely in determination, that it pushed on him a semblance of normality. His natural mien was a snapping, fussy jerkiness. This stillness he had suddenly assumed, the expression

243

of cold patience which lay on his face with a peculiar, biding malevolence, shrivelled her own hysteria. In a moment it was gone, replaced by a watchfulness and a beating, wary heart.

In silence they stared at each other.

"There is the poker," he said raising his hand stiffly and pointing to the fireplace. "Kill me! Well? What are you waiting for? Kill me!"

She made a slight, hopeless movement.

With a wild gesture he began to speak, the words tearing from his throat.

"I am——" he said. "I am as good . . . All my life," he said gasping, "I have lived for study. And you say . . . *I have reputation*," he burst out. "Why have so many come around me? Eh? Tell me that! All these years they come to discuss, to ask of me my opinion. You have seen all your life . . . Well? Can you deny? Do not so many come to me? For advice, for learning . . ."

She found it impossible to answer him. For, just as the smallest organism can be found to attract to itself a host of even minuter satellites, so, in her father's circle of ineffectual, muddle-minded old men, he was their leader. She hesitated, the words "worthless, worthless" trembling on the verge of utterance. But the brutal impulse had spent itself. Already she was weakened, shaken, with the backwash of remorse.

"You are trying to destroy me," he said all at once, compressing his lips and nodding his head. "You will not succeed. That I can tell you. You think to destroy me as our enemies think to destroy the Jews; as your sister thought to destroy what I live for. *You* will go down; all of you. Not me!"

She gazed at him in silence.

"Yes," she said to herself. "That at least is true. You will bend and bend . . . and never break. I will break, not you. There is a power of the ego I know nothing of; a force beyond reason; a grip beyond truth."

Taking out his handkerchief he wiped his forehead, his hands and lips trembling. She watched him, a strange mixture of pity and admiration, awe and shame welling in her heart.

She walked to the window and looked out from the grey, hot, melancholy room at the brilliant, dying, evening sun full on the shabby houses across the street.

"I should not have spoken like that," she said at last, turning round. "No, I should not have spoken like that."

"I could have . . ." he began again but could not finish. It was she, still at the window, who finished his sentence for him.

"Yes. You could have, father. I am wrong. It is your life, the circumstances of your life which are all wrong. Not you."

And she thought, even as she spoke these comforting, lying words, that they were not after all such lies. That his flaws and failures were not altogether due to the material of which he was made but to the general waste of nature. If only, she thought with a prick of anguish, his qualities could have been properly used. And she saw how his pride, under no necessity to inflate, would have been proportionate: his self-respect—recognized, unbattered—less flaming in its demands: his iron stubbornness used for right: his foggy passion for ideas channelled, the laughable element in all his claims and aspirations, gone.

There *was* something in him. Even now, when he had refused truth, wrecked two daughters' lives, there was, she saw, a kind of ruined potential, a power in his nature which he had had no idea how to use, a vitality which—not allowing his ego to rest—had pushed him on to folly, had made him more ridiculous, more dangerous, more vulnerable, infinitely easier to despise than the truly cloddish. He was more than many. Certainly he was more than many.

# Chapter Nine

## I

LEO DID NOT SLEEP VERY WELL DURING THE WEEKS THAT followed his visit to the Gabriels though it was not so much a mental condition which took away his rest as a physical one, a feeling of dry hollowness which no amount of food or drink seemed able to abate. He got through the days and read most of the nights. The only activity which gave him any sense of being alive was that—accidentally discovered through a visit he was obliged to make in the East End of London—of walking the streets either of that neighbourhood or of the nearby City.

Though he had known them perfunctorily for years, the streets of the old Jewish quarter now fascinated him and day after day he returned, usually at early evening, to walk and walk through the dirty little alleys where the first great waves of Jewish immigrants had clustered towards the end of the last century. As he walked a curious strength of feeling, a kind of passionate affection went out from him to the mean, decrepit little houses, the tiny, frowzy provision shops, the poultry stalls, the very refuse in the gutters. When, now and then, he passed a new, clean block of council flats or a raw, modern factory, he frowned with displeasure. Then he would catch sight of one of the old, Jewish, black-garbed men, venerable and bearded, now so few in the quarter but still occasionally to be seen, and his heart would lift with a kind of passionate nostalgia as if through such men he could still touch the certainty, the vitality, the rough, innocent, ambitious, swarming life of those early immigrants with so much before them of promise. He felt also a great pride. Searching for an imaginary companion his roving thoughts hit on Dean Mitchell and to him on these solitary evening walks he gave long explanations full of love and names; how the inhabitants of these very slums and blackened tenements, so sad and desolate now in the soft, golden evenings, had risen to eminences, given birth to greatness, preserved microcosms of civilization and order, revered

246

and striven for knowledge. Passing a tiny Synagogue, no more than a couple of rooms in a tumbledown, converted house, tears would come thickly to his eyes. "You see . . . you see . . ." he would stammer to the imagined Mitchell, ". . . the strength. The obstinate, stiff-necked strength . . ." And so the East End with its intimations of strength, its very smells a recollection of conviction, drew his weakness to it evening after evening.

A comfort of another kind he found, oddly in wandering round the City of London itself. This he would only do in the afternoons while the streets were still crowded. There his acute yet dulled suffering receded as he made himself part of the endless throng and movement of the neighbourhood: Cheapside, Mansion House, Throgmorton Street, Ludgate Hill. What pleased him most was to sit in one or other of the cafeterias or milk bars and watch the little, pretty, perky typists and clerks seeming to him so innocent and bird-like, so blissfully normal and simple, their chirpy little painted faces so profoundly reassuring as to the everyday of life that he would smile to himself with pleasure.

## 2

One evening there was a ring at his door. He had had a tiring day devoted entirely to ministerial work. In the morning there had been a meeting of one of the innumerable Synagogue Committees still haggling over the Building Fund: the afternoon he had spent on his hospital round. Since tea time there had been a succession of tiresome callers; an old, fanatically orthodox woman with a chicken which she suspected of not being kosher and which he had had more or less to dissect before she would go away satisfied; another woman who wanted him to prevent her son getting engaged to a perfectly suitable girl on the grounds that the girl's grandfather was reputed to have died of consumption.

"*You* speak to my Bernie," she said. "To me he won't listen. All he knows he's in love. I tell him a thousand times, Bernie, I says, if the family's not healthy d'you think what you're doing is the right thing? So today you think you're in love. Bernie, I say, listen to me. So you're *in* love. So your wife is ailing six months after you get married. What then? What's your life? Rabbi Norberg, I ask you, is it right he should tie himself up, a fine, healthy boy, to a not well girl?"

It had taken him all his time—and patience—to reassure her on the principles of heredity and the marvels of modern medicine.

She had hardly been gone five minutes when his housekeeper ushered in a tall, brown-skinned young man, very broad-shouldered, his fair hair cropped closely to his head. With a kind of heavy, dulled surprise the Rabbi recognized Dov Benari, the young Israeli to whom Sophie was engaged. He lumbered to his feet and with a wary, sagging politeness congratulated him. The young man accepted his remarks with a casual air and, before Leo could ask him to do so, sat down.

"I guess you know what I'm here about," he said, his voice strongly foreign-accented yet—as with many Israelis—with a definite American twang.

"Anything I can advise you on I should of course be only too——"

"It is for the wedding. Sophie has suggested I call on you."

"You wish to have the ceremony in my——?" began Leo, feeling almost light-hearted at the prospect of such stupendous irony.

"No. No. If I had the choice I don't mind telling you I prefer here, but Sophie insists on to go up . . . down? which is it . . .?"

"I should think 'down'," said Leo.

". . . down to Wales for to get married. But the procedure I don't know so much about. Where do we start? What is the first thing?"

During the ensuing conversation the Rabbi kept his eyes steadily on the young man, noting his good but rather broad features, accentuated by white pointed teeth, and the narrow, casual-glancing eyes set slightly slant in his face. Like many young Israelis he looked, with his broad, flat cheeks, rather like a sandy Chinaman. There was no old-fashioned, Oriental nonsense regarding courtesy about him however. He was not rude but his manner was off-hand, casually confident, talkative to the point of cockiness. Leo was struck all over again, as he had been in Israel, with the curiously alert, vibrant quality of the young Israelis, the *sabras* as they are called. They had often reminded him of the American boys he had met so many times during the war, but with a special quality of toughness, purpose and articulateness which American youth—so often soft-centred—does not have.

His questions answered, Dov seemed in no great hurry to go but sat talking on in his assertive, sometimes satirical, unillusioned way, telling Leo about his experiences at the law school and describing with sardonic gusto the English students all clustered in vague in-attention at the back of the lecture hall while the front seats were thronged with eagerly listening black, brown and yellow students. Whenever he referred to England and the English he did so with a hard, impatient scepticism which, for all his own criticism of English behaviour in the Middle East, irritated Leo.

"Yes, yes," he said at last, "but leaving all that on one side, you are badly under-rating the valuable elements in British ways of life."

"Yes. For instance the boiled cabbage——"

"No," said Leo firmly. "I am referring to such things as our comparative political stability——"

"Becoss what Englishman is politically minded anyway?"

"The Welfare State . . ."

"Such an investment repays itself. It is a good thing," said Dov with an upward, sarcastic flourish of his hands, "from a quite com-mercial point of view. The British Government gives to the people what it onn—ly wishes to give—for its own benefit. But the ordinary man in the street of course, he like to think the Government nice, kind, Father Christmas."

"Ach!" said Leo angrily, "And on what does Israel base her economy?"

"We too," cried the young man with a comical look and shrug-ing his shoulders very high, "we too have our Father Christmas—if a Rabbi will forgive my mentioning again such a person! A great many in fact, all coming and going till they don' know from left to right!"

"There is another English virtue which we might mention," said Leo "and that's gratitude."

"Ah yes, gratitude," said Dov putting a forefinger into one nostril and looking thoughtful. He sniffed sharply, pressing his lips to-gether. "To this one, that one . . . For what? For being allowed to stay alive? Europeans may feel grateful for such privilege. We in Israel are not. To us it is not a privilege. It is our *right*. In Israel," he

249

said lifting up a finger at Leo with a mischievous, chiding look, "you see . . . we think we are *entitled*. That is a big thing, you know—to feel entitled."

He gave Leo a grin, still cocky and sardonic but with a kind of scoffing sweetness as well, which made him turn away with a sudden throb of the heart. For one instant he felt a love like that of a father for the tough, sweet, mocking boy. The wrench back to the truth gave him a feeling as if blood were pouring from him in a stream of pain.

The young man stood up to go and thanked him for his advice and for: "being good enough of giving your time tonight. There! Correct, English gratitude! I used the right words, yes?"

"How is Sophie by the way?" said Leo as he accompanied Dov to the front door.

"Fine. The only thing I have found in England which I wish to take back with me to Israel. But then of course—she is *Welsh*!"

"Give her . . . my best wishes," said Leo.

The following day he went off to a summer school in Scotland for a week as guest lecturer. It was when he arrived home from there that he found the letter from Joel saying that he was marrying Zella Harris at the end of the month.

# Chapter Ten

## I

NORTH, WEST AND SOUTH OF MANOR CROSS, WHICH is the focal point of the whole suburb of Manor Green, the busy, glossy shopping streets sooner or later run into residential neighbourhoods, tree-lined streets of clean, bright, well-kept houses. Only the road to the East deteriorates as it goes along, skirting the garden suburb without ever quite touching it and ending up for the last two miles of its considerable length as the rather surprisingly dingy and somehow forgotten-looking High Street of Manor Green East.

About half-way along this street, between a dairy and a cheap milliners stood Mr Gabriel's bookshop; narrow, rather dusty, brown-painted, its stock of Hebrew books old and new overflowing everywhere, candlesticks and prayer shawls mixed together on the shelves.

One late afternoon not long before the two days of the Jewish New Year which that year fell at the end of the first week of October, Dr Gildheim walked into the shop. He found Sara there alone. Rather relieved though he knew that Mr Gabriel was not likely to be around, he said to Sara with all of his usual, soft-voiced, Austrian charm: "How very nice to see you! But I thought I would find your brother-in-law here?"

"He's gone down to the West End on some business," she said, a slight trace of embarrassment in her manner. She had neither seen nor spoken to him since the night her father had made so appalling a scene on the telephone.

Betraying no hint of remembering it however, he drew up a chair on his side of the counter and, sitting down, made himself comfortable with the ease of the always popular, his movements rather too graceful for him ever to be mistaken for a man brought up in England. Although his hair was almost silver, his eyes shone blue and gay in his square, Slavonic, deep-grooved face. He drew out his cigarettes, offered her one which she refused, saying with a smile that she did not often smoke, and lit one for himself.

"I've come in for a prayer book," he said, "but if you don't mind I'll give myself a few minutes to cool off before looking at any. It is *so* hot. But very nice and cool in here."

She looked out from the shop, dark even at the height of the day, to the blazing, shabby street outside. "Of course," she said. "Would you like . . .? I was just going to make some tea . . ."

"Good heavens! What a luxury! Yes indeed. But only, *only* if you're making one for yourself."

"Yes, I am. This is our busiest period in the whole year just now, before *Yomtov*. I didn't have time the whole afternoon."

She gave him a friendly smile before disappearing into the small, back room with its rusty gas ring and cold water tap.

"And who," he called out to her between draws on his cigarette, "is looking after your father while you are here?"

"My married sister is with him for the afternoon," she called back "though actually it is quite all right to leave him alone for an hour or two—only we never do! It was only a very slight stroke you know. It's left him a little stiff in one leg, that's all."

"Yes, I know," he said rather rapidly. "It's all the same lucky that there are four of you to take turns."

"Four?" she said from inside the back room. "But perhaps you didn't know? Fagy, my youngest sister, is not at home any more."

"Really?" said John. "No, that I didn't hear."

"She went to France for her summer holiday and managed— I have no idea how she manages these things!—to get herself a job in Geneva while she was there. She came back, packed up and flew —literally flew!—to Switzerland almost before we knew what was happening."

She came back into the shop with a jam jar half full of sugar and a packet of biscuits and put them on the counter.

"That was really quite a clever thing to do," said John approvingly. "Before anyone could object. Yes, that was very sensible."

"Oh yes," she said absently fingering a pile of prayer books. "Fagy was always very sensible.

"Was?" said John. "You sound as though she has gone for ever from your life."

252

"Yes, well, I think she probably has," she said. "There was no stopping her, you know. Father——" she half-looked at him with a kind of vulnerable blink of her eyes but his expression showed only a calm interest. "She'll be working," she went on, "for a Jewish organization there. Perfectly respectable. He had no arguments you see. He couldn't stop her. He didn't have a leg to stand on." She laughed slightly. "Almost literally, as it turned out!"

"Surely she did not go off and leave him—and you!—just when——"

Sara looked at him with a smile of genuine amusement.

"No, no. Her luck . . . bless her! Fagy's luck . . . it is quite extraordinary, it is enough in itself to make you believe in God! There *must* be another world to redress the balance of this one! No. Her luck held and father's timing was out. I suppose it has always been out," she added half to herself. "No, she had been gone some hours——"

The telephone rang and with a lift of her eyebrows indicating that she had half expected it, she lifted the receiver. John looked round the shop while she was speaking first to her sister whose voice came through resigned but exasperated, then to her father whose loud, impatient quack reverberated from the mouthpiece.

"Yes," she said. "Yes. As soon as I possibly can. But I'm . . . No. No. Not long."

She hung up at last and said with an apologetic look: "He doesn't get on very well with Rebecca these days. She is so placid and ordinary he can't stand it! She doesn't allow him to make any drama out of his illness."

"And you do?"

"It's better to," she said.

"*Better* to!" he said with an unbelieving jerk of his head backwards.

"Even you . . . a doctor . . . surely *I* don't have to tell *you* that this . . . this need to make capital from a small illness . . . that *is* an illness. It is a symptom of need. People, I think, are in general too severe, too cruel in their censure of this kind of behaviour. Hypochondria is a cry for love. But Rebecca has no understanding of this at all. Anyway, just this once I won't hurry. She's staying another hour."

The kettle whistled and she went back, made the tea and came into the shop with two filled cups. "Not exactly the Ritz," she said, "But we don't bother for here."

"Better than!" said John, "better than! I would not change this tea at this moment for . . . for all the tea in China!"

"I think," she said looking at her watch, "that we might as well have it in peace. It's closing time anyway. Please don't hurry," she added quickly. "There is absolutely no need to rush. But I'll just lock the door and hope no one comes clamouring at it." She bolted the door and came back to her chair behind the counter.

"Fagy came back on a Tuesday, booked her plane seat for Thursday afternoon," she went on, stirring her tea intently, "then someone, a friend she met in France, got her a returned ticket on the plane they were taking: Wednesday evening. There was hardly time to say goodbye. And no time for father . . .

"But he was very frightened," she said, "when it actually happened. The stroke I mean. In the middle of the night. Fortunately I wasn't asleep. I don't sleep very well lately," she said in an abstracted voice. "I heard something and went in."

She had not in fact taken as long as usual that particular night to fall asleep. In order to relieve the strange, light aching in the back of her head and in her cheeks, she had taken some aspirin and fallen off almost at once. Two hours later she had wakened to a kind of soughing, black, smothered sadness, the black plumes of it curling and furling around her, a sensation as of heavy weeping dragging down from her heart. Then she was wide awake, the tears not in her eyes but seeming to pluck and sear at her eyelids.

Without having made any decision about it she got out of bed and walked in her bare feet, tall and pale in her long, thin nightdress, out of her room, along the landing and down four stairs into the room Essie and Fagy had shared.

The two single beds had been stripped of linen. Fagy's bed lay now beneath blankets slightly awry, the cotton bedcover stretched carelessly across. Essie's bed, neatly covered, was by the window. There had been one of their rare disputes between the two of them about this; they had both wanted the window. Fagy in fact had *taken* it, in her curiously calm, hardly noticing way. She had always

254

had this habit of taking, smoothly and rapidly, anything she liked and making any contestant look selfish and feel foolish if they disputed it. "Please yourself," with a cool shrug had been one of her catch phrases, catch actions. But in the middle of that particular argument she had—and this too she had done before—capitulated with a genial, naïve good humour, had been Fagy, their baby again, leaving the rest of her family, none of whom were blessed with this ability to shrug off and leave alone, more affectionate and more wary towards her than ever.

Fagy, who was fond of hats and had had a collection of them, had made a hasty choice to take with her and left at least half a dozen lying about. Immaculate to look at she had often been curiously untidy at home. Sara picked one up, a red feather helmet they had all strenuously declared to be far too old for her. She and Essie had combined to tease her out of wearing it but nothing could disturb Fagy's calm, bland over-riding of anyone's opinion but her own. Then, suddenly, she had discarded the helmet and never worn it again. There had always been something ungraspable, arbitrary about Fagy's actions, an unpierceable, opaque glass surrounding her essence. Sara had sometimes wondered if she had any feeling at all for any of them. Once or twice of late years she had even begun to suspect that her youngest sister was one of those women who remain for ever cool in emotion, who do not love, or enjoy friendship or desire to need or be needed; but who are at the same time profoundly sensual.

It was strange how their father had never seemed to notice in his sharp, spying watch over herself and Essie how often Fagy had come in late with flushed cheeks and swollen lips. But she had always got away with everything and always would. "There *are* people like that," said Sara to herself, turning the hat round and round in her fingers. "She is the person we all think we are going to be when we are young."

She moved across to the wardrobe, intending to put the hat away but as she opened the door an old dress of Essie's, imperfectly hung up, swung out at her and with its touch the immense, lowering sadness with which she had awakened again fell on her. For the first time since Essie had gone she allowed herself—indeed could not hold back—the full knowledge of loss.

255

Where there had been a family there were now broken ends.

Reproaches, images, regrets streamed across her mind. Essie! What was she doing? How had she spent that day, that night? Talking? Eating? Shopping? In her husband's arms? What words had she spoken, what strange streets had she walked on? And Fagy . . . in what bed was she now lying, what colour of walls surrounded her, what world would she step into tomorrow morning?

A feeling of such isolation from the common stream of life, a sense of having been passed by unwanted by any world, good or bad, so unexpectedly swept her with pain that she gave a kind of gasped "Ah!" She stood there in the bedroom, one hand still on the wardrobe door, feeling with breaking heart that a kind of insult had been dealt to herself and the house and the room. The room— recently so full and alive with all the chatter and paraphernalia, the clothes and cosmetics, magazines and hair clips of two young women—now smelling already of desertion. Breaking repeatedly across the anguished rhythm of her thoughts, an image kept reappearing of the dinner table that evening after Fagy had gone. A knife, a fork, a spoon, a plate. It had been like that for weeks since Essie had gone and Fagy had been away. But now, she realized, it would be for ever. There would be no particular time for the meal; her father, often erratic, took his own food, ate when he pleased. No one would be coming in, hungry and talkative after a working day. She would not automatically, at a quarter to six on winter evenings, stoke up the fire so that they would find the living room warm. She would seldom go to the cleaners now, to the shoe repairer, to the chemist. The routine of her life would shrink. There would only be her father's demands and inadequacies to bear, pity to be dredged with constant effort from a weary heart, the drab, silent house to be held together.

"They have gone away," she said aloud. "They have found something, some other . . . They have left me without a frame."

What we call love (she felt rather than thought) is really no more than this: the *presence* of others, their noise, their needs, their occupancy of the terrifying empty spaces of our daily lives. We use even our best beloveds only as stars by which to plot our own positions.

"But me, *me*," she said to herself frantically. "I too am alive.

*I* live. *I* have rights . . . They have all found something: only I have nothing." Leo came to her mind like a flashed pinpoint of light instantly doused again. Elements quite foreign to her nature, rebellion, assertion, demand, seemed to pour upwards from her centre, disturbed like monsters, long thought extinct, from secret depths. "I will go too," she said aloud, her fingers, which were still holding Fagy's hat, gripping and twisting along the brim, pressing the feathers back against the grain. The hard stalks bent and twisted but did not break. With ferocious intensity she tried to pull one out but, too firmly attached to the crown, it only slipped, fragile and spiky, into crooked shape. For a moment she wrestled with it, breathing harshly, but the hard, glassy tube in the centre of the brittle tendrils resisted.

An unexpected sound coming from the next room—her father's —caught her ear and she paused. There was again silence. Her heart began to beat furiously at the thought that he was spying on her. A cloudburst of clenched rage seemed about to break and thunder from her throat. Then she heard the sound again and it occurred to her that he was crying; that Fagy, his youngest and dearest, Fagy, his one pride in his children, had gone. That she had gone coolly, imperturbably, leaving him no room for drama, only a bare situation to cover as best he could. She stood listening by the open wardrobe door, her hands unconsciously smoothing the feathers back into place, straightening the stems, stroking the soft, frail edges even between finger and thumb. She pressed her lips together, trying to pit the fact of her suffering against the fact of his. He will get over it, she thought, as he has other things. And she pushed to the forefront of her mind the fact that he had been much milder since she had thrown "failure" in his face, been almost humble so far as it lay within his natural manner to be, so that she had almost begun to hope that he had learned something at last of how to deal with his life. Then she heard for the third time her father moan and, suddenly alarmed, ran to his room. But in the split second between his cry and her body moving in answer, the truth broke in her mind and she realized that whatever was awaiting her in her father's room she should have expected. That he had had no intention of letting her go unpunished for what she had done to him. His docility, his quietness, his humbleness had all been false; a

257

deep-gripped, neurotic, iron-like determination on revenge, a *reculer pour mieux sauter*. She was the only bank from which he could draw the debt of life owed him. And now her payment was about to begin.

"He is better now though," she said looking up. "And really I don't see why I should bore you with my family affairs. What . . ."

John, who had been smoking casually, his eyes on the floor, now looked across at her with a professional, assessing look, noting that her austere face, though more hollowed than before, had also acquired a curious, fine mobility, her features less harsh, her skin transparent yet with something marble-like in its texture.

He moved his shoulders suddenly and said in a brisk voice: "Yes of course. I actually came in to buy a new prayer book. Not for myself; for my mother."

"Your mother?" she said in surprise. "But I thought you were entirely . . . that you lived alone."

"So I do. At least—it is the same thing, almost—I have a flat in my partner's house. But I have a mother still alive you know. But of course you *didn't*. Many people think as you do; that I am completely on my own, very carefree, very free . . ."

"I suppose she lives somewhere like Whytecliffe Sands?" she said.

"No, not at all. She lives right here in London."

"You *do* surprise me," she said. "But in that case, why——?"

"Why does she not live with me—or I with her?" he finished. "Well, that is easily explained. I keep her (at considerable expense I might tell you) living apart from me in a very pleasant room with some kind people, solely because I do not wish to commit suicide as well as murder." He laughed with a look in his eyes at once, teasing, sardonic and watchful.

"You have not the faintest idea what I am talking about, no? I will explain. My mother and I are the only two members of my family left. What more natural than we should live together? And yet, I assure you, to do so for me would be suicide. *All* parents are possessive, some for one reason, some another. My mother because she was a success, very gay, beautiful, very spoilt by my father. And now . . . now she is old she cannot believe it is all gone. She wishes" (speaking, as he seldom did, with strength, from the heart, John's sentences became noticeably more foreign in form, his accent more broken) "to make *me* her husband for to spoil, to dance attendance . . . If I allowed her to my life" (he gave a characteristically foreign, upward jerk of his chin), "I would be committing suicide. But by *not* allowing her I am killing her. I know it. I see this every time I go to visit her. By not letting her live with me I am committing murder. You understand what I mean. Don't you?" he said lifting an eybrow at her.

"Yes."

"Besides," he went on, "I have every hope of marrying; *some* day! As soon as I tire of being gay bachelor I *shall* marry," he said with a mischievous look. "But if she lives with me I know this all becomes immediately impossible. So it is absolutely necessary that I keep open the door. It is *necessary*," he added in an unexpectedly stern and unmistakably warning voice. "It is a mistake for *any* child to sacrifice his or her self to a parent. I cannot express myself too strongly on this matter. And I think particularly this wrong for a daughter. We must be realistic. For a man such a position is easier. To be a bachelor . . . it carries, you know, less stigma. There is less . . . well . . . you know what I mean. Come, I will be straight out, John Blunt as the English say: I am referring specifically to your own situation. Sara, I know what your father is like. Now the others have escaped; and I tell you that you too must escape before it is too late, while you are still . . . not too old. Your father has had his life. Good or bad he has had it. You must not throw away yours. I am not interfering without good feeling towards you, believe me. I have told you of my own problem to show that I have some experience of yours, that I am not advising from the outside, so to speak. You are not angry?"

She raised her eyes which had been downcast for some minutes and, looking not quite directly at him, she said: "I knew of course that you were speaking to *me*. But of course not angry. I think it a great compliment—" her voice faltered slightly and he sensed that tears had come to her eyes, "that *anyone*, anyone at all should give any thought to my position in the world, my feelings . . ." She paused for a moment and, swallowing, regained control of her voice, then went on.

"You say you are not speaking from the outside; that you understand my problem from within. But that is in fact where I must straight away contradict you. You *are* looking at this matter from outside. That is, you are outside *me*. You see my situation as terrible. But from inside me it does not feel so terrible really. Since my father took ill I have had some time in which to think. I have faced my position. After all, I have assets . . ." He frowned slightly as if surprised to discover that she intended to boast, then relaxed as she went on: "One of my great blessings is a temperament which does not wish for rebellion. I like order. I do not mind being *told*. And when I am told from a source I can respect, from religion, from history, from the first instincts of the heart, then I do not find it hard to obey. It is not easy *always*; but not hard."

"To resign oneself," John said rather testily, flicking his thumb rapidly with his little finger, "that is the worst——"

"No, it is not resignation," she interrupted him quickly, "it is not that I have given up feeling or desiring . . . there are still hours when I see myself as you do. And when that happens it is a great anguish——" She stopped and put a hand unconsciously clenched to her heart. "But then it passes," she said. "The boundaries settle into shape again. I stop looking over the wall.

"You see," she said, "there is a point at which you go wrong. You say . . . my father has had his life. That I am younger and therefore more important than he. You think my life more important than his; more worth the saving. This is where you go wrong. This is the great error the world makes. His life is *just* as important. And —because he is old—more so. *More so*. You too," she smiled at him in a kind of apology for contradicting him but went on firmly, "subscribe to the great sentimental fallacy; that the young are more important than the old. 'Look after the children.' That's the cry, isn't it, all over the world? Always the emphasis is on the children. Will it shock you very much if I say that I am not greatly concerned for children? Children are tough. Children are hopeful, resilient. A child's ego is unbattered. They have youth, energy, all life before them They can look after themselves," she said with a half-smiling, quizzical nod of her head towards him. "It is the old whose need is strong. The old have nothing. The old are beaten. The old are the Jews of life; despised for what they cannot help, forced by life itself into what they are and then resented for it; provokers of guilt because they suffer. *They are entitled to their suffering*. And, more than that, we must take notice of it. You think their suffering doesn't count because they are not important any more. That is where you are wrong; that is where you are *Fascist*. Suffering *bestows* importance. My father . . . I have no illusions. I see him for what he is, vain, selfish, absurd, trying in the extreme: there is no dignity to him and—this is his particular tragedy—there never was. But then I think—really I do," she added with a simple, frowning earnestness which affected John so that he gave her an almost loving, tender smile as to a clever child, though he was not profoundly interested in her ideas (like many kind, well-meaning people he was only interested in *stopping* pain, not in evolving ways of enduring it); "I think," she said, "that there is probably very little dignity inside anyone when they are stretched on their particular rack. The fact is that all suffering at the moment of experiencing it is ignoble. But we must take it seriously wherever we find it," she continued vigorously. "Do you think because we are foolish, selfish, ignorant, played-out, that therefore we suffer less? On the contrary. If my father were brilliant, successful, respected, whatever happened to him would be less piercing in its effect. It is *because* of his inability to cope with life, *because* of his raw, feeble, pettish, done-for struggle that he requires——" she hesitated then with a certain defiance brought out the word, "love. Love and high seriousness. My father is not to be written off because he is ineffectual. His suffering—or anyone's—we must give a place to."

"He behaves so badly," said John doubling his chin and sighing down into his shirt.

"It's the only way he can get what he wants."

"Oh my dear Sara," he said impatiently jerking his head up again. "Can't we all say that? But we don't, do we? We have all learnt some control."

"*You* have. *I* have—a little perhaps. But he hasn't. You still don't understand. You jump over too quickly what is in fact a great gap. There are some people (a great number I sometimes think) who have not only never learnt to control their demands from life; they don't even know about the *necessity* for control. My father is in this strange state of what I can only call innocence. His egotism, his selfishness is that of a child's or even a baby's. It is not badness; it is unknowingness, a kind of peasant ignorance of the spirit. He has

261

this curious, destructive innocence because he does not know there is any other way to be. He reads Jewish philosophy because he enjoys reading words in books. He simply does not know how to apply it in life. He can't *relate*. He does not *see*. But stupidity does not rule out suffering. We must take it seriously . . . or we are all destroyed by the snigger of the universe."

John said, running a finger round the rim of his empty cup: "You know . . . you should have been a doctor, Sara. Did you ever think of——?"

"Yes," she said abruptly, a quick flush staining her face, turning to look at him with the first sign he had seen of ordinary, human, vulnerable distress. "That is . . . well, what does it matter now? That is the thing I most wished for. But you are the only person in the world who has ever had the same thought . . ."

He said nothing for a few moments, only looked down through the glass top of the counter to the display inside it of highly coloured, illustrated productions for children; books of Jewish history, tales from the Bible, stories of the Festivals.

"They didn't have all these when I was a young boy," he said. "Pictures, comic strips, everything, all modern, all very bright, all the latest advertising techniques. All to teach them . . . what?"

"Judaism as it should be," said Sara with a somewhat wry smile.

"And for that we need books like *these*? But why should we stop there? I cannot think why we don't buy time on television. 'Try the *Jewish* Orthodoxy'," he cried in a television advertising voice. " 'Established six thousand years! Our methods are *guaranteed*. Make your soul shining white with conforming *Judaism*, the all-purpose, up-to-date, moral cleanser. Try it today. Why not *be Orthodox*? Be Orthodox! Orthodoxy is best.' Ah now! you are not cross wiz me because I joke?" he said letting his accent slip and smiling at her in the undeniably taking, foreign-charmer way which he could not help using on occasion.

She could not help smiling in return, giving him a chiding, affectionate, rather teasing look as she would to a frolicsome brother.

"Ah! that's better! It suits you, you know, Sara, to be responsive!" He flicked a finger towards her and had opened his mouth to tease her further when she said, without self-pity, only stating a fact: "I am obliged to give up response."

He could not help feeling a touch reproved and this immediately bored him. Nevertheless he took up her remark.

"Are you really willing to lose all chance of life for yourself?"

"I suppose you are really equating the word 'life' with the word 'marriage'," she said. "Most people do. Yet that is such *conventional* thinking, really. I have not noticed in many of the married women I know who have so much, homes, husbands, children, health and wealth . . . I have not noticed great happiness in these women. On the contrary—there seems to me to be a great deal of downright misery."

"That may be," he said argumentatively feeling all at once (as Leo had often done) rather prickly, rather put out by her austere, somewhat unappealing good sense. "But there are some happy marriages. And of course . . . you know . . . there are other necessities . . ."

He gave her a merry, meaning look as if half hoping he'd shocked her, but she surprised him again, as she had once surprised Leo, by her immediate, forthright candour.

"Oh, the sexual relationship," she said almost impatiently. "Really, there is more . . . The impression I get from married women is not one of great joy. From the confidences I've heard from time to time I've come to the conclusion that that relationship is often the most unhappy part of marriage. There is so much grief, humiliation, bitter destruction there. I don't think I am missing so much. Perfect sexual happiness . . . that would be . . . but the chances are so greatly against finding it, anyway. And as for children—the other great argument." She smiled at him. "Well, you have heard my unnatural opinions——"

"Everyone wants children," he said. "I don't believe you. It's a natural thing. Ah, I see what you are going to say before you say it! 'Then why don't you get married and have some?' "

"Well why don't you?" she said laughing outright. "There are so many girls! In the Guild alone there are at least half a dozen very pretty girls. There is even Lillie Stiel!"

"Good Heavens!" he exclaimed, "that reminds me! I have to meet her this evening. I have a present for her."

"A present?"

"Yes. Beautiful Italian nylons. I brought them from Rome a week ago and I must give them to her."

She looked at him but with characteristic delicacy did not question him and, the matter being quite unimportant to him—the nylons were a present for some particular secretarial job Lillie had undertaken, indeed offered to do for him while he was away—he did not think of explaining. It did not occur to him (he was always giving presents to girls) that Sara might interpret his gift in some other way. Rather disliking Lillie if anything, though her antics in pursuit of himself had sometimes amused him, he couldn't be bothered talking about her and, changing the subject, said almost at random: "I think nearly everyone has finished with summer holidays now. Even Leo is back. I don't know what can be the matter with that man, he has hardly sat still this year. He came back from Scotland, stayed one day in London and went straight off to the Continent. I believe his congregation were very much annoyed for him taking such long holidays as *they* do! Anyway, now he is back and forgiven. Well now . . . I must choose this prayer book. What have you suitable for an old lady who is very particular, very snob?"

She had turned to the shelves behind her and was pulling out some volumes. John suddenly looked over at her tall figure as she stood there, her back towards him. Her movements were neat and normal, her face when she eventually turned round no different in expression than before. And yet there was something . . . something which had caught his attention. Then he realized what it was: an alteration in the rhythm of her breathing, very slight, almost undetectable, had been caught by his doctor's ear.

Successful, popular, handsome people like John Gildheim often have kind hearts possibly because they can afford them. Contact with grief or failure does not harm or diminish them.

Comprehending—quick-witted in the Continental fashion regarding affairs of the heart—that he had knocked accidentally against a bandage concealing a hardly healing wound—he saw that nothing would avail save complete ignorance on his part. All he could do, as soon as she had wrapped the book he chose for him, was to insist on taking her home in his car, chatting unceasingly of his patients and his girl-friends and Guild affairs and finally leaving her at her door; though not without a great relief that her father did not see him.

Roughly twenty-four hours later Leo was driving along this same High Street of Manor Green East. He had passed the Gabriels' shop but the sight of it had focused his attention—rather unwillingly— on that family. Lately back from travelling, he had still not adjusted himself at this dead end of summer, to the ordinary routines of his life. Questions, attitudes . . . all lay in limbo as they had done during his restless moving about Europe these last weeks. Beyond a brief note of congratulation and a present, he had not communicated with Joel nor—being abroad—needed any other excuse for not going to his wedding. But this had left him ignorant of the couple's plans and suddenly one day, sitting beside a Swiss lake, it occurred to him that they might have chosen that same resort for their honeymoon. Immediately, impelled by a desperate, shrinking fear of meeting them, of the shame of being alone when they were two, he left Switzerland for Italy, only to be pursued by the added terror of meeting anyone whom he knew at all. To be alone as he was . . . this condition now appeared to him as the greatest shame; only supportable if no one knew. Travelling restlessly from place to place, tied as he was to Jewish hotels and restaurants in whatever country he was in, he found himself in a perpetual state of stretched nerves and constant reconnaisance.

He did not envy Joel his bride; only his state. When he allowed himself to think about it the emotional pattern of his friend's life touched him with its hint of ironic repetition. Zella Harris was exactly such a one as Joel's first wife had been. And Joel, the eternal fat-man, sucker, had fallen into exactly the same situation all over again. Within six months she would have him humiliated and begging; hard, impatient and uncaring to his sad, melancholy softness. Yet, even while he saw the inevitable, humiliated unhappiness awaiting his friend, he also envied him, had a strange feeling that Joel had betrayed him, had gone off and joined a successful opposition party leaving him to continue a losing battle alone.

He drove on along the hideous, main shopping street of Manor Green East with its shabby hopelessness made more lowering by the dirty, yellow heat of the late afternoon. Some of the shops had already closed but most of the food shops and greengrocers were still open. Where the street widened out for a few hundred yards to accommodate the kerb side stalls of the local, rather inadequate market, he drew up behind one partly dismantled stall and getting out went into a tobacconist for some of the Perfectos he smoked when he smoked at all. He was just settling himself behind the driving wheel again when he caught sight of Sara, a string bag on her arm, making some purchases from a fruit stall a little further along. He watched her waiting for some apples to be weighed, her tall figure rather too stiffly held for grace, her shoulders a little gaunt and bent. With her long neck and severe head she looked, even in the always ungraceful act of marketing, somehow unapproachable. As an attitude, it was, he realized as he sat watching her through the windscreen, at once her only defence and greatest hindrance. Given her circumstance she had no choice save between withdrawal and indignity.

"Face!" he thought. "Face. How important it is. How much more than love in the end. We Orientals know that, all of us. It is the stupid, western politician with no nerves, with his blank unrecognition of this supreme fact, who is responsible for so much damage to world order. From reasons for war to reasons for marriage, the ultimate, bedrock facts are those of status. The great humiliations are not the actual hungers and poverties of peoples but the lack of standing which hunger and poverty and loneliness force on us. How many go to war for real hate? How many marry for real love?"

Sara had moved to another stall and was buying potatoes.

"Could I marry her?" he asked himself directly for the first time.

She had lifted the heavy string bag from her wrist and, balancing it rather awkwardly, was rubbing the red weal the handle had left on her arm.

"*Should* I marry her?" he asked himself.

The stall-holder poured the potatoes in on top of the shopping bag before she could stop him and Leo saw the slight, tolerant frown with which she extricated a bag of something easily crushed, eggs? tomatoes? from underneath. Burdened with the weight on her arm she struggled to open her handbag and get at her purse. The stall-keeper stood waiting bad-tempered and surly till, smiling and saying Thank you as she did so, she paid him.

For the life of him Leo could not endorse her restraint which seemed to him unbearable in its meekness even while he recognized its strength. "She *is* strong," he said to himself as she disappeared inside a newsagents. "She is strong, but not in the *world*; and that is where I need strength. I am weak in the world, in the outward social forms and manner of life. I cannot face any more the struggle of each day's affairs, the pity which will soon begin, the struggle to appear powerful, the endless battle to make myself suffice. I need help, power, hardness behind me, a wife to make a wall. I cannot lift or shield myself; how can I battle for her as well?

"I am not much, am I?" he suddenly exclaimed to himself with great bitterness. "I know what I should do. But . . .

"Do I love her? Yes, yes, in a way, in a way, I love her. She can bring me peace—but only afterwards. She cannot make my happiness—only ease my unhappiness. To marry her would not be life. She provokes no ache in me, no sense of the fever of living, no untidy, splashing disports of the heart. Her gift is for the soul."

Sara came out of the newsagents and went into the Post Office next door.

The soul! this word it was his professional duty to face every day of the week and every hour of the day. It was from this word that he shrank. He could not will himself to make or face the effort of spirit which would be needed to change the relativity of Self, to bring himself up into a higher, larger, differently shaped universe. Only the small, faulty, highly personal world mattered because there he had failed and this he could never forget or overlook or leave alone.

He thought again of the Gabriels and tried to imagine himself into alliance with them but his imagination collapsed. He knew that he could not take them on. He was not strong enough. For all his position and authority in the community it had always been something of an effort to keep himself in line with John and the others. He was always being nearly left out of their affairs, their comings and goings. It had always been a struggle to avoid being unclassified, a "fringe" man, cut off partly by his profession but more, far more, by his age and type and bearing, from their social lives. He had never really had a proper place: not married or settled, too old to be one of the boys, too much the prisoner of his calling to be a gay bachelor, perpetually in a vague state of uncertain, social acceptance. Eligible . . . yes. Desirable . . . no, not by a long chalk. What he had once told Joel was true: he did not want "the nice girls". But he wanted a *place*.

To ally himself with the Gabriels would mean the undertaking of an enormous work of social construction for which he did not have the moral strength. At the thought of having to integrate Mr Gabriel into the intimate pattern of his life, of beginning the uphill, hopeless task of keeping him in order, confining his wild plungings and flauntings as *the Rabbi's father-in-law*, his spirit wilted. If Sara had been young and beautiful and lively it could perhaps have been done. But as she was he would have to fight and make her way for her too.

If I lived, he thought, in a state of permanent crisis, then I would always need her. But life is not like that. It is the day-after-dayness, the perpetual smallnesses (which are not small at all but collectively form the sum, colour and pattern of our lives) which count. How well the ancient Rabbis knew this. How well they formulated—and knew the necessity of—that immense body of laws for the every day. *They* knew the grain of human nature.

It was no use, no use. She was no use to him, too expensive a luxury. She was like a rich, mineral deposit, useless to mine because so inaccessible it would not be economic to do so. His moral resources were too low to afford her.

Sara came out of the Post Office. He saw her looking up and down the street to see if a bus was coming. He watched her hesitate between walking on to the next stop and walking back, past where he was parked behind the empty stall to the stop beyond him. Deciding, she walked as rapidly as she could, encumbered with her shopping, towards him. As she came up to the stall which obscured him from her vision he leaned over, opened the door of his car and called to her. She came on a few steps, saw him, and hesitated. "Come on," he called, "I'll give you a lift."

Not wanting to seem ungrateful though it was evident that she would rather have refused, she got in, thanking him.

"Not at all, not at all," he said, busying himself with signals and gears as he drove off. "What a long time it is since I have seen you. How are you getting on? And your family?"

"My father has been ill. Perhaps you hadn't heard," she said composedly.

"I'm very sorry to hear that," said Leo, who, absorbed in soothing down his Synagogue officials, genuinely hadn't known. "What has been the matter?"

"He had a slight stroke. Not very serious. But enough to make some difficulty at home; especially as my younger sister is now in Geneva."

In answer to his questions she explained what had happened.

"But then you have had no holiday," he suddenly exclaimed, interrupting her as though he hadn't really been listening.

"That doesn't matter very much. D'you know," she said turning to him in surprise as he drove steadily through the hot streets, "I hadn't realized it! What with one thing and another I completely forgot that I had had no holiday this year!"

"Does it ever occur to you to think about yourself at all?" he said in the hectoring manner he had always enjoyed using to her.

"Oh heavens," she said rather crossly but with all her old ease with him, "of course I do. I assure you I am no saint."

"To your——" (family you are, he had been going to say but stopped himself from this dangerous remark in time).

"To try to behave with as much understanding of other people's miseries as one can . . . there is nothing remarkable in that."

"Isn't there?"

"I cannot claim any kind of good conduct medal for myself," she said. "If I had been presented with a choice, now, and had deliberately chosen . . . well that would be different. But I have not been burdened with any real agony of conflict. That at least I have been spared: I have had some luck after all. There was no choice," she said mildly.

Leo stirred uneasily but with her sometimes curiously blinkered vision it did not occur to her—for she had already put him away from her life—that he was thinking that he could have provided her with choice. "Perhaps it's just as well," he thought with cross, guilty relief. "I would only have made things worse for her." Then shame at this easy assuagement swept him again and he longed for her to *demand* from him, to force charity from his heart and love from his soul, not to leave it to him.

But all she said was: "When you are presented with a *fait accompli*—a life from which there is to be no deviation, laid out like a railway line in front of you—there is nothing to do but accept."

"But——" he began, then stopped and sighed, seeing that in a way she *was* lucky. "Acceptance," he thought, slipping over the full implications of the word with the belittling ease with which we endow other people's struggles, "is easy for her."

"All the same," he said, feeling to his shame a kind of begrudging envy that she who had so little should have this, "all the same," he repeated, not knowing quite what he was saying, "you should have had a holiday."

"Oh well," she said, "never mind. Perhaps next year. I must say I should very much like to go to Italy. John Gildheim was in the shop yesterday and was telling me about it on the way home. He gave me a lift."

"But I was in Italy . . . I didn't know he was going there," said Leo frowning. "D'you happen to know what part?"

"Rome, I know definitely, because he told me he'd bought some stockings there for Lillie."

"For *Lillie!* Lillie Stiel?"

"Yes."

Leo changed into fourth gear with rather unnecessary violence and accelerated. "I wonder why he did that?" he said.

"Well I rather wondered myself," she said, slipping unconsciously into their old, pleasant, gossiping tone. "D'you know," she went on, "I wonder if there's anything between them? He was taking her out last night, I know."

Leo made no reply but as they were at her gate and he had stopped the car she did not notice.

"Thank you for the lift," she said, looking at him fully for the first time since they had met. Like a muffled gong, reverberations of a feeling she would never now allow herself to know in full, vibrating sound, broke and trembled within the confines of her deepest heart. Then she hauled the heavy shopping bag out of the car and leaving Leo walked up the path to her home.

In his way he loved her. Yet, lashed by ropes of jealous resentment, he hardly noticed at that moment that she had gone. He drove on, feeling again the high tides of loneliness sweeping up on him at the thought of John and Lillie marrying each other. Alone. Alone. I shall be left alone, his brain muttered to him continuously. Blows, nothing but blows all round. Those two married he would be bereft of all company, not even anyone left in the same boat with him. Sophie . . . Joel . . . and now those two! He felt that the walls of his house were breaking down all round him, that soon there would be no shelter left. No sooner had he got home than an uncontrollable urge to know the worst sent him to the telephone. He rang up Lillie and asked her if she'd like a run in the car. He had often done this in the past. She was agreeable enough company in her frosty way.

She was lively that evening and, pleased to have someone beside him for an evening drive, he felt a sudden gush of warm feeling towards her and towards the normal, even tenor of life which she represented. A kind of disgust seized him at the thought of the dark, anguished misery of the last few months.

"How's John? I haven't seen him lately," he said noticing with detached astonishment the jealous shiver which ran through him as he waited for her answer.

"He's very well. He had a wonderful time in Italy. He says it's honeymoon country." She spoke flatly enough, she was only repeating John's exact words but to Leo they sounded like the clap of doom. The word "honeymoon" in conjunction with the two of them was more than he could bear. Not even knowing what he was saying through the dull, swinging ache in his head he said: "We'll have to take a trip there one of these days, you and I."

"Well, how about it?" she said flirtatiously. "I'm game!"

"Perhaps you'd rather go with John?"

"You'll do!" she said archly.

Conscious only of the fact that nothing so far had been irrevocably settled between them, relief as strong as a pain flooding into him, he said at random: "Lillie, why don't we really go there?"

Hardly slowing down for a roundabout he slew the car round and accelerating violently up the straight said: "I mean it. Let's get married."

She gave a start of surprise. It was the last thing in the world she had expected to hear.

"Oh I know it's sudden for me to ask you like this. We've seen so little of each other lately. But it's time I settled down. Time you settled down too," he added, too brutal for tact.

"Well!" she said, looking astonished, then added: "Well for heaven's sake slow down a bit! You can't propose to me at seventy miles an hour."

"We know each other pretty well. Oh come on!" he said roughly, still driving very fast, his eyes glued in vacant concentration on the road. "You don't have to be coy with me. What d'you say?"

"Well, I don't know," she said laughing. "What a proposal!"

"Is it yes or no?" he shouted at her above the noise of the wind.

"Yes," she said.

All the time in the days that followed he repeated over and over to himself her virtues: Pretty. Efficient. Smart. Over and over again. Every night when he got into bed he lay staring into the darkness with burning eyes, his thoughts formless, only the same words, like an obsessional chant which he dared not stop repeating, echoing over and over: Pretty. Efficient. Smart.

3

The announcement of Leo's engagement appeared on a Friday. The following day was not only the Sabbath but also the first day of the Jewish New Year. Striding into the Synagogue that morning he accepted somewhat brusquely the congratulations which greeted him and, climbing rapidly into the pulpit, remained there raised above his congregants while cantor and choir between them went through the service. He kept his eyes steadily on the big prayer book before him, even delivering his sermon that way, so that it was not until he had finished it that, looking up involuntarily as he pronounced the final blessing, he saw Lillie in her place in the Ladies' Gallery. By some horrible irony she was sitting in a seat directly in front of Sara Gabriel so that he could not look at one without seeing the other. Quickly he looked down again, his heart burning and wretched. As if emerging from a nightmare circus into a quiet street, directly he saw Sara his thoughts immediately ran together, coherent, fluid, agonized.

272

"What have I done?" he said to himself, standing exalted in his white robes above his people.

The great, hot, crowded synagogue murmured with prayer.

"What have I done?" he said again. And, even as he asked himself, knew that it would never be undone, that he would marry Lillie, that he had made his choice; that he had ultimately, finally betrayed the possible goodness within him which now would wither and die.

Rosh Hashanah, the Jewish New Year, is nearly always, by some miracle, fine and sunny. The congregation streamed out after the service into the bright mid-day, gathering in the drive in great clusters, well dressed, well groomed, the air loud and busy with hand-shakes and New Year greetings.

Mrs Goldenbird, her newest mink floating from her massive shoulders, Doris sturdily in tow, caught Leo as he stood with Lillie receiving congratulations from all sides.

"Delighted. I'm delighted," she said in her large, nasal voice. "You've set all the other bachelors a real good example, Rabbi Norberg. Shake them all up a bit, let's hope."

Leo thanked her absently. Standing alone at one side of the crowd he could see Sara evidently waiting for her father. One of Mr Gabriel's most doddery but also most insubordinate old cronies, the one always most ready to argue against his pronouncements, had come up to him on the way out with a comment on the sermon which Mr Gabriel had fully intended making himself. Obliged to swivel right round and hotly contradict old Oppenheimer he was now deep in fiery argument.

Not even bothering to answer one startled well-wisher whom he left with outstretched hand unshaken, Leo began to press through the gradually thinning groups towards Sara with no idea in his head of what he wished to say. All he knew or felt was a kind of acute, physical regret and shame, an apology of his whole body. His head did not seem to exist, there was only this sense of the body in abasement, a kind of enormous, silent, physical groan.

"Pity me. Pity me," he wanted to say.

Before he could reach Sara, however, he saw John Gildheim detach himself from what was left of the crowd and join her, making some remark which immediately made her smile. Though she was tall she had to look up at the doctor and her eyes, open and sad and shining even as she smiled with her pale, delicate lips, brought to Leo's heart such a pang that he stopped dead, then turned and went back to where Lillie and her parents were waiting for him. With an exaggerated gesture he took Lillie's arm and walked her flamboyantly, deliberately, with rage and agony, right across Sara's field of vision and out through the left-hand gates of the drive.

The semi-circular path before the synagogue was almost empty now. John remained, still talking to Sara while Mr Gabriel and the little knot of old men who had gathered round him continued to argue. A few minutes later, seeing that her father's group was beginning to break up, Sara said good-bye to John and, falling into step with a couple whom she knew who were going the same way, walked slowly towards the main gates chatting desultorily.

The doctor had half turned to go out by a side entrance which would shorten the distance to his home when he saw Mr Gabriel, whose limp had been much in evidence when he came into the synagogue that morning, shoot past him, his thin little legs going at speed, no sign of a limp, till he came up to his daughter. With a fierce, reproachful, violent gesture he took her arm, hanging on it heavily, his limp coming on again at full strength. It was obvious that he'd thought she had been going to walk off without him.

Still watching, the doctor saw Sara turn and smile down at her father, putting her left hand over his left hand where it gripped her arm. "As though I would leave you," the gesture seemed to say.

They walked slowly out of the gateway and on to the pavement, the small man holding on to the tall, thin girl.

Propelled by some instinct, some goodness of heart, some guilt perhaps of his own, John suddenly turned and, running across the gravel, joined them, walking on Mr Gabriel's other side. And so the little man walked on along the street, ignoble, wrong, stiffnecked, absurd . . . protected on the one side by his daughter and on the other by the doctor: and perhaps, around him, by the Spirit of God also.